FROM THE PERVY HEART OF THE AUTHOR

My Cupcakes... Thank you for being my ride or die this last year through all the chaos and clusterfucks. I appreciate your patience, understanding, and encouragement more than you'll ever know. I adore you all and I'm grateful for each and every one of you.

Brynne Asher and Sarah Curtis, you keep me sane. Well, let's not get carried away. You keep me sane-*ish*. Thank you for being the best friends a gal could ever ask for and for being there for me—always, but especially this year. Here's to more years, more booze, and more bombshell secret pets...

Lindsay, thank you for always cracking the whip and being there for me! You're an absolute treasure, and I'm so lucky to have you as a friend.

Dark Water Covers... Every time I think you can't top a previous cover, you do it. Thank you for the perfect Maximo cover. I love it!

All the other authors, bloggers, Bookstagrammers, and readers in my life... I couldn't do anything without you all. The patience, support, understanding, and LOVE this community shows is a constant reminder that the world isn't a complete dumpster fire. I appreciate all you do.

And M, this year has been the lowest of lows and the highest of highs. Through it all, you've been there. My rock. My best friend. My everything. I love you whole bunches.

LITTLE *Dove*

LAYLA FROST

DEDICATED TO BABY SPRINKLE

Thank you for the insane pregnancy hormones that made this book possible. You're not even born yet, and I already owe you one. I also already love you. Spent years waiting for you, and I just know you're going to be worth every second.

CHAPTER ONE

Our White Castle

JULIET

"GET IN."

"What?" I asked, taking rapid shuffling steps to keep up as my father gripped my shoulders and propelled me backward. I stumbled, nearly falling, but he didn't stop.

Throwing open the small pantry door, he shoved me inside. "Don't come out no matter what you hear. Got it?"

I had no idea what was happening, but I knew better than to question Shamus McMillon, especially when he was in a *state*.

His graying red hair was in disarray and his wild eyes kept darting to the side. Each breath he huffed my way smelled like cheap whiskey and a keg of Guinness.

So instead of the fifty-billion questions that danced on my tongue, I said, "Okay."

"I mean it, Jule-bug. Don't open the door until I say so." He scanned my face, his expression tense and anxious. With a sigh, he closed the door, leaving me in darkness with stale crackers, canned Spam, and likely a mouse or two.

I'd just gotten home from errands and grocery shopping when Dad had dragged his butt off the couch to raid the food. His eyes had gone toward the front window before he'd dropped the peanut butter jar to the ground in order to push me into the pantry.

I had no clue what he'd seen that'd freaked him out. We lived at the end of the long dirt road behind Dad's gym and the only visitors we got were his buddies.

If anyone should be freaked by that, it was me. His friends were ass-holes who gave me the creeps.

Whatever this is, I hope it's fast. I splurged on ice cream, and Vegas doesn't seem to understand February is winter. My precious cookies and cream goodness is probably melting right now.

Maybe it's dinner delivery and I don't have to cook for once. Or maybe it's the few people I like from the gym bringing cake to go with my ice cream. Maybe, just maybe, my father didn't actually forget my seventeenth birthday and is trying to surprise me.

And maybe I'll find a rainbow in the box of stale, store brand Lucky Charms and ride it to a pot of gold.

I knew better than fanciful dreams. It wasn't the first time my dad had forgotten my birthday. The fact it was on Valentine's Day should've taken the guesswork out of it, but he'd still have to care enough to re-member.

He never did.

There was a pounding on the front door before it opened so hard, it banged into the wall.

"Boys!" Dad greeted, his voice traveling easily through the pa-per-thin walls. "What brings you to my castle?"

I barely held in a snort.

If this is a castle, it's owned by the Burger King.

And his Dairy Queen.

It's their humble White Castle.

I'm so hungry.

"If ya wanna book me," Dad said, "ya gotta call my girl. She sched-ules my fights."

I rolled my eyes. He always gave that line, like he had some big-time agent or manager handling his fight bookings.

I was his girl. Just me and a tattered desk calendar in the backroom of the training gym he owned.

2

"We had a meeting today," a deep voice rumbled—calm, cool, and collected.

Whereas my dad sounded nervous, jittery, and forced. "Oh! Was that today? Must've slipped my mind. What'd you need?"

"Rough loss on Saturday," whoever said.

Wait. I thought he won.

He hadn't said as much, but he also hadn't gotten blackout drunk— or worse—like he always did after a loss.

"Yeah, that sp—kid," he said, catching himself before he used the slur, "has a helluva right hook."

There was a lot to despise about Shamus McMillon, and his casual racism was high on the list.

"That's funny," the mystery man said in a tone that made it clear there was nothing humorous about it. "'Cause I talked to Jose's trainer. He said his right hook is weak. Not only that, but he sets his left foot. Everyone knows about it. He's trying to break him of the habit."

"Must've missed it. I'm gettin' old, not as sharp as I used to be."

"That so?"

"Yeah, I've actually been tossing around the idea of hangin' up my gloves and focusing on training the young guns at the gym."

That was news to me.

Dad gave a chuckle. "But if you're interested in booking my grand finale fight, Max, I'll—"

"Maximo," the voice rumbled.

"Huh?"

"My name is Maximo. *Not* Max."

The name didn't sound familiar. Knowing who my dad associated with, I could just picture the wannabe hotshot with a pot belly and greasy face who thought he was one of the Rat Pack.

I just hoped, whoever Maximo was, he hurried up and said what he needed to say. I had to eat, and after being on the go all day, my feet were killing me.

"Right, right, Maximo," Dad said. "I'll get you my girl's number, and she can help you out."

As if my dad hadn't spoken, Maximo continued. "After I talked to Jose's trainer, I went to see someone else."

"Who?"

"Carmichael. He had a lot to say about you, Shamus."

3

"Yeah?" A pitch of nerves hit Dad's voice. "We're old friends. Haven't seen him in a while. Probably about a year or so."

That was a lie. Mugsy Carmichael was one of the wannabe gangsters Dad liked to run with. He came by the gym all the time and totally creeped me out. He'd just been there earlier that week.

"You know what I hate, Ash?" the man—Maximo—asked.

"What, boss?" a new voice answered.

"Liars. Fucking hate them."

Something slammed against the wall, making me jump.

"You took the fall," Maximo bit out, his volume low, though he might as well have been shouting. There was a bass rumble to it that I could almost feel.

"I'd never—" Dad started, but based on the sound of flesh hitting flesh—the soundtrack to my life—someone punched him before he could finish.

"Don't lie to me again," Maximo said. "You took the fall after you bet on Jose."

My dad was a lot of things. A drunk. A gambler. A racist. A crap father.

And greedy.

I hadn't thought he was a cheat, though. His name, title, and reputation in the boxing world were the most important things he had. He valued them above all else—including his only daughter.

"Your loss cost people a shit-ton of money, Shamus. People who are not happy. People who are accusing me of running crooked fights. I don't like liars or cheats, and I sure as fuck don't like being accused of either."

"I didn't fall," Dad claimed.

But it was a lie.

And the sound of punches meant they knew it.

I reached out and gripped the doorknob before hesitating.

It wasn't the first time someone had come to rough Dad up. He had his share of enemies. In the fight world. In the casinos. All across the US.

I wouldn't be surprised if the sisters at Mother Mary's in New York spit when they heard his name.

At least whoever was out there had gone straight to Dad instead of roughing me up in his place. It wouldn't have been the first time that'd happened, either.

Dad was a professional boxer. He could take care of himself. There was nothing I could do except put myself in danger for nothing.

I let my hand drop from the knob.

"I can make it right!" Dad shouted, and the commotion died down.

"I think you're underestimating how pissed people are. They want their money back."

"I just need a little time, but I'll pay." Dad's panic was growing, and he didn't try to hide it. "I'll find a way. Sell the gym. Do something."

Oh, Dad. What'd you get yourself into this time?

"Pit me against one of your new guys," Dad pleaded, "and I'll do whatever. Win or throw the match, whatever you want. I'll make it believable so no one knows."

"Are you fucking kidding me?" Maximo roared, the sound rattling in my ears. "What part of 'I hate liars' does he not get?"

"No clue, boss," whoever said.

"Let's get this over with."

"Whoa, fellas. Max…imo. Maximo, man, sir. Come on." Dad lowered his voice until I had to press my ear against the shared wall to hear him. "The gym, the car, *everything*. You can have it. Take it."

"I don't want your shit, Shamus. It's as worthless as you are."

"C'mon, man, seriously, I get it. I fucked up. I'll find a way to pay and then I'll retire. I'll steer clear of the tables. But if you kill me, you'll be out the money. Dead men can't pay."

Kill?

Did he just say kill?

I threw open the door and launched myself into our small kitchen. I turned toward the entryway to the living room just as a boom filled the tiny house. Filled my head. It bounced around, leaving a ringing in my ears.

But I barely noticed the echo it left behind.

Because my focus—the entirety of it—was on my father.

My dead father with the hole in his head and his brains splattered on our crappy couch.

I'm never going to get that stain out.

I'd thought my words were in my head, but I must've spoken them out loud because every set of eyes shot to me.

Well, every set except Dad's.

Vomit lodged in my throat.

"Shit," a black-haired man bit out.

The man to his left lifted his gun and pointed it at me.

Right.

At.

Me.

I had nowhere to go. There was no way I was getting through three goons and a monster of a man. The old backdoor behind me didn't open anymore. If I jetted down the hall, I might be able to break one of the painted-shut windows, but it was more likely I'd be shot in the back.

If I'm dying, running will not *be the last thing I do on this earth.*

Trapped like a defenseless mouse surrounded by vicious predators, I stayed where I was. I steeled my spine and raised my chin.

I waited for death.

"Wait," the black-haired man said, pushing the other man's arm down. He studied me with dark eyes, running a tattooed hand through his hair and then across his stubbled jaw. Seeming to reach a conclusion, he gave a single nod. "She comes with us."

Oh no.

At that, I did turn and run.

There were fates worse than death.

And if that was what I was facing, I'd take a bullet in the back instead.

I took them by surprise and gained some distance, but my short legs were no match for the goon's much longer ones.

Thick arms wrapped around my waist, and I thrashed. I screamed. I bit. I kicked and punched and clawed.

I'd fight.

I'd die.

But I'd never go with them.

"Fucking hell," the man cursed, squeezing me like I was the rabbit Lennie pet too hard.

I caught him with a lucky kick to the junk. His hold loosened enough for me to wiggle free and punch him in the throat.

I started to turn to take on whatever was behind me, but before I could, everything shifted. The world went sideways.

And then it went black.

CHAPTER TWO

Pretty Broken Girl

MAXIMO

"WHAT'RE WE GOING to do with her?"

That was the million-dollar question.

I glanced in the rearview mirror even though I couldn't see the unconscious girl lying on the backseat of my Navigator.

Shamus' daughter.

Last time he'd gotten behind on repaying his gambling debt, he'd thrown the blame on being a single father with no other family to help. I'd assumed it was yet another of his bullshit lies.

I'd been wrong.

She was a tiny, pretty thing. Ballsy, too. She may have learned her scrappy fighting from Shamus, but her brass balls sure as hell hadn't come from the coward.

I focused on the road just in time to swerve to avoid some drunken asshat who'd decided jaywalking across the busy street was a smart choice.

Ash flipped the guy off. "This is why I drive."

"No, you drive so I can work."

"Plus, having your badass bodyguard drive you around makes you look like a badass VIP."

I raised a brow. "I don't need help with that."

"True," he agreed. "Tell me the plan."

I would have, except I had none. No ideas. No damn clue.

And I was a man who meticulously planned everything.

Shamus' death.

Packing up enough of his stuff to make it look like he'd run away from his problems.

Even down to the exact spot where I was going to bury his body so no one would find it.

I'd accounted for everything but the girl. She'd been a twist I hadn't anticipated.

"Can't exactly dump her on the side of the road," Ash said. "She's seen us and heard your name."

That was true. I had friends on the force, but there was only so much they could do. Especially if she went to the media. They loved a pretty, broken girl. And Shamus' daughter—with her huge green eyes, dusting of freckles, and long strawberry-blond hair—would be ratings bait.

More than that, if we dropped her off, she'd be left to fend for herself against wolves.

"Too young to leave on her own." I ran my hand through my hair. "I doubt that bastard had any savings. She'd be fucked even without people coming to collect Shamus' debts."

And they would come. Happily. Greedily. Eager to take their pound of flesh from the pretty, broken girl.

I knew too fucking well what it was like to suffer for the sins of the father. I wasn't leaving her to deal with Shamus' clusterfuck.

"So you're keeping her," Ash surmised, no question or judgment in his tone.

"Yeah, I'm keeping her."

JULIET

I COULD SLEEP for twenty hours.

Still half-asleep, I kept my eyes closed as I stretched and rolled before burrowing into the pillows and blankets. I must've been even more exhausted than usual because rather than a flat pillow with its threadbare case and a lumpy mattress with broken springs, I felt like I was sleeping on a cloud. Clean and fresh and *lush*.

And that's what woke me. Because nothing in my life was clean, fresh, or lush.

My mind catapulted into consciousness, the memories flashing through my brain like scenes from a horror movie.

My dad was dead.

Shot.

Murdered.

I'd been kidnapped. And drugged?

The thought launched me upright. I was still in my clothes and nothing felt out of place. No aches or pains that would take this from a nightmare to hell on earth.

I jumped from the bed, barely seeing the room as I scanned for an exit. Finding three doors, I tried the closest one, but it led to a bathroom. The second door was to a walk-in closet.

Let's see what's behind door number three.

I frantically turned the handle on the last one, but rather than a hallway, it led into another room. There was yet another door on the opposite side, and I ran to it, yanking the handle.

It didn't budge.

Panic set in, and I banged my fist over and over again. "Let me out! Let me out of here!"

No one came.

I pressed my ear to the thick wood, hoping to hear voices or movement, but it was silent.

Okay.

Okay, I need a plan.

First, I needed a weapon. Then an exit. Then I'd haul ass out of there. Then...

Well, I'd figure that out.

I turned back to search the bedroom more thoroughly.

Oh Toto, we're not in Kansas anymore.

There's no place like home... And this is definitely no place like home.

My actual bedroom was the size of a closet, and a small one at that. It barely fit my twin bed, and I had to keep my broken dresser in the bathroom. My walls were a faded pee yellow, stained and likely filled with lead. And the rust-colored carpet was worn away, left scratchy and stained—a common theme through the whole house.

Wherever I was, it was the exact opposite of all that.

The room was huge. Bigger than our living room and kitchen combined. The walls were a pretty gray-blue, no fading or stains in sight. The white, four-post bed was oversized and covered with puffy pillows and a plush comforter the same color as the walls.

There was also a white armoire, two bedside tables, and a long bench in front of the bed that matched the rest.

Our furniture at home never matched—not even two pieces, let alone a whole room. It was all cheap thrift shop finds or even cheaper curb finds.

I checked the armoire and the drawers on the bedside tables, but they were empty. Searching the bathroom next, I hoped for a razor, chemical spray, or even a plunger, but there was nothing.

I tried to lift the frosted window, but it wouldn't budge—and not because it was painted shut.

Damn.

Heading back into the bedroom, I decided to try the window that was behind the bed. Standing on the soft mattress, I pushed the pale blue curtains aside as best as I could with the headboard in the way.

The fenced-in yard—if it could even be called that—stretched far and was filled with more plants than I'd ever seen in Vegas, minus some of the casinos' gardens. They were healthy and vibrant, something that was hard to achieve in the dry heat. Off to the side, amidst all the greenery, I could see part of a pool. Beyond the tall wooden fence, there were beautiful trees and distant mountains, making a gorgeous backdrop to the picturesque landscape.

It looked like something straight out of a magazine.

Actually, it looked like a luxury resort.

I'm in a hotel. That makes sense.

Kinda.

Other than why I'm here, it makes sense.

I tried those windows and was unsurprised when they were locked. I could've broken one, but hurting myself on the glass would make me more vulnerable. Not to mention, I was on the second story. Jumping would almost certainly lead to a broken bone or worse.

Backtracking to the sitting room, I scanned each inch as if my life depended on it—because I was pretty sure it did. It was the same size as the bedroom, though more sparsely decorated. A plush couch faced a TV hanging on the wall with a long coffee table positioned in front of it. But that was all. No desk or chair. No mini fridge. No logoed pad of paper and pen. No phone hanging from the wall, a relic mainstay in all hotel rooms—or at least the motel rooms Dad and I had stayed at.

There was a rush of emotion I didn't want to face, so I bottled it up.

I had to be smart.

If nothing else, Shamus had taught me to watch out for myself.

There were no windows and only two doors—the one to the bedroom and the locked one. I inspected the locked handle for a discreet latch, but there was nothing.

Hotels locks are on the inside *of the room.*

All the cool I'd gathered disappeared. Fear seized my heart as I yelled, "Let me go! Please!" I knocked, again and again until my knuckles hurt, and then I switched to slapping the thick wood. "Please, please, please!"

I'd just given up to rest my knuckles when I heard it.

Footsteps.

I scurried away from the door as the knob began to turn.

This is how I die.

I'm the slutty cheerleader in the horror movie of life, screaming my way to an early grave.

Wishing like hell I'd found a weapon, I braced as the door opened.

It wasn't the boss or one of his goons, thankfully. Instead, an older woman came in with a tray. My eyes went behind her, but before I could make my move, the door slammed closed.

She set it down and smiled. "Pretty girl," she said with an accent. "Eat. You're too thin."

"I'm not hungry," I lied.

Tsking, she shook her head. "He does not like liars. You haven't eaten since you got here yesterday, you must be starving."

I rocked back. "I've been here since yesterday?"

That meant it'd actually been two days since I'd eaten because I hadn't had anything before running my errands the day before.

"Yes, you were tired."

"I was *drugged*," I hissed.

There was no shock on the woman's face. No confusion. No denial.

She merely shrugged. "That only lasts a few hours. You slept the other sixteen because you were exhausted."

Sixteen hours?

"What time is it?"

"Ten. I was told not to wake you until noon, but the men said you were awake." She gestured to the food. "Eat."

"I'm not hungry." My growling stomach contradicted my repeated lie.

"He *hates* liars," she emphasized, a heavy warning in her tone. It lightened when she began fussing with the dome on the tray. "The food is good. Mr. Freddy only uses the best ingredients. Better than sludge and bland microwave porridge."

I didn't want to eat. I wanted to be stubborn and petulant and on guard. But the food smelled so good, my resolve quickly weakened.

It would be stupid not to eat. I can't escape if I'm too weak. I need my strength.

Nervously approaching like she was going to jab me in the neck with a needle, I asked, "It's not poisoned?"

She looked at me like I was an idiot. "If Mr. Freddy hears you ask that, he won't cook for you again. *Ever.*"

"Got it," I mumbled. Lowering myself to the couch, I removed the metal dome to reveal a pile of food. The large plate was piled high with eggs, a mountain of home fries, toast, and a stack of bacon. A separate bowl of fruit sat next to the plate with little containers of butter, jelly, honey, and some sort of thick cream. There were also small glasses of OJ, apple juice, and milk.

It was more than I ate in one day, much less one meal.

Still, a vital piece of my DNA was missing. I would need the caffeine boost if I was going to find a way to escape, so I tentatively asked, "Would it be possible to have coffee?"

Thankfully she didn't call me greedy or take the tray away. She just gave me a motherly smile—or what I guessed was a motherly smile, I didn't exactly have a reference. "No, coffee is bad for young girls."

Tell that to Starbucks' main demographic—high school girls who can't live without their daily frappe or PSL.

"It'll stunt your growth," she continued.

Yeah, I've been five-three for two years. I'm done growing.

Keeping my thoughts to myself, I dug in.

"Do you have food allergies?" she asked.

"No, ma'am."

"Call me Ms. Vera," she corrected.

"Juliet," I said because it seemed like the right thing at the time. After I said it, I wished I'd given a fake name.

I suck at this.

"Pretty name for a pretty girl. Do you have any foods you hate?" she asked.

"Breakfast sausage, squash, and tuna. Oh, and oregano and rosemary, but that's it."

Her brow raised. "Ones you don't *like*?"

I picked up a perfectly cooked piece of bacon, crunchy but not too crunchy. It was thick, not the cheap, thin stuff we microwaved. I shook my head. "No, ma'am. I'm not picky."

She gave a soft sound of acknowledgment but otherwise left me to eat as she fussed with righting cushions and wiping down surfaces that were already immaculate.

I could only eat a quarter of the delicious breakfast before I was stuffed.

When the woman—Ms. Vera—came back in from the bedroom, she eyed my tray disapprovingly.

"I'll eat the rest for lunch," I said automatically, not wanting to piss anyone off. Realizing my response made it seem like I'd still be there in a few hours, my tone was hopeful and nonchalant when I added, "I'll take it home with me."

My hope was quickly dashed when Ms. Vera said, "You're not leaving."

"For how long?"

"Until Mr. Maximo says you can."

I was supposed to be playing it smart, but I couldn't stop myself from shouting, "That's kidnapping!"

Again, she shrugged like it was no biggie that she was an accomplice to kidnapping and unlawful holding and whatever else it was.

"I'll scream until someone calls the cops."

"No one will."

Disappointment sank like a boulder in my belly. "The other hotel guests?"

"Mr. Maximo owns four hotels, but this is not one of them." There was no anger, ridicule, or venom in her voice. It was matter of fact. "And no one will help you."

13

He owns hotels?

And this isn't one?

Then where the hell am I?

Pulling out a little drawer in the coffee table, she grabbed a remote and turned on the TV before handing it to me. "I'll be back with your lunch in a few hours."

"Wait!" I stood up. "What am I supposed to do?"

She tilted her head toward the TV. "There are hundreds of channels, I'm sure you can find something to watch."

As she approached the door, I readied myself to bolt. But when the door was opened, two goons were there.

I may have been able to knock her over, but I had no chance against them.

Flinching as the door clicked closed, I scanned the room, zeroing in on the little drawers I'd missed during my first inspection.

I pulled all three completely out, turning them over as if I was in an escape room and needed to search for clues. Which wasn't far from the truth. Only, instead of fighting the clock, I was fighting for my life. I went into the room and checked the armoire and nightstands, feeling around the back and under the drawers.

Empty.

Shit.

I was well and truly trapped.

Conserving my energy so I was ready when the opportunity arose, I went back to the sitting room, grabbed the remote, and flipped through the channels.

Hundreds and hundreds of channels.

CHAPTER THREE

And The Oscar Goes To...

JULIET

"*HAS HE* SAID when I can leave?"

I didn't speak his name. I never did.

Two full days.

I'd been there for two long, boring days. That might not seem like long, but when being held captive and waiting for my fate to be revealed, it was an eternity.

In my real life, I worked at the gym. I kept the house running. I did chores, ran errands, and then worked at the gym some more.

I didn't watch TV for hours on end. I didn't nap. I didn't eat huge, gourmet meals three times a day.

They were playing some kind of game with me, I knew it. Lulling me into a false sense of security with relaxation and beauty before pulling the rug out from under me.

What other explanation was there?

Each time I saw her, I asked if *he'd* said when I could leave. Each time the answer was the same.

"No," Ms. Vera said simply.

Damn.

Weighing my words for fear of losing what little entertainment I had, I asked, "Can I have something else to do? Some books or magazines."

"I'll ask."

"Did he say if I could have real clothes?"

When she'd brought me breakfast the day before, she'd also dropped off toiletries and a new set of clothes. Unfortunately, they were over-sized PJ pants and a tee that fit like a dress.

As comfy as they were, there was no way I'd be able to run in them.

And I needed to be able to run.

"Yes," she said.

That was something.

"Now eat." She removed the dome from my breakfast tray.

It wasn't my leftovers. It never was, no matter how many times I insisted on eating them.

Instead, there was a slice of thick bread covered in smashed avocado and a poached egg with fresh herbs. As always, there was a big bowl of fresh fruit salad, but only one glass of OJ.

Someone paid attention to what I ate and how much.

I sat and began eating the fruit. Ms. Vera shook her head, muttering that I was too skinny, but she otherwise left me alone as she went about her daily task of cleaning what was already clean.

I heard rustling from the bedroom and rolled my eyes. Like the day before, I'd made the bed only for her to undo it and make it again.

Unlike the day before, though, there was a knock on the door.

My heart raced as I bolted up, wondering who was there, what they wanted, and, most of all, if I could finally leave.

Ms. Vera came rushing in as the door opened, but it was just the goon who always ignored me.

As far as I'd seen, there was a rotation of three different ones.

The brown-haired guy in the doorway was smaller than the other two, but still a goon. He never even glanced my way, which was fine by me.

The big, bulky meathead with the dark hair always glared like he wanted to snap me like a twig.

The last seemed nicer—the handsome goon with a dimpled smile. He was tall, tattooed, and bulky with buzzed hair and a blond beard. He didn't look at me much, but at least he offered a smile when he did. It

16

beat being death glared.

Then, of course, there was *him*, but I hadn't seen him since that first night. He had black hair that was buzzed on the sides and left longer on top, scruff, a bunch of tattoos, and evil black eyes.

Monster's eyes.

"Oh good." Ms. Vera held out her hands and took the bags I belatedly noticed he held.

The ignore-me goon didn't speak or look my way before leaving—surprise, surprise.

Ms. Vera retreated to the room with the bags. As curious as I was to know what they held, I stubbornly fought the urge to ask. Sitting back down, I cut and ate a few bites of the delicious avocado toast, but I'd filled up on fruit.

When Ms. Vera came back in, she didn't comment about my left-overs as she gathered my tray. "There's some new soaps in the bathroom and a fresh set of clothes on the bed."

"Thank you." I stayed on my best behavior and didn't bite the hand that feeds.

Not yet, at least.

When she left, I went into the bedroom to check out what had been left. Sure enough, the bed had been remade, each line and fold precise. A pair of gray leggings, a white cropped tee, plain underwear, and a bra were set out on it.

When I'd asked for clothes, I'd figured I'd get... I dunno, something that looked like a prison jumpsuit or a thrift store special. I hadn't expected anything cute or soft.

Going into the bathroom, I saw the built-in shelf had been stocked. I'd gotten soap, shampoo and conditioner, and a toothbrush and tooth-paste the morning before, but there was even more of it, plus bubble bath, face wash, and a thick paddle brush.

I was tempted to soak in the tub but stuck with a quick shower. I dried off, brushed my teeth, got dressed, and waited.

I had a plan.

Thankfully, my lunch a few hours later included the usual bottle of water. Despite the nerves and anticipation clenching my stomach, I forced myself to eat all the food but tucked the bottle next to me so Vera didn't clear it away. I waited another tense hour before slipping on my worn-out shoes.

I was fed and had water.

I was rested.

I was dressed in clothes that allowed movement.

It was time.

The darkness of night may have been easier to hide in, but it also meant I'd have to navigate in said darkness.

Daytime was my best bet.

Heading to the main door, I knocked hard. "I need help! My stomach hurts so bad. I think something is wrong." When there was no response, I added a sob that was only half-forced. "Please, help."

The door clicked before opening. I thanked my lucky stars it was the ignore-me goon again and not the nasty one.

"What's wrong?"

"My stomach," I groaned.

He took a step in.

And I took my opening—literally. Like one of Dad's boxers, I ducked and weaved, dodging the man. I squeezed out the door before slamming it closed with him locked inside.

The room was at the end of a hall, leaving only one direction to go. I ran, passing door after door until I turned a corner and saw them.

Stairs.

I nearly tumbled down the slick hardwood as I skipped steps in my rush. Hitting the foyer, I wasn't being careful, taking it slow, or checking my surroundings, and I didn't care. My eyes were on the prize—the front door.

Throwing it open, I hauled ass off the porch and toward the road.

Like the backyard, there was a tall fence completely surrounding the massive property. An iron gate blocked the entrance of the winding drive. Knowing that would be easier to climb than the fence, I raced for it.

After a quick glance to confirm there was no secret button to easily open the gate, I tossed the water to the other side and squeezed my feet between the bars to climb the rattling metal. The decorative spears at the top scraped my belly and legs as I pulled myself over, but I didn't care.

I was almost free.

Landing on the other side, I picked up the bottle and took a moment I didn't have to glance around.

Nothing.

Just sprawling land with no buildings or houses I could run to or hide behind. The road was empty—not even the distant sound of traffic.

Picking a direction, I took off at full speed, pumping my legs until they ached. Rocks dug into my soles, my thin canvas shoes offering little cushioning.

But I didn't slow.

I ran until my lungs burned and my vision began to tunnel. Only at the threat of passing out did I switch to a fast walk.

The stretch of empty desert was much bigger than I'd anticipated. There were no marked trails or people. I kept going, waiting to see buildings or a road in the horizon, but each step took me deeper into nothingness.

With no sounds of anyone following me—and there was no way those big guys could be silent—I slowed further. Even with my reduced pace, the sun beating down on me made sweat drip. I stopped to rest in the shade from a boulder but worried my scent would attract bugs.

Or worse.

As more time passed, my unease grew. I looked over my shoulder, but there was no sign of the house or road.

In front of me, to the sides, in back—desert.

I should've gone for the road.

But there was no turning back.

MAXIMO

LEANING BACK IN my chair, I stared at the man sitting on the other side of my desk.

Mugsy Carmichael.

Or Ronald Carmichael, according to his birth certificate and license.

Stupid name change for a stupid man.

The longer we sat in silence, the more flop sweat dripped down his fat jowls and the more my limited patience drained.

I had four resorts to run—Moonlight, Sunrise, Star, and Nebula. I had meetings and emails and a shit-ton of headaches that came with running those four resorts. And I had a little dove to watch.

My gaze drifted to the blank security monitors that hung on the wall behind him just as he found his balls and spoke. "After we talked, Shamus McMillon, uh, disappeared."

19

"Okay." My face nor my voice gave anything away. And he was watching for confirmation that the two things were connected. Confirmation I'd killed him.

"His little girl is gone, too."

Again, I gave away nothing. "Okay."

Mugsy ran his hand through his black-dyed hair, the greasy pieces doing little to cover his ever-growing bald spot. "I know Shamus fucked up. He screwed you over—"

"*He* did?"

"Fine, *we*. I helped him, but only because he was about to lose everything. He'd gotten in bad—"

"I don't give a shit what problems he had. I give a shit about getting fucked over by a cheat and a liar."

"I said I'd make it up to you. I'm your eyes and ears. You'll get first call about new fighters. Whatever else you want, I'll do it." He inhaled deeply, gathering his courage.

What a pussy.

"Juliet," he started, saying the only thing that would interest me.

I played dumb. "Who?"

"Shamus' little girl. She's a sweet kid. A good kid."

She was a tiny thing, but she was far from the pigtailed middle schooler Mugsy was trying to paint her as.

"What about her?"

Mugsy looked nervous, and I was beginning to think I'd have to disinfect the chair when he left. Or maybe just throw the thing out. I doubted the stench of sweat and B.O. would ever fade. "She had nothing to do with Shamus' actions. She doesn't deserve to be punished."

"What are you insinuating?" I bit out.

"Nothing, nothing. I'm just saying, she's gone, too."

"If she has any sense in her head, she got as far from Shamus' bullshit as she could."

He hesitated, seeming to war with himself. "She has no other family. It was just her and Shamus. She's only seventeen."

I already knew that. Cole was finding out everything there was to know about Juliet, but it'd been a slow trickle. Shamus hadn't kept meticulous records. No birth certificate, no school records, not even a damn tax return.

I'd only agreed to Mugsy's meeting request on the off chance he had something useful to say for once in his pathetic life.

I should've known better.

Standing so fast my chair slammed into the wall behind me, I put my palms flat on my desk. "I don't know who the fuck you think you're talking to, but I'd reconsider your insinuation."

"No, no. There's no insinuation," he backpedaled. "I'm just bringing up my concern so you can keep an ear out in case anyone has seen her."

Liar.

Still glaring at him, my voice was even. "If you ever cross me again, I'll make you pay. I don't give a shit how noble you think your reasoning is, I'll make you wish for death."

"It'll never happen again."

My cell rang, but I didn't look as I hit ignore. "And if you ever come into my office and even hint at an accusation, I'll cut your tongue out and feed it to you. Are we clear?"

Before he could respond, Ash stuck his head into my office. "Answer your phone."

As he spoke, it started ringing again.

Picking it up, I saw it was Cole and connected the call. "Yeah?"

"She's gone."

My gut clenched. "What did you say?"

"She ran outside, cameras showed her heading east."

I kept my cool, but just barely. I wanted to shove my phone down Mugsy's throat to kill two pains in my ass at once.

"I'll call you back." I gave Mugsy my attention, needing him gone. "Are we clear?"

"Crystal," he choked out.

"Get the fuck out of my office."

He jumped up, and sure enough, a slick of back sweat clung to the chair.

Marco was waiting to escort our unwanted guest out.

Ash came in. "I'll go—"

But I was already up and grabbing my shit.

Ash and I walked from my office as Marco and Carmichael boarded the public elevator. I scanned my thumb at my private one.

Once we were inside, I called Cole back. "How the hell did she get out?"

"She was screaming about her stomach hurting and said she needed help."

"And so you opened the door and let her go?" I growled.

"No, I went to check on her and... Marco was right, she's fast. She dodged me and locked me in. I had to call Freddy to let me out."

"Fucking hell."

That Juliet had kicked Marco's ass at her house and then not only dodged Cole but locked him in the room was amusing. Or it would've been, had worry not sat heavy in my gut.

I should've been worried about myself since I'd added kidnapping to the murder she could pin on me.

But my concern was solely for Juliet.

My house was secluded, surrounded by nothing for miles. Going left she'd have some shade from boulders, brush, or Joshua trees, but there were no marked trails or paths to guide her. There were, however, coyotes, rattlesnakes, and the occasional scorpion.

"I'm on my way. Start searching," I said before hanging up.

I'd known her shy mouse act was just that—an act. I'd been waiting for her to try to make an escape or take revenge.

But her timing and sense of self-preservation were shit.

If I hadn't left the house.

If I hadn't turned off the monitors to deal with that dickhead.

If I hadn't taken her in the first damn place.

CHAPTER FOUR

The Predator

JULIET

WHAT WAS I THINKING?

I had no clue what time it was, but it was late.

And dark.

And cold.

And scary as fuck.

The patch of desert was *not* a patch. Nor was it a plot. It was never-ending—just desert followed by more desert surrounded by more desert.

My body ached to the bones, far beyond any exhaustion and soreness I'd ever experienced. Every step I forced wore on me like a mile. Even though I'd taken advantage of every hint of shade I'd come across, my skin was tight and painfully sunburned. And I was thirsty. So thirsty.

I wanted to go back.

But I kept moving because I had to run into civilization eventually.

I hoped.

Unable to see where I was going, my foot caught on a jagged rock. I tumbled forward, but my shoe was stuck, making my ankle twist painfully as I fell.

"Shit," I hissed, tears of pain and frustration burning my eyes. "Ow, ow, ow."

My shoe ripped and excruciating pain tore at my ankle, making me wonder if I'd broken it.

Using a boulder, I was able to stand, but as soon as I put weight on my foot, pain ripped up my leg and it gave out.

Left prone on the ground, the enormity of how badly I'd fucked up sank in. I was alone. No phone. No weapon. No food. Although I'd sipped at my water, it was long gone.

And no one would be looking for me because I had no one.

The monster and his goons likely knew I'd get lost and die, taking care of their problem without them having to lift a finger—or a gun.

I was stuck alone in the middle of the desert with bugs, wild animals, and God knew what else.

After a few minutes, I found out what else. Because as I sat, something moved over my foot.

No, it didn't move.

It *slithered*.

Slowly.

Purposefully.

And stealthily.

I hadn't even noticed it'd circled me until it was too late. Until I was surrounded by its long length.

Freezing, my breath caught in my lungs as I clenched my jaw to keep from screeching.

Even if I were uninjured, it was unlikely I could get away before the snake attacked. Being injured pretty much sealed it. How could I run if I couldn't even stand?

I couldn't.

Slow and cautious, I reached behind me for the jagged rock that'd gotten me into that mess. Once I had it, I felt for the sharpest point. I strained to see in the dark, but when I was fairly certain I saw the head, I slammed the rock down.

The snake let out a horrid, pained hiss and I let out a sobbed scream before hitting it again. And again. Even though my heart ached, I slammed the rock one last time, assuring it was dead.

Dropping the rock, I quickly scrambled away before scavengers came for both of us. Once I'd scooted enough to put some distance between me and my reptilian victim, I got control of my emotions as I racked my brain for a plan.

I couldn't just sit around and wait. There was no rescue coming. An hour of rest wouldn't make a difference to my ankle, but it would increase my chances of another predator discovering me.

And, that time, I might not be so lucky.

That left one option.

I had to crawl.

Moving slow, I ignored the coarse sand digging into my palms, the bugs relentlessly attacking, and the pain in my ankle. I wasn't making good time, but I was moving, and that's what mattered.

Always pushing.

Always fighting.

Always trying to survive.

I was so damn tired of it.

Why did I run?

Lost, scared, and in pain, a sob ripped through me as regret clawed at my chest.

I left behind a gorgeous room, three delicious meals a day, and zero responsibility... for what? To make it on my own like I always have? To barely survive?

Because I wasn't here by choice, being homeless was somehow better?

Shaking my head, I reminded myself that I didn't know what they'd planned to do to me. They could've been traffickers or pimps—a huge industry in Vegas. I wasn't sure why they'd have fed me and set me up in a beautiful room, but who knew how monsters worked.

And *he* was a monster. A murderer.

It didn't matter that Shamus was an asshole who'd been horrible to me.

It didn't matter he'd deserved worse than a quick death.

All that mattered was Maximo was capable of murder, and that meant I needed to get away.

Right?

I only made it a short distance on my hands and knees before a cramp tightened my stomach, stealing my breath and ability to move. I rolled to sit on my ass, keeping an eye on my surroundings.

I'm gonna die out here.

Alone.

Always alone.

Once my cramp subsided, I started crawling again.

But not forward.

No, I crawled in the direction I'd come from. Toward where I wanted to be. For all I knew, I was going sideways, heading farther into the desert, but I didn't care.

My arms shook with the strain of supporting my weight. My cuts were coated in sand, burning and tearing at the already painful wounds. My skin was covered in itchy bug bites. My sides hurt, my knees felt like they were going to shatter, and my clenched stomach was set to a constant growl.

I'd kill for one of Mr. Freddy's trays right now.

Using the image of a fluffy omelet and coffee to drive me on, I started crawling faster until I reached the small patch of Joshua trees I'd rested by earlier.

I'm going the right way. Maybe I'll actually survive the night.

My progress was cut off suddenly when my knee came down on something sharp. It pierced my already raw skin, stabbing in so deep, it felt like it embedded in bone

"Shit," I hissed. I fought to be strong, but each time I put weight on it, the pain grew. I sat on my ass and pulled my muddy leggings up. With no light to see, I ran my hand over my knee but nothing was there. That didn't mean there wasn't something below the surface, though.

I couldn't walk.

I couldn't crawl.

I couldn't do anything.

Just a little breather. Then I'll find a way to keep going. I'll drag myself if I have to.

Hugging my bent legs, I rested my cheek on my non-injured knee. I gave my vigilant eyes a break, allowing them to close as I inhaled deep.

And because I was so still, I heard it.

A roar.

It faded, but it wasn't silent for long.

The snap of a twig.

The rustle of brush.

Something's here.

My stomach dropped, and I froze in terrified indecision. Did I crawl? Did I try to run, further injuring my ankle and likely making a lot of noise that would alert them? Or did I stay still, allowing whatever predator was out there to track my scent and be done with it?

I didn't know, but I had to try something. Anything.

Hands to the ground, I worked to push myself to my feet, but I didn't even get the chance to test my bad ankle because my legs gave out.

I barely choked back my pained cry.

The sounds grew closer, and my eyes scanned for the predator.

Surprise and relief flooded me when I saw a dim light just before it cleared the shadows.

Maximo.

"You came," I forced out through the lump in my throat.

"*Jesus*, little dove," Maximo whispered gruffly, rushing over. His expensive slacks and white tee were still pristine, as though the dirt didn't dare touch him. Only his dress shoes showed signs of his journey, the shiny black leather scuffed and dusted with sand. Crouching in front of me, he pushed my filthy hair out of my face. His alert eyes moved between studying me and scanning our surroundings. "Are you hurt?"

I pointed to my foot. "I twisted my ankle."

"Let me see." Grabbing my calf, he began to straighten my leg, but pain zipped up the muscle, and I tucked it close. "Juliet."

I didn't even know he knew my name.

At his firm tone, I bit my lip and let him extend my leg and gently touch the swollen joint. His shadowed expression was thunderous, but his voice was soft when he chided, "What did you do to yourself?"

"I'm sorry," I said reflexively.

He stood and handed me the flashlight. I waited for him to pull me up, but instead, he lifted me in his arms.

Since I didn't want him to trip while hefting me around—not to mention, I was filthy and smelled—I insisted, "I can walk."

I think.

He didn't respond verbally, just shot me a quick look before his gaze returned to where he was stepping.

"Really, I only need a little help," I tried again.

"No."

"But—"

"Juliet." His tone was filled with warning again, as if that were the

27

only way he could say my name.

I held my tongue for as long as possible before muttering, "I really should've gone for the road."

Maximo stopped, and I worried he'd dump me on the ground. Since he was more than a foot taller than me, it wouldn't be a short fall. Instead, he tightened his hold and aimed his glower my way. "That route is harsher. You'd have been walking for miles with no trees or boulders to offer shade. You wouldn't have made it far before passing out from heatstroke." He adjusted me in his arms as he began walking again. "Or worse."

"Oh."

He made a noncommittal grunt.

After a few more minutes of tense silence, we reached a waiting four-wheeler. He set me down before grabbing the side pack and handing me two sandwiches and a bottle of water. "Eat."

He didn't have to tell me twice. I dug into the PB&J like it was the best thing I'd ever tasted because, right then, it was. I polished off both and the glorious water within minutes.

My stomach hurt from eating so fast, but it was better than it hurting from hunger or fear.

Once I was done, he took my garbage and shoved it in the pack.

"What time is it?" I asked.

"Almost midnight."

God, I'm so stupid.

I'd gotten lost, sunburned, injured to the point of incapacitation *twice*, and had been forced to kill a snake.

And it'd only been half a day.

What would've happened had he not come? Would I have survived the next day? Would I even have survived the night?

But I wouldn't have to find out because Maximo had come for me when he could've easily left me out there to die.

Unable to choke down my gratitude, I blurted, "Thank you for looking for me."

"Juliet."

"I thought... I just... I was—"

"Shut up."

"Shutting up," I whispered before he changed his mind and left me.

Maximo climbed behind me before the four-wheeler roared to life.

A headlight lit the way, but he seemed to know where he was going, his speed eating up the distance until his house finally came into view. He stopped next to his gate and killed the engine before standing. Pulling his cell from his pocket, he touched the screen a few times. "Call them off, I have her." I jumped when his hand landed on my head, but he just absentmindedly stroked my hair as he stared toward the house. "Yeah. Get the car, meet me on the street."

The car?

Of course they're not going to let me go back to the house.

Of-fucking-course they're not.

I'd been a witness and then a prisoner. Trying to escape had shown them I was a loose end who needed to be cut before I unraveled everything. Maybe he'd rescued me just so he could make sure I died.

The fear that'd disappeared after my rescue came back times a hundred.

I didn't bother arguing when he picked me up. I didn't ask the millions of questions that swirled in my head. I didn't voice my fears.

Because none of it mattered.

Lost in thought, I stayed silent as an SUV pulled out of the driveway and stopped in front of us. Handsome goon got out, his eyes on us. I waited for him to glare like the mean one, but he didn't. If anything, he looked happy to see me. He opened the backdoor, and Maximo set me on the seat.

When the door closed, I buckled up on instinct, numbly going through the motions.

Rather than driving or sitting in the passenger's seat, Maximo opened the other back door and climbed in, moving over until he was in the middle. He reached over, unbuckled my seatbelt, and pulled me into his lap.

Maybe this will be like the old gangster movies where he throws me out of a moving car.

How well can I tuck and roll?

Handsome goon got in and began driving.

"Is everything ready?" Maximo asked him.

"All set and waiting."

Separating myself from the terror and pain, I stared out the window.

There was a lot of nothing. Just as Maximo had said, that route was desert for miles and miles with no houses, buildings, boulders, or even brush around.

As if reading my thoughts, he whispered, "Told you."

I nodded but couldn't find any words.

The farther we drove, the more my panic took hold. Rather than pointless begging, I decided to use my time to curse my bastard father. If he hadn't lied and cheated and lied some more, none of this would've happened. I would be asleep in my shitty bed in my shitty home in my shitty life.

I still wouldn't have been safe—I never was—but I was used to that. Defending myself against assholes, drunks, and creepers was easier than taking on the elements, bugs, and snakes.

"You okay?" Maximo asked, bringing his hand to my forehead. "You're shivering."

It was with rage, but I didn't share that. "I'm fine."

He met the driver's eyes in the rearview mirror.

The goon lifted his chin. "I could go a lot faster if you'd put her down so she can buckle up."

"No," was all Maximo said, and the goon didn't argue.

If I were a different girl who'd lived a different life, I may have let myself believe his concern. And that concern would've given me hope. But I knew better.

Hope was an empty word on the way to disappointment.

Exhausted—mentally and physically—I wanted to rest my head, but I couldn't. The pain made it easy to stay alert as I sat stiffly in the silent car. Staring at my hands in my lap, I sank further into myself as I used the time to build my walls against whatever was to come.

If I was about to die, I'd go out with my pride—it was the only thing I had to my name.

If he was about to dump me back into the shithole that was my life, I'd figure it out.

I always did.

After a while, the car turned and turned again. It slowed, but only when it came to a stop did I look up.

What the hell?

CHAPTER FIVE

Fine, Fine, Fine

JULIET

A HOSPITAL.

He wouldn't take me to a hospital if he were going to kill me. That'd be like giving a manicure to someone before hacking off their fingers—a pointless waste of time.

My eyes darted from the Emergency Department sign to Maximo.

His face gave away nothing as he climbed out before readjusting me in his arms and carrying me into the packed waiting room. Rather than joining the lengthy line, he paused for a moment.

A man pushed through double doors to our right. "Mr. Black."

Maximo walked over to him. "Doctor Pierce."

Maximo Black.

I wonder if that's his real name or an alias.

The doctor gestured. "This way."

We followed through the double doors, down a winding hallway, and into a private room rather than a curtained stall. Maximo finally set me down on the exam table, but he stayed close.

He must be making sure I don't tell the doc I was kidnapped.

I wouldn't. For one, they clearly knew each other. Even if I told the truth, the doctor might not believe me. I'd just further piss off Maximo for nothing. I was fairly certain he wasn't going to kill me, but I didn't want to push my luck.

Beyond that, if the doc did take my side, he'd call the cops. I was seventeen. I had no family. Bringing the authorities into it was a one-way ticket to foster care.

I'd rather take my chances alone.

"What happened?" the doc asked.

"I had the brilliant idea to explore by myself. I got lost and tripped on a rock." I pulled my leggings up to reveal my bruised knees.

"Christ, dove," Maximo bit out, horrified.

He had every reason to be. My legs looked awful—especially my knee that was swollen, angry red, and hot to the touch.

"After I hurt my ankle, I tried to crawl and stabbed my knee with something."

The doctor opened a drawer and pulled out an ugly gown. "Undress to your underwear and put this on. We'll be right outside."

"I'm not leaving," Maximo said, his gaze still locked on my battered legs.

"Mr. Black," the doctor said pointedly.

Hesitantly, I touched Maximo's arm, his eyes shooting to mine. "Please."

He ran his hand through his hair before nodding. "I'm coming back in."

The challenge in his dark eyes dared anyone to argue, but I wasn't going to. I didn't know why it mattered to him. I didn't know why he was acting so nice. I did, however, know I must've lost my mind out there in the desert.

Because after the day I'd had, I found a monster's company comforting.

They left the room, and I hurried to shed my filthy clothes. I pulled on the thin, scratchy smock and sat back on the exam table.

The door opened a moment later and both men came in. The doctor pulled various things out of cabinets, lining them up on a metal tray. He put on a pair of gloves and gave me a reassuring smile. "We need to get you cleaned up for an x-ray."

Shit. I just want to eat and sleep—and not necessarily in that order.

I'll be here forever.

My dad had broken his finger during a match the year before, and it'd taken hours to get x-rayed and more hours to get the results and needed splint. It'd been a different hospital, but they were all backed up at night.

Drunken injuries were as much a Vegas mainstay as showgirls and Barry Manilow.

All thoughts of time flew from my head as the doctor began vigorously scrubbing my leg.

"Ow!" I cried on a startled gasp.

"Pierce," Maximo growled, the same warning in his tone he used with me.

At least I'm not the only one who irritates him.

The doctor froze, but I shook my head. "I'm fine. I just wasn't expecting it to sting so bad."

"I'll put in an order for pain meds as soon as I'm done. Are you allergic to anything?"

I shook my head.

When he went back to cleaning the dried dirt, I sat as still as possible, choking back tears and pleas to stop. The only movement was the rapid rise and fall of my chest.

"Dove," Maximo whispered soothingly, stroking the top of my head. I wanted to lean into his touch, but I couldn't.

Shouldn't.

My muscles were so tense, my bones ached, but I stayed quiet and stoic as the soap stung my wounds and the scrubbing rubbed my skin raw.

It felt like a hundred hours later when the doctor finally sat back and surveyed my red skin. "That's the best we'll be able to do. I'll get transport in here to take you to x-ray."

The doctor left, closing the door behind him.

Maximo came to stand in front of me, his hands gripping the edge of the exam table as he leaned down so we were face to face.

Avoiding his gaze, I looked to the side. There was a tattooed point that crept up his neck, but I couldn't figure out what it was.

"Look at me," he ordered, making my gaze shoot from his mystery ink to his eyes. "Are you okay?"

"I'm fine," I said automatically.

"Juliet."

"Really, I'm fine. You can go."

His dark eyes narrowed, and I scooted back on the table. He added a clenched jaw to his glare, but before he could speak, a woman in green scrubs pushed a wheelchair in.

Her eyes went huge when she saw Maximo, and it took her a moment to drag her focus to me. "I'm Mia from transport, here to take you to x-ray. Ready, sweetie?"

"Already?" I asked.

"Doctor Pierce ordered it," she answered with a smile, though I could see matching surprise and confusion in her expression.

Maximo didn't seem to share our confusion. He picked me up before I could climb down, lowering me to the wheelchair.

"I could've handled the three steps," I said.

He didn't respond verbally, just gave me another *look*. That seemed to be his go-to move when he didn't deem something worthy of a reply.

Mia moved to push the wheelchair, but Maximo got there first. She didn't bother to argue—smartly saving herself from *the look*—and led the way through the halls, swiping her badge periodically to unlock doors and summon the transport elevator.

Once we reached the ground floor, Mia gestured to a spot against the wall. "Park the chair over there. They'll be right with her, so if you'd like to get a snack or coffee, now's a good time." Her smile changed from professional to something that made it clear *he* was the snack she wanted to eat. "I can show you where the cafeteria is."

Maximo didn't look at her. "I'll wait."

In the face of his coldness, she was right back to professional. "Okay, good luck."

As she walked away, Maximo asked me, "Are you in pain?"

"No, I'm fine."

"You're scowling."

I am?

"I'll have Pierce get you the pain meds now."

Grabbing his arm, I shook my head. "I'm fine. Honestly."

"You only had those sandwiches, are you hungry?"

"Can I have a coffee?" I asked, desperate for the bitter goodness and the needed caffeine jolt after such a rough day.

"A small one."

I'd suck on a used coffee filter right now, so anything is good.

"Sugar and cream?" At my nod, he said, "I'll be back."

After a quick yet uncomfortably positioned x-ray, I got into the hall to find Maximo waiting with a small coffee cup in his hand. I grabbed for it as soon as it was within reach, but he pulled it away. When I went for it again, Maximo lifted it near his head. Since he was over a foot taller than me *and* I was sitting, it might as well have been on the moon.

"Please," I tried because I was willing to beg.

He kept hold of it for a long moment before finally handing it over.

I grinned as the bitter scent filled my nose. "Oh yeah, that's the good stuff."

The same transport woman came over, using the condescending voice and name again. "Ready, sweetie?"

Yes, bitch.

"Yup, *hun.*" I may not have said what I wanted to, but I also wasn't able to completely bite my tongue.

Mia gave a tight smile before staring ahead of her.

Shit, I know better than to be petty.

I glanced up at Maximo, hoping he wasn't pissed or embarrassed, but a barely-there smirk curved his lips. He met my eyes and winked before looking ahead.

For a monster, that was hot.

Wait, what?

Shut up, self. You're delirious.

When we returned to the room, Dr. Pierce and a nurse were already waiting. Maximo lifted me onto the table, and the nurse took my coffee, setting it on the counter before handing me a little paper cup of pills and a cup of water. "For the pain."

"Thanks." I gratefully swallowed the pills and chugged the water. If I couldn't have my scalding coffee, the cold, refreshing water was the next best thing.

The nurse opened a packet and a sterile swab, dipping the swab into the goo before passing it to the doc. He rubbed it across a nasty gash on my shin.

"Shit," I hissed. The burn didn't dissipate—it grew and grew. It spread across my skin like lava. The heat was so bad, I expected to see my skin bubbling or melting away.

Tears welled, and I reached out to clutch something so I wouldn't punch the doctor.

I didn't even realize I'd grabbed Maximo's forearm until he pried my fingers away before my nails gauged chunks out of his tattoos. I was in too much pain to feel embarrassed or apologize, but I did release my death grip. Before I could pull my hand out of his, he adjusted his hold. His tattooed fingers wove through mine, giving me a reassuring squeeze.

And I squeezed the hell out of his.

I was beginning to worry I'd pass out when the doc finally leaned back.

I survived. We're done.

"You've got a few bad cuts on your back," he said, bursting my bubble.

Stupid crop top.

If my shins hurt, the thin, sensitive skin of my back killed. I'd have cried out, but I didn't have any air in my lungs to force out.

Thankfully, the torture only lasted a minute before Dr. Pierce moved away.

"Are we done?" Looking up at Maximo as tears trailed down my cheeks, I asked him, "Can I go home now?"

But Maximo didn't have time to answer before movement stole my attention.

My chest tightened as I watched Dr. Pierce lift a pair of giant tweezers off the tray. "I need to check your knee."

My hand shot out to grab Maximo's, my entire body tense as I watched the doctor adjust a light so it was shining on me. The tweezers touched the angry wound, and my shoulders slumped in relief.

This isn't too bad. Definitely not as bad as the ointment.

But then he began moving them. I was positive half the sharp tweezers were through my leg. Stabbing. Gauging. *Digging.*

My eyes darted down to reassure myself he wasn't actually peeling muscle from bone, but at the sight of the open flesh—*my* open flesh—my head swam and spots floated across my tunneled vision.

I'd grown up in boxing gyms all across the country. I'd seen torn brows, cheeks, and lips. I'd even patched them up.

But it never got easier to see.

I must've looked as nauseous as I felt because Maximo put his hand on the back of my head and pushed my face into his side so I couldn't see anything.

It was a million years—or maybe a few minutes—until the pain finally eased.

Pushing against Maximo's tight hold, I watched as Doctor Pierce held up the tweezers. A jagged chunk of wood was pinched at the end.

"That was in my leg?" I wheezed, growing lightheaded again.

Something beeped, but my horrified gaze was locked on the wood.

"Perfect timing, your x-ray results are in." Dr. Pierce typed something into a computer attached to the wall. A medical file loaded, and my eyes landed on my name on the top of the screen.

Dove Black.

Ha. Maybe now that I'm on my own, I'll change my name.

Be someone other than a worthless McMillon.

With another few clicks, fuzzy black and white images popped up. I studied them as though I had any clue what I was looking at.

"Good news," the doctor said, solving the mystery for me. "You've got a grade two sprain, but no break. Your knees are fine, though."

"What do I need to do for the ankle?" I asked, knowing too much about wrapping injuries.

"We'll get you a brace. Stay off it as much as possible for the next two weeks, at least." He clicked a few buttons. "I'll print out discharge paperwork with more instructions, things to watch out for, and the name of a lotion for your burns."

"Thank you," I said sincerely. Even though he'd caused me insane pain, it would've been a million times worse had I left the cuts untreated.

Especially the tree trunk in my knee.

The doctor shook my hand before shaking Maximo's. "I trust you'll be purchasing a table at the hospital's fundraiser next month."

"I always do," Maximo said, not bothered by the thinly veiled extortion.

Shit, this has probably cost a fortune and my insurance barely covers a Flintstones vitamin and a prayer.

It wouldn't be the first bill to go to collection, and I knew it wouldn't be the last.

After the doctor and nurse left, I didn't speak and neither did Maximo. My thoughts were on what was to come.

He clearly wasn't going to kill me. My guess was he'd drop me back at home—likely *after* he threatened me to stay silent.

Maybe it made me a shit person or a shit daughter—or both—but I wouldn't go to the cops. It was doubtful they'd even care about Shamus' death. It wasn't worth ending up in foster care. Or worse, having them think I was responsible for his death.

A quick interview with some of his buddies would show I had a lot of motive.

My plan was to go back to my house, focus on how to survive, and pretend the last few days never happened.

The nurse returned with the brace and showed me how to slide it on my foot, even though I already knew. She handed Maximo my discharge and prescription papers before recapping the doc's orders.

By the time she finished her spiel, the pain meds had hit my brain. *Those pills were* not *Motrin...*

My head was a floaty balloon, and I was exhaustedly loopy. *Have the lights in here always been so bright and annoying? And has Maximo always been so hot? No. Definitely not. It's the drugs. Monsters aren't hot. I need to get out of here. I'm pretty sure my balloon head can just float me away.*

Not waiting for help, I stood and wobbled, both from the meds and my foot.

Maximo looked ready to throttle me. "Careful."

"I'm fine," I said for what felt like the billionth time that day. So much so, the word didn't even sound real anymore. "Fine, fine, fine."

"I'll let you get her home. Contact us if there are any issues." She looked at me. "Feel better, Dove."

I didn't like her calling me that. I didn't like her voice.

But it was better than her calling me sweetie, so I wasn't bitchy. "Thank you."

"Let me see if I can find you some clean clothes to wear," she said as she headed for the door.

"We're set," Maximo told her.

My eyes darted to my crusty clothes and I grimaced. I'd rather stay in the open butt hospital gown than try to put that mess back on.

When she opened the door, handsome goon was standing in the hall. He tossed a bag to Maximo and left just as fast.

Maximo pulled out a pair of fleece PJ pants and a gray tee.

Oh, thank God.

He tore the tags off the shirt and handed it to me before turning around.

I slid the scratchy gown off before pulling on the super soft shirt. "Pants, please."

"Sit," he ordered.

Right. It'd be kind of hard for me to put them on when I can't even stand.

I wiggled onto the exam table. Maximo took a step closer but stopped suddenly. He handed me the pants before giving me his back again.

Once I had my pants on, I stood to pull them the rest of the way up. I tried to take a step toward the wheelchair—I wasn't a total irresponsible dummy—but Maximo picked me up. "I can walk."

"And look where it got you."

"Fine, I can ride in the wheelchair."

"Or you can be quiet and let me carry you."

I narrowed my eyes but stayed quiet. If he wanted to waste his time and energy hefting me around, that was on him.

It beat the scratchy wheelchair fabric against my back.

When we got outside, the goon was waiting with the SUV. Like the ride there, Maximo got in and settled me on his lap before handing the goon the prescriptions. "Get these filled."

"I can do it," I argued.

"Ash has it handled."

"There's a pharmacy on my street. I'll bring them in tomorrow when I go shopping."

"Your street?"

I nodded through my yawn, exhaustion and pain meds double teaming my brain. "You didn't throw me out of the car. Or take me somewhere to kill me."

"You thought I was going to kill you?"

"Uh, yeah," I said, the *duh* going unsaid but highly implied. "But you didn't, so that means you're dropping me off at home."

His body went tight. "You're not going back there."

"I live there."

"Not anymore."

"What do you mean? It's all I have."

"Not anymore," he repeated.

I was trying to keep up with the conversation, but it made no sense in my medicated haze. "The point is, you saved my life. I won't go to the police. We're even. You can just drop me off wherever."

His voice was firm and angry. "I'm not dropping you off anywhere."

"I can't just stay."

"That's exactly what you're going to do."

"Why?"

"Because you're seventeen, and I'm not going to drop you at that dump so you can be homeless in a few days."

"Homeless?"

"That shithole is in foreclosure."

The familiar money stress settled on my chest, but I breathed through it like I always did. It wasn't a new occurrence. I'd been managing that anxiety since I was ten and first understood how royally fucked we always were. "I'll figure something out."

I always did.

I always held it together. I always made it work. I always survived.

"I'm not having this fucking argument. You're not going to live alone in that slum. You'd be dead by the morning," he bit out, shaking his head. "Christ, I'm offering paradise and she wants hell."

I was about to ask why it mattered when it hit me.

He felt guilty.

I wouldn't be a charity case. I didn't want his pity. But he wasn't offering out of the goodness of his heart. He was offering to clear his conscience.

If I stayed for a bit, I'd have time to figure out my next step and his guilt would be alleviated.

It was a win-win.

"Maybe for a few days," I agreed after a thoughtful moment. If things went downhill, I'd cross that bridge when I had to.

"Hear that, Ash? She'll tolerate paradise for a few days."

Everything caught up to me, and I couldn't keep my head up. It dropped to his shoulder as I gave a soft laugh. At least I thought I did.

I wasn't really sure.

MAXIMO

JESUS, SHE'S STUBBORN.

And deadweight.

I cringed at the phrase. Juliet had thought we were driving to her death. And yet she'd sat, quiet and brave.

It made me wonder what she'd lived through that made her grow so strong.

Or maybe what she'd lived through that made death seem not so bad.

And made *me* seem not so bad.

Because she didn't hate me. I'd watched for it, expecting loathing in her gaze. I'd waited for her to scream or shank me with a broken tongue depressor. But she hadn't. She'd smile at me. She'd reached for me when she was in pain.

She'd wanted me there.

Ash hit the brakes suddenly, and I tightened my hold. I should've put her down so she was buckled.

I should've put her down so she could sleep comfortably.

I should've put her down because I was a thirty-two-year-old man who had no business holding a seventeen-year-old in his lap.

I didn't put her down.

Thinking she was asleep, I readjusted her when she murmured, "Ash."

His surprised eyes went to the rearview mirror. "Yeah?"

"Your name is Ash."

"Yup," he said, amused.

"That's a better name than *handsome goon.*"

Ash started chuckling before catching himself and disguising it as a cough, but I could see his cocky smirk in the mirror.

She thinks he's handsome?

"You're off door duty," I bit out, pissed and irritated for reasons I didn't want to think about.

"Whatever you say, boss," Ash muttered, not even trying to hide that chuckle.

Bastard.

CHAPTER SIX

Nemesis

JULIET

I HURT.

Every inch of my body was sore and burning and throbbing. I rolled over in bed, wanting more sleep, but something had woken me.

No—*someone.*

"Good morning," Ms. Vera's accented greeting pushed through my muddled brain.

"Sleep," I groaned.

She flipped a switch and the curtain slid open, letting in all sorts of stupid light.

I groaned again and buried my head under the pillow.

"You need your medicine and cream," she insisted, tearing the puffy cloud of a blanket off of me. "Then, you need to eat."

The meds and cream sounded awful. The food, though? That was worth waking up for.

I sat up and saw a glass of water, pills, and the ointment lined up on the bedside table. I was in the middle of swallowing the meds when she smiled.

"That was easy," she said. "I thought I'd have to tell you there was coffee to get you out of bed."

Nearly choking in my excitement, I wiped my mouth. "There's coffee?"

"A small cup." She tutted her disapproval. "Too young, but Mr. Maximo said he owed you."

My coffee yesterday. I forgot about it.

Who have I become?

I reached for the ointment, but Ms. Vera shook her head. "Shower first. *Carefully.*"

Shower and coffee?

Oh hell yeah.

I removed the brace and was going to use the wall to get into the bathroom, but Ms. Vera wheeled something over. It resembled a scooter, just with the flat part higher up. "Put your knee here."

I stood and put my shin on the pad, my foot hanging off the back. Steering with the handle, I was able to easily wheel into the bathroom. I was tempted to soak my muscles in the bath with some salts, but everything had been rearranged and I didn't feel like searching.

Plus, coffee was waiting, and I wasn't about to miss out again.

I let the hot water pound my skin as I shampooed my hair until my head was raw. I conditioned and washed as best as I could without irritating the scrapes.

When I got out and dried off, I coated my face and arms in soothing aloe before cracking the door to see clothes set out for me.

I pulled on the large tee and oversized joggers, grateful they weren't constricting. Tugging the pant leg up, I got the ankle brace on when Ms. Vera came back in.

I pushed the other pant leg up over my knee and slathered the ointment on my shins and knees. Bending forward, I tried to reach the tender spots on my back, but I was pretty sure I was disinfecting the shirt.

"Let me do it," Ms. Vera said, taking the tube from me. She was gentle and quick as she treated the scrapes.

I wondered if Maximo blamed her for my escape, and guilt hit me hard.

"You didn't get in trouble, did you?" I asked even though I wasn't sure I wanted the answer.

"You need to eat." I thought she was dismissing my nosy question, which did not bode well, but then she added, "And I'll tell you a story."

Using the scooter, I got myself into the sitting room and flopped onto the couch. I didn't bother to lift the metal dome and just zeroed in on the coffee. It was small, but better than nothing. I added some sugar and cream before clutching the warm mug as I sat back to savor the deliciousness.

Vera didn't sit and instead flitted around the room to do her dusting as she spoke. "There was a very mean, crooked man. He worked for bad people and did bad things."

Is she talking about Maximo?

"One of those bad things he did was come to America to try to spread his boss' power. When he was caught—and it happened fast because he was not a smart man—he fled home, bringing the danger to his wife. A wife he cheated on, beat, and was cruel to."

Definitely not *Maximo.*

But poor Ms. Vera.

Why did the men we trusted to take care of us—albeit in very different ways—fail us so miserably?

"The man he'd tried to ruin came and killed the evil man, but he didn't kill his wife. Knowing she was a victim of her husband's cruelty, he offered her a choice and a threat. She could stay there or she could come work for him."

"And the threat?"

"That if she ever crossed him or even thought about avenging her husband's death, he'd kill her with zero hesitation."

"But you never did."

It wasn't a question, but still Ms. Vera dropped the façade and answered. "Never. He offered me kindness instead of cruelty. A job." She gave me a pointed look. "A home instead of a hovel. Life instead of pain and struggles."

Not-so-subtle message received.

"To answer your earlier question, he did not punish me for your actions. The fact you are here is proof that Mr. Maximo is a fair man who doesn't believe in punishing people for others' mistakes." She paused, scanning the beautiful room before continuing. "And running was a mistake. One I hope you don't make again, sweet girl. Because along with being fair, Mr. Maximo is no fool. And next time you will not be as incredibly lucky as you've been."

Not-so-subtle threat received, too.
"Now eat," she ordered. "I'll be back."
As Ms. Vera left, I pulled the dome off and grimaced.
Sausage patties and egg whites.
I guess someone decided I need to be extra-healthy when healing.
Damn them.

I drank my coffee and ate my small bowl of berries before choking down the eggs and the sausage. When I'd eaten all I could, I scootered into the bathroom to brush the sage taste out of my mouth. And then I scootered around because I was bored.

When my legs hurt too bad to continue, I went back to the couch to watch TV.

But it was just my luck that the one time I wanted to watch, the cable was out. I flipped through fuzzy channel after fuzzy channel, but I only had access to a few crappy daytime talk shows or fake court dramas. I settled in to wait for *The Price is Right.*

Maybe I'll just doze.

IT FELT LIKE I'd just drifted off when Ms. Vera was back with a goon. Unfortunately, it wasn't the handsome one. Extra unfortunately, it was the guy who used to ignore me but had taken to glaring.
Apparently, he's holding a grudge about being locked in a room.
I was about to apologize but bit my tongue and returned his glare.
Now he knows how it feels.
He picked up my old tray and left as Ms. Vera put down the new one.
"I just had breakfast," I pointed out.
"Four hours ago."
Okay, so I did more than doze.
Ms. Vera left before I could mention the cable being out.
Oh well, I'll ask at dinner.
Since my breakfast had been less than appetizing, my stomach grumbled, happy to eat again. I removed the dome and my empty stomach sank. Thick white bread sandwiched lettuce, tomato, cheese, and—so gross—tuna salad. It smelled like low tide on a hot day, and my stomach churned.

Holding my breath, I scraped off as much tuna as I could before adding the small portion of chips to the topping sandwich. It took all my stubbornness, but I got it down without losing my lunch *and* breakfast.

The bowl of berries was even smaller than that morning's, but I savored each delicious bite.

I'd just finished when someone knocked and the door was opened. Ignore-now-glare man came in to get the tray. He tossed something to the couch next to me.

"What's that?" I asked, not tearing my eyes from him.

I didn't think he'd attack me, but I wasn't sure. I didn't trust anyone, but especially not people I'd ticked off.

"From the boss," was all he said before leaving.

Once the door clicked closed, I looked at the box next to me. A beautiful iridescent bow was on top of the pretty gray wrapping paper. I took the bow and slapped it on my head before tentatively unwrapping the paper. It took me a moment to figure out what I was looking at.

An iPad.

He gave me an iPad.

I lifted the lid from the box to find a shiny, sleek tablet. It was so pretty. I wasn't sure if technology was supposed to be pretty, but it was. My experience with gadgets was limited. My old cell had been a laggy brick. The computer at the gym was one step above a hamster-powered machine.

The iPad was the opposite of both.

Careful not to drop it, I took it out of the box and spotted a note underneath.

A belated birthday present

-M

How did he know about my birthday?

I pressed the power button to find it'd been set up and was ready to use.

Out of curiosity, I tried to download Facebook, only to find it—along with every other app—had been blocked. Most of the internet was unavailable, too, but I could visit some sites. Bringing up Google, I typed in *Maximo Black* to find it completely restricted. No websites, no pictures, no news stories.

No surprise.

It was worth a shot.

I went to the bookstore app but wasn't able to download anything, even the freebies. When I checked out iBooks, there were already some mysteries and historical nonfictions downloaded.

Since libraries were free, books had been one of the few sources of entertainment I'd had access to no matter where we'd lived. I preferred serial killer biographies or true crime, with the occasional fantasy thrown in, but desperate times called for desperate measures.

Turning off the soap opera I'd barely been following, I opened one of the books and settled in.

I didn't care that it was locked down tighter than a thirteen-year-old boy's laptop. I didn't care that the book selection sucked. It was an iPad and it was *mine*.

My fingertips ran across some ridges on the back, and I flipped it over to see an engraving.

Happy Birthday, little dove.

I wonder if he knows how few presents I've received in my life… and that this is, by far, the best one.

"Do you know what's up with the TV?" I asked Ms. Vera when she returned with dinner later.

I'd finished one of the mystery novels, despite it being boring, long-winded, and so predictable, I'd correctly guessed the clichéd villain in the second chapter.

My brain needed a rest.

"What's wrong with it?" she asked.

"None of the channels are working."

She glanced at it. "I'll ask one of the men."

"Thanks."

She set down the tray. "It's time for medicine and cream."

Damn.

"Okay," I muttered.

I scootered after her into the bedroom. Like the morning, I took the pill and did my legs before she helped me reach my back.

"Thanks," I said when she finished.

She offered me one of her motherly smiles. "Go wash your hands

47

then eat."

I didn't argue because my disassembled fishy sandwich had left a lot to be desired.

When I returned to the sitting room, Ms. Vera was already gone. Loneliness swirled around me.

A familiar feeling.

Sighing, I flipped through the three channels that worked. Two were playing the news and one had a decade-old syndicated sitcom. Leaving it on that, I lifted the dome to reveal a huge piece of roasted chicken. I didn't even care that it was accompanied by a few roasted carrots and a butt-ton of disgusting yellow squash coins. The chicken was massive and would be more than enough on its own.

Cutting a big piece, I stabbed it with a fork and shoved the whole chunk into my mouth.

And then I spit it back out into a napkin.

Rosemary.

The smell I hadn't been able to place was my nemesis herb. My mouth tasted like I'd just made out with a Christmas tree.

I peeled the skin back and picked at the meat. The flavor was still there but not as strong. I ate the carrots before trying a piece of squash out of desperation. The texture and taste were as off-putting as I remembered. More so, actually.

There was no fruit, just a glass of milk I chugged to clear away the pine tree taste.

Ms. Vera must not have told Mr. Freddy what I hated.

Hopefully he's still paying attention to what I've left behind.

Like after lunch, there was a knock on the door before the newly-glaring guy came in. He was silent as he grabbed the tray.

"Uh, hey—" I started, wanting to ask for something else to eat. When his angry eyes aimed at me, though, I changed my mind. Putting my knees to my chest like a shield, I wrapped my arms around my legs and stammered an apology. "Sorry, forget I said anything."

His expression went scary hard, but his tone was gentle when he asked, "What do you need?"

"Nothing." He glowered, and I scooted into the corner which just made him glower more. Since he didn't seem willing to leave until I spoke, I said, "I, uh, wanted to say I'm sorry about yesterday. It won't happen again."

His expression stayed tight, but he lifted his chin and left.

Okay then.

Apology accepted?

THE NEXT MORNING, it wasn't Ms. Vera who woke me. It was the OG glaring goon and he showed up even earlier than Ms. Vera did.

I was grumpy at the early wakeup after having tossed and turned the night before.

I was even grumpier when I got to the sitting room to see there was no coffee on my tray.

And I was damn disgruntled to see my breakfast was a frittata filled with squash, mushrooms, and chopped breakfast sausage.

I ate around the squash, but it was cut small, infiltrating every damn bite. The rest of the frittata was a work of delicious art, so the inclusion of the squash was even more infuriating.

I hate Mr. Freddy.

DESPITE THE FACT I'd started reading during breakfast, I was only a handful of chapters into a dull book about ancient civilizations when the goon brought lunch.

Desperate for human interaction, I set down my iPad to say hi to him, but he put the tray on the table and hauled ass out again like the room was on fire.

Do I smell bad?

At the thought of unpleasant odors, I inhaled, my shoulder slumping in relief when I didn't catch a whiff of tuna from under the dome. I excitedly whipped it off to see another sandwich. I wasn't sure what it was, but it wasn't tuna, so that was a step in the right direction.

I took a tentative bite before grimacing.

The rosemary chicken.

All the times I offered to eat my leftovers, and they finally took me up on it with rosemary freaking chicken.

49

I opened the sandwich, willing to eat the lettuce, tomato, and cheese again, but there was nothing but the awful rosemary chicken salad.

Pushing it aside, I grabbed the small spoon out of the orange half that was in a small bowl.

Who gives someone half an orange and a weird spoon?

I scooped out a chunk and popped it into my mouth only to quickly realize it wasn't an orange at all. It was a bitter, tart, disgusting grapefruit.

Stupid grapefruit, piggybacking off a grape's good name to trick people into thinking it's delicious, too.

Giving up on lunch all together, I picked up the iPad to read the stupid book.

There's only so much Mesopotamia a girl can handle before she wishes she was wiped out by conquerors.

CHAPTER SEVEN

Sick Fuck

JULIET

I CAN'T DO IT.

I just can't freaking eat this.

I glared at my dinner—a triple whammy of slices of sage pork covered in a rosemary sauce with sautéed squash. I'd lived on small, crappy meals for years. I should've been able to suck it up and choke down the gross food, but I couldn't do it again. I just couldn't.

For an entire week, all my meals had consisted exclusively of food I loathed. Tuna sandwiches. Rosemary chicken. Sage pork. Omelets filled with sausage and covered in oregano. Sides of squash and gross grapefruit—something I hadn't known I hated but I very much did.

I was being punished.

I'd suspected it after a couple days, because, really, what were the chances they kept serving me my most hated foods? But it'd seemed egotistical that meals would be planned around messing with me.

Then it became obvious it wasn't a coincidence.

It was planned and precise torture.

Because it didn't end at the food. The TV no longer worked at all. My iPad had disappeared, and I hadn't been able to ask Ms. Vera because *she'd* disappeared, too. My clothes were back to oversized and my bath stuff had been cleared out and replaced by the same cheap stuff I'd used at home.

I was hungry for something that actually tasted good.

I was exhausted thanks to the goons waking me with the sun every day.

I was stir-crazy from being stuck in the room with no TV or books.

And because Ms. Vera had been replaced with silent goons, I was lonely. Gut-wrenchingly lonely.

So I snapped.

Scootering to the door, I banged on it. When no one came, I shouted, "I'm not eating this!"

No response.

"I'm hungry!" I tried, hoping someone would take pity on me and my inability to force down the sage and squash mess.

But still nothing.

"I hate you all so fucking much! Just give me some damn toast. Actually, just give me bread. I don't care, assholes!"

Nothing.

I'm alone.

I'm always alone.

Trapped and suffocating, the four walls I'd been stuck within felt as though they were closing in. A choked sob tore through me, and I cursed my weakness. I should've been stronger. I should've been able to hold out.

I shouldn't have broken.

But that was exactly what I did.

MAXIMO

FUCKING HELL, I need sleep.

I'd spent the night at Moonlight, lining everything up for an impending Pay-Per-View fight. One of the main-event boxers was being a diva and a pain in my ass.

Once I'd had that under control and had been about to leave, security at Star had paged to report a possible sighting of Viktor Dobrow.

Dobrow was a scumbag club owner who had aspirations of Vegas power. Since he was also stupid and a shitty businessman, he worked to achieve that goal by being a loan shark, pimp, and dealer. He'd tried multiple times to get me to allow his drugs and women to be distributed in my casinos. Rejected every time, he'd stopped asking and had tried running that shit behind my back. Since nothing happened at my properties without my knowledge, it hadn't been long before he'd been caught.

He'd thought I'd see my cut and reconsider.

He'd been mistaken.

In addition to a broken arm and smashed face, Dobrow had been banned from my resorts and fights.

I'd driven to Star to search the place myself, but it'd been a waste of time. If he'd been there at all, he was long gone by the time I'd arrived.

Climbing the stairs, I ran my palm down my face. If I were smart, I'd steer clear of my office and go right to my room to crash.

I wasn't smart, though. Not when it came to her.

I turned down the hallway to see someone sitting on the floor, looking at their cell.

"Just me, boss," Cole whispered.

He wouldn't have been sitting in front of Juliet's door unless something was wrong.

Swear to Christ, if she tried to escape again, I'm gonna tie her to the damn bed.

Ignoring my body's response to that inappropriate thought, I asked, "What's wrong?"

"She had a rough night. Figured I'd stay close in case she needed anything."

"What happened?"

He stood. "She's not too happy with your stunts."

"Neither are Vera or Freddy."

Vera didn't like not being allowed to see Juliet. Freddy was disgruntled at cooking the same shit every day, especially when so much of it went untouched. He was a chef whose ego depended on people loving his dishes. Normally they did, so the mostly untouched meals were a blow he wasn't accustomed to.

Cole shook his head. "I mean she's *really* not happy."

"Good." Truth be told, I wasn't sure how long I could keep it up. There was a good chance I'd break before the stubborn, ballsy dove did.

"Watch the footage." Stretching, he started for the stairs. "I'm crashing in the pool house."

He usually did.

Rather than getting the sleep I needed, I went into my office and sat, grabbing the remote.

Security monitors hung on the wall opposite my desk in all my offices—including my home. I could switch between my casinos, the back offices, and outside my house.

And Juliet's sitting room and bedroom.

I hadn't turned on the bedroom camera. Not that I was a saint. Unless someone was with me, her sitting room was always on the main screen. Watching her had become a sick obsession.

I turned on the camera to see her sleeping on her couch with the light on and no blanket.

Standing back up, I went down the hall to her room. I opened the door, quietly closing it behind me so I didn't wake her. She didn't look comfortable, and I was tempted to carry her to bed, but I didn't. Moving the coffee table, I grabbed her blanket and covered her.

And then I turned off the lights and got the hell out.

Returning to my office, I grabbed a tumbler and a bottle of Johnnie Walker Blue. I drank as the footage from the night slowly rewound.

When she moved from sleeping on the couch to the door, I pressed play.

Like Cole said, she wasn't happy. I'd have smiled at her calling us assholes had it not been for the emotion threading her words.

She's killing me.

I was about to wake her and feed her whatever the hell she wanted when it happened.

She broke.

"I'm sorry, okay?" Her crying grew louder. *"I'm sorry I ran. I'm sorry I didn't appreciate what I had before."* Her forehead hit the door with a thud. *"I tried to come back! I tried to crawl back to you!"*

She'd tried to crawl back to me.

Not *the house*. Not *here*.

Me.

Fuck, that went straight to my dick.

I should've gone to sleep. I should've at least turned off the camera. I didn't do either.

Instead, I took a quick shower and changed clothes before returning to my office and my whiskey.

And Juliet.

ITCHY, FLAT PILLOW. Neck hurting. Scrunched positioning on a lumpy bed.

I'm back home.

Still mostly asleep, I stretched and rolled.

And then I fell.

"Oof," I wheezed. Sitting up, I rubbed the sleep from my eyes to see I wasn't home—or what used to be home. I was on the floor of the sitting room.

Thankfully, one of the goons or Ms. Vera had moved the table and covered me with the puffy blanket that offered a bit of cushion. Otherwise, I'd have likely hit my head or hurt myself worse than I already had.

As it was, pain radiated from my hip bone.

I moved my hand around to feel for my scooter in the dark, but there was nothing.

Well, shit.

Before I could pull myself back onto the couch, the door opened, light filtering through from the hallway.

I expected one of the goons, but it wasn't. Instead, Maximo stood in the open doorway. Wearing only a pair of low riding joggers, he was shirtless, showing off his insane muscles. Guiltily, my eyes darted up from his abs to his disheveled hair. I wondered if I'd woken him with my fall, which made me also wonder how close his room was that he'd been able to hear. With the light behind him, I wasn't able to make out the details of his expression, so I didn't know if he was pissed at being disturbed.

"I fell off the couch in my sleep," I said feebly when the silence stretched. I glanced around before pointing to where my scooter had ended up. "Can you push that to me?"

He didn't move.

"Never mind," I muttered. "I'll figure it out."

I was going to climb back on the couch to sleep there for the night. It wasn't as comfortable as the bed—especially without a pillow—but it beat the floor.

When I shifted, he finally walked toward me but stopped a foot away.

My eyes caught on his torso and the tattoos there. His arms were a mix of designs, but the left side of his torso was all Vegas. The sign. Chips. His upper chest and part of his shoulder were covered with a king—the playing card kind. A spike on the king's crown was what stretched onto Maximo's neck.

Hoping the poor lighting hid my inspection of his tattoos—and his cut muscles—I tipped my head back to look at his shadowed face.

"You can go back to bed," I tried, not even sure he was actually awake. I used to sleepwalk as a kid—a side effect of stress. Shifting onto my knees, I was about to pull myself onto the couch when his hand stroked my head, his fingers combing through my hair.

My breath seized in my lungs at the unexpected and gentle touch. I wasn't sure what was happening, but I wanted it to continue. Even as my heart raced and my palms grew sweaty, I stayed as still as possible so I didn't break the spell.

His hand was gone just as quick, but before I could mourn the loss, he bent to pick me up. Only instead of cradling me like he'd done before, I was positioned with my front to his. He took a step and my legs automatically wrapped around his waist as my hands clutched his shoulder.

He froze and inhaled deeply, letting it out in a harsh rush.

Whiskey.

With my face close to his, I could smell the smokiness of the liquor on his breath. It wasn't the cheap, turpentine kind I'd often smelled, but I still recognized it.

No wonder he's being so weird.

He's drunk.

I tried to drop my legs, but he lowered one arm from my back to hold my thigh and keep it in place. Carrying me into the bedroom, he set me on the bed before going back into the sitting room. He returned a moment later, leaving the scooter within reach and tossing the blanket on the bed.

And then he left, never saying a single word the whole time.

Definitely drunk.

Being drunk explained his weirdness. It didn't, however, explain my body's reaction to him. To his body. To his touch. My heart still raced in my chest, and my legs shifted restlessly, wanting to ease an ache I shouldn't have felt. I could've blamed it on my loneliness or that I was far too tired to use my brain. But it was more than that.

It was the feelings he evoked. The pull. His tender touch.

It was just Maximo.

And that was proof I'd lost my mind.

Life held enough disappointments, I wasn't big on setting myself up for more by building up fantasies in my head.

And I wasn't Belle going all Stockholm Syndrome for a beast.

Because, sure, Maximo—with his tattoos, pelvic muscles, and broodingly dark eyes—was the most gorgeous man I'd ever seen in my life, but that didn't matter. Appearances weren't everything. He was a bad man.

Which is what I kept telling myself, over and over as the tension in my belly tightened like a coiled spring. I ignored it and tried to sleep but kept tossing and turning like I was back in my tiny twin bed with uncomfortable threadbare sheets. My mind fought my body.

And my body won.

Kicking the blanket off, my hand went down my pants to cup myself between my legs. I blanked my thoughts as I touched my clit with hurried, practiced circles, but it didn't work like it usually did.

I tried cupping my breast, but even needy and on the edge of the cliff, it wasn't enough to make me dive.

Past the point of no return, desperation kicked in and I let the fantasy I'd been fighting take over. I imagined Maximo in bed with me. Guiding my touches before replacing my hand with his tattooed one. I pictured the perfection that was his tall, muscular body as I ran my fingers along the deep vee I'd seen above the waistband of his joggers.

His joggers.

They look exactly like the ones I wore a few days ago.

I'm wearing his clothes.

I'm touching myself while wearing his clothes.

Something about that did it for me in a big way. I came hard, hoping I wasn't making any noise but too lost to truly care. My body shuddered as I rubbed myself through one orgasm and into a second, my fantasy blooming as I imagined his body covering mine.

I could've gone for three, but with the edge taken off, shame replaced horniness.

I just got off thinking about Maximo.

That was so hot.

I mean, stupid. That was so stupid.

Getting out of bed, I used the bathroom and cleaned up, avoiding my reflection in the mirror.

I'm a pervert.

A happy and satisfied pervert.

MAXIMO

PANTING, MY LIP curled in disgust.

I'm a sick fuck.

After my shower, I'd returned to my office to drink away my restless energy. The whiskey had sat mostly untouched, and I'd watched Juliet instead. Thank fuck I had, because after she'd fallen off the couch, I had no doubt she'd have tried to walk and hurt herself worse.

After carrying her to bed, I'd turned on the camera in her bedroom for the first time. I could've said I'd been making sure she settled okay, but I didn't lie, even to myself. I'd wanted to climb into that damn bed with her so I could count every last sexy freckle on her body. Since that wasn't an option, I'd settled for watching.

When she'd tossed and turned, I'd been about to offer her food, assuming hunger was keeping her awake. I sure as shit hadn't expected to see her hand slide down her pants—*my* pants. My dick had gone rock hard as I'd watched her touch herself.

Not once—not even for one damn second—had I thought about turning off the camera.

I'd been too busy holding my waistband down with one hand so I could stroke myself with the other.

Too busy fantasizing she was thinking of me the same way I thought of her.

Too busy giving in to the sick need that seemed to grow with each passing day.

Too busy coming harder than I ever had.

Grabbing a handful of tissues, I wiped the come from my stomach and chest and tossed them out. Then I grabbed my whiskey and drained the glass before pouring another.

I might not have felt guilt during, but I sure as hell felt it after.

I kept the camera going when she went to the bathroom. Once she was back in bed, I turned it off and picked up my cell, bringing up my texts with Ash.

Me: Disconnect the bedroom camera tomorrow.

I switched to my ones with Freddy.

Me: Regular menu for J tomorrow.

I thought for a moment before adding one more order.

Me: And a large mug of your good coffee.

I'll talk to Vera in the morning since she doesn't check her phone.

Putting my cell down, I knocked back whiskey until I was too drunk to do something stupid.

Or stupid*er*.

JULIET

I WOKE SLOWLY, feeling rested and not nearly as sore as I'd been.

What time is it?

The men had been getting me up early every day, but I had the distinct feeling it was late.

After taking off my ankle brace, I stretched my foot. A jolt of pain still shot up my calf, so I played it safe and used the scooter to get to the bathroom. By the time I showered and got back to the room, there was a new outfit waiting on my bed.

Black leggings, a gray, slouchy tee, and undies with a matching bralette that were different than the basic cotton ones I'd been given.

Is this just another layer of cruelty meant to build my hopes before shattering them?

I hurried and dressed—though my cheeks heated as I realized how much I missed *his* joggers. When I scootered into the sitting room, breakfast was already sitting on the table with two domes on the tray. But that wasn't the most exciting part.

Ms. Vera was.

"You're back." I grinned, happiness flowing through me.

"Hi, pretty girl," she greeted. "Sit."

I did it immediately, not wanting to give her any reason to leave. She handed me water and my antibiotics before inspecting my scrapes. They were all healed or scabbed over, so there was no need for ointment.

Once she was done looking me over, she moved toward the door. I opened my mouth, ready to beg her to stay, but she just grabbed her cleaning supplies from a carrier.

"Eat," she ordered as she started dusting. Usually it was a pointless chore, but since she hadn't been coming, there was actually a little buildup. Not much, but something.

Doing as she said, I checked out the two domed tray. Lifting one revealed eggs Benedict on an English muffin with a side of delicious looking home fries.

No sage.

No rosemary.

No oregano.

I was almost nervous to lift the other dome, like there'd be a note announcing the food was fake or poisoned. But when I tentatively peaked under, I saw a large bowl of fresh fruit salad and coffee.

A *big* coffee.

The delicious aroma flowed free with the heavy barrier out of the way.

I looked up and grinned at Ms. Vera. "This looks amazing."

"Don't just drink that coffee, you need to eat. You're far too skinny." Returning to get something out of her carrier, she gave me a small smile as she tossed my iPad onto the couch. "Why don't you read?"

My heart surged at seeing my shiny precious again. As excited as I was to have it back, being able to have a conversation was even better.

"How are you?" I asked.

While she cleaned, Ms. Vera talked about errands and a good book she was reading. I happily listened and dug into the food, eating almost the entire plate. Not even a single drop of coffee went to waste. I savored it as I ate and then sat back, holding the mug under my nose.

Ms. Vera came from the bedroom and picked up my mostly empty tray. When she was almost to the door, she tossed over her shoulder, "Relax. Read. Maybe even watch some TV."

TV?

Before I could speak, she was gone.

I already got Ms. Vera, my iPad, delicious food, and even better coffee. Could I possibly be lucky enough to have TV back, too?

Holding my breath, I hit the power button on the remote. When the TV turned on, it whooshed out in a small, "Yay."

Not only did I have TV, I had *all* the stations again.

I couldn't decide whether I wanted to watch TV or read, so I decided to do both. Picking a movie I didn't have to pay close attention to, I opened iBooks before nearly dropped my precious.

I can't believe it.

Rather than dull mysteries and stodgy nonfiction, there were hundreds of choices downloaded.

Hundreds.

Dystopian Young Adult. Biographies. Ones that looked like school textbooks. Serial killers, romances, paranormal, fantasy, and everything in between.

That time, my yay wasn't soft. It was loud. As was my shouted, "Thank you!"

I wasn't sure if anyone could hear me, but I said it anyway.

And then I curled up on the couch with the good mug of coffee and a good book.

CHAPTER EIGHT

Ring-O-Fire

JULIET

"DO YOU THINK I could do tricks with this?" Even though I didn't need it anymore, I scootered in circles around the couch. "Maybe a sick kickflip or some ramps. Oh! I know. I could try to scooter my way through the ring-o-fire."

"Ring-o-fire?" Ms. Vera asked, setting my lunch tray down.

For a glorious week, I'd devoured amazing food. Devastatingly, the coffee had been a one-time treat, but lunch had started including a mini can of Diet Coke. Coffee was my first love, but Diet Coke was a close second.

I'd taken baths with bombs and salts and oils and whatever other fruity fragranced items my bathroom was stocked with. I'd binged movies. I'd read.

As amazing as it'd been—especially compared to my real life or a slow death in the desert sun—I was beginning to go stir-crazy again. A happier stir-crazy than last time, but still.

"Sit and eat," Ms. Vera said.

"I will. I just need to finish my laps. I'm training for the scooter X

Games and since my ankle is better, my time is limited."

She rolled her eyes. "Your lunch time is limited today, too."

"Why?"

"Because Mr. Freddy made you a BLT and soup, and if you don't eat it, I will." I almost believed her until I saw her smile.

I was good at reading people. Dad had taught me all about tells and cues, and I'd gotten good at picking up on them to avoid getting whaled on.

Ms. Vera had a big one.

Her mischievous smile.

My eyes narrowed. "What do you know?"

"Nothing. Now eat."

"I'll eat when you tell me what you know."

She sighed. "Fine. Starve. Mr. Freddy's broccoli cheese soup is my favorite."

"Never mind," I said, scootering over so fast, I nearly knocked into the table. I sat and removed the dome.

Holy shit, I could've sworn my birthday was a couple weeks ago, but maybe it's today.

Picking up the soft white-bread sandwich, I bit in to the salty, tangy, fresh BLT and moaned. "Sometimes the basics really are the best."

She gave me a pointed look for talking with my mouth full. "Manners."

"Yes, ma'am," I said, extending my pinkies.

"You're a silly girl today," she said, but I wasn't sure she meant it as a compliment.

"I'm in a good mood," I said. Probably a better one than I had any right being in, all things considered.

Darkness pushed in, threatening to steal my appetite *and* good mood.

Into the box.

Into the box.

There.

Crazily enough, I was pretty sure Ms. Vera read my internal battle because she busted out the big guns to distract me. "There's a visitor coming tomorrow morning."

Maximo.

I hadn't seen him since he'd carried me to bed. Which was probably for the best because I doubted I could face him. I'd promised myself I'd never think about him when I touched myself again. It was wrong and stupid and more than a little sleazy.

But I still did it.

"Who is it?" I asked.

"A tutor."

Shit.

Shit, shit, shit.

They know.

A pit in my belly grew even as a thrum of excitement buzzed through me.

"Why?" I asked, playing dumb.

"He's going to see what areas you need help with so you can graduate."

All areas.

Shame burned my cheeks. I didn't want anyone to know how far behind I was.

I didn't want them to know I was a high school dropout who'd only made it partway through tenth grade before her asshole father had decided school wasn't a priority.

Appetite dead and gone, I nearly gagged on the bite of sandwich that suddenly felt like a chunk of asphalt. "I appreciate it, but I've already graduated."

Ms. Vera's eyes flashed with anger, and her easygoing, motherly disposition was gone. Or maybe she became more motherly because she looked ready to ground me. "Listen to me. Mr. Maximo hates liars. Learn this lesson and learn it fast. Learn it until it becomes as ingrained in your head as your own name. He will *not* tolerate liars. Not ever. Do you understand?"

I nodded because what was there to misconstrue?

"An education is important," she continued. "A priceless gift that others die for."

Finding my courage, I asked, "He knows I dropped out?"

"He knows you were," she lifted her hands to make air quotes, "*homeschooled.*"

"That's really embarrassing," I muttered.

"No, embarrassing would be having this opportunity and then turning it down because of stupid pride. Men throw away their lives for pride. Women are smarter."

She has a point.

I focused on the excitement that flowed through me, allowing it to dim some of the shame. I'd always told myself I'd go back for my GED. Getting a tutor meant I wouldn't have to wait.

My stomach loosened enough that I could eat a spoonful of the amazingly creamy soup. Then another. And a bunch more until the bowl was empty.

Only after I was full to bursting did Ms. Vera speak again, her expression somber. "Mr. Maximo is trusting you to work with the tutor in the dining room."

"I won't do anything stupid," I vowed truthfully.

I'm not interested in a painful death in the scalding sunlight.

She gave a single nod. "The tutor owes Mr. Maximo a large sum of money. He's agreed to work with you to settle those debts. He will not rescue you. He will not go to the cops. He knows you're not here by choice, and he does not care. He cares about himself and staying alive."

But I am here by choice now.

Wait, what?

Shut up, brain.

Keeping that insane thought to myself, I repeated, "I won't do anything stupid."

"If, for some reason, he tries to help you, he'll be dealt with and so will you, sweet girl. Last week will seem like a vacation by comparison."

With that ominous warning, she grabbed my tray and left.

Ms. Vera was only gone for a half hour before she returned, carrying a canvas tote.

"What's up?" I asked, surprised to see her so soon. Usually she only came at mealtimes.

"I said you had plans this afternoon." She reached into the bag and tossed me something.

I looked down to see what I'd caught.

A razor.

Well, it has been a while since I've been able to shave, but I don't think it'll take all afternoon.

She pulled something else out.

A pretty mauve two-piece.

"I can go outside?" I asked. "I can go swimming?"

She nodded and handed me the suit, plus a pair of flip-flops and a coverup. "Go change."

Don't gotta tell me twice.

I rushed into the bathroom and stripped down. Sitting on the side of the tub, I shaved my legs as quickly as I could without nicking myself and bleeding out just as I was about to get a taste of freedom. I pulled on the bottoms and ran my fingers along the scalloped edge. The top had the same detailing on its square neckline.

I'd have gone out in my underwear or a garbage bag if it meant swimming, but it was still nice to wear something so cute.

Throwing on the coverup and sliding on the flip-flops, I literally ran back into the sitting room. "Ready."

She gestured for me to spin around. "Sunblock."

"Good idea."

My painful sunburn from my failed escape was not an experience I was jonesing to repeat. Nor was the itching, disgusting peeling that'd followed.

Ms. Vera rubbed the coconut-scented lotion into my back before handing me the bottle to do the rest. I was just finishing turning myself into a human piña colada when no-longer-ignoring-me goon—or Cole, as I'd learned—opened the door.

He'd stopped glaring and had started half-smiling at me, so I'd taken that to mean he'd forgiven me for the room fiasco. Even glaring goon—or Marco—had warmed up to just ignoring me.

Progress all around.

Since Cole had ditched his suit for slacks and a tee, I wasn't surprised when he followed Ms. Vera and me.

The only time I'd been in the hallway, I'd been drugged, high on pain meds, or running for my life. Since I was awake and not fleeing at top speed, my eyes darted all around, trying to take in everything at once.

There was beautiful Vegas themed art and photography on the light-gray walls. The plush carpet was white and shockingly spotless.

And there were doors. *Twelve* doors.

Who has twelve doors in their upstairs alone?

Two of them had weird locks that looked like something from a spy movie.

Intriguing.

I looked over my shoulder to see my room had one, too.

Are there other people held here?

No, I'd have heard.

Right?

After going downstairs, we turned toward the back of the house, passing the living room, dining room, another living room, and some closed doors. I gawked at the size of the place.

Who lives like this?

It was masculine and though it was lavish, there was an emphasis on comfort and coolness. It reminded me of the houses on old episodes of MTV *Cribs* that were decked out and upgraded with every feature available.

Reaching a sliding glass door at the back of the house, Vera opened it. The dry heat hit like a wall.

Even after living in Vegas for a couple years, I wasn't used to the weather. I'd spent most of my life in places where blizzards in March were common, so it being hot enough to swim was bizarre.

Glorious, but bizarre.

I stepped outside and shielded my eyes from the blinding sun as I craned my neck to take in the house.

No, it wasn't a *house*. It was a mansion. No. It was whatever was bigger than a mansion. I had no idea how many rooms there were, but there were a hell of a lot of tinted windows. One appeared to be floor to ceiling and was the width of three other windows combined.

I wonder what's in there?

Spinning back toward the lawn, excitement buzzed through me as if I'd chugged four cups of coffee. I wanted to touch and smell every plant. I wanted to spread out on one of the thickly cushioned lounge chairs and soak in the sun. But more than anything, I wanted to dive into the gorgeous blue water and swim until I was a wrinkly prune.

As I followed Ms. Vera and Cole to the patio, I realized that what I could see from my window was a *very* small fraction of the unusually shaped pool. The thing was massive. It even had a wide waterfall pouring from a rounded, stacked rock mound.

I kicked off my shoes and tossed my coverup onto a lounger before walking along the stone deck, occasionally dipping my toes into the warm water. When I got to the other end, there was a rectangular planter of rocks that separated the pool from a hot tub. I got a little closer and realized the planter was actually a fire pit that could be accessed from either side.

This is insane.

Seriously, who the heck lives like this?

The stone path continued to a small building that had the same color scheme and style as the house.

"What's that?" I asked Vera.

"Pool house."

That's the...

No.

A pool house is the size of a shed. That's a condo that would cost a few grand a month.

"You know how to swim?" Ms. Vera asked, sitting on a patio couch under the shade of an overhang.

"Yup."

When we'd lived in NYC, my grandparents had taken me to the YMCA all the time.

"Have fun then." She pulled a floppy hat out of her Mary Poppins bag of tricks and put it on before taking out a book with a shirtless, kilted man on the cover.

Jumping into the pool, I swam laps until my lungs burned and my arms ached. I floated around for a while before going to check out the waterfall. When I inched through the cascade, I expected to hit a pool wall, but there was a small alcove instead. I moved farther in before banging my knee on the underwater stone bench that curved around the space.

Sitting, I stretched my legs out and enjoyed the cool mist that came from the waterfall.

Just a teeny tiny bit better than the pool at the Y, with its fungusy mats, annoying kids, and speedo-clad old men.

Going back out into the pool, I felt like a mermaid in a lagoon. It was a fantasyland out of an epic fairy tale, but I couldn't shake the feeling that the story would end soon.

And, contrary to most fairy tales, there'd be no happily ever after.

I used that to keep my walls up.

This isn't my life.
This is a reprieve from hell.
And it'll end.
Everything ends.
Until it did, though, I'd savor the paradise for what it was.
Temporary.

CHAPTER NINE

Normal

MAXIMO

"SHE'S BRIGHT."

I glanced up at the man sitting across my desk who was wasting my time by telling me things I already knew. "I'm aware."

Peter Reed ran one of the top private schools in the nation. He also had a penchant for high-stakes cards, top-shelf liquor, and high-class call girls. And he used the school's money to fund his habit. He usually made back what he borrowed before anyone noticed it was gone, but a string of bad luck had him over his head with the school and me. Lucky for him, he was of use.

I didn't know how he explained the new online student, and I didn't care. That was his problem.

Peter flipped through a leather-bound notebook. "It's no surprise she's behind with as often as she's moved around. She missed a lot of school before officially leaving halfway through tenth grade."

That wasn't news to me.

According to the file Cole had found, the education department in Texas had made a half-assed effort when she'd become truant more often than not, but after a short time, her case had fallen through the cracks.

"Did she say why?" I asked, something no amount of Cole's research could drag up.

"She didn't seem to want to talk about it."

"What else?" I asked.

"For the four core subjects, I combined chunks of placement exams ranging from eighth to twelfth grade so I could get an idea of where she was. The good news is, she didn't score as poorly as I'd expected. World and US History were strong." His brows lowered. "She did exceptionally well on ancient civilizations, which was surprising."

Since I'm the one who loaded her iPad with the dullest books I could find, including multiple on the topic, I'm not surprised.

"Her English scores were off the charts. She could pass both courses today with ease. Actually, she would likely pass some college courses. Her comprehension is great, her writing skills aren't fine-tuned but they're good, and, as I said, she's bright. She can piece together what she doesn't know."

"What about science and math?"

"In science, if she could use common sense to figure out, she did fine. Earth Science topics were done well since she'd completed ninth grade, but Chemistry and Biology weren't as strong. A lot is knowledge that can only come from doing the specific research, experiments, and memorizations. If she passed, it would be just barely. But that's a big *if*." His eyes darted to where Marco stood by the door then back to me. He fidgeted with some papers and cleared his throat.

Growing impatient, I bit out, "What?"

"She's, uh, very behind in math. She can't use common sense and accrued knowledge to solve problems. It's all formula based. Rigid. If you don't know the operations, it's impossible. Online lessons will help, but it won't be enough."

"Teach her then."

He cleared his throat again. "I can handle getting her caught up in the sciences, but math isn't my strength, either."

That's not surprising given how often he loses at the tables.

"I can recommend some tutors, ones I think could be bought. But I don't have the ability to teach her what she needs."

"I've got it handled," I said with a sigh.

"She needs to pass the subject to graduate."

"She will. Is that all?"

Standing, he handed me a printout. "Here's a supply list she'll need."

I set it to the side and nodded.

"I'll begin sending her online resources and video lessons when I get to my office. And I'll be back Saturday morning to work with her."

As he left, I picked up my cell.

Me: How'd you like a promotion?

Ash: The only position above mine is yours, and you couldn't pay me enough to take on that headache. So what's the promotion?

Me: Math tutor.

Ash had a gift for numbers. His wasn't as advanced as *Rain Man*, but if he were a gambling man, I'd ban him from my casinos.

If anyone could get Juliet caught up, it was Ash.

The bastard.

Ash: Does that mean I'm no longer banned from being around her?

I ran my hand down my face, knowing what was coming.

Me: Yes.

Ash: Good. It's been a while since anyone's called me a handsome goon.

Before I could respond, either to tell him he was dead or fired, he texted again.

Ash: I'll start tomorrow after breakfast and work with her every morning, unless we have something going on.

Me: I appreciate it.

Ash: Hey, the promotion includes a big pay raise I gotta earn.

I shook my head but didn't argue. If he got her caught up, I'd pay him a shit-ton on top of the already generous shit-ton he earned.

Me: She's behind.

Ash: Not for long.

Ash: Now excuse me while I go piss on Shamus' unmarked grave, the dumb asshole.

Every time I thought we'd discovered all the ways her piece of shit father had fucked up her life, another thing came along to show what a scumbag he'd been.

Guessing where she was after such a long day, I pressed the button to open my blinds before spinning my chair to look out the floor to ceiling window.

All the windows in the house were coated with a dark tint. It protected against the heat and sun damage and allowed privacy. It also meant I could watch Juliet without her knowing—a growing obsession of mine.

Just as I'd guessed, she was floating in the pool. If she didn't have to eat and sleep, I was certain she'd spend the entire day out there.

I watched her long after I should've gotten back to work. Long after it became outright creepy.

And long after my body reacted in a way that it definitely should not have.

Disgusted with myself, I spun back around and closed the blinds.

But it did nothing to erase the images in my head.

JULIET

"WHAT'S THIS?"

Ash pulled out the dining room chair next to mine and sat. His brows lowered when he slowly said, "A computer."

I rolled my eyes. "I'm not that poor, I've seen a computer before."

Of course, not one this sleek and pretty.

He shrugged. "You're the one who asked."

"I meant what is it for?"

"Your schoolwork."

"Mr. Reed said I could run the programs on the iPad."

"And Maximo said this would be better." Ash opened it. "It's a Mac, so it's synced with your iPad. If you end up doing any of the work on there, it'll transfer onto here."

"Cool." I dragged my finger along the touchpad, but I had no clue what to click. Everything was different compared to a PC, especially compared to the ancient one I was used to.

Ash turned it toward him, clicked a few things, and then twisted it back. "This is the site your work will be added to. Everything can be done online and submitted."

"Got it."

"Any other questions, ask Cole. He's the computer guy. I can show you how to check your email, read the news, and watch—" His words cut off abruptly.

"Netflix?" I supplied, though we both knew that was *not* what he'd been about to say.

"Yeah. Netflix." He closed the computer and pushed it across the table. He replaced it with something far less exciting.

A binder filled with math worksheets.

"This may as well be Latin," I muttered.

He handed me a graphing calculator. "That's why I'm here."

I lifted a brow. "You're going to teach me how letters fit into math?"

"Yup." He smirked. "Hey, don't look so shocked. I'm more than my handsome-goon face."

My jaw dropped. "What? How?"

"Pain meds make people say crazy, yet true, things." He tapped a pencil on the worksheet. "Now show me what you can do so I know where to start."

Then, in a dining room of a mansion that belonged to a powerful and deadly man, a goon taught me math better than any teacher I'd ever had could.

And it wasn't torture.

BEEP! BEEP! BEEP!

I swatted to hit snooze on my alarm clock only to hear it crash to the floor.

Jolting up, I hung my head off the bed and saw my iPad beeping away on the floor.

Nooo, my precious.

In my rush to grab it, I tumbled off the bed, landing with a hard *thud*.

The sitting room door slammed before my bedroom one was thrown open.

Marco, gun drawn and alert, scanned the room for whatever dastardly enemy had caused such a ruckus.

My cheeks burned red as I jumped to stand. "I, uh, fell out of bed."

His eyes narrowed in suspicion as he slid the gun into a holster hidden beneath his suit coat. He stormed over and stuck his head into the bathroom before checking behind the curtain. "What were you trying to do?"

I held up the iPad. "Grab this from the floor without getting my lazy butt out of bed."

He looked at the tall bed then back to the not-tall me. "Your feet wouldn't even touch the ground, let alone your arms."

"Hence why I fell."

Smirking, he shook his head and checked his watch. "Why're you up so early?"

"I wanted to get into a routine with the school stuff."

For some reason, I expected him to call me a nerd and maybe give me a swirly in the toilet. I didn't have a locker, but he could probably shove me in the armoire instead. He seemed like the type.

But I was wrong.

"I'll tell Ms. Vera to start bringing your breakfast earlier," he said. "You can't concentrate on an empty stomach."

Stunned by his consideration, I didn't respond as he walked from the room.

Ohhhhkay then.

Definitely better than him glaring.

Gently tossing the iPad onto the bed, I went to shower and get ready for the day. When I opened the armoire to grab my clothes, I saw my leggings and tees were still there.

But so were new pajamas, bathing suits, bralettes, undies, and socks.

On a hunch, I checked the formerly empty closet and found tops, a few pairs of jeans, and some shorts.

For the briefest moment, it felt like too much. Like it was wrong to accept them. But clothes were a necessity, and since Maximo was the one who'd insisted I stay, it was up to him to provide them. Plus, as comfortable as leggings were, it would be nice to have some variety.

After tugging on a pair of jeans and a tee, I turned to leave when my eyes landed on the floor under the clothes.

Tucked tight against the wall, there were a pair of sparkly sandals, a pair of gray and white sneakers, and—my personal favorite—a pair of gray canvas slip-ons.

He's trusting me with shoes.

Shoes I could run in.

I won't, but I could.

Even though I was just going into the sitting room, I slipped on the canvas ones—unsurprised they fit perfectly.

Something about being dressed in real clothes made me happy. I felt normal.

I wasn't sure if that was a good thing, but right then, I really didn't care.

CHAPTER TEN

Code-Fucking-Red

JULIET

"*I* NEED A snack."

Ash tapped the paper. "You need to solve for X."

I didn't feel great. I was exhausted, meh, and seriously hungry despite the bagel and fruit I'd had for breakfast.

"My ex can solve his own problems. I need a snack," I repeated.

Shaking his head, he stood. "Let's go see what Freddy has stashed."

Eagerly following him down the hall and through a doorway, I was stupidly excited to check out the kitchen.

My excitement was warranted.

It looked right out of a restaurant. There were oversized appliances, shiny surfaces, and stacks of different sized pots, pans, and other utensils. The setup was overkill for the handful of people who were usually around.

We turned a corner to see a man stirring something in a pot.

"Ay, Freddy," Ash said. "We've come for snacks."

The man turned and did a double take when he saw me, and I probably did one, too.

I'd expected Mr. Freddy to look like Chef Boyardee or the French chef from *The Little Mermaid*—with the thin mustache and everything.

But Freddy was in his mid-twenties—maybe a little older—and heavily tattooed. He looked like the hotshot chefs from Food Network shows.

He recovered quickly, stirring with one hand while he gestured to a door behind him. His accent was tinged with a hint of French and something else when he said, "She can raid away."

Well, I had the French part right.

Having tasted the amazing food that'd come out of that kitchen, I was anticipating snacks of every salty, sweet, tangy, sour, and spicy variety. But when Ash turned on the light to the pantry, it was barren, like an apocalypse had hit and the shelves had been wiped out.

"Maximo isn't a snacker," Ash explained.

Based on his cut, muscular physique, that's not surprising.

"Is there any chocolate?" I asked.

"In the box of bran cereal," Freddy shouted from the stove.

Ash pulled out a wide candy bar that was wrapped in shiny purple foil and tossed it to me. I tried to read the brand, but it was in a different language.

"You sneaky bastard." Ash stuck his head out. "What else have you been hiding?"

"Cheetos in the protein powder jug. Starburst in the whole wheat pasta box. And beef jerky in the Cornflakes."

"What's in this big box of anchovies?" Ash grabbed it down and opened the flap. "It's actually anchovies. Who the fuck needs so many anchovies?"

"Caesar dressing," Freddy called.

Ash put them back and asked me, "Anything else?"

"Just the chocolate."

He grabbed the jerky for himself before heading out. I followed, my nose going wild at the scent of garlic.

I hope that's dinner.

Freddy was still stirring away.

Ash waited until we were across the kitchen before saying, "Thanks for the jerky."

"Hey, I said *she* could raid away." His accent was thicker in his anger. "You put my jerky back."

"Come get it," Ash taunted.

Freddy looked disgruntled, his eyes darting between the pot on the stove and the jerky. "I can't leave the risotto. It has to be stirred constantly."

"Is that dinner?" I asked, my tone hopeful.

Other than seeing chefs fail on *Chopped* when they attempted it, I had no clue what risotto was. But it smelled so good, I was sure I'd love it.

"No, this is a test batch of a new recipe."

"Freddy develops recipes for the upscale restaurants in the boss' properties," Ash shared.

From the very limited amount Ms. Vera and Ash had shared, Maximo owned four hotel and casino resorts. I had no clue which ones and a Google search on my MacBook had been as unsuccessful as the one on my iPad.

"I thought he was the…" Not knowing the correct phrasing, I went with, "House chef?"

"I am," Freddy said. "I develop. I cook. I train. I slice, I dice, I even julienne."

"That is a lot."

"I like to feed people." He tapped his spoon on the pot. "If this is good, I'll serve it for lunch."

I grinned, my stomach growling before twisting.

I'm hungrier than I thought.

Freddy looked pleased with my reaction. "You like my food?"

I almost gave him shit about the rosemary nightmares, but that would've been unfair. He was likely following orders.

I went with honesty, bordering on enthusiastic food fangirling. "I love it."

His chest puffed out. "Good. Is there anything you'd like me to make this week?"

"I thought you didn't take requests," Ash grumbled sullenly.

"I don't for bastards who steal my jerky." He tilted his head toward me. "But if she appreciates the food I make with my own skilled hands, she can choose whatever she likes."

Ash crossed his arms. "I appreciate your food."

"You dipped an exquisitely marbled, dry-aged porterhouse in A.1."

"I had a taste for it." Ash stormed back into the pantry and reemerged with the Cheetos, giving Freddy a wide berth so he couldn't reach him without abandoning his risotto. "You won't take my requests, I'm taking your Cheetos."

"Asshole." Freddy's tight expression smoothed out as he looked back to me. "What would you like?"

Since it seemed like this was a one-time, rare-as-a-blue-moon thing, I considered my options carefully before deciding. "I'd love some mac and cheese."

"Done," Freddy said with a firm nod.

My stomach did another grumble and flip in anticipation.

"Ready to get back to the exciting world of variables?" Ash asked me.

"You and I have *very* different ideas of exciting," I mumbled. I started to follow him before turning back to Freddy. "Thanks for the chocolate."

"It's straight from Belgium. If you like it, I'll get more."

My mouth watered as I returned to the table with Ash. I sat and was about to rip into the package when my stomach twisted. Only that time, it was followed by a clench that stole my breath.

Oh shit.

No, not right now.

Staying in the house, all the days had begun blurring together. I'd lost track.

"What's wrong?" Ash asked, his snacks forgotten as he went alert.

I jolted up before things got real embarrassing, real fast. The quick movement caused another cramp to squeeze my stomach like a vise. Wrapping my arms around myself, I blinked away tears.

"Juliet." Ash stood and held my shoulders, panicked. "Are you sick? Does something hurt?"

Yes, my uterus is rioting and tearing apart the baby nursery it spent a month making.

I shook my head. "I need Ms. Vera."

"I can help, just tell me what's wrong."

Yeah, not happening.

The situation was quickly deteriorating, and my panic went into overdrive. I probably looked like my head was going to start spinning around like the girl from *The Exorcist*. "Send Ms. Vera to my room."

Realization must've dawned because his eyes widened. "Ohhh, got it. She'll be right up." Moving fast, he headed through one of the mystery doors.

I hauled ass as quickly as I could while keeping my thighs pressed tight together, waddling like a penguin.

We're at critical levels of oh-shit. Code red.

Code-fucking-red.

No longer waddling, I took off at a run and didn't stop until I was in the bathroom.

Stripping down, my stupid hormonal tears irrationally increased when I saw my cute polka dot undies were ruined. My leggings hadn't fared much better.

I turned the shower on as hot as I could stand before stepping under the scalding jets.

It felt glorious.

My muscles loosened as I turned my back toward the hard spray. I leaned my forehead against the wall, taking slow, deep breaths.

I'd just relaxed when someone knocked. Tension tightened my body again as I braced. "Who is it?"

"Ms. Vera. Can I come in?"

"Yes," I called since the glass was frosted and she couldn't see anything.

The bathroom door opened and closed. "Mr. Ash said you needed me. Is it *that* time?"

"Yes."

"There are supplies in the second drawer under the sink."

"There's already supplies?"

"Of course. We're women. Women bleed. Men would die from their first cramp."

I laughed through an emotionally charge sob.

"Stay in the shower as long as you need. Where are your clothes?"

"I'll take care of them," I insisted. "I've been doing laundry since before I was tall enough to reach the buttons."

"Where are they?"

"I can handle it."

"Where?"

"In the hamper. But I can wash them," I repeated.

"You relax, sweet girl."

The door opened and closed again as Ms. Vera left me to my shower.

Aiming the showerhead lower, I sat and wrapped my arms around my bent legs, letting the water hit my back until the last of the tension eased away.

I should've grabbed that chocolate bar.

MAXIMO

As I WALKED into my house, I caught a brief glimpse of Juliet's back as she raced up the stairs.

What the hell?

Passing by the dining room, I saw Juliet's MacBook still open with papers and a calculator next to it. Along with her school stuff, there were snacks and chocolate.

Freddy.

I went into the kitchen to find Freddy dumping ingredients into the stand mixer. Ash leaned against the counter next to him, his arms and ankles crossed.

"What the hell happened?" I asked.

"You saw Juliet," Ash surmised. "She's good, boss, it's just that time."

I glanced at my watch. "What time?"

"She's a woman." Freddy raised his brows. "*That* time."

Shit.

I was an idiot. In my defense, I'd never lived with a woman before—not counting my ma. But not in my defense, I was a fucking idiot to not take into consideration something that happened to almost half the population on a monthly basis.

"My sisters called it shark week," Ash said. "Four older sisters, all synced. Made it easy to work out why Juliet was upset and needed Ms. Vera." He gave Freddy a pointed look. "No wonder she was holding that chocolate bar like it was her one true love."

"I'll run to the store. What does she need?" I asked, feeling out of my element.

"Ms. Vera was prepared."

"And I'm making her mac and cheese and," he gestured to the mixer, "chocolate cake with chocolate chunks and cream cheese frosting. If carbs and chocolate don't help, nothing will."

Since there was nothing I could do, I was out of my element *and*

82

useless—two feelings I wasn't familiar with.

"Let me know if something changes." I backtracked through the house, snagging the unopened chocolate on my way up to my office. I'd barely sat when someone knocked. "Come in."

Vera opened the door. "Juliet is not feeling well."

"Ash told me. Does she need anything?"

"She's in the shower now. I'm going to bring her some medicine and a hot pad when she's done."

"I'll do it."

She tilted her head, and I thought she was preparing her argument. "It seems to be heavy. Painful. She should be on the pill. It helps. It would be smart to start sooner rather than when it's needed later. Call your doctor friend to prescribe it." Then, not giving me the chance to process what she'd said—or the heavy implication in her words—she turned, still speaking as she left. "I'll leave the supplies in front of her door."

I sat back in stunned silence.

That was unexpected.

After a few minutes, I got up and headed to my room to grab a pair of my sweats and a tee. At the memory of what she'd done—what I'd watched her do—the last time she'd worn my clothes, my body reacted. I tucked my dick into the waistband of my slacks, the hard length stretching up my stomach. The fabric cutting in nor the uncomfortable angle did anything to lessen my hard-on, but at least it was hidden.

I carried the clothes to her room and picked up the waiting items before unlocking the door.

The little dove didn't even lift her head when I entered. Her eyes tracked me as I approached where she was curled on the couch, but she stayed in her ball.

"I brought you water, pain meds, a hot pad, and a change of clothes."

Her eyes dropped to the bunched fabric. "I can't wear those."

"Why?"

"Because."

I looked at her fitted PJ pants and top. "It'll be less constricting."

She opened her mouth then closed it. Her lids closed, too, her cheeks flushing.

"I don't give a damn if you leak on them. It happens." Her eyes shot open but I kept going. "And Vera can get anything clean."

And she's got experience with blood stains.

A small tear dripped from her eye. She swiped at it as she sat up and grabbed the clothes. "Thanks."

The loose comfort must've been needed because she didn't wait until I left before closing herself in her bedroom. She returned a minute later, wearing my clothes. They were huge on her, but that was the point.

I waited until she took the pain pills before passing her the heating pad and plugging it in.

She pressed it to her stomach and curled around it. "Thanks."

I reached into my pocket and pulled out Freddy's Belgium chocolate.

Her pretty green eyes went huge and she licked her lips.

Jesus.

Before my tenuous control snapped, I handed her the chocolate and got the fuck out of there.

I need to stay the hell away from her.

CHAPTER ELEVEN

The One With The Time Jumps

JULIET

Three Weeks Later

I WAS BORED.

Beyond bored.

So bored, I was voluntarily working ahead on my schoolwork. Sitting on my bed with my computer, I flipped through my remaining assignments and sighed when I realized I couldn't do anything else yet. I closed it and got onto my knees, moving the curtain aside to look out the window.

Still raining.

Damn.

I walked into the sitting room and knocked on the door.

Cole opened it. "What's up?"

"I'm bored."

"Want Ash to give you more math?"

"God, *noooo*," I drawled dramatically. "I said I'm bored not that I want to be so bored, I'll die."

He half-smiled. "What do you want?"

"To *do* something. I feel all fidgety."

"It's still raining." Holding the door with his body, he gestured out. "Want to walk around the house?"

Surprisingly, I didn't.

With the exception of some off-limit areas, I'd already been around the house a bunch. Gorgeous room after gorgeous room had been exciting the first few times, but the appeal had faded fast.

I preferred my area to the rest of the house. It was the first time in my life I had my own space—even if temporarily.

Sometimes, late at night when dark thoughts took root and wove through my brain, I wondered if they were even keeping me locked in anymore.

Or if I was doing it to myself.

"Will you show me the forbidden rooms?" I asked even though I knew the answer.

"No. Want to use the gym?"

"Yuck, definitely not."

He chuckled. "Media room?"

I shook my head and hooked a thumb over my shoulder. "I've got movies here."

"Yeah, but not the big screen with recliners and popcorn."

"Still not active enough."

"You've gotta give me a little more to go on."

"I want to… I dunno. Draw. Knit. Mess with clay. Hell, I'd try macramé and I don't even know what that is. I just want to do something."

He didn't make fun of me or roll his eyes that I was asking a big badass to procure arts and crafts supplies. "I'll see what I can do."

The door closed and, since desperate times called for desperate measures, I grabbed my iPad and played some of the math games Mr. Reed had recommended.

Nothing about math was fun and games, but at least it took my mind off my boredom for a while.

Or, like, fifteen minutes.

I switched to iBooks, but nothing grabbed me, so I turned on the TV and flipped channels.

When I was sitting on the couch with my legs up the back and my head hanging upside down off the cushion, the door opened again.

"You really are bored," Cole said, setting two loaded plastic bags against the wall.

In my excitement, I sat up so fast, my head swam. "I just do it for the sweet, sweet headrush."

"Man, if you think that's a headrush, wait until you try tequila."

"Is that an offer of a shot or ten? Extra lime and salt, please," I joked.

"No thanks, I don't feel like getting shot today."

"Huh?"

"He doesn't even like you having caffeine. If I gave you liquor, he'd shoot my kneecaps." He bent and extended his leg. "And I like my kneecaps."

"I thought Ms. Vera was the one limiting my caffeine."

Not only did Cole not respond, he avoided looking at me.

Ah, just like old times.

I got the feeling sharing any info was a big no-no. Taking pity on him—and not wanting to return to being ignored—I let it go. "I bet I'm more of a piña colada gal anyway."

He still didn't speak, but he did shoot me a half-smile. Holding the door with one foot, he reached into the hall for more bags.

Can't they do anything half-assed?

I flung my hand toward the purchases. "I just wanted a thing of yarn or some colored pencils or something. I didn't need all this."

He shrugged. "Now you've got options. Yell if you need anything else."

What else could I possibly need?

When he left, I pulled everything out and lined it up, hoping inspiration would strike. There were a dozen yarn bundles of different textures and colors, knitting needles, and some hooky thingies of various sizes, plus a couple adult coloring books with colored pencils and gel pens.

Going for the yarn, I grabbed the brightest color and two of the needles before loading a beginner tutorial on YouTube. I discovered how much fun it was to create.

I also discovered how incredibly, horribly, horrendously unskilled I was.

Still fun, though.

Two Weeks Later

GEARED UP IN a pretty pink halter bikini, my flip-flops, a ton of sunblock, and a floppy hat, I hefted my tote up my shoulder.

Since my period was *finally done,* it was time to hit the pool. To be fair, thanks to Ms. Vera's recommendation I start the pill, it had been the best—or maybe least bad—one I'd ever had. However, I'd still spent nearly a week on the couch with the heating pad.

I was ready to swim until my muscles ached before sitting in the hot tub until I turned to goo.

I knocked on my door and backed up.

"Yeah?" Marco called from the hallway.

"Swim time!"

"Okay," he said, but the door remained closed.

I waited a couple seconds longer before asking, "Can you open the door?"

"Open it yourself."

Shit, what'd I do to piss him off?

Marco may not have been as friendly as Cole or Ash, but it'd been a while since he'd been a jerk to me.

"Please, can you open the door?" I tried.

"Open it yourself," he repeated.

"I'm just trying to go swimming."

"Juliet." And that's when I heard it—a hint of amusement. "Open it yourself."

My heart kicked into overdrive, hammering in my chest.

I'd already lost the men tailing me like prison guards. They weren't even stationed outside my door. I was on my own, free to go anywhere but the off-limit rooms. But in order to take advantage of that freedom, I first needed to be let out.

Permanently unlocking my door would be major.

My breath froze in my lungs as I reached for the handle. It whooshed out in a weird squeal when I easily pulled the door open.

Marco was standing outside my door. "Took you long enough."

"It's unlocked now?"

He lifted his chin.

"Like, from now on?" I asked.

"Don't fuck it up."

I watched him storm down the hall, put his thumb to a lock, and head into the room.

He's all bark and… okay, he's probably all bite, too. But it's not aimed at me anymore, so whatever.

Hiking my tote up my arm, I hightailed it to the pool and hot tub.

I was total goo by the time I returned to my *unlocked* room.

MAXIMO

Three Weeks Later

"GET THIS AREA cleaned up."

"Yes, sir."

Walking slowly through the kitchen at Moonlight's buffet, I checked every corner and crevice. My chefs and staff didn't mind the health department's inspection, but they loathed mine. I was a hardass when it came to cleanliness, order, and image.

Heading out of the restaurant, I knew the other kitchens would be spotless by the time I made it to them. Whoever I hit first tipped the rest off. I didn't give a damn so long as the job was done.

"Maximo." Serrano jogged over to catch up to me. "How bad was it?"

"Some clutter and spills. Not bad."

"Did you put the fear of God in them anyway?"

"No, I put the fear of *me* in them."

He chuckled. "How're things for Friday?"

"Georgie says it's going smooth," I said, referring to Star's Tournament Director. "Rooms are ready, tables will be set up Thursday night, kitchen and bar orders have been adjusted for the influx. Registration is already full."

The poker tournaments tended to be easy. A few bickering fights, a few accusations of cheating, and a few small-town big shots who thought they deserved the VIP treatment. Other than that, people played cards, collected their winnings, and then hit up the tables and slots for the fun of gambling rather than the competition.

My cell vibrated in my pocket. I pulled it out to see a text from Cole.

Cole: She wants a keyboard. A musical one, not the computer kind, so I'm no help.

89

I couldn't hold back the small smile that tipped my lips.

Juliet liked to create.

She'd crocheted—badly, according to the men. Her knitting had been even worse. Coloring books had been a mild success, though the bar had been set low.

Despite her lack of ability, she had fun. Which meant I'd give her whatever the hell she wanted.

Me: Then get her one.

Cole: Given her track record, I'm getting the kind that hooks to her headphones. Because if she's badly bopping some Backstreet Boys shit, I'm off guard duty.

Me: Unless she's time traveling back to the late nineties, I think you're safe.

Cole: What?

Me: Backstreet Boys are on the oldies stations now.

Cole: Shit.

I pocketed my phone and turned back to Serrano. "Call me if anything comes up, otherwise I'll see you this weekend."

I walked through the other restaurants and the food court in Moonlight.

And just as I knew they'd be, all were spotless.

A Week Later

Looking up at the knock on my door, I called, "Come in."

Marco opened the door and came in. "Keyboard ain't her thing, boss."

I wasn't surprised. While she'd used the art supplies for hours, the keyboard had gone untouched after the first day.

"She want lessons?" I asked.

He shook his head. "Apparently listening to music is more fun than trying to make it. She's worried about pissing you off, so she said she was going to work at it."

His displeasure was clear.

Even after being there as long as she had, she was still skittish. She walked on eggshells. Worst of fucking all, there were times when she braced like she was preparing to get hit. Like she had experience with that.

And I was willing to bet her piece-of-shit father was to blame.

I'd long ago stopped wondering why Juliet didn't hate me for killing him. The more I learned about her life before me, the more it made sense. One day when she trusted me, I'd make her tell me everything.

And then I'd dig the bastard up and find a way to kill him again.

"Tell her we can return it. No harm, no foul," I said.

"On it."

"Has she said what she wants next?"

He shook his head. "I get the feeling she thinks she's pushed it enough already."

"Find out and get it for her."

"On it," he repeated, leaving the room.

Sweet little dove, still so fucking broken.

JULIET

One Week Later

"To A B." Ash lifted his Diet Coke float that was mostly vanilla ice cream with only a few drops of Diet Coke.

Sitting on the kitchen counter, I raised my float that was heavy on the Diet Coke *and* ice cream. "To being done with ratios!"

Vera and Freddy added theirs, clinking the glasses.

"Units of measurement and fractions will be better anyway," Ash said, holding in a smile that his dimples betrayed. "We'll get started tomorrow."

I dropped my head back. "Whhhhhy? Just let me enjoy my treat and pretend we're done with math forever."

"Just think," Freddy said, making quick work of his float instead of savoring it like I was. "Once you learn those, you'll know how to double and triple ingredients to bake cookies with me."

Few things could get me excited about math, but cookies did it. Especially if they were sugar cookies coated with sprinkles.

My gaze shot to Ash. "Want to dive in when we're done? Maybe we can knock off the whole section in one afternoon."

"Tomorrow."

"Fine," I drawled.

Conversation moved from math to the much more exciting topic of favorite cookies. I didn't speak as I soaked in the happiness surrounding me.

Vera, Ash, and Freddy had busy lives. They had better things to do than to hang around the kitchen, drinking Diet Coke floats with me.

But they took the time to do it anyway. They noticed my hard work and celebrated my accomplishments, even if it was only a B. I'd never had that before, and it made me feel like Freddy's hot coffee was in my veins, warming me from the inside out.

Conversation cut off as the kitchen door opened suddenly.

Wearing his signature suit and cold expression, Maximo walked to the fridge and grabbed a bottle of water before leaning his hip on the counter near where I sat.

I wasn't expecting to see him. I actually rarely saw him. If he wasn't at work, he was locked away in his home office.

But at his nearness, shame and arousal bloomed through me in equal measure.

"What's your favorite cookie, boss?" Ash asked.

I figured he'd say none since he wasn't big on snacks, but after a long moment, he said, "Chocolate chip, but only the chewy kind."

"A classic. Though thin and crunchy is superior." Freddy set his empty cup in the sink and checked his watch. "I've got to run. I'm training the chefs not to butcher my beautiful risotto recipe."

Ash scraped the last of his ice cream before adding his cup to the sink. "I've gotta get going, too." He paused to give my shoulder a squeeze. "Good job again, Juliet," he said before following Freddy out the door.

Even Ms. Vera was suddenly hellbent on escape, putting down her barely touched float. "That laundry isn't going to fold itself."

Oh no, I wonder if they're in trouble.

I was sure Maximo paid them a lot to do their jobs, not drink floats with me. Maybe he was mad they were sitting around on the clock.

But when I caught a glimpse of Ms. Vera's profile, it wasn't fear or nervousness on her face. It was her sly smile.

What's that about?

Before I could ask, she rushed out like the safety of the world depended on her folding laundry right that second.

Leaving me.

With Maximo.

Alone in a giant kitchen that suddenly seemed the size of a broom closet.

Before I could make my escape, Maximo asked, "You like the dress?"

Suddenly forgetting what I was even wearing, I glanced down at the casual skater dress. It'd been left on my bed a few days before with a note from Maximo congratulating me on the A I'd gotten on a Geography test—one of my strengths thanks to having moved so much.

It wasn't the first time I'd been surprised with a gift for a good grade. Like the float celebration, it wasn't the items themselves, but the thought behind them that meant so much.

"I love it," I told him, "but you don't have to—"

"Say thank you, Juliet."

At his tone, my body tightened in a not unpleasant way and a tremor ran down my spine. My hands grew so clammy, I worried my drink would slip from my hold. I did as he ordered, my voice airy and softer than intended. "Thank you."

He didn't respond as he eyed me with an unreadable expression.

The room no longer felt like a broom closet. It was even smaller. And someone had sucked all the air from it. There was none left. *That* was why I was suddenly lightheaded and breathless.

I needed to get out before Maximo heard how embarrassingly loud my heart pounded.

Or before his too sharp eyes noticed the effect he had on me.

Gripping my cup, I started to slide off the counter. "I'm going to get started on—"

His tattooed hand came down on my bare thigh, his fingers curling around to keep me in place and send a rush of emotion—and inappropriate arousal—through me.

My wide eyes shot to his arctic dark ones.

"Stay and finish your ice cream," he ordered—calm, collected, and unaware of the riot he'd started within me. "You earned it."

His hold tightened before he removed his hand and stalked out.

Holy.

Shit.

I had work to do, but I wasn't sure I could walk on my Jell-O legs or focus on anything other than the phantom sensation of his hand on me.

Staying where I was, I grabbed Freddy's handwritten recipe book and flipped through to the baking section.

And then, for reasons I didn't want to acknowledge, I searched for *chewy* chocolate chip cookies.

CHAPTER TWELVE

The One With Even More Time Jumps

MAXIMO

One Month Later

WALKING AROUND THE empty makeshift arena, I double checked that everything was in place.

It was going to be a wild night.

If boxing at Moonlight brought out everyone's primal side, the matches I held at the warehouse brought out their basest instincts.

No-holds-barred.

No bet restrictions.

No regulations.

The first two bouts were amateur. It gave my guests a sneak peek at up-and-coming fighters. Ones who were desperate for a sponsor to get them on the map.

And the rich motherfuckers who would pack the seats were desperate to live vicariously through them.

The event was exclusive. No one got through without an invite. Every guest had to be vetted. Security was tight and unbreachable.

That VIP feeling, the knowledge they were a *have* and not a *have-not*, added to the night. As did the less-than-ideal surroundings. It was dirty and raw.

Wrong.

The illegalness was the high the bastards needed to feel something again.

Checking out the other side, Serrano met me in the middle. He gave a low whistle. "It's going to be a moneymaker. Ortiz said one of the guests has already dropped a couple hundred grand at the blackjack tables."

"Good. Hopefully he's got enough left to lose here, too."

The heavy door opened, and my hand went to my Glock until I saw it was Ash.

"One of your VIPs at Nebula wants a meeting with you," he called to me.

"Handle it."

Because I sure as hell don't want to.

"I tried, but he insists on talking to the big boss."

I dragged my hand down my face.

All my properties were upscale, but Nebula was my luxury resort. It was the best of the best, which was why it cost a fucking shit-ton to stay in a basic room. A night in one of the suites or penthouses was more than most people's mortgage for a couple months.

The majority of my guests were happy to make their own trouble, but there was always one who wanted to feel like the ultimate VIP.

"Did he say what he wanted?" I asked.

"No, which means Mr. Dicky-doo probably wants pussy, dick, drugs, or all three at the same time."

"Mr. Dicky-doo?" Serrano stupidly asked.

"It's when his stomach sticks out more than his dicky do."

"Fucking hell," I muttered, shaking my head.

Ash smirked, but it was about more than giving me the heebie-fuck-ing-jeebies.

I almost didn't want to ask. "What else?"

"She wants to learn to cook with Freddy," he shared, not having to say who he was referring to.

The same *she* I hadn't allowed myself to see—in person, at least. Not since I'd fucked up by wrapping my hand around her thigh, finally feeling her soft skin.

"I'll have a different chef come by," I said.

"Tried that. She wants to cook with Freddy."

I scowled.

Between his kitchen skills and his accent, Freddy had women throwing themselves at him. He could get even more if he was so inclined, but his passion was food.

I trusted him, but I still didn't like the idea of her spending time with him. And his accent. In his kitchen.

Especially when I knew how easy it was to lose control in there with her.

It was wrong to be jealous, but it was there like a punch to the gut.

"Fine," I gritted out. "Tell him to keep his damn hands to himself."

"Already done."

"Then why're you here?"

His smirk spread to a shit-eating grin. "And miss seeing your panties in a twist about it?"

"You're fired," I said though he didn't look fazed.

"Worth it." Heading toward the door, he called over his shoulder, "Don't forget to deal with Mr. Dicky-doo. I'll text you his room number."

Fucking Christ.

I need a vacation on an island with no cell service and a supply of whiskey...

And a pretty dove.

JULIET

Three Weeks Later

I DID IT.

I stared at the screen, blinking rapidly to see if it changed. When everything remained the same, I rubbed my eyes.

Still the same.

Even pinching myself didn't change anything.

I graduated.

Not gray-area-graduated or symbolic-graduated.

I actually graduated from Melbrook Academy.

Mr. Reed may have finessed logistics behind the scenes, but working morning, noon, and night had earned me the credits. And all my studying had prepared me for finals.

I'd been stalking the online grades, and they finally posted.

"Well?" Ash asked from the doorway.

I'd planned to give him the sad face and pretend I'd failed. But when it came time to execute my prank, I was too excited.

Jumping out of my seat, I turned the computer to face him. "I passed!"

"Even math?"

I'd cut it close with a seventy-six, but didn't matter—a pass was a pass was a pass.

A huge grin split my face, making my cheeks hurt. "Even math!"

Ash came over and pulled me into a bear hug. "Proud of you."

Maybe it was because I hadn't ever heard those words before.

Maybe it was because I was so damn happy.

Maybe it was because I couldn't remember the last time anyone had hugged me.

Or maybe it was just because Ash had worked hard to find a teaching method that clicked in my brain and then had busted his ass to make sure I could pass.

Whatever the reason, tears streamed down my face as I choked out, "Thank you for helping me."

He pulled away to grip my shoulders. "Hey, this was all you. You were so determined, you'd have done it with or without me."

I laughed and hiccupped, wiping my cheeks with the back of my hand.

There was a throat clearing behind him, and he dropped his hands like my shoulders had burned him.

When Ash moved to the side, I saw Maximo standing on the other side of the table, his arms crossed over his broad chest. "Well?"

When I didn't answer, Ash nudged me. "Tell him."

"I passed," I said, grinning despite being completely intimidated by Maximo and his brooding black eyes.

"Everything?"

"Everything. Mr. Reed said I've officially met the criteria to graduate."

"Reed keeps his knees then," Maximo said, as if that were a normal comment.

At the reminder of all he'd done for me—from extorting... er, *uti-*

lizing Mr. Reed's debt, to buying my supplies, to roping Ash into help-ing—I did something stupid.

Rounding the table, I got into his space and wrapped my arms around him. I *hugged* him.

His body was rigid and his arms were still crossed.

I didn't care.

In that moment, the hug was for the hugger, not the huggee.

He uncrossed his arms and lowered them to grip my waist. I thought he was going to shove me away, but his palms slid to my back as he wrapped his arms around me and returned my embrace. "I'm proud of you, little dove."

Ash hugging me and telling me he was proud had meant a lot.

Maximo hugging me and telling me he was proud meant the *world*.

Letting me go, he backed away. "Do you want to walk the stage? I'll arrange it with Reed."

I'd had to physically go into Melbrook Academy to take the proc-tored final exams. The kids had gawked and whispered, and the over-whelming smell of Axe body spray had given me a headache.

I had no interest in walking the stage with people I didn't know in front of an audience of strangers.

"No," I said. "I'm good."

"You'll still celebrate," he stated, sounding more like a threat than a plan.

"I'm going to ask Freddy to teach me his mac and cheese recipe and then beg him to make me funfetti cake."

Freddy had said it was an abomination against his French ancestry, but I'd graduated. That had to count for something, right?

"He'll do it," Maximo said, his tone again making the words sound like a threat. He gave Ash his attention. "Ready?"

Ash nodded but shot me another smile. "Congrats again, Juliet."

"Thanks."

I watched them leave before plopping onto the chair.

Well, shit. Now what do I do?

CHAPTER THIRTEEN

The Last One With The Time Jumps

JULIET

Four Months Later

WELL, DAMN. THIS *sucks.*

After showering, I'd gone into my closet to get dressed, only to find a couple new items. It wasn't the first time, but it never failed to surprise me.

One of the outfits was a gray romper I'd immediately tried on, but the fit was all wrong. I was too petite, so everything hit at the wrong spots.

Frowning, I checked myself out in the mirror to see if it was really as bad as I thought.

It was worse.

I looked like a kid wearing her older sister's clothes.

Actually, thanks to the weird poofiness at the butt, I looked like a toddler with a full diaper.

Maybe I can ask to have it altered.

Or maybe I can alter it...

I had no clue if I could even do it. It'd been a while since I'd sewn anything—and that'd just been small mending or patching jobs.

But it'd also been a while since I'd tried a new hobby. I was getting restless.

After finding out I'd graduated, I'd looked up some colleges. I hadn't known how the logistics would work since I was a penniless minor, but it hadn't mattered. I'd been far too late to apply for fall semester. Without school to focus on, I'd rotated through a variety of hobbies I'd never had time or money to try.

I'd given the keyboard another shot, that time with lessons from a patient music teacher. It hadn't taken long to figure out lack of instruction hadn't been the problem.

Not by a long, badly-rhythmed mile.

I'd practically handcuffed myself with yarn when I'd tried knitting.

Crocheting had been better, but not by much. Even going slow with a video guide, my scarf was less scarfy and more knots and tangles forming an abstract rectangle.

Freddy had taught me to cook and bake some basics—including *chewy* chocolate chip cookies.

It was time to try something new.

After changing into clothes that actually fit, I headed into the hall.

I was pretty sure Maximo was home, but I didn't go to him. As odd as it was since he bankrolled the whole shebang, I didn't feel comfortable asking him for anything. It was easier to pretend things just magically showed up.

Like I had unlimited wishes from a genie.

Going downstairs, I searched for one of the men or Ms. Vera but had no luck. The kitchen was empty, too, and I swiped a couple Starbursts for my trouble. I was about to leave when Marco came in.

He looked guilty until his eyes narrowed. "What're you doing in here?"

I hid the candy behind my back as I shot back, "What're *you* doing?"

"Just looking for Freddy." He picked up a big pot like he was casually checking it out.

"Freddy moved the Oreos."

"Dammit. Where?"

I shrugged.

"What'd you go for?"

"Starburst. In the flour canister."

"Thanks." He grabbed a much larger handful and pocketed them. "What're you up to?"

"Can you get me a needle and thread?"

His eyes went alert and he scanned me like he was searching for an injury.

I wonder if he's ex-military or a commando or something.

I rolled my eyes. "I'm not looking to do battlefield stitches, I actually want to sew."

"Need fabric?"

I shook my head. "Just gray thread."

"Got it." He grabbed another handful of Starburst and checked one more pot before leaving.

And I went upstairs to plan my new hobby.

MAXIMO

"WHAT IS SHE doing?"

Juliet sat on her floor, her body hunched over, but I couldn't see what had her attention.

Ash didn't need to glance at the screen to know. "She's altering one of her outfits."

"I can have my tailor do it."

"Marco already offered when he dropped off the supplies and saw what she was working on. She said she wants to do it herself."

Since she'd barely moved in hours, she was determined enough.

"Why'd Marco tell you?" I asked.

"To give me a heads-up she was armed with sharp-as-fuck fabric scissors."

I wasn't worried—and not just because I wasn't home to get shivved.

She'd had countless opportunities to leave. She wasn't locked in her room. The front door was unguarded. Hell, she had access to Freddy's knives and could've used one to demand a car to aid her escape.

She never tried.

My little dove likes her gilded cage.

I pulled my eyes away and moved on to a topic that was far less enticing. "Any new Dobrow sightings?"

He shook his head. "Nada."

There'd been a handful of suspected sightings, but they could've been cases of mistaken identity—wannabe Bond villains were a dime a dozen in Vegas.

But I didn't trust it.

My eyes went back to the monitors over Ash's shoulder. "Have Cole run an optics check on the security systems as a precaution."

He stood. "On it."

When he left, I leaned back in my chair and ran my palm down my face. I couldn't shake the feeling shit was about to go sideways.

And my gut was never wrong.

JULIET

A Week Later

HOLDING UP THE fabric, I inspected my handiwork.

After adjusting the romper's straps so they fit without drooping, I'd watched a ton of tutorials before turning the shorts into a skirt.

And it'd worked.

Kinda.

My stitches were janky, my hem wasn't quite even, and there was a good chance none of the seams would hold.

But so long as I didn't look too closely and barely moved, it'd worked.

Running into my closet, I changed into the dress and did a spin in front of the mirror.

I actually did it.

I slid on a pair of wedge sandals and went in search of Ms. Vera. I didn't have to go far. She came out of one of the guest rooms as I neared it.

Catching sight of me, she stopped and clutched her hands against her chest. "Beautiful! It's much prettier as a dress."

"I think so, too."

I'd been working on the project, fixing and refixing until my back was numb and my fingers were stabbed more than a pin cushion.

And I'd loved every frustrating second.

Finishing was bittersweet because I didn't have another project yet. I'd looked through all of my clothes, but minus altering my tees into crop tops or extending my crop tops into tees, there was nothing I could do.

"Can I have some regular fabric to mess around with?" I asked.

"Make a list, and we'll go tomorrow."

I nodded even though I had no clue what I was going to do, let alone what I'd need to do it.

Only one way to find out.

Returning to my room, I grabbed a notebook, pen, and my MacBook. Then in my pretty dress, I sat on the floor and researched all afternoon, through dinner, and until I was falling asleep at the coffee table.

CHRISTMAS

KNOCK.

Don't even knock. Just say 'Merry Christmas' then go eat breakfast. Two words. No big deal.

Walking down the hall, I stared at the closed office door. My steps slowed as I neared it.

Ms. Vera and the men are off. He's probably gone, too.

Using that flimsy excuse to chicken out, I sped past and went downstairs.

'Twas the morning of Christmas, and all through the big-ass mansion, no one was around, which made it eerily quiet.

Not quite as charming as the original.

Going into the kitchen, I opened the fridge to find heat-and-eat meals stacked for me. I grabbed the two labeled for Christmas morning and opened them, practically drooling at the sight of fruit salad and breakfast casserole.

I popped the casserole into the microwave and turned to grab a fork when my eyes landed on something.

Something magical.

Something with my name on it—literally.

It's a true Christmas miracle.

Freddy was already on my *Nice List* since he'd promised to teach me to make beignets when he returned from visiting family in New Orleans.

Him leaving me a stash of coffee put him on my *Super-Duper Nice List.*

I followed his written directions to brew it using the pour over thingy.

A Mr. Coffee would've sufficed.

When it finished, I took a sip.

Never mind.

This is the nectar of the gods and Mr. Coffee is a sin against coffee.

I didn't bother eating at the big table since it was just me. I sat on the counter and ate, enjoying the delicious food and *loving* the coffee.

To some, it would probably be a shitty way to spend Christmas morning.

But to me, it was the best Christmas I'd ever had.

I had food that wasn't a frozen turkey dinner.

No one was drunk.

There was no random cocktail waitress cooking me expired eggs because she felt bad I was eating dry cereal in a house with no decorations or presents.

Instead, I was warm. I was fed. I was caffeinated.

And, most of all, it was peaceful.

A smidge creepy in all its expansive emptiness, but still better than drunk screaming—or worse.

Full and happy, I backtracked upstairs. I was trying to decide whether I wanted to take a nap or watch one of the fifty-billion Christmas movies on TV when I noticed something.

One of the normally closed doors was ajar.

That wasn't open earlier.

Was it?

I wasn't sure. My focus had been aimed at Maximo's office, which was opposite the ajar one. It was entirely possible I'd missed it.

I slowed to sneak a peek.

It's probably just storage.

Or yet another boring guest room.

Or it holds government secrets, hostages, and Jimmy Hoffa.

But when I glanced in, I saw none of those.

I saw something even more unbelievable.

Positive it was a hallucination, I pushed the door all the way open and stared.

In the center of the room, there was a L-shaped desk with a sewing machine on top. Two of those headless torso mannequins were positioned next to it. The wall was lined with racks filled with all sorts of bits, doohickeys, and bolts of fabric.

So much fabric.

It was a lot.

Too much.

Beyond anything I'd asked for.

It was beautiful and amazing and perfect.

Too perfect.

There's no way this is for me.

No way in hell.

My type got toys from a family who picked a name off a charity tree.

My type got cheap presents from church handouts.

My type had a dad who pawned all the donated gifts because he was feeling lucky and claimed he'd be able to win enough to buy better gifts.

My type had a dad who *never* replaced any of the hawked gifts, let alone with better ones.

My type was poor trash who didn't get a spectacular life, even temporarily.

I don't know who it's for, but it's not me.

Even as the denials raced through my pessimistic mind, something else bloomed in my heart.

Hope.

That stupid emotion I'd thought I was too smart to feel grew as I took in the details. The oversized green and red bow stuck to the top of the sewing machine. The cotton sleep shorts I'd been hand sewing positioned on the desk. The notecard with the familiar masculine scrawl.

And the canvas prints on the wall.

A handful of different sized pictures were hung around the room. They were simplistic, just a single white dove with a gray backdrop, but that minimalism was what made them breathtaking.

Even without the note or the bow, the doves made it clear this room was meant to be mine.

Like it was armed with boobytraps and I was trespassing, I took a tentative step inside. Then another. And another. Once I reached the desk, my heart pounded so hard, I was surprised it didn't beat right out of my sternum. I grazed my fingertips along the machine that was loaded with so many buttons and settings, I couldn't imagine all it was capable of doing.

I picked up the card.

Merry Christmas, little dove.

It's actually for me.

No.

No, no, no.

As much as I loved the room—and I loved every single aspect of it—I couldn't use it.

I'd stayed to ease his guilt.

I'd taken his help getting my diploma because I wasn't stupid enough to turn down the priceless opportunity.

I'd accepted the clothes because clothes were a necessity. Plus, the cost for all of it was likely less than a payment on one of his cars.

Even the hobby supplies I'd asked for were meant to be cheap and inconsequential.

Temporary.

Just like me.

A sewing room was not something I could bring with me when I turned eighteen.

And if I allowed myself to use it—if I fell in love with it—how was I supposed to return to janky hand sewing?

Turning to leave the room, I froze.

My movements.

My breathing.

My thoughts.

Hanging on the wall opposite the sewing machine was the largest canvas print.

A dove in an intricate cage.

In black and white, the gleaming bars of the ornate cage and the bright white dove contrasted with the dark background. It looked beautiful, each bit of shadow and light playing perfectly against each other.

The beauty of it twisted in my gut for reasons I couldn't fully comprehend, let alone explain.

I was pretty sure that was how good art was supposed to make people feel.

Dragging my eyes from the canvas, I looked out the open door to the closed one across the way.

He needs to return everything.

All of it.

Except maybe this print. I'll let myself keep this one.

I steeled my spine and marched across the hall, rehearsing how to turn down his thoughtful gifts without sounding ungrateful.

But when I got to the door, it wasn't my fist that hit it. It was my forehead landing with a gentle thud.

Because in that brief delay, I'd thought about how supported I'd been. With my schoolwork. With my reading or swimming. With my less than successful hobby attempts. And with sewing.

It may have started as a way to kill some time and alter a romper, but it had grown into something I loved.

And someone had noticed that.

Choked with emotion, my raw words didn't insist he take it all back. They expressed the deep, heartfelt gratitude that filled me. "Thank you. I love it."

For all I knew, I was talking to an empty room, but that was okay.

I'd said what I needed to.

Turning, I headed for my room and my iPad.

If I want to learn how to use that sewing machine before my birthday, I'm going to need to watch videos.

I thought about all the switches and buttons and settings I'd seen.

A lot of videos.

CHAPTER FOURTEEN

Happy Birthday

JULIET

"*H*APPY BIRTHDAY!"

There was *nothing* happy about any of my birthdays, but especially not that one. I wanted to climb back into bed, pull the covers over my head, and pretend the day—and the entirety of the outside world—didn't exist.

When I'd gotten up, Ms. Vera had been waiting in my sitting room with breakfast and a birthday hug.

"Thanks," I said, forcing a smile I did *not* feel.

She gestured to the couch, a little bounce in her step as she moved. "Sit. Eat."

She seems extra chipper.

I, on the other hand, was a gloomy cloud raining on my own parade.

The dreaded day had arrived.

I was eighteen.

An adult.

Able to live on my own, make my own way, all that jazz.

It was time to leave.

"What's the, uh, *plan*?" I asked.

She pointed at the food. "Eat. It's a little chilly, but Cole already adjusted the pool temp so you can swim."

I smiled, and it was only a little forced.

Of course, they're not going to boot me out on my birthday.

I would have to ask again later because I needed time to plan and pack. For right then, though, I'd greedily savor my last day in paradise.

Lifting the dome off the tray, the smell of Cajun seasoning and jalapeños burned my nose and made my mouth water. Along with the spicy omelet, there was a piece of toast, a bowl of strawberry and banana slices, and coffee.

A *big* mug of coffee.

All my favorites.

Happy birthday to me.

MAXIMO

HEADING TO TALK to Freddy, I stopped as Juliet came out of the kitchen, her strawberry-blond hair in a high ponytail and her body barely covered by a white bikini. She didn't notice me as she turned toward the backdoor, giving me a view of her rounded ass cheeks peeking out.

Since that meant Freddy had gotten the same view, I clenched my jaw. "Having fun, little dove?"

She spun around, and her startled gasp went straight to my cock. As did the way she breathed, "Maximo."

Christ, what I wouldn't give to hear her say my name like that when I'm buried deep inside her.

"Having fun?" I repeated.

She nodded, that damn ponytail bobbing.

"Good." I was about to turn away when my gaze caught on something.

As I closed the distance, Juliet backed away until she was pressed against the wall, her green eyes locked on me like a pretty doe eyeing a circling wolf. That didn't put me off.

It turned me on.

I only stopped when I was close enough to count the freckles smattered across her nose. Slowly, I skimmed my bent finger down her side, her skin so damn soft.

As I reached the hem of her bikini bottoms, her breath hitched.

With fear?

Or something much different?

I ran my thumb along the thin, puckered scar above her hip bone.

I knew what it was.

I had enough of them.

I'd given even more.

Still, I rumbled, "Where'd you get this scar, little dove?"

She swallowed hard, her voice uneven when she lied, "I don't remember."

"Don't lie to me."

She hesitated before admitting, "My dad owed money. They came after me as a warning to him."

"Who'd he owe?"

"Everyone," she said with a small, sardonic laugh. "But in this case, it was the Sullivans."

The Sullivans were small-time loan sharks and big-time gun runners.

"Didn't Patrick Sullivan box with Shamus?"

She nodded. "That's why they let me off easy."

She thinks that's getting off easy?

"Patrick did it?" I asked.

"No, one of his goons."

"Is he dead?"

If her piece-of-shit father had cared about anything other than himself and his vices, he'd have slaughtered the bastard responsible in a way that made it clear Juliet was off limits.

Her pretty eyes went wide at my question. "Not that I know of."

"He will be."

She shook her head, but it wasn't an objection to the violence. "It wasn't worth the headache."

How badly did Shamus fuck her up that she thinks she's not worth it?

I gripped her hip and stooped so my eyes were level with hers. When she tried to glance away, I ordered, "Look at me." Once I had her eyes again, I spoke slow and clear so there was no misunderstanding. "No one hurts you. If they do, I'll make sure they spend the limited time they have left on earth regretting it. It will not be a headache. I'll enjoy making it clear what happens to anyone stupid enough to touch you."

"This conversation is insane," she whispered.

"No, what's insane is you thinking a knife to the gut isn't worth re-taliation."

"Dad said it would mean war with them."

"Then I'll start a fucking war 'cause you're sure as fuck worth it. You need someone to take care of you."

Her spine straightened as she lifted that stubborn chin of hers. "I can take care of myself. I always have."

"And that's exactly the fucking problem." My plans to ease her in shot right out the damn window. Seeing the residual pain, betrayal, and sadness that shadowed her eyes, I muttered, "Fuck, you need a Daddy bad."

Juliet scoffed, rolling her eyes. "No, thanks. I had a dad and he caused more than enough problems."

"I didn't say a dad. I said a *Daddy*."

Her eyes went big as her full lips parted. Chest rising and falling, she shook her head. "I know Shamus fucked me up, but I don't have daddy issues. I'm not that damaged and dysf—"

"Watch your words carefully, Juliet. This has nothing to do with dys-function and everything to do with letting someone take care of you for once. And based on the way your pulse is pounding, you know that."

"I'm not interested in that kind of thing," she claimed, despite her body's reaction contradicting her words.

"Don't lie to me. More importantly, don't lie to yourself."

I couldn't stop myself.

I didn't even try.

Giving in to the twisted need that'd haunted me for a whole fucking year, I pressed my mouth to her lie-filled one in a hard kiss.

She tasted like sunshine and Diet Coke, and I wanted to plunge my tongue in and memorize the flavor.

But I didn't.

Pulling away, I stepped back. "We'll talk more later."

Dazed, she nodded before hurrying out the backdoor.

I'd done the honorable thing.

I'd waited for her birthday.

I'd been patient.

And I was done.

JULIET

112

A DADDY.

He kissed me.

A freaking Daddy.

What'd that mean?

He freaking kissed me.

What did that mean?

My thoughts whipped around as I sat in the hot tub. My muscles were so tight, it was a wonder my bones didn't turn to dust. I was tense and confused and surprised and...

Needy.

I was needy and restless and the kind of hot that had nothing to do with the water temp and everything to do with the thrumming between my legs.

God, for such a quick kiss, it'd been amazing. Intense. Controlling. As dominating as his personality.

I couldn't deny I wanted Maximo. Ever since the first night I'd thought of him while I'd touched myself, he'd turned into a secret fantasy.

An *unattainable* fantasy.

Or so I'd thought.

But thanks to his abrupt change—going from avoiding me to kissing me—I wasn't so sure he was as cold and unattainable as I'd believed. Add in his *Daddy* comment, and I wasn't even sure which way was up anymore.

Giving up on relaxing, I climbed out and wrapped a towel around myself. Maximo had said we'd talk more, and before that happened, I needed to get my racing thoughts together.

And that meant I needed to do some research.

I was relieved I didn't run into him as I hurried to my room because there was no way I'd be able to hide how affected I was by our conversation or his kiss.

Grabbing my MacBook, I started by Googling the most important thing.

Daddy kink equals daddy issues?

I was relieved to see that, like Maximo had claimed, it had nothing to do with anything revolting. Therapists and experts agreed it was about the power dynamic of one partner being in charge and the other being submissive, with an emphasis on care and nurturing.

I wasn't sure about all that, but I was relieved it wasn't indicative of some secret desire that would have made me barf up everything I'd ever eaten in my entire life.

Broadening my search, I skipped past the erotica that came up and focused on the real-life blogs and articles.

All of it was gross.

It did nothing for me.

It was *wrong*.

That's how I *should* have felt.

Because in actuality, there was a lot I found appealing.

It did so much for me, I couldn't stop from shifting and squeezing my thighs together.

And even if my brain was trying to tell me it was wrong, the idea of Maximo taking care of me the way the blogs described filled me with this sense of… rightness.

Not that I was into all the things people described. I knew I would hate any form of humiliation. Trading partners or sharing made me feel sick *and* pissed off. And I didn't judge, but age play was definitely *not* for me.

After a while, my head was swimming with information, and I felt even more confused than when I'd started researching.

Did Maximo want a sugar daddy thing? Was he into age play? Did he want to trade his partner or watch them with others? Was he a Dom who liked the occasional 'scene'? There'd been a couple guys at the gym whose girls had called them papi, and those guys were selfish assholes who slept with anything that breathed. Maybe Maximo just liked being called Daddy and there was nothing more to it. I wasn't sure it would do anything for me, but I could probably just say it for him.

That was, of course, if I decided to do it.

It was not a one-size-fits-all kink, and there were so many variables and variations. I couldn't decide if I was interested until I found out what he was interested in.

Someone knocked on the door, and I slammed the laptop closed like I'd been looking at something dirty.

Which I kinda had.

Ms. Vera opened the door and tsked. "You're still in your suit. Go get ready."

"For what?"

"Go shower." She shooed me. "Hurry."

"Okay, okay," I said, rushing into the bathroom to shower.

Standing under the hot spray, my thoughts on what I'd read, Maximo, and his kiss, I wanted to touch myself. But I could hear footsteps outside the door, and that acted like a bucket of ice water.

Once I showered and dried off, I wrapped a bathrobe around myself and opened the door to see Ms. Vera waiting with a blow-dryer and round brush. She marched me back into the bathroom, sitting me on the closed toilet before going to town on my hair. It felt like it was going to have some eighties height, but when she let me look, I saw there was just a little volume and flip to my usually straight locks.

It was pretty.

"Do your makeup." She gestured to my stash. "You only have fifteen minutes."

"Until what?"

"Your birthday dinner."

"Aren't I just eating up here? Freddy said he was making something special."

"No, downstairs tonight." She shooed me again. "Makeup."

"Has anyone told you that you're bossy?"

"Yes, but only a few lived to tell about it." She winked, but I wasn't positive she was joking.

Erring on the safe side, I jumped up and did as she said.

Walking out to my bedroom, Ms. Vera wasn't there but a garment bag and a shoebox were.

Since I'm leaving soon, one last present won't hurt, right? Who knows how long it'll be before I get one again.

I unzipped the bag to see a gorgeous little black dress. One side had a long sleeve but the other was completely bare. After pulling on panties, I slid the dress over my head and tugged it gently into place.

I grabbed the silver pumps from the box and put them on before walking to the mirror in my closet.

Oh, I have to learn to sew this because I want one in every color.

It was overkill for dinner in the dining room, but I didn't care. I loved it.

"Time's up!" Ms. Vera called from the sitting room.

"I'm coming!" I hurried out and opened the door.

Ms. Vera gave a small gasp. "Pretty girl."

"Thank you. I love how you did my hair."

"Of course. I'm very good." She fluffed her short hair for emphasis. "Now go."

Hours in the pool meant I was so hungry, I almost missed it.

Her tell.

I eyed her skeptically. "What's happening?"

"Nothing. Go before you're late."

"Why would that matter?"

"Because if you're late, Freddy is going to eat your mac and cheese."

"Freddy made me mac and cheese?"

"Yes, now *go*."

I may not have trusted her, but the mention of mac and cheese was enough to put some fire in my steps as I rushed downstairs.

When I turned into the dining room, all that fire moved somewhere *much* different, and I came to a halt.

Maximo.

Sitting at the head of the table in a black suit and white dress shirt with the top button undone, he looked like an ambitious businessman about to take over the world.

And all that arrogant authority was focused on one thing.

Me.

Standing, he came over and put his palm to my lower back before kissing my cheek. "You look beautiful."

"Thank you," I forced out.

He put some gentle pressure on my back, guiding me to the table and pulling out the chair to the right of his.

Why is he here?

There's no way I can eat with him.

I can't even look at him without thinking of... everything.

Seriously, why is he here?

"Relax," he said, easily reading my freak out. "This is just dinner. Nothing more."

I still didn't think I'd be able to stomach any food, but my shoulders lowered slightly as I exhaled. "Okay."

Freddy came out from the kitchen carrying two shallow bowls. His accent was exaggeratedly thick as he announced, "Two salads," before disappearing.

Silently, I picked at my salad, mostly eating the blueberries and feta.

I should've said something—*anything*—but my brain was blank as blank could be.

"Tell me what you're making."

My gaze shot to Maximo's. "Pardon?"

"Your sewing. You finished the shirt for Vera. What's your new project?"

My brows shot up that he knew about the top, but I hurried to answer since I got the feeling he was a man who didn't like to repeat himself. "I'm trying the sleep shorts again. Last time I messed up the elastic and the leg holes were different sizes."

"Are you having better luck this time?"

"So far. I learned a new measuring trick that's more accurate."

"What other plans are on your list?"

Before I could answer, Freddy came in with two plates. As he set them down, he did his accented spiel. "Lobster mac and cheese with buttered French breadcrumbs, lemon goat cheese, and a sherry reduction. Plus, roasted green beans that no one is going to eat but that needed to be included for color. Enjoy." He looked at me and added, "But save room for dessert."

Usually that wouldn't be an issue, but as I drooled down at my plate, I wasn't sure I could stop myself from eating my serving *and* Maximo's.

Picking up my fork, I speared a few cavatappi noodles when what I really wanted to do was shovel all of it directly into my mouth.

"Your list?" Maximo prompted.

"Ms. Vera brought me some really soft fabric that I want to make pillowcases with. I also have a dress pattern, but I think I want to try making it as a skirt and top. It should be easy so long as I don't mess up the elastic again. I have this really pretty color in mind."

You're rambling. He doesn't care about this.

"And it should be nice," I finished lamely.

"That's it?"

"What?"

"You've been working in that room from the time you get up until dinner, and you've only got two things on your list?"

"Well, no, but—"

"If I ask you a question, Juliet, it's because I want an answer. And I expect to get one." He picked up his water and drank, his throat working in a way that was distracting and weirdly sexy. "Now what else do

117

you have planned?" At my hesitation, his tone was filled with warning. "Juliet."

"I'm just trying to get my thoughts in order. Sheesh."

His dark eyes narrowed as he muttered, "Brat."

The way he said it made me squeeze my thighs.

I took another drink before answering. "I've only been sewing with patterns, but once I get better, I want to try designing my own items. It'll probably be a while before I get to that stage, but it would be fun."

As we ate, Maximo asked more questions, encouraging me to go into details about things I knew he didn't give a damn about. Even still, I talked and talked and talked, happily sharing the ideas that constantly floated through my head. I didn't know what it said about my life that someone taking an interest in me was so unusual, but it was.

Once I was dangerously close to being too full for whatever majestic dessert Freddy had whipped up, I pushed my plate away.

Maximo had already finished his dinner, including the green beans. He pointed to the untouched pile on my plate. "Eat."

"I'm saving room for dessert."

"You can't just have mac and cheese for dinner."

"I also had a salad."

"You had blueberries and feta."

I shrugged. "Still healthy."

His jaw clenched as he rubbed a tattooed hand across it, but he didn't say anything.

A few minutes of charged silence ticked by before Freddy came out to clear away the plates.

"You've outdone yourself," I told him.

His chest puffed at the compliment. "Just wait, chéri," he said with a wink.

"Freddy," Maximo bit out.

But he didn't look fazed. "Be back."

When Freddy left with our plates, I shifted in my seat so I was facing Maximo. "Do you always say people's names like that?"

"Like what?"

"Like you're warning them."

He lifted a shoulder. "Usually I am."

"I think I'll start saying your name like that."

"That I'd like to hear."

118

I didn't get the chance to try before Freddy came in with clean plates, forks, and a big knife. He left again before returning with a cake loaded with so many sprinkles, I couldn't see the frosting under them. He placed the cake tower in front of me and lit the tall pink candles. "Make a wish."

I didn't bother to make a wish, but I did blow them out so we could hurry to the good stuff.

Freddy sliced into the beauty, putting a hefty wedge on my plate. Like the outside, the inside was filled with so many sprinkles, there was hardly any white.

"You made me funfetti cake." I grinned up at him. "I thought it was an insult to cakes."

"It is. But I made this one from scratch, so it's not as bad. I guess."

I grabbed my fork and took a huge bite before noticing Freddy had left and Maximo wasn't having any. Swallowing, I asked, "You don't like cake?"

"No."

"That's crazy. Who doesn't like *cake*?"

He smirked. "I don't care for most desserts."

He doesn't snack. He doesn't like most sweets. He eats his green beans.

Weirdo.

Freddy came back to drop off a cup of black coffee to Maximo.

"May I have one?" I asked Freddy, but it was Maximo who answered.

"It's too late for you to have caffeine."

I thought Freddy would maybe shrug or roll his eyes, but he didn't look surprised by Maximo's denial.

"It's not that late," I argued as Freddy left.

"It is."

"Then why're you having it?"

He took a drink, as if to rub it in my face. "Because I can."

I glared.

"It's after seven." He gave me a pointed look. "What would happen if you drank coffee this late?"

"Nothing," I lied.

"Juliet."

"Maximo," I shot back with the same dramatic warning.

He didn't seem amused as he stared me down.

"I wouldn't be able to sleep," I grudgingly admitted.

Maximo smirked, his stupid, handsome face looking even more handsome. "Exactly."

"Is this part of your whole... *thing*?" I asked impulsively before wishing I could rewind and eat my words.

"Yes," he said simply.

And even though I regretted awkwardly bringing it up, I found myself disappointed he didn't expand.

I picked at the amazing cake that beat the pants off any box mix, but my mind was on what I'd read online.

Questions bounced through my head and swirled across my tongue until I couldn't hold them in. "So, your thing..." At his quirked brow, I amended, "The *Daddy* thing."

"What about it?"

"Is that just an endearment you like to be called?"

He gave me *the look*. "No."

I waited for him to elaborate, but he didn't that time, either.

There was a glint of anticipation and enjoyment in his dark eyes, and I got the feeling he enjoyed forcing me to voice my questions.

Since I was far too curious to back down, that was exactly what I did. "Is it, like, a sugar daddy arrangement?"

"I don't need to pay for a date."

That means it's the actual kink, but how extreme does he take it?

I moved on to my make-or-break questions. "Are you into age play?"

He froze with his cup at his mouth. "What do you know about age play, little dove?"

"I did some research," I admitted.

His eyes flared, but he shook his head. "No, I don't do age play. I know people who do, but it's not for me."

"What about, like, humiliation stuff?"

"Not my personal preference but I'm flexible. Is that something *you'd* like?"

I rapidly shook my head. "I can't even watch awkwardness on TV. I get secondhand embarrassment."

"Noted."

Maybe I shouldn't have admitted that.

"But you *do* like to tell your partner what to do?" I asked.

He studied me carefully. "Yes."

I thought about what I'd read, both online and in fiction. "Why do you like it?"

"Are you asking if something shaped my preferences?" At my nod, he said, "No. There's no tragic backstory. No outlandish reasoning. I like control in all areas of my life. It's what I've always preferred and who I've always been. Simple as that."

Nothing about this seems simple.

"Are there rules and a contract?" I asked.

"There are rules, but I'm not big on wasting time and energy producing a bullshit contract that isn't worth the paper it's printed on. We'd communicate like any other relationship."

I flipped the fork back and forth, pressing the prongs down on the cake crumbs as I gathered my nerves. "Do you, uh, share or loan out your—"

"Fuck no." Maximo's eyes blazed as he pinned me with an intense stare. "If you're mine, you're *mine*."

That was all well and good, but it didn't mean there weren't a dozen other women spread about, loyal to him while he alternated between them.

I swallowed. "And you're…"

"Every fucking bit as much yours."

I had to force myself to breathe past the hammering in my chest and the thrumming of my clit.

Maximo must've misconstrued the tension that'd infused my body because his expression softened. "We can finish this conversation another time. Eat your cake and relax."

I nodded but didn't eat, my thoughts too busy racing. After a minute, I asked, "Is it only in the bedroom? Scenes or whatever?"

"No. It's not playtime for kicks and giggles. It's twenty-four-seven. If you agree, it will be your life until you decide you don't want it to be anymore."

"How would that work once I move out?"

His jaw clenched. "You won't be moving out."

"I can't stay here."

"Why the hell not?"

"Because I'm eighteen."

"And?"

"And I'm old enough to be on my own. Get a job. All that. I can't just stay here and… what? Be your whore?"

Slamming a palm down on the table, he held up two tattooed fingers on his other hand. "That's twice now you've insinuated I need to buy it. I don't pay for pussy, and you're sure as fuck not a whore. Whatever asinine notion you've twisted around in your head, get it out of there. Now."

His words helped wipe away the shame that'd been festering. The little voice in my head that'd said I was wrong to be intrigued by what he offered. That I was a whore for wanting it.

I focused on my plate. "I just don't understand this."

"Look at me." Once I did, he asked, "What part?"

"What would I do?"

"You'd do what I say. Beyond that, swim. Read. Sew. Do whatever the hell you want."

"What do you get out of it?"

"Other than you? I get to take care of you."

"And that's worth all this?" I asked, not understanding how taking care of me was beneficial to him.

Leaning back, he rubbed his jaw, his thumb sweeping across his bottom lip. "Oh, little dove, it's more than fucking worth it."

If it were possible to spontaneously orgasm, I was sure I would have.

Trying to stay on track, I asked, "The stuff you'd tell me to do… is it unusual? Like, do you have a fetish?"

"Fucking Christ," he muttered, but he didn't sound insulted, so that was good. "No, Juliet. I'm not going to ask you to dress in a gimp suit and beat the shit outta me or anything like that."

"Gimp suit?"

"Never mind. What I'm saying is, all things considered, my tastes are fairly tame."

"Except you like complete control over everything," I deadpanned.

But Maximo didn't take it as a joke and merely lifted his chin in agreement. "Except that."

I was glad he wasn't into anything weird, but I still wasn't sure I could do the basics. I'd never had sex. I could be awful at it.

It was entirely possible he was going all-in to win a five-buck pot.

Inhaling deeply, I blurted in a rushed whisper, "I've never had sex or done much of anything."

At his quiet curse, a pit formed in my belly.

He's gonna change his mind.

And I'm disappointed.

Why am I so disappointed?

"Look at me," he ordered.

And what is his obsession with eye contact?

Still, I did as he said and was relieved to see a satisfied smile curving his lips. "I'll teach you what I like." His smile grew into a wolfish grin. "More importantly, I'll teach you what *you* like."

Definite spontaneous orgasm.

At my silence, he prodded, "What else are you confused about?"

"It seems abrupt."

"It's not."

"We don't know anything about each other," I pointed out.

"What would you like to know?"

I thought for a moment before starting with the basics. "What's your favorite color?"

His lips tipped. "Gray."

Makes sense since that seems to be where he lives.

"How old are you?"

"Thirty-three."

That was about what I figured, but it was still surprising.

"That's young to own resorts and," I gestured around, "all this."

"I inherited three of my four properties, though I've worked hard to build them up and make them my own." He gave a similar gesture around. "And they do well."

That's an understatement.

"Is your family around?"

I couldn't imagine family dinners happening while I'd been locked upstairs, but I had no idea.

"No. I'm an only child and my mother passed away seven years ago."

"And your dad?"

"He died when I was nineteen." He took another drink of his coffee before setting it down. "We've talked enough tonight. Go get some sleep."

Since I wanted to go do more research, I didn't argue.

When I stood, he ordered, "Kiss me goodnight, dove."

I hesitated, not because I didn't want to, but because he'd caught me off guard.

He pushed his chair away from the table, his air of authority filling the room until I felt like I couldn't breathe.

Or like I was breathing him in.

"Now."

I jolted and stepped closer to stand between his spread legs. Bending, I pressed my mouth to his. When his tongue teased my lips, I parted them and involuntarily moaned at his taste.

And then the kiss went wild.

Spearing his fingers into the sides of my hair, Maximo cupped my head in both hands. He held my mouth to his as he stood so fast, his chair fell back with a clatter. Backing me up until the table dug into my thighs, he devoured my mouth. His kiss tasted of rich, dark coffee and something even better.

Him.

He released my head to grip my hips and lift me onto the edge of the table. His hands dropped to my thighs, spreading them before running his palms up.

I wanted him to keep going. I wanted him to touch me. I wanted it all.

But Maximo had more control than I did. He tore his mouth from mine and stepped away, his gaze locked on my parted lips. "Go to bed."

Shimmying off the table, I tugged my dress back into place and walked on shaking legs.

I was at the threshold when he called, "Juliet."

I looked over my bare shoulder to see he was sitting, casual and chill like he hadn't just rocked my world with a single kiss.

"This isn't a choice between me and homelessness. If you don't want this," he motioned between us, "you can stay here, same as it was before today. If you want to move out, I'll get you your own place somewhere safe and help you. You can take your stuff with you, no strings attached."

Again, it didn't say good things about my life that his kindness surprised me. It also made me choked up and suspicious at the same time.

"Why would you do that?" I asked.

"Because I like you." Even at the distance, I could feel the heat from his gaze. "And you need someone to take care of you for once."

My emotions and thoughts were so jumbled, I didn't even know what to say, so I remained silent.

"Happy birthday, little dove."

"Thank you," I whispered before hightailing it out of there.

CHAPTER FIFTEEN

A Taste

JULIET

I CAN'T DO IT.

It'd be crazy.

The whole thing is wrong.

Right?

Kicking off my heels, I paced my room.

I shouldn't have been considering it. He'd offered me two easy—and generous—outs. I should've been deciding between them.

But I wasn't.

Because I wanted him and what he offered. I just wasn't sure I was brave enough to accept.

Going to the sitting room, I grabbed my MacBook and brought it to my bed. I opened the browser and searched what a gimp suit was.

And then I laughed before quickly exiting out of that tab.

Well, thank God he's not into that.

I switched to the tab I'd been reading when Ms. Vera had come in earlier. It was informative, talking about the power dynamics of the relationship and what each person got from it.

As helpful as it was, they were just words. They didn't tell me how I'd feel. Whether I'd enjoy it or hate it. I could think something sounded great in theory but hate it in practice.

Or I could assume I'd hate it and end up missing out on something incredible.

Closing the MacBook, I showered before pulling on a tank top and sleep shorts. I climbed into bed and closed my eyes, but my mind wouldn't turn off.

And neither would my body.

I was overheated and restless. Sliding my hand into my shorts, I didn't even try to keep my thoughts blank. They were filled with Maximo and his kiss. The way he'd touched me. The way he'd moved me. The way his eyes had blazed with want.

And the way he'd ordered me around.

Even though I was soaked and desperate for a release, I couldn't find it.

But I knew who could.

MAXIMO

NOT FOR THE first time, I seriously fucking regretted making Ash disconnect the camera in Juliet's bedroom.

By the time I'd turned on her sitting room camera, she'd already been in her bedroom. I'd thought maybe she was asleep, but a short time later, she'd stormed out to grab her MacBook from the coffee table before closing herself back in.

I wanted to see what she was looking up.

I wanted to watch her response to it.

I wanted to know what made her full lips part, her thighs squeeze, and her pulse go wild.

Or if it made her do more than that. If her hand went under her dress so she could make herself come.

If she were mine, I'd control that, too.

Groaning, I turned off the monitors before reaching for a bottle of whiskey and pouring a glass as I replayed that damn kiss in my mind.

When I'd told her to kiss me, I'd wanted to see if she'd even do it. I'd intended for it to be a small one. A taste.

But then she'd let out that soft, sexy moan, and I'd lost my mind.

I pushed away from my desk to go to bed.

Or, more accurately, to go stroke my dick while picturing Juliet.

I was about to stand when there was a tentative knock at the door.

What is my little dove up to?

"Come in," I said.

But the door remained closed.

"Open the door, Juliet." I waited a few moments before adding, "Or I'll do it."

It swung open, and Juliet stood in the doorway. She'd showered and changed into a tank top and a pair of shorts. Her damp hair was pulled into a high ponytail.

It was a stark contrast to how she'd been dressed at dinner, but it was just as sexy.

"What do you need?" I asked.

"Just came to say I'd like coffee in the morning. Okay, bye."

She turned away but stopped when I said, "Juliet."

"Maximo," she muttered in a mocking tone, not turning back.

Oh, this is going to be fun.

I stood and walked to her. "What do you need?"

"I told you—"

"A lie. And you know how I feel about lying. I'm not going to ask you again."

She spun to face me, and that's when I saw it.

Her flushed skin.

The pieces that'd come loose from her ponytail.

Her unfocused, heated eyes.

My dick throbbed. "Were you touching your pretty pussy, little dove?"

Her eyes went saucer big, but shocking the hell out of me, she didn't try to deny it and only nodded.

"Because of what you were reading?"

Thankfully, she didn't ask how I knew she'd been reading. Instead, she shook her head.

"What were you thinking about?"

She ran her tongue across her bottom lip before whispering, "You."

Fuck, she's killing me.

"Did you come?" I asked, my voice gruff.

Shifting her legs, she looked desperate and wild. "I couldn't."

"Are you here to ask your Daddy to make you come?"

A volcano of need erupted in her eyes as she nodded instantly. "Please."

Cupping the back of her head and gripping her hip, I kissed her hard as I walked us to my desk. I lifted her onto the edge, spreading her thighs to stand between them.

My hand pushed under her shirt and ran up her side, stopping with my thumb curved just below her braless tit.

Juliet whimpered and tried to shift so I was touching it, but I dropped my hand. When I brought it back, she did it again, so I lowered it farther.

The next time my hand trailed up, she remained still.

So fucking perfect.

I stretched my thumb up to tease her hard nipple. Her moan went straight to my dick.

I wanted to drop to my knees and eat her until she came all over my mouth. Until she was the only thing I tasted for the rest of my damn life. But I knew if I did that, if I tasted that sweetness, I wouldn't be able to stop myself from fucking her.

Feeling her come on my fingers would have to do.

Moving my hand between her thighs, I hooked a finger in the fabric and pulled it aside, my dick aching when I realized she wasn't wearing any panties.

Tearing my mouth away, I leaned back to look.

Juliet tried squeezing her thighs closed, but I moved my hand from her tit to hold her legs open. "Don't ever hide yourself from me. I plan on spending hours and hours staring at this pussy. Show it to me."

She swallowed hard, her pulse going wild and her legs trembling, but after a few moments, she spread them.

And gave me a view of heaven that was even more perfect than I'd envisioned.

And I'd envisioned it far more often than I should've.

"So fucking pretty," I groaned. Running my thumb through her wetness, I stopped with it pushed against her clit.

Juliet rocked her hips, but my hold on her thigh tightened, my fingertips digging in.

"Please," she whispered, her voice pained.

"What do you need?"

"To come."

"Ask me."

"Will you make me come?"

Hearing her sweet voice asking that made precum drip from my dick, but I didn't give her what she wanted.

Not until she asked correctly.

When I didn't move, she looked so frustrated, I thought she might cry or start throwing punches.

Taking pity on her, I gave her a hint. "Who am I to you now, dove?"

What I wanted must've clicked into place because Juliet didn't hesitate. She met my eyes and begged, "Please make me come, Daddy."

Fucking hell.

I'd spent countless nights with my fist around my cock, imagining her asking me that. Reality was far better than any fantasy.

Deep breathing to gain control, I focused on rewarding her. I circled her clit with my thumb. Moving my other hand from her thigh, I teased my middle finger into her tight hole.

"This is mine now," I growled, watching my hands work her. "You don't come unless I say so. You don't play with yourself without me. If you want to come, I'll give you what you need. Do you understand, Juliet?" When she nodded, I said, "I need to hear it."

"Yes."

I stopped.

"Yes, Daddy," she amended.

My thumb stroked her clit harder. Faster.

Leaning back on her arms, Juliet dropped her head.

"Keep your eyes on me," I ordered.

She did as I said, her dazed gaze on me as she rocked her hips. Her walls pulsed around my fingertip.

Her quiet pants grew to sexy moans. She cried out, her neck arching and her body tensing.

But she kept her eyes on me as she came from my touch.

Easing the pressure, I gave her just enough to ride the wave but not enough to overwhelm her. Once she was done, I took my finger away.

Shoulders slumped, her face was relaxed and sated.

And happy.

"Better?" I asked, gathering her close.

"Much."

"What do you say?"

A small smile curled her fuckable lips as she blinked up at me. "Thank you, Daddy."

Dipping my head to kiss her, I muttered, "I'm already addicted to hearing you call me that. You're an obsession."

Not knowing how strongly I meant that, she gave a soft laugh that turned into a yawn.

"You need sleep." I released my hold and stepped back.

Juliet stood and shot me a small smile. "Good night."

She started for the door but yelped when I picked her up, her legs automatically wrapping around my waist.

"Where do you think you're going?"

Her brows lowered. "My room."

"No." Gripping her ass, I carried her down the hall and opened my door before flicking on the light. "I want you here with me."

From now on.

Surprisingly, she didn't argue as she glanced around. "Bathroom?"

I pointed to a door. "Do you need anything from your room?"

She shook her head.

After she closed herself in the bathroom, I stripped down to my boxer briefs. She came out a minute later and stopped in her tracks when she saw me.

As tempted as I was to tease her for staring, I remained silent as I went to brush my teeth and take a leak. After washing my hands, I opened the door to see Juliet sitting with her gaze aimed my way.

Waiting for me.

Finally in my bed.

Now who's staring, asshole?

Turning off the light, I got into bed. Juliet lay stiff as a board next to me. So much tension radiated off her, I almost let her go to her room.

Almost.

Rearranging us so she was on her side with my body curved around hers, I curled my arm up to cup her tit. Her sharp inhale made my dick jerk. I draped my other arm over her and slid my hand down her shorts, teasing my middle finger along her slit.

"What're you doing?" she asked, even as she rocked her hips.

"Helping you relax." Tweaking her nipple, I kissed her neck, biting down hard enough to make her cry out and grow wetter.

"This is not making me relaxed," she breathed.

I ground my palm into her clit, shifting it back and forth as best as I could in the tight confines before freezing suddenly. "So I should stop?"

"No, no, no, definitely not."

My lips and tongue trailed her neck before I bit down again. "Then hush." I started moving my hand as I played with her nipple, her breath catching. "Let me take care of you."

Her nod was cut off when she arched her neck, her body tightening in my arms. She cried out and tried to tilt her pelvis away, but I pinned her in place, grinding harder until I was sure she'd given me everything.

Moving my hand up from her tit, I rested it at the base of her throat and kept the other in her shorts, cupping her.

Even with my possessive hold, she was relaxed and quiet. I thought she was asleep until she whispered, "I've never slept in the same bed as anyone."

"Neither have I."

"You haven't? But you've—"

"And then I've left. I like my space when I sleep."

"But you want me here?"

I need you here.

"Yes," I said instead.

She grew quiet again before pushing her ass against my hard-on. I heard her shaky inhale and braced for whatever she was about to say.

"I could touch you," she whispered.

No amount of bracing could have prepared me for that.

"Swear to Christ, Juliet, you keep saying things like that, and I'm not going to be able to stop myself from fucking you."

"Okay."

"Juliet."

"Maximo," she mocked.

"I'm going to spank your ass raw."

"I don't know if I'd like that." There was a hint of a smile in her voice as she continued. "But I think I'm willing to try."

"You're killing me," I groaned. "Go to sleep."

"Fine." She gave a dramatic sigh, but within minutes, her body relaxed and her breathing grew even.

It took me and my dick much longer to settle.

CHAPTER SIXTEEN

Everything's Better In Black

JULIET

"JULIET."

I opened my eyes then squeezed them shut when Maximo switched on the lamp. "Hmm?"

"I've got to leave."

Blinking rapidly, I peered up at him.

He was showered and dressed in a dark gray suit with a navy dress shirt unbuttoned at the neck.

"Do you wear ties?" I asked.

"Not if I can help it. Did you hear me?"

"You're leaving, got it. What time is it?"

"Six."

"In the *morning*?"

"Yes. Go back to sleep. I want you to take it easy today."

"Okay," I said, closing my eyes to get right on that.

"I'll be home after lunch." I was vaguely aware of the light flicking off. "We'll talk then."

"'Kay."

It took a couple hazy minutes for his words to sink into my exhausted mind. My eyes shot open and I bolted upright, but he was gone.

Don't tell me to relax and then tell me we'll talk later. I can't do both!

I flopped back, pulling the covers up.

I had no clue what we needed to talk about. I thought we'd said everything that needed saying the night before. We'd talked at dinner, I'd made my decision, and I'd gone to him even though I'd been terrified.

What else was there to say?

Maybe he changed his mind.

I dismissed the thought immediately. Or I tried to. Because once it entered my brain, it took root, filling me with panic and unease.

I didn't want him to change his mind. The night before had been amazing thanks to his skilled hands, but it'd been more than the mind-blowing release he'd provided. He'd known what I needed and had taken care of me without expecting reciprocation. Then he'd held me tight until I'd fallen into the best sleep of my life. He'd been patient and tender and rough and demanding and *perfect*.

And suddenly he was back to cold.

My mind continued replaying his words until I knew sleep was a lost cause. I was tempted to use his amazing shower I'd seen the night before. The blue-tiled room had a double bowl sink, a bath the size of a hot tub, and a shower that was so big, it had multiple heads and part of the wall was cut away to make a bench.

But the longer I spent in his room, the more likely it was someone would discover I'd pulled a Goldilocks by sleeping in someone else's bed.

Opening the door, I peeked my head out to make sure the coast was clear. Hightailing it to my room, I showered and started brushing my teeth before wiping the steam from the mirror. I caught my reflection and my jaw dropped, my toothbrush falling into the sink with a clatter.

A hickey.

Maximo had given me a hickey.

Not a full-blown one, but there were a few light marks.

Who even does that?

And why is it so hot?

I'm losing my mind.

At least I have a new project… I'm gonna have to convert my tops to turtlenecks so I can hide these marks.

I finished getting ready before heading to the closet to put on ripped black jeans and a cropped tee that was covered in tears and holes. I loved the ultra-distressed look and that I could see glimpses of my bra underneath.

Forget the turtlenecks, I'm going to try replicating this top.

Excitement bubbled through me as I went to my sewing room and got to work on a black version.

Everything's better in black.

HOURS LATER, NEARLY asleep at my desk, I checked my progress. I needed to research how to prevent the rips from growing or the thread from unraveling, but the top was coming along better than anticipated.

I fed the fabric into the machine to double stitch the neckline.

The door opened, and my eyes snapped up, but it was Ash not Maximo.

Taking in his concerned expression, I asked, "What's wrong?"

"Watch your fingers." I turned the machine off, and he asked, "How long have you been in here?"

"I dunno. Since six-thirty or so. Why?"

"We thought you were still sleeping. I went in to wake you, and you weren't there."

And I wasn't there all night.

But then he continued. "Or in your room."

Wait, he knows I slept with Maximo?

Well, slept in his room, not the other kind of slept with.

Yet, at least.

"Juliet," he said, not looking happy.

I jolted again. "Sorry, were you saying something?"

"You skipped breakfast and lunch, and you look exhausted." He shook his head. "You shouldn't be in here when you're so tired, you'll end up sewing your fingers together. Go nap."

"I'm fine," I said, even though I was exhausted. I glanced at the time on my iPad. "Maximo said he'd be home after lunch."

"That's why I was coming to find you. He wanted me to tell you he got held up and won't be back until later."

Shit. I'd been counting down until we could talk.

"Oh, okay," I said. "I'll just keep working then."

"Go rest."

My eyes narrowed. "I'm fine."

Ash pulled his phone out of his pocket and typed something. It rang half a minute later and he handed it to me.

I glanced at the screen and saw who it was.

"You tattled on me?" I asked.

"Yes, now answer or he'll be pissed."

I accepted the call and put the phone to my ear. "Hello?"

"You've been up since I left and skipped breakfast and lunch?" Maximo said by way of greeting.

"Hello to you, too. How's your day?"

"Juliet."

"Maximo."

"Christ, do you want me to spank your ass until you can't sit down?"

Yes.

Wait, what?

No, definitely yes, I maybe certainly want to consider having that happen.

"I'm fine," I tried.

"Ash says you're not."

"Ash is a snitch."

"I'll have the snitch bring you a sandwich and then you need to rest."

The concern in his voice was reassuring but it wasn't enough. "I couldn't sleep because you said we'd talk later."

"Shit," he muttered. "I meant we'd talk to see how you're feeling after last night. If you wanted to change your mind."

"I thought you'd changed your mind," I whispered, surprised by how dejected that made me feel.

"Never," he bit out in an intense way that scared me but mostly made me wet.

"You didn't kiss me goodbye." Remembering I wasn't alone, my eyes darted to Ash's, but he didn't look surprised in the slightest.

Huh.

"I was giving you space in case you had regrets, that's all. Go get

135

some sleep. We're going to a fight tonight, and it'll be a late one."

Even though I'd become a homebody who liked the security of my little world, I had left the house. But errands were much different than going out with Maximo.

Especially going to a *fight* with Maximo.

Excitement zipped through me. Not wanting to fall asleep during the action, I relented. "Okay, I'll eat then rest."

"Now."

"I will, I will. Sheesh."

"I'm going to redden that sweet ass."

"Promises, promises," I blurted before hanging up.

I'm going to regret that.

When I handed Ash his cell back, he asked, "Want a sandwich?"

My stomach growled at the thought. "I can grab it."

He gave me a look that wasn't as powerful as Maximo's *the look*, but it was still pretty effective.

"Turkey, please."

"Got it."

I finished what I was doing while he grabbed the sandwich. When he got back, he shot me a disapproving scowl but didn't say anything.

He did, however, stand there while I ate. As soon as I finished the last bite, he tipped his head toward the door. "Nap."

"Is it a rule that you have to be bossy to work for Maximo?"

"Work for him? No. Work closely with him? Yes. Now go."

I sighed, and my dramatics would've been more effective had a massive yawn not snuck out.

I was down the hall when Ash called, "Juliet."

Glancing over my shoulder, I saw him open Maximo's bedroom.

He knows.

He definitely knows.

Does everyone?

Since it was pointless to deny it—not to mention, Maximo's bed smelled like him and that sounded heavenly—I turned around and headed in.

Once the door closed behind me, I stripped off my jeans and flopped onto the bed, not expecting to sleep.

I was out within minutes.

THIS IS THE best dream.

Ever.

Lips, teeth, and a tongue trailed across the back of my neck. I tilted my head—or thought I did, at least—to give better access.

If I was dreaming, it could only be one person.

"Maximo," I moaned softly.

A hand pushed under me, cupping me over my undies. Hardness pressed against my ass, and I arched into it.

"You awake?" he whispered in my ear.

I shook my head. "No, this is definitely a dream because dream-you has an unreal, massive..." Just in time, my brain pulled out of its fog before I finished my sleepy rambling.

"Massive what?" he asked, amusement in his cocky tone.

"Ego," I finished. "An unreal, massive ego."

He flipped me to my back. My startled laughter died when his hips fell between my spread legs, his dick pressing against me.

The sleeves of his shirt were rolled, the muscles of his tattooed forearms defined as he held his weight off me. "I promise my *ego* is very real and just as massive in real life as it is in your dreams." He smirked, but his eyes were filled with an inferno not humor. "But I like that you dream about me."

I shrugged as best as I could. "Dreams, nightmares. Po-tay-to, po-tah-to."

"Brat." He dropped his head to kiss me. Unfortunately, it was just a quick one. "Sleep okay?"

I nodded. "What time is it?"

"Almost four."

"In the afternoon?" I tried to scooch away so I could sit up, but he gripped my hip. The movement pressed him harder against me, and I forgot about getting up.

And thinking.

And breathing.

And basically anything else that didn't involve how good he felt.

Maximo's dark eyes scanned my face. "You okay after last night?" At my nod, he prompted, "I need to hear the words."

"I'm good." I hesitated, my heart pounding as I added, "Daddy."

His groan rumbled against me and he dropped to take my mouth in a kiss that was *not* quick. He took his time, slowly tasting me until I was rocking my hips, needy for more.

Pulling away, he rested his forehead on mine. "Christ, you drive me wild."

It may not have been a flowery compliment, but it was an effective one.

He lifted his head, his gaze dropping to take in the smile I couldn't hide. Moving suddenly, he got out of bed. I was about to ask what was wrong when he said, "If I stay in bed with you smiling that fucking smile, we won't be going anywhere."

Sounds good to me.

Sitting up, I figured it was best to keep that thought to myself.

"We're going to dinner before the fight. Go get ready." Maximo watched me climb out of bed like it was the most interesting thing he'd seen. Giving him my back, I shimmied into my jeans. Before I could turn back around, his arms wrapped around my waist and he pulled me against him.

He didn't speak as he held me, so neither did I. I leaned into him and soaked up his warmth.

When he slowly pulled away, he hooked a finger in my belt loop and twisted me toward the door. His palm landed a sharp slap on my ass.

"Ouch!" I yelped, rubbing the sting that really wasn't that bad.

"Promises, promises, remember?" His hand connected again. "We leave in an hour."

"I'm going, I'm going."

He took a step closer, and I burst out laughing, hurrying out of spanking range as I bolted out the door.

Like the day before, a garment bag and shoebox were waiting for me.

Unlike the day before, a rectangular black box with a pretty silver bow was sitting with them.

Unable to fight my curiosity, I hurried to open it.

Holy shit.

Too much.

This is definitely too much.

138

The velvet lined box held a delicate tennis bracelet made of oval diamonds. Afraid to even breathe on it, I closed the lid and carefully set it down before unzipping the garment bag. Silver with a hint of shimmer, the gorgeous dress had long sleeves, a faux-wrap closure, and a belt that tied around the waist.

It looks like the world's fanciest bathrobe.

The shoebox held a pair of open-toed heels with a thin ankle strap.

As much as I loved it, it was too much. I didn't need clothes or jewelry or presents.

The only thing I wanted was him.

Setting everything down, I hurried to tame my bedhead and do my makeup before getting dressed.

Thankfully, the dress didn't look like a bathrobe once it was on. It was short, fun, and sexy—especially when I walked and the fabric separated to show more thigh.

I put the shoes on, grabbed the jewelry box, and went to find Maximo. As I headed down the hallway, he came out of his office.

He'd showered and changed into a black suit with a black dress shirt, and the effect of all that darkness was breathtaking and panty soaking.

He looked sinister and wicked.

Sinful.

Running his tattooed hand across his jaw as his thumb swept his bottom lip, his eyes blazed as they traveled my body. "Fucking perfection. Do you like your Valentine's present?"

My brows lowered. "What?"

Like a tiger stalking a gazelle, he approached and took the box from me. He pulled the bracelet out and tucked the empty case under his arm before grabbing my wrist and securing it in place. "I planned to give it to you last night after dinner, but then you," he glanced at me, "distracted me. Today works better anyway. I'm sure it's not fun sharing your birthday with a holiday."

I didn't tell him my dad had rarely remembered my birthday, let alone Valentine's Day. He'd certainly never celebrated either.

"Do you like it?" he asked again.

"It's beautiful, but the clothes and this... It's too much. You don't have—"

"If I felt like I had to do anything, your sweet ass would be out the door. I do things because I want to. Because I want to take care of you.

Spoil you. I don't *have* to do that, I *want* to do it. What I don't want is an argument every time I give you something. You need to learn to let me take care of you."

Easier said than done.

I'd been taking care of myself for as long as I could remember. I'd never learned to let someone else do it because I'd never had someone try.

Not until Maximo.

Letting go of the awkwardness that came from the unfamiliar, I smiled. "I love it. Thank you."

"You're welcome." His gaze dropped to my neck, zeroing in on his bite mark. The low rumble of his voice sent a tremor down my spine when he muttered, "Didn't see this until now."

I worried he felt guilty for biting me so hard, but when he backed me against a wall, it became obvious that wasn't his reaction to seeing his mark on me. His erection pressed into my belly as he dropped the empty jewelry box. I thought he was going to kiss me, but instead he grudgingly muttered, "We've got to go."

"Okay."

For a flash, he looked uneasy as he studied me. He opened his mouth before closing it again, his lips pressing into a thin line. Stepping away, he grabbed my hand and silently walked to his waiting SUV.

His grip stayed tight the whole time.

CHAPTER SEVENTEEN

Hungry For It

JULIET

GETTING OUT OF the car, I scanned the windowless building Maximo had parked in front of. "I thought we were going to one of your properties."

He hadn't said as much, I'd just assumed.

"We are." Taking my hand, he started walking toward the doors.

"This is one of your casinos?"

I'd picked Dad up from a variety of nontraditional casinos, including the airport, gas stations, and even an old church that'd been converted into a strip club *and* casino. This wasn't even in the top ten strangest setups I'd seen, but I was still surprised.

He burst out laughing and his steps stopped so suddenly, I nearly lost my balance. He grabbed my waist to steady me. "This is *not* one of my casinos. I own the warehouse."

"Well, how am I supposed to know?"

"Do I look like the kind of man who runs a casino out of a warehouse?"

No, you look like the kind of man who runs the whole damn world.

I lifted a shoulder. "No?"

"Is that a question or an answer?"

"An answer?" At his narrowed eyes, I held my hands in the air. "I don't know what that kind of man would look like."

Gripping my hand again, Maximo started walking. "Jesus, I'm taking you to my actual resorts ASAP so you don't think this piss-poorly of me."

Yay.

Taking in the empty lot and horror movie vibe, I couldn't help asking, "Why do you hold fights here?"

We stopped outside a set of metal double doors. The dim overhead light played with the darkness, adding shadows to Maximo's defined jaw and cheekbones. He looked menacing and *hot*. There was something unreadable in his expression as he curled his hand around the side of my neck, his thumb stroking across the bite mark. "You'll see."

With that ominous answer, he released me to touch his thumb to a keypad similar to the ones at home. There was a beep and a click before he opened the door, gesturing for me to enter first.

It may not have looked like an arena from the outside, but the inside sure did.

And a nice one, at that.

Rows of empty padded folding chairs surrounded the ring in the center of the humongous room. Speakers and lights hung from the high ceiling, stocked bars lined the walls, and a blank scoreboard was suspended over the ring.

With a hand at my lower back, Maximo guided me around the edge of the room and down a long hallway. He put his thumb on another lock and opened the door to an office.

He grabbed a remote off the desk and turned on a small TV. "Stay here while I check on everything."

"I can help," I offered, not wanting to miss a moment of the excitement. There were a lot of things I hated about my childhood, but boxing wasn't one of them. It was thrilling and primal and beautiful in a violent way.

"Maybe next time. Marco will be outside the door."

And then he left.

I scanned the office, but it was just beige concrete walls, two doors, a metal desk, and a few metal filing cabinets. Trying one of the drawers, it loudly slid open.

Empty.

Boring.

I opened a door to find a tiny bathroom that'd seen better days. I used it anyway, scrubbing my hands like a surgeon when I was done. Flopping down on the desk chair, I spun around a few times before leaning back to watch the TV.

After forty-five minutes—or a sitcom and a half in TV time—there was a ruckus in the hall.

People must be arriving.

I cracked the door to check it out, but the only view I got was of Marco's broad back.

He glanced at me over his shoulder. "Need something?"

"No, I—"

"Then close the door."

Rolling my eyes, I said, "I just wanted to see."

"Close the door, Juliet."

"Fine." Since I couldn't see anything past the human door that was Marco, I closed the actual one. I climbed onto the desk and flicked through the stations, growing more and more envious of the people in the arena.

The air was always wired before a match. The blood lust and violence. The adrenaline. The savageness. It was unlike anything else.

Instead of experiencing that high, I was stuck experiencing the low that came from shitty TV.

After another sitcom, the door swung open, the low rumble of chaos growing louder. Maximo stood in the doorway, his expression blank.

I turned off the TV and approached, his sharp eyes tracking my every movement. When I got within reach, he hooked a hand behind my neck and tugged me so I slammed against his chest. His head lowered and his lips pressed against mine in a bruising kiss.

There was a desperation to it I may not have understood, but I liked. A lot. His kiss wasn't as cold and aloof as he'd been. It was hot and fervent.

Pulling away, he held my hand but didn't speak as we left the room— not that I would've been able to hear him anyway. Conversation and laughter traveled down the hall at a steady roar. Since there was no cheering or flesh hitting flesh mixed in with the noise, I knew the matches hadn't begun.

When we reached the main area, my steps faltered before stopping completely.

It was...

Insanity.

Chaos.

Wild.

There were beautiful women in various stages of undress hanging on men. Minidress clad waitresses navigated through the crush with practiced ease. The heavy stench of liquor and cigars clung in the air, mixing with wired adrenaline—a cocktail for depravity.

Noticing I'd stopped, Maximo paused, too, his eyes on me as a muscle in his jaw twitched. After a long moment, he tugged my hand as he continued down the aisle.

As we moved, I glanced around at people talking, drinking, and smoking. No one was dressed casually. It was all pristine suits and sexy dresses, and the smell of money filled the air just as strongly as the tobacco.

When I caught sight of an older, bald man openly groping a redhead's breast, I dropped my focus to my feet.

Maximo stopped at the first row. Clearly for VIPs, the chairs had extra padding and there were small tables between each one.

He sat in the aisle chair, and I started to squeeze by him when he pulled me into his lap. Settling me on his thigh with my legs between his spread ones, he wrapped an arm around me.

Surprised by the intimate hold, my eyes shot to his, but his stony stare was aimed outward at everyone else.

He was a king, daring anyone to challenge him for his throne.

No sooner had we settled than a pretty blond cocktail waitress appeared at our side. "Usual whiskey, Mr. Black?"

He didn't even glance her way. "Two waters."

"Yes, sir." She sped away, ignoring anyone who tried to flag her down.

I sat stiffly on his lap, my spine steeled and my hands clasped so I didn't fidget.

Never give away more than you want them to know.

Well, I definitely don't want this lion's den to sniff out my discomfort because they'll pounce on the show of weakness.

144

Movement on the other side of the aisle caught my attention, and I watched as a woman leaned forward and lifted her short skirt to expose her ass. The man she was in front of ran his hand along the top of her ass cheeks. Only when he bent forward did I realize he'd been spreading a line of coke. He happily snorted it before running his tongue along the residue. He smacked her ass and she stood upright, tugged her dress into place, and walked away.

When I got a view of his face *not* coke deep in someone's ass, I recognized him, though it took me a moment to place from where. He was a politician. I didn't know what kind, but I'd seen his face plastered on billboards and the election ads that repeated every other commercial.

I shifted my gaze *far* from him and was careful not to let it settle in one spot for too long. Surrounded by drugs, alcohol, beautiful women, and rich men seeking a thrill, I was betting there was a lot happening I didn't want to see.

The waitress returned and set the water bottles on the small table next to us. She didn't wait for acknowledgment before moving on to serve someone else.

Maximo grabbed a bottle and released me just long enough to open the lid and hand it to me. I took a sip, but the cold water sat heavily in my stomach. He took it back and set it next to him.

"Thanks," I whispered.

He just lifted his chin.

It wasn't long before more people filled the seats.

A couple stopped in front of us. The man's surprised eyes landed briefly on me before focusing on Maximo. He extended his hand. "Black."

"Adams." Without releasing his hold on me, Maximo used his free hand to shake before making introductions. "Juliet, this is Tony and Ella Adams."

Ella smiled at me, offering a little wave. "I love your dress, Juliet."

"Thanks, I love yours, too." It was sexy and red, with a Jessica Rabbit-esque slit up the thigh.

"It's fun to get dressed up every now and then." She took the seat two over and Tony took the one on the other side, leaving an empty chair between us. I was relieved I wouldn't have to make or listen to small talk all night.

All conversation quieted as the room turned electric.

Like everyone else, I felt the morbid anticipation of what was to come. My heart raced and it took everything in me to sit still.

A light-haired man climbed into the ring, gripping a microphone as he walked around. "Ladies and gentlemen, betting for bout one is officially closed. You can place wagers on the other two until ten minutes before they begin, so if you're feeling lucky, get your ass up and put your cash down. It's gonna be a helluva night!"

Loud music blared through the speakers as a parade of people came down the aisle right next to us. In the midst of them was a boxer in green shorts, but there were no sponsor emblems attached to them.

That's weird.

He climbed into the ring with part of his crew, the rest setting up outside their corner.

The music changed suddenly, thumping bass shaking the ground. Another parade of people and another fighter with no sponsor emblems on his blue shorts went past, rounding the ring for his corner. Unlike his opponent, he climbed in alone as his people raced around to get everything set up.

The music cut off and the emcee introduced the boxers. Green shorts was The King. Blue was God of Death.

My money was on blue, and not just because his name was better. He may have been smaller, but bigger wasn't always an advantage.

A bell dinged and it was on.

And it was *ugly*.

I wasn't sure why the ref was even there because he wasn't calling a single thing. King fought dirty, aiming for low blow after low blow. God of Death was quick with a dodge and a jab, though he'd yet to connect a good hook.

When the round ended, I tilted my head toward Maximo's ear. "Who're we supposed to root for?"

"Doesn't matter with this one. Who do you like?"

"God of Death."

"The King is favored to win."

"And he knows it. He's too cocky. Death is hungry."

He lowered his head so his lips grazed the shell of my ear. "I agree."

A shiver went down my spine, goosebumps spreading across my skin. Since his arm was still wrapped around me, I doubted he missed it.

He never missed much.

146

The bell rang, and I shifted so I was facing outward rather than sideways.

Death took a couple kidney shots before King dropped his gloves. It was just inches. Just for seconds.

But it was the opening Death had been waiting for. With energy he'd been conserving, he went at him until King was against the ropes.

The ref was close but he wasn't pulling Death off. He wasn't forcing the TKO. He wasn't even trying to get him to back away.

Death is gonna kill him.

Holy shit, he's gonna kill him.

My frantic eyes turned to Maximo, but he just stared ahead like a robot. The only reaction he gave to the savagery unfolding was his hold tightening so I couldn't move.

All around me, depravity flowed free and bloodshed went unchecked. It was clear the rules were different there.

Because there were none.

Like it was a train wreck happening in slow-motion, I couldn't tear my eyes away from the devastation. I watched as Death threw a right cross, twisting his pelvis so all his strength went into it.

King slammed to the mat, not even trying to break his fall.

Like deadweight.

My breath froze in my lungs. It whooshed out when King lifted his glove just enough to tap out.

And that was it.

Second round.

Victory by submission.

And no one died.

Shoulders slumped, I grabbed my water and drank half in one go. My heart rate slowed from hummingbird speed, though I was still amped on adrenaline and relief.

It wasn't the first time I'd seen a no-holds-barred fight. I'd grown up around violence—and not always the spectator kind. It ran in my veins as much as blood.

Rich people betting on fights to the death would've pushed me beyond my violence threshold, but as long as everyone left the ring breathing, I was good.

There was a rush to prepare for the next match.

I turned to talk to Maximo, only to find him already watching me.

147

When he didn't speak, I bragged, "I called it."

His lips just barely tipped, but I caught it. "I agreed with you."

"Yeah, but I said it first."

He lowered his head to kiss me before returning his focus to the preparations. "So you did."

The second match went longer, making it to round five before ending in an exciting knockout. And, once again, it was *ugly* but no one died.

During the last break, the emcee hyped the final bout. His efforts worked and more attendees went to place their bets before it was too late.

"That man deserves a fat bonus and a good raise," I muttered more to myself than Maximo.

Still, he lifted his chin. "Noted."

Whatever further commentary I may have had died in a lusty fire when Maximo moved to rest his hand on my thigh. There was something about the contrast of his large tattooed hand encircling my pale skin that sent a jolt of need through me. As though he knew the effect he had, his fingertips teased up my inner thigh.

I tilted my head to look at him, but his expression was blank, his eyes hard and alert. In a room full of powerful people, he made it clear he was in charge. That he held the cards and wouldn't hesitate to take someone down. That he'd *enjoy* it.

It scared the hell out of me how someone could look so icy and ruthless, but I couldn't deny it was also crazy hot.

So long as it wasn't aimed at me.

The emcee climbed the steps and swung under the ropes. "You know what time it is, folks. I hope you've put your money down because you could be leaving with stacks on stacks."

The frenzy grew, everyone's amped-up energy feeding off one another. It was always like that on fight nights, especially before the main event. With the addition of the other vices, it was magnified tenfold.

Music started—loud and pounding. The first boxer climbed into the ring and circled the mat, hitting his glove to his chest a few times. The waistband of his red and orange shorts touted sponsor logos, but I couldn't see what they were.

The song faded, a new one starting slow and low before growing louder as the bass and tempo increased. The other boxer entered with his crew around him. I didn't have to strain to see if he had sponsors because he stopped right next to us, giving me a clear view of the single logo on his black shorts.

Black Resorts.

He held out his glove, and Maximo tapped his fist to it. When the boxer lowered it toward my hand, I did the same.

Returning his focus to the ring in front of him, he stretched his neck. And then he grinned.

It wasn't cocky.

It wasn't aggressive.

It was the kind of grin that said he was damn excited to throw fists.

As he climbed in, the emcee finished intros and sponsor rundowns.

Orange was Alek 'The Finisher' Findlay.

Black was Mateo 'Kid Wonder' Torres.

Oh, both good nicknames.

Kid Wonder is better by a hair, though.

I shifted on Maximo's lap and waited for him to give me his ear. When he didn't, I cupped his cheek and tilted his head. "I guess I don't have to ask who we're cheering for. He'd have been my pick anyway."

"Yeah?"

I let go of his cheek and nodded. "He doesn't just want the victory, he *likes* the fight. That makes a difference."

I had no clue why, but at my words, Maximo cupped the sides of my head and kissed me. His fingertips dug in as he tilted my face to deepen the kiss.

He speared his tongue in to taste and take and devour.

And, like there was no one else in the whole world but the two of us, I let him.

I hadn't noticed the bell ringing, but he must've because he tore his mouth away just as the fight began.

Taking a shuddering breath, I focused on the match and *not* Maximo, his kiss, and the way my body reacted to him.

Okay, I split my focus between Maximo *and* the match because they were both engrossing.

Some people thought boxing was barbaric. A fake sport for muscle heads and steroid dummies whose only talent was taking a punch.

But they were wrong. Maybe not about it being barbaric, but about no skill being involved.

Each fight was like a dance. A boxer had to know when to lead and when to follow. They had to be light, agile, aggressive, passive, strong, quick, and in tuned with themselves and their opponent.

It was a sport.

And, when done right, it was an art.

The way Finisher and Kid Wonder fought?

It was a masterpiece.

Evenly matched, neither let the other run the show for long. They may have bided their time, but then they took any opening to go on the offense.

Each time I thought one of them had it, the other fought for the upper hand.

I missed this thrill.

Turning, I grinned at Maximo. "This is such a good fight."

Before I could turn back, he palmed the back of my head and tugged me closer so his lips were at my ear. "Glad you think so."

At the graze of his lips, goosebumps spread across my skin. Before I could do something stupid—like beg him to trail his lips across other areas of my body—I twisted to face forward, but my ass slid from his thigh to his lap.

Oh God.

Maximo was hard.

Not kinda.

Or slightly.

Or semi.

Long and thick, it stretched down his other thigh.

It may not have been the first time I'd felt it pressed against my ass, but it was the first time in public. I tried to shift back to his thigh, but his hands gripped my hips, keeping me in place.

Sitting on his thigh had been intimate enough, but with my ass firmly on his hard-on, I was keenly aware of how few layers separated us.

We wouldn't even have to take them off. Just tug down his zipper and pull my panties to the side. Done.

Before I lost my head and did something insane, I tried again to return to his thigh.

Maximo wrapped his arms around my waist, pressing my back against his front. His voice rumbled right in my ear when he ordered, "Watch the fight."

"I am."

I wasn't.

"Relax."

"I am."

I wasn't.

He bit down on the spot that already displayed his mark. "Don't lie to me."

"I'm not."

I was.

Maximo went silent, and so did I. I forced myself to watch the fight because I had no clue when I'd be able to see another one, let alone one so good.

Kid connected a killer right hook to Finisher's jaw. He took the advantage, coming on strong and landing blow after blow. His technique was perfect, each punch landing at a different location, making it hard for Finisher to block while also inflicting damage to a widespread area.

The crowd went wild, growing louder with each show of unfettered brutality. Like the two previous bouts, the ref was there, but he didn't interfere. Not even when Finisher was being held up by the ropes rather than his own two feet.

My hands clutched Maximo's forearms as I stared at Finisher's gloves.

Come on, man, tap. Kid is not going to stop.

Tap, tap, tap!

I leaned forward, unsure if he was even conscious and able to tap out.

Kid's fist connected with Finisher's eye, tearing open a cut until blood *sprayed* Kid's face and chest.

And Kid laughed.

A twisted, cruel, gleeful laugh.

A chill went down my spine at the sound.

I must not have been the only one to realize how crazy he was because Finisher *finally* tapped.

Almost everyone erupted in applause, though there was some angry bitching from those who'd lost their hefty bets.

Clapping until my hands stung, my cheers cut off suddenly when Maximo spanned my hips and ground my ass into him, lifting his hips to press harder. "Ready to go, dove?"

Yes.

No.

Maybe?

Using his hold to lift me to my feet, he kept me close so when he stood, my back was pressed to his front. His arm went around my chest, keeping me pinned to him as we waited.

Kid catapulted off the top rope like he'd joined the WWE before jogging over. He shook Maximo's hand before gently booping my nose. "Thanks for the good luck, doll."

I'd have congratulated him, but Maximo spoke first. "I'll be in touch tomorrow.'

"Cool." With the strut of a winner, he headed toward the long hallway, stopping occasionally when someone grabbed his attention.

Especially if that someone was of the female variety.

Maximo released his hold on me and took my hand. He didn't stop to talk to anyone as we walked, just lifted his chin in the briefest acknowledgement. When we reached the crowd that'd formed at the exit, security guards I hadn't noticed forced a path for us.

At least the arena is safe in its lawlessness.

Unlocking his SUV, Maximo opened my door but didn't meet my eyes once. He got in, started the car, and began driving.

I'd thought his withdrawn mood was because he was preoccupied with making sure the night went smoothly. As far as I could tell, it had, yet he was still on edge.

Giving him space, I looked out the window as we made the long drive in awkward silence.

Only once we were home and standing in the foyer did he finally break it. "Did you change your mind yet?"

Startled, I asked, "About what?"

"This. *Us.*"

"What?"

Speaking slowly, he enunciated each word. "Did you change your mind about us yet?"

Yet?

Was he trying to scare me away?

That asshole.

CHAPTER EIGHTEEN

Worth Every Second

JULIET

RAGE SIMMERED IN me, and I worked to tamp it down. I would not show him how he affected me. I would not feed his unreal, massive ego by letting him see how crushed I was. I would not be pathetic and weak by begging him to keep me.

"Is that what you want?" I asked.

It was his turn to be confused. Or play dumb, I wasn't sure which. "What?"

"Did you bring me there to scare me away?" My hold on my temper slipped, and I shook with anger. "Were you hoping I'd go running because you didn't have the balls—"

"Watch yourself, Juliet."

"Go to hell."

His eyes narrowed. "Been there all night, worrying you'd change your mind when you saw what I do."

That stole some fire from my belly, but I clutched to it. Anger was easier than sadness. It was a hell of a lot safer than hope.

I crossed my arms. "Why would a few boxing matches make me

change my mind?"

"Those weren't regular fights," he pointed out.

"Pshh. I've seen worse."

The muscle in his jaw ticked. "The whole setup is illegal."

"Again, I've seen worse."

He lifted his hand to count off, raising one tattooed finger after each item. "Minimal rules. Drugs. Women."

I lifted my hand and counted right back. "I've. Seen. Worse."

"Christ, what kind of life have you had?" he muttered, his own fire burning in his eyes.

"Not a good one. Not until you."

The words were out before I could think. Vulnerable and raw, I wanted to inhale them back. I *needed* to keep my pride—it was the only thing I had.

Maximo's body went tight, his face so scarily blank, my brain screamed at me to look away. To run.

But I couldn't.

He started talking, his voice even and cold. "The fights aren't the worst thing I do."

"You act like this is the first time I've seen you do something illegal. Are you forgetting how we met?"

"I want to make sure you know that wasn't a single blip in an otherwise saintly life."

I hated to think about *that* night. It put me in a dark place—but not for the reason it should've. I'd locked the memory deep inside, and I'd rather it never saw the light of day.

But I forced myself to talk about it for the first time. "The night we met, you made it unmistakably clear who you are and what you do. But I'm still here. With you. *Because* of you."

His dark eyes glittered as he rubbed his hand across his jaw. Thumb dragging across his bottom lip, his voice was low with warning. "Make sure you know what you're saying, little dove. I'll control you. Completely. Every damn aspect of your entire life. You'll follow my rules. When you break them, I'll punish you until you hate me and then fuck you until you don't." As he stalked toward me, I stood my ground. It made his lips twist into something between a smirk and a sneer. "Too stubborn for your own good."

My heart raced, slamming so loudly, it should've echoed around us.

My stomach was a tight knot, my thoughts were racing, and my blood rushed in my ears.

And I was wet.

So unbelievably, stupidly wet.

Gripping my waist in one hand, he speared his other into my hair, twisting the strands as he fisted it. He tugged my head back, making my scalp sting. "I'll take care of you until you're just as wrapped up and addicted to me as I am to you."

No hesitation. No bracing. No thoughts or worries or pride.

Automatic and honest, I whispered, "I already am, Daddy."

The cold, aloofness he'd carried himself with all day was gone. Like his blank mask had been torn away, lust, happiness, and relief flowed unencumbered across his face.

He'd been worried.

That was the desperation in his kiss. The distance he'd placed between us.

He'd been scared I'd leave.

He doesn't want to lose me.

Mouth crashing down on mine, his tongue didn't tease my lips, coaxing them open. It forced its way in, taking what he wanted. What was his. What I'd willingly given.

When he released my hair to palm my ass and lift, I wrapped my legs around him. He tore his lips away like it physically hurt, and I whimpered, stretching to get them back.

"Not going to risk falling down the damn steps and hurting you," he explained, starting up them.

Since his mouth wasn't an option, I kissed, licked, and nipped at his throat and jaw.

"Fuck me, you're gonna make me shoot off in my pants."

There was something so heady about knowing the effect I had on a man who was as controlled as Maximo. A shiver went through me, and I bit harder, making him groan.

Speeding up, he carried me to his room, unlocking the door and letting it slam behind us as he lowered me. My feet had barely touched the floor when he kissed me, his large hands cupping the sides of my head.

It was possessive and dominating and intense.

Just like Maximo.

Ending the kiss, he took a step away so he could untie my belt. His fingertips teased my thighs as he gathered the material of my skirt and lifted the dress over my head, leaving me in my bra, panties, and heels. His searing gaze started at my feet and slowly moved up, as though he were trying to memorize each freckle, dip, and curve of my body.

Shrugging off his jacket, he dropped it to the floor with my dress. He toed off his shoes before ordering, "Undress me."

I hesitated, unsure my shaking fingers could undo a single button, much less the line of them.

"Once I have you naked, I won't have the patience to strip. So unless you want me to fuck you while I'm fully clothed, I suggest you undress me. Now, Juliet."

I liked the visual he created—and the swirl of need *it* created—but I wanted to see and feel all of him.

My shaking fingers managed the buttons before pushing the shirt off his broad shoulders.

God, he was beautiful. Each cut line. Bumped ridge. Splash of color. Even the marks that marred his skin—the puckered scars and faded slashes—added to his perfection.

I undid his belt and slacks, letting them drop before glancing up at him.

"Everything, little dove."

Happily, I shoved his black boxer briefs down. His chiseled pelvic muscles led to neatly trimmed dark hair and a hard cock that was as mouthwatering as the rest of him.

Holy shit.

Maximo kicked the bunched fabric to the side before adding his socks to the pile, but I couldn't tear my eyes away from his intimidatingly impressive erection.

This explains why he's so damn arrogant. He's got enough to back it up.

And then some.

Total Big Dick Energy.

After removing my bra, Maximo knelt in front of me to undo the delicate straps of my shoes. I stepped out of them before he hooked his thumbs in the sides of my panties and slowly slid them down my legs.

"Christ, you're perfection," he murmured before leaning forward to kiss the sensitive skin under my navel.

But one small kiss wasn't enough.

Dipping lower, he parted my legs and pressed his mouth against me. His tongue darted out to taste, his groan vibrating through me.

Holy shit.

Holy shit.

I clutched his head, partially to keep from falling but mostly to keep his mouth locked on me.

When he pulled away, I wanted to yank him back and demand he finish what he started. But at the fire in his hooded eyes, I knew it was just the beginning.

And the best was yet to come.

Standing, he kissed me again, my taste on his tongue. He backed me up but my small, shuffling steps must've taken too long because he lifted me. When my back hit the mattress, Maximo covered my body with his. His arms supported him and his abs pressed between my spread thighs.

His mouth left mine to tease my neck, his lips softly kissing before he bit hard enough to make me cry out. Hard enough to make me wetter.

Hard enough to leave his mark.

Continuing down, he licked, kissed, sucked, and nipped my breast, his skillful mouth touching everywhere but my nipple. Each time I arched and shifted, silently demanding what I needed, he moved farther away and started the process again.

He's killing me.

Finally, the very tip of his tongue swirled around the hardened peak. My breath caught, and I gripped the sheets to keep from moving, but he didn't give me more. The light touch of his tongue was more torment than relief.

No, I'm gonna kill him.

I hadn't realized I'd spoken the words out loud until Maximo replied, "If this is the way I leave this world, little dove, it'd be the perfect death."

Whatever retort I may have scrambled together was lost and forgotten when he sucked my nipple. His teeth scraped across the sensitive skin as he slowly pulled away before sucking it in harder, his tongue swirling.

No amount of control could stop my hips from grinding against him. I didn't care that I was soaked. I didn't care that I was rubbing all that wetness on him.

I didn't even care that he could feel it.

All that mattered was easing the ache that grew low in my belly.

"Jesus," Maximo bit out, moving suddenly. I braced, worried I'd done something wrong, but he just shifted down the bed so his head was between my legs. He didn't tease as he had with my breasts. His thumbs spread my lower lips and he speared his tongue in. Deep and rough, he groaned like he was the one receiving pleasure after being tormented.

My legs trembled, trying to close. I wasn't sure whether it was to get away from the intensity or to hold him in place.

His hands moved to grip my inner thighs, keeping me open so he could eat me.

Devour me.

In tune with me and my body, he knew exactly how to build the tension while keeping me teetering on an edge that rose higher and higher.

I'd never experienced such a beautifully frustrating pleasure.

Sliding a hand up my thigh, he eased a finger in. Then another, stretching me. With his mouth and hand working me in unison, my orgasm hit suddenly, launching me over the edge I'd been chasing.

My pulse thumped at the base of my throat.

My thoughts went hazy.

My eyes squeezed shut.

And I exploded, coming completely undone.

Maximo continued his fervent pace as he wrung everything from me then demanded more. My orgasm faded just to start building again before I even had a chance to catch my breath.

It was too much.

Too intense.

But as I fisted his hair, my hand abruptly switched from tugging him away to clutching him closer.

Because the overstimulated feeling faded, leaving *need* in its place.

"Maximo—" I started, my word turning to a sharp cry when he bit down on my clit and slammed his fingers in.

He lifted his head to look at me. "Who am I?"

"Daddy," I corrected. "I need…"

His fingers pumped in and out, his thumb stroking my clit. "What do you need?"

"More," I pleaded, mindless and restless and a million other *lesses* that I was too turned on to think of. "I need more. You."

"You're so fucking tight. I've got to get you ready to take me."

"If I was any readier, I'd flood Vegas."

"Christ. Jesus fucking Christ, you really are killing me." Sliding his fingers free, he moved up my body to search my face.

If he was looking for doubt or reluctance, he wouldn't find it. I wanted him. Badly. I'd never been more sure of anything in my entire life.

Maximo kneeled between my thighs, his spread legs pushing mine wider. He fisted his cock, lining up the head with my ready pussy.

I didn't want there to be a barrier separating us, but I also didn't want to be stupid.

"Have you been tested?" I blurted.

Maximo froze at my question. "I'd *never* risk your safety, Juliet. I've never been with anyone bare, and I haven't been with anyone since I was last tested."

"I'm on the pill," I said, wanting to hug Ms. Vera for that. "And, you know, I haven't… So I'm good, too."

"Do you want me to use a condom anyway?"

I shook my head. "I want to feel *everything*."

"Don't say shit like that when I'm already working not to come." He positioned himself again. With one last searching gaze, he lowered his eyes to raptly watch as he slowly pressed in.

Inch by long, thick inch.

Even as prepared as I was, it stung as he stretched me. I was so full, I thought I'd burst. I hissed out a breath at the unfamiliar intrusion.

But I wanted more. All of it. All of him.

I lifted my hips, pushing him in farther and crying out.

"I should warm your ass for that." His muscles were tense, his breathing short and harsh. "But that would involve pulling out of heaven, so it'll have to wait." Holding my hips, he thrust in and planted himself fully.

He stayed like that for long moments that felt like long hours. My body adjusted as best as it could considering his size, and the restless neediness returned times a million.

I rocked my hips, but he squeezed them, pinning me to the bed so I couldn't move.

"You gotta give me a second," he said gruffly, his expression pained as he closed his eyes. "Told you it's been a while, and your perfect pussy is squeezing me like a damn vise, I don't wanna come in less than two pumps."

"How long of a while?" I asked before wishing I could choke on the stupid question.

Or, depending on his answer, choke Maximo.

Opening his lids, he stared down at me. The look in his brooding, blazing eyes twisted deep inside me, imbedding in my soul until I knew I'd never forget it for the rest of my life. I could be on my deathbed at the old age of a hundred, and I'd still remember the way he was looking at me.

"A year, little dove."

A year?

Holy shit, a year is a long time.

It's also exactly how long I've been here.

That can't be a coincidence.

My brows shot up, but before I could form a response, he *finally* moved. Slow, long strokes, pulling his length out before sliding back in.

Panic hit me as I realized I had no clue what to do. Did I move? What was I supposed to do with my hands? Was he expecting me to bend, twist, and throw my legs over my head like a Cirque du Soleil performer? Was he bored or disappointed?

My freak out—and all other thoughts—flew from my head as his pace increased. Raw desire filled his expression as he watched me take him, his hold on my hips digging in.

This is all he wants.

Just me.

Lowering himself, Maximo put one of his forearms flat to the bed near my head. His other kept hold of my hip as he slammed into me. His body brushed mine with each thrust, his cock pounding so hard, I would've been propelled up the bed had he not held me in place.

He surrounded me. Touched every inch of me. Overwhelmed me, but in the best possible way.

All I saw was Maximo.

All I felt was Maximo.

All I needed right then was Maximo.

There was no chasing the edge. I was launched off it, plunging into pure bliss that zipped through my veins like molten lava and a charged electrical current.

I forced my lids open to find Maximo's intense eyes on me. They were wild. Unhinged. Filled with so much desire, I couldn't believe it

160

was aimed at me.

Lowering his head near my ear, his breathing was harsh as his pace slowed but his force increased. With a few more brutal thrusts, he came with a groan.

That rough, unbelievably sexy groan imbedded itself in my memory, too.

Breathless and exhausted, my thoughts were fleeting, bouncing from everything to nothing. At the feel of Maximo's cock slipping free, I was able to grab a thought.

I want to do it again.

He got up and padded to the bathroom. Giving a languid stretch, I stood and began gathering my clothes.

"What the fuck are you doing?"

I jumped at the anger in his quiet yet somehow booming voice. "Uh, going to my room?"

"This *is* your room now." He glared. "Now get your ass back in bed because you're going to be sore enough without me making it red."

I couldn't argue with that.

I also didn't want to.

When we climbed back into bed, I belatedly noticed the damp cloth Maximo held. When he tried to wipe between my legs, I reached to do it myself, but his glare intensified.

"I take care of you, dove. You know the rules. Spread your legs for Daddy."

I'd already come so hard, I wasn't sure my body could take anymore, but a surge of arousal shot through me anyway. I did as ordered and was rewarded by his wicked smile. When he finished, he sat back. "What do you need from your room?"

"I can grab it." When his only response was *the look*, I said, "My toothbrush and face wash."

Once we finished our nighttime stuff, we climbed back into bed. My back had barely hit the mattress when he rolled me on my side and wrapped his body around mine.

I felt warm and safe and content—three things I didn't have a wealth of experience with.

"Juliet."

At the tone of voice, my tired eyes snapped open and I went alert. "Hmm?"

"You're in here every night. Your clothes and all your things will be moved."

"I have a lot of stuff," I pointed out as if he wasn't the one who'd bought it all.

"I have a shit-ton of room."

I hoped my voice was nonchalant and cool, and not the excited giddy squeal I felt like giving. "Okay."

"And if you ever try to leave after sex, I'll take that to mean I haven't fucked you hard enough. I'll make sure to rectify that until you can't even think about standing. That, or I'll tie you to the bed."

Either sounds good to me.

I didn't share that.

"Okay," I repeated.

Like the night before, his hand moved to my throat and the other cupped my tender pussy. The hold was hot and oddly comforting. "You're not a whore who leaves right after. And your pussy isn't the only thing I want or the only thing I like."

"You don't even know me," I pointed out through a yawn.

"I know more than you think." He nipped my neck. "I may know you better than you know yourself."

My eyes got heavy, and I hovered between consciousness and sleep.

"Thank you for giving me you," he whispered.

"Thank you for wanting me," I whispered back.

And then I was out.

MAXIMO

'THANK YOU FOR wanting me.'

Fuck me, her sweet voice whispering those words ricocheted around my brain like a bullet in my skull.

Except her words did more damage.

My broken girl.

She'd thought I didn't want her. That I'd changed my mind, which would also mean I'd lost my damn mind.

I'd taken her to the fight with no warning or explanations so she wouldn't have time to form walls, expectations, or justifications. I needed it to be crystal fucking clear who she was agreeing to be with. Who she was giving herself to. I was a ruthless asshole who didn't hesitate to

162

do what was needed—or what I wanted.

And that included pulling strings to manipulate Juliet without her realizing.

My obsession had been growing for a year—a year I shouldn't have been looking at her much less thinking the things I had. A year I'd spent planning and plotting, each action and response meticulous.

A year I'd spent waiting for her.

With her body pressed to mine, her pussy in my hand and her heart beating under my other palm, I knew two things down to my bones.

It'd been worth every second.

And I was never letting her go.

CHAPTER NINETEEN

Got It Bad

JULIET

*W*AKING UP THE next morning, I knew I was alone because Maximo wasn't pressed to my back like he'd been the whole night. I rolled and stretched. And then I smiled at the dull ache between my thighs.

I had sex.

With Maximo.

And it was better than my fantasies, which is saying something.

I can't wait to do it again.

Climbing from the bed, I winced as the ache grew.

Okay, I can't wait to take some Motrin and then do it again.

Padding across the room, I used the bathroom and was washing my hands when I looked up.

What the hell?

I leaned forward to inspect the love bites in the mirror. Bites, *plural.* Two more marked my neck and a dark hickey was on my breast.

This is ridiculous and immature and possessive and... Who am I kidding?

I like it as much as he does.

I finished washing up before brushing my teeth. I didn't want to pull my dress back on, so I raided his armoire and threw on a pair of joggers and a tee.

Just like old times.

Opening the door, I didn't bother with my stealth routine since everyone already knew. I headed for my sewing room but slowed when I saw Maximo's office door was open. Unfortunately, he was on the phone, so I continued across the hall.

Sitting at my desk, I felt inspired. I grabbed a pad of paper and colored pencils and closed my eyes, visualizing what I wanted.

And then I sketched it. Badly.

But it would do.

I was sorting through my fabric when the door opened.

Maximo paused in the doorway. A warm, small smile pulled at his mouth as he checked out what I was wearing. Walking over, he hauled me to him and kissed me so hard, it was a wonder our lips didn't fuse together. He pulled away but kept his face close as he studied mine. "You good?"

"Very."

"Sore?"

"Yeah." I hoped my meaning came across when I added, "But not *too* sore."

His groan showed he got what I was saying. I thought I'd get his mouth back, but instead he gave me a stern expression. "If I'm working from home, I expect you to come kiss me when you wake up."

"You were on the phone," I said.

"I don't give a damn. You can always interrupt me. I would've welcomed it during that call."

Noticing the lines on his forehead and the way his jaw clenched, I asked, "Is everything okay?"

"Just the usual bullshit. Which is why I could've used your sweet mouth as a distraction."

"If you want to go back and pretend to be on a call, we can have a do-over."

He looked genuinely disappointed when he shook his head. "I was waiting for you to wake up so I could check on you, but I've got to run for a meeting at Sunrise."

"Is that one of your casinos?" I was excited to get that tidbit of info.

He lifted his chin. "Sunrise, Moonlight, Star, and Nebula."

My jaw dropped to the floor. "I didn't realize those were yours. I've never been, but they're always on the lists of the top places to stay off-Strip."

He smirked. "Glad my PR team earns their salaries."

Maximo owns four hugely popular resorts and I own…

Nothing.

Yeah, that's not an imbalance at all.

Maximo cupped the sides of my head in the possessive hold. "I'm sending someone up with lunch."

"Lunch?"

"It's almost noon."

"I didn't realize it was so late."

"You were wiped. You didn't even twitch when I kissed you before getting up this morning." His smile was cocky and wicked and packed with male satisfaction.

He kissed me before getting out of bed.

A bed we shared.

And now he hung around so he could make sure I'm okay.

His eyes narrowed. "You sure you're good?"

I was better than good.

I was *happy*.

"I'm sure, Daddy," I said instantly.

When we'd first talked, I'd figured the name was only for him and it wouldn't do much for me.

I'd been wrong.

Calling him Daddy did a *lot* for me.

The more I said it, the more I liked it. I was still a little flustered and a lot awkward, but I'd get more comfortable.

Especially if saying it meant I got to see the look of fiery lust and warm affection he was giving me.

He kissed me again before heading for the door. Stopping when he reached it, he looked over his shoulder. "Make sure you eat, Juliet. And keep this door open from now on."

Before I could ask why, he was gone.

I shrugged and went back to finding fabric.

A few minutes later, Marco came in carrying a full tray service. There was a ham sandwich, a small salad, a bowl of fruit, and two Diet Cokes.

Two.

Seems it's my lucky day for various reasons.

"Thanks," I said, cracking right into one of those bad boys.

I watched Marco's face carefully, searching for any sign he was judging or disgusted or any of the other bad things I worried people would feel.

He looked stoic and bored—business as usual.

"Shout if you need anything." When he walked from the room, he started closing the door behind him before stopping and opening it fully.

Apparently, Maximo shared his new door policy.

Running to my room, I grabbed my iPad and headphones before returning to my sandwich. As I dug in, I brought up Google and did a search.

Nebula Vegas NV

Unsurprisingly, the screen loaded to tell me to contact the network admin. I was pretty sure Cole handled all the tech in the house, and I wasn't asking him to help me snoop on his boss.

Exiting out of the browser, I put on music as I finished eating. Once I was done, I laid out the fabric I'd chosen and started measuring it. It took much longer than usual because I kept glancing at the open door.

There was no one there, but I worried someone would walk by just as I was making some huge mistake. Or as I was dancing and lip-syncing—something I did often.

With a sigh, I went and closed the door.

He's not even home.

What's the worst that could happen?

MAXIMO

WALKING THROUGH THE isolated building, my anticipation grew with each step I took.

Ordinarily when someone crossed me, I brought them to the basement of Moonlight. But Jack Murphy hadn't crossed me.

He'd hurt Juliet.

Which meant I didn't need a secure room with a private exit to a waiting vehicle. I needed the industrial tools, cleaning system, and disposal unit of a former meat-processing plant.

It was going to get messy.

And I couldn't fucking wait.

Opening another door slowly so it would creak and groan, I stepped in and let the slam echo around the room. Ash sat silently in a chair, but my gaze went to where Jack Murphy hung from a meat hook, his pale torso bare.

"Who's there?" His words were slurred with the residual effects of Ash's drugs. He moved his head back and forth as if he could see past the blindfold.

Lifting my chin at Ash, I leaned against the wall and pulled out my phone. I scrolled through emails and my calendar, patient to wait until the drugs were out of Murphy's system. Otherwise, they'd diminish the pain. He didn't deserve that.

Plus, anticipation was half the fun.

Every time Murphy sank back into a stupor, Ash or I would make a noise to set him off again. It was another hour before his voice was normal, no hint of impairment. Completely alert, his movements grew frantic as he worked to escape the bindings.

It wouldn't happen—Ash was an expert.

It also wouldn't happen because he would be in too much pain.

"Jack Murphy," I said, pocketing my phone. "Lowlife, scumbag-for-hire, crony." I glanced at Ash. "Am I missing anything?"

"Gemini," he added. "Oh, and woman beater—professionally and personally."

"What the fuck is this, some jacked version of *This Is Your Life*?" Murphy croaked. "Untie me or else—"

I tugged off his blindfold and whatever blustered threat he was about to spew died abruptly when he saw me. "Fuck."

In the face of his panic, my lips tipped but I didn't speak.

The longer the silence stretched, thickening the tension in the room, the more agitated Murphy became. "Why the hell am I here?"

"Do you like beating women, Murphy?"

"I don't know what—"

"Are you too much of a pussy to take on men so you go after their daughters?"

"Fuck you, asshole."

Circling his hanging body, I slid on gloves and an apron before grabbing a small knife from the set that hung on the wall. There were bigger ones—ones that would do the job quicker.

But I wanted to take my time.

I ran the blade down his side, hard enough for him to feel its sharpness, but not enough to puncture skin. "Does it get you and your tiny prick off to stab them because you can't get inside them any other way?"

"We've got no beef with you, Black," he gritted out, his body tense and his breathing shallow so the blade wouldn't cut.

Keeping it pressed tight, I rounded him so I could see his face. His jaw was tight, fury warring with fear.

"But I've got a lot of fucking beef with you," I said, my tone cold and impassive. My expression was blank as I stabbed him, just above his hip.

Right where he'd stabbed Juliet.

"Fucking shit! What the hell? Fuck!"

"Does it feel like I'm letting you off easy?"

"What're you talking about?" His body shook as he fought to stay still so he didn't make the pain worse.

He didn't have to worry, I'd take care of that for him.

Sliding the knife free, I pressed the tip to the same spot above his other hip. "Shamus McMillon."

He shook his head rapidly, confusion tightening his features. "We cut ties with Shamus over a year ago. Before he took off. We've got no clue where he is. If he owes you money, try Carmichael—they were tight."

"But he owed you?"

"The Sullivans. But he squared up his last debt a couple weeks before he took off."

I stabbed hard enough to puncture the skin before slowing down so the blade inched in.

"Fuck, fuck, fuck," he chanted, his eyes dazed at the pain.

"Shamus owed. *Shamus*. Yet you stuck your knife in his daughter." I buried mine to the hilt. "You couldn't take an old man so you went after a teenager?"

"What's she have to do with you?" he asked before he gave a weak smile. "You nailing the frigid bitch? I'm sure that uptight, barely legal cunt is worth a lot, but is it worth going against the Sullivans?"

I didn't hesitate. "Abso-fucking-lutely."

"You gonna dump me at the bar as a warning? A declaration of war?" There was more than a hint of hope in his pale face, and, fuck me, I loved crushing it.

"No. I'm going to kill you. Slowly. Painfully. I just wanted to make sure you went to hell knowing why."

"The Sullivans will come after you."

I smirked. "Who do you think told us where to find you?"

I'd been prepared to go to war, but when I'd gone to their bar, Patrick had eagerly turned on Jack Murphy. Unlike their watered-down drinks, Jack paired up with a different kind of *coke*, and he'd been dipping into their supply. They were happy to have their headache gone.

And I was happy to accommodate.

Murphy's mouth opened and closed—betrayal and anger mixed with pain in his expression before it grew frantic. He tried to throw his boss under the bus. "Patrick's the one who sent me after her."

Patrick said he'd sent Murphy to give Juliet a *verbal* message to pass to Shamus. He'd wanted Shamus to know he could reach her but had sworn it'd been an empty threat.

Murphy's knife work had come after Juliet had rejected him in a loud, insulting, and embarrassing way.

That was my ballsy girl.

Before I'd left the bar, I'd made it clear to Patrick and his brothers that Juliet was off-limits. If having Juliet's ass on my lap at the fight hadn't spread that message, Patrick Sullivan's big mouth would.

"I can get you information," Murphy tried. "An in with the Sullivans. Loans, drugs, enforcers."

I looked back at Ash. "Why does every shithead think I want that garbage in my resorts?"

Ash scowled at Murphy. "And why the hell is he trying to outsource my job?" He scoffed. "I'm sitting here reading NFL trade rumors and he's hanging from the ceiling. You tell me who the better enforcer is."

Done talking, I sliced across the shitty Clip-Art tattoo that covered Murphy's gut. I moved to his back, carefully carving before grabbing the container of salt behind me. Scooping a handful, I pressed it against the bloody wounds that made up the abstract dove.

It wasn't perfect since my canvas pissed himself and kept choking on his own vomit, but I knew what it was supposed to be.

I methodically sliced. I stabbed. I carved. I gave him breaks, ensuring he didn't pass out from the pain or bleed out, only to start again.

After what likely felt like an eternity to Jack Murphy, I was done.

I buried my knife deep in his side, right at the spot where he'd stabbed

Juliet. I twisted it and left it there as he took his final breath.

"The dump idea isn't a bad one," Ash pointed out as he stood. "Make sure the Sullivans got your message."

It was tempting, but not worth it. For the Sullivans, the connection to my casinos was worth far more than Murphy's life. They wouldn't risk severing it to avenge a fucker they wanted dead, too.

I pulled my bloodied gloves and apron off. "They got it."

"Disposal it is," Ash said as he circled around to get his first view of Murphy's back. He laughed, shaking his head. "A dove? Christ, you're sick. And you've got it bad."

I didn't bother to argue.

He was right on both counts.

JULIET

WHEN I'D CLOSED the door, I'd asked myself what the worst that could happen was.

Hours later—how many, I wasn't sure because I'd stupidly lost track of time—I learned what.

Because Maximo was glowering at me from the doorway.

Glowering.

I took my headphones off to hear him ask, "What did I say about this door, Juliet?"

Oh no.

Shrugging, I went for evasive, but it came out like a question. "I don't remember?"

"Really? Because it seems like you do. Which means along with me spanking your ass for disobeying, I'd be forced to spank it again for lying."

Spank?

Yes, please.

I mean, no way.

"Why did you close it?"

I shrugged. "I felt weird with it open."

His body went rigid. "Why?"

"I was self-conscious."

His shoulders dropped a little, but he still didn't look happy. "Get over it."

171

He did not…

"Did you just tell me to get over it?"

"Yes," he said simply.

I crossed my arms over my chest and glowered at *him*. "You can't just tell me how to feel."

"That's exactly what you agreed to when you came to my office. It's what you agreed to again when you gave me you."

I hadn't thought Maximo would notice the door being closed, and I definitely hadn't thought it was a spankable offense.

But the hardness in his eyes told me I was wrong.

"Let's go, little dove."

I swallowed hard. "W-where?"

"Our room."

My stomach would've gone all swoony at him calling it *our* room had it not been for the impending punishment.

When I didn't move, he tilted his head, thoughtful for a moment. "I could always bend you over the desk and do it in here."

He's not really going to…

Right?

Yeah, there's no way.

He's just trying to scare me.

"I won't close it again," I promised.

"Good."

Relief and a surprising surge of disappointment warred within me. I didn't want to be in pain, but at the same time, I was intrigued by being spanked.

Maybe even looking forward to it.

I was granted a reprieve, so why am I thinking of asking for my punishment anyway?

I've clearly lost my mind.

"Here or our room?" Maximo asked, making me realize my internal dilemma was for nothing. I wasn't being spared at all.

My brows shot up as my relief and disappointment quickly pivoted to dread and excitement. "I said I wouldn't do it again."

"Which is good. But I told you to keep the door open. You didn't listen. You earned these consequences. Now, I'll ask you one last time. Here or our room?"

"How about I stay in here and you go—"

"Juliet."

"Our room works."

Just like me, he seemed to like the sounds of that.

Either that, or I'd made him develop a tic that tipped his lips.

Grabbing my hand, he pulled me from the room, unfazed by my slow, trudging steps. He closed us into the room and sat on the bench in front of his bed. "Pull your pants and panties down."

I didn't do as ordered and instead tried to bargain. "How about if we just forget this happened and start fresh? Clear the slate."

He studied me, his gaze too intent and sharp. "Do you not want this?"

I wasn't sure if 'this' was referring to the punishment or the whole dynamic.

Either way, my answer was the same. "I do. I'm just nervous. This is all unknown territory for me." I inhaled before softly admitting, "And I feel wrong for wanting it."

"Why?"

"Because it's not… typical."

"Fuck typical. Fuck normal. Fuck what anyone else says. The only person who can tell you what to do is *me*. And I said pants and panties down."

His words quieted the nagging voice of doubt in my head. Actually, his words held a pillow over doubt's face and smothered it.

Because he was right. It didn't matter what anyone else thought. All that mattered was what we wanted. And, even though I was unsure I'd enjoy it, I wanted to try.

Since I wasn't wearing any panties, I eagerly shoved the joggers off.

Maximo's gaze followed the fabric, before shooting back up. Finding me bare, he said, "Wouldn't have been able to leave had I known you were wearing my pants with nothing underneath." He reached his hand out. "Come here."

A shiver of lust and fear and anticipation went through me.

What the hell am I doing?

But even as I thought it, my feet carried me to him. My body was stiff, but he easily bent me over his knee.

Maximo's large palm gently stroked my ass. It felt good, and I wasn't the only one who thought so. His cock grew hard under me, pushing against my belly.

I raised my head to look over my shoulder, but he put his hand on my back, keeping me in place.

"I'm going to go easy for your first time and only give you five for closing the door," he said.

Five. Five's not so bad.

Probably.

Maybe?

"And then ten for lying," he continued.

"Fifteen? That's not going easy!"

"I can make it an even twenty if you'd prefer."

I bit my lip to keep any further complaints to myself before I made things worse.

"Fuck, I love this ass." I lost his soothing strokes just before his palm came down.

Hard.

"Ow!"

The sting radiated and increased when his hand landed again.

He wasn't deterred by my pained cries. No, he *enjoyed* them. His cock jerked with each one.

I didn't try to hold in my sobs. It was impossible. Every time his palm connected, the sting and burn grew—especially when he hit an already heated spot. I lost count of how many he'd delivered and panic set in.

What if he lost track, too?

What if he gets carried away?

I'll never be able to sit again!

But with one last smack, Maximo stopped. He rearranged me so I was sitting upright in his lap, and I hissed at the roughness of his slacks against my raw ass.

And my ass wasn't the only thing that was raw. My emotions were flayed open and whatever dam held my tears broke. I wasn't sure the last time I'd really bawled, but all of a sudden, I couldn't stop.

Needing to be closer, I straddled Maximo so I could bury my face in his chest, huge sobs wracking my body. The more I tried to choke them down, the worse they became.

He tenderly rubbed my back and whispered, "You did good, little dove. So good."

It was stupid to be delighted by praise for my ability to take a palm to my butt, but that didn't stop me from feeling proud. His words warmed my insides almost as much as his hand had warmed my ass.

Getting control of my tears with only a few shuddering hiccups remaining, I whispered, "I'm never breaking the rules again."

Maximo chuckled. "Somehow I don't believe that." He cupped my head and leaned me back so he could study me. After the pain he'd enjoyed inflicting, it was unexpected to see such deep concern. "How're you feeling?"

That was a good question.

I was starving.

Exhausted.

And, surprisingly, horny.

Even more surprising, however, was the feeling of peace that'd settled into my soul. I was content, the cathartic cry had washed away years of emotional drought.

"I'm fine," I told him honestly.

"I need more than that."

"It hurt worse than I expected, but at the same time, it wasn't as bad as I thought it would be." I fell forward, resting my forehead on his chest. "That doesn't make sense."

"It does." His hand rubbed down my back, over my heated cheeks, ending between my thighs. He slid a finger through the arousal that pooled there. I stiffened in his hold, but he just wrapped his other arm around my waist. "Shh. Let me take care of you."

From behind, two of his fingers pumped into me until I was rocking against him. Fucking myself on his fingers.

I was close, but I needed more.

Slipping his fingers free, he used the wetness that coated them to circle my clit. It wasn't long before the pleasure zipped through me, not canceling out the pain, but mixing with it. Like two sides of a coin, one couldn't exist without the other.

I came hard until I was a boneless mess, leaning on him to stay upright.

"Better?" Maximo rumbled.

"Mmhmm."

Setting me on the bench, he grabbed the joggers from the floor and crouched, slipping them up my legs. He stood and pulled me up before securing the oversized pants around my hips. "Let's go feed you."

"'Kay."

"You're agreeable after you've come. I'll have to remember that."

That could be bad.

Really, really good, but then bad.

Walking downstairs, dinner was already on the table. My stomach growled at the scent. I started pulling out my chair, but Maximo snagged me first, tugging me into his lap.

"What're you doing?" I asked.

Keeping an arm around me, he used his free one to grab his fork. "I like you on my lap."

"Another rule?"

"Yes."

I reached for my fork and froze.

My place setting was already in front of me. Not at the other chair but positioned right next to Maximo's. Like Freddy knew I'd be sitting on Maximo's lap.

How often has this happened?

Jealousy swelled in my stomach, the black tendrils weaving through me, its roots taking hold. No matter how much I tried to shake the thoughts, they burrowed deeper.

I had no clue how many partners he'd had or how many other *little doves* he'd been Daddy to. I didn't *want* to know. But the idea it'd been a regular enough occurrence that Freddy knew to rearrange the settings bothered me.

A lot.

It doesn't matter.

It doesn't matter.

Don't be stupid and dramatic.

He hasn't been with anyone for a year. What happened before me doesn't matter.

"What's wrong?" Of course he noticed my body going tense.

Forcing myself to loosen, I picked up my fork and stabbed the salad. "Nothing, why?"

"You know how I feel about lying. Do you need another ten?"

"Nope, definitely not."

Curling his hand around the side of my neck, he tilted my head so I was forced to meet his eyes. "Then what's wrong?"

I scrambled for an excuse. Anything. Literally, any half-plausible reason would work.

But I came up empty.

"I asked you a question, and I expect an answer."

Unable to meet his eyes, I focused to the side when I muttered, "My place setting was already here."

"And? Juliet, I told you things would be done my way. I'm not going to ask unless it's something major and even then, I likely won't."

"That's not what I meant." Jealous—*and* frustrated with myself for being jealous—I explained, "Freddy knew to put my plate here."

"Yes, because I told him to."

"You did?"

"I knew you closed the door, which meant I knew dinner would be delayed. I told him we'd be a half-hour late and how to set the table. What does that have to do with why you're upset?"

"I thought..." I averted my eyes again as I rushed, "I thought he set it like this because it was your usual routine."

His brows lowered before understanding hit him.

And when his stupid sexy mouth curved in a stupid sexy smirk, I wanted to hit him, too.

"You were jealous," he stated.

I opened my mouth to deny it, but then I caught the expectant gleam in his eyes.

He wanted me to lie because he wanted to punish me.

I pressed my lips together.

"Lies by omission are still lies, Juliet."

"You didn't ask a question," I pointed out.

"True. Were you jealous?"

Shit.

"Yes."

But he didn't leave it at that. "Why?"

"Because I didn't like the idea this has happened with other women so frequently, Freddy knew what to do." Despite not having eaten the bite on my fork, I stabbed more lettuce just for an excuse to stab something.

"I like you jealous."

My startled gaze shot to him to see if he was being sarcastic. "You do?"

He lifted his chin. "It's good for my unreal, massive ego to know you're as possessive of me as I am of you."

"You get jealous?"

I wasn't sure why that surprised me so much. Maybe because he was usually so cool and collected to the point of frigid aloofness. Or because he could get any woman he wanted with a crook of his skilled finger and smirk of his sinful lips. Actually, it wouldn't even take that much.

Or because he was all he was and I was just... well, me.

His thumb rubbed along my jaw. "Of everyone who's lucky enough to look at you."

The tendrils of jealousy in my stomach turned to melty goodness at his sweet words.

But he wasn't done. "I told you I've never slept in the same bed with a woman, which was easy because I've never brought women here. Not for dinner or anything else. Understand?"

I nodded.

"Good. Even though I like your jealousy, I don't like you upset. Talk to me. Don't let shit fester."

After a moment, I asked, "You already knew I closed the door?" At his chin lift, I asked, "How?"

"Marco."

That rat.

He dropped his hand from my neck and picked his fork up. Tapping my plate, he ordered, "Eat."

I finally ate the salad I'd been murdering. After a few silent minutes, I opened my mouth to ask about his day.

That was what I'd intended to ask.

But what shot out was, "Did you call other women *little dove*, too?"

I didn't have time to regret asking because his patient answer was instantaneous. "Never. Not even dove. That's all yours."

The last of the tension flowed from my body. Past or not, I wanted to be his only dove.

I hoped my voice was nonchalant and super casual when I said, "Cool."

Nailed it.

I both felt and heard his chuckle. "You're fucking cute."

Okay, maybe I didn't nail it.

Oh well.

CHAPTER TWENTY

Rattle The Cage

Maximo

It's going to be a good day.

After I'd spanked Juliet's ass the week before, I figured she'd shove a wedge under the door to make sure it didn't close an inch. It'd been wide open that morning when I'd popped in to taste her mouth and tell her the men and I would be gone until late.

Unfortunately for her, my mind had been on her sweet mouth and I'd left the house without my cell. I'd stopped home between meetings to find her door closed.

I was willing to bet she'd closed it as soon as my car had cleared the driveway.

I opened the door, but she didn't notice—her headphones were on and her music was cranked so loud, I could hear it. Working at the side of the L-shaped desk, her head was bent over the fabric as she carefully slid pins into place.

I leaned against the jamb and crossed my arms, taking the minute I didn't have to study her profile.

Fuck, she was beautiful. Her high ponytail bobbed as she mouthed along with the song. A small smile curved her lips.

After a minute, she finally glanced my way before doing a double take. My already thickening cock quickly hardened as her expression morphed from surprise to fear to panic.

"What're you doing here?" she shouted. I gestured to my ear, and she slid her headphones off before quietly repeating, "What're you doing here?"

"The more important question is why was the door closed?"

Ballsy girl didn't try to lie or claim she hadn't noticed. "I closed it."

"Why?"

"Ms. Vera's off for the week, and you said the men were going with you. I didn't think it mattered since the house is empty."

"You thought wrong."

Her face set in the prettiest pout as she muttered, "I know that now."

"Let's go, Juliet."

"Don't you have a meeting? I don't want to keep you. We can pencil this in for a later date."

"And when would that be?"

"February thirty-first?"

Christ, she's funny.

Even with all the shit Juliet had been through in her life, she was still soft. Still happy. She could've justifiably turned bitter and jaded, but she hadn't. She stayed sweet.

Too bad that didn't make me lenient. It was the opposite. It made my need to control and keep her even stronger.

"Here or our room?"

She sighed, her shoulders slumping. "Our room."

Dramatic as she was acting, she didn't put up much of a fight as she followed me into the hall.

If I didn't know any better, I'd think my little dove was just rattling her cage to see if she could get away with it...

Or maybe she wants *to receive the punishment as badly as I want to give it.*

As we entered the room, her steps slowed. She wrapped her arms around herself. "I don't get why it matters that the door was closed."

"Because I said so."

"Yes, but *why?*"

I wasn't used to explaining myself. I said something, it was done.

Simple as that.

But treating Juliet with those same expectations had been a misstep. She wasn't used to it, and until I had her trust, she wouldn't blindly obey.

There'd be other orders she'd need to follow without explanation, but the door rule was one I could clarify.

Curling my hand around the side of her neck, I used my thumb to tilt her jaw up. "I want it open so when I'm sitting at my desk, I can see you."

"But you weren't even home," she pointed out.

"And look how long it took you to notice me standing there." My jaw clenched. "It was dangerous."

"This place is locked down like Fort Knox. Cole installed that panic button on the wall literally a foot from my desk."

"If you've got the door closed, how would you know you needed to push it until it was too late? And while we're at it, no wearing head-phones when you're home alone. I'm adding to the rules."

Surprisingly, she smiled and stepped closer. "The only person after me is a big, angry Daddy who wants to spank my ass."

Fucking hell, she's out to kill me.

Gripping that tight ass, I pressed her body flush to mine. "The door stays open and no headphones when I'm gone. Understood?"

She nodded, and her eyes darted to the side to focus on the bench. "Since I didn't know *why* you wanted—"

"Nice try, Juliet." Releasing her, I sat on the bench. "Lower your pants and panties, but keep them around your ankles." Once she had, I positioned her over my legs. "Ten today."

"Ten? It was only five—"

"I can make it thirty." I rubbed my palm over the curve of her ass, pausing and starting again so I could hear her breath catch. Just as she began to relax, I lifted my hand and brought it down on the center of her ass cheek, the sharp sound breaking through the calm silence.

"Ow!" she cried, trying to sit up.

Placing a hand between her shoulders, I held her still as my palm connected again, aiming for the same spot.

She cried out again. "That hurt!"

"That's the point." I spread the next seven around before the last landed on the same spot as the first two.

By the time I was done, her pretty pale skin was bright red. My hand went between her thighs to find her just as wet as the day before, if not more.

I stroked two fingers through her slit before slamming them in. Finger fucking her, I moved my other hand from between her shoulders to her hair, gripping her ponytail and turning her head so I could see her.

Blinking up at me with tears in her eyes, her face flushed and damp, Juliet was never more beautiful. Because she was at ease.

Happy.

She's made for what I give her, and I'm the lucky bastard who gets to show her that.

Juliet made a murmur of protest when I slid my fingers free and sat her upright. Unlike the day before when I'd played with her at the bench, I stood and carried her to the bed.

Because her punishment wasn't over.

Setting her down, I said, "Lie back, feet together, and drop your knees."

After only a few seconds of hesitation, she did as I said, spreading herself for me.

I undid my belt and slacks, shoving them and my boxers down just enough to free myself. Fisting my cock, I stroked slowly.

Juliet's eyes heated, her pink tongue darting out to wet her fuckable lips.

I was tempted to make use of those lips, but if I got them wrapped around me, I'd want to take my time.

I started going faster, and her hand moved between her legs.

"No," I bit out.

Frustration tightened her features. "Why can't I touch?"

"Because you broke the rules."

"And you punished me."

"And now I'm finishing your punishment."

My intentions set in and her gaze narrowed. "You're not going to let me come?"

"No."

"That's… that's torture!"

"Trust me, little dove, staring at that pussy and not fucking it is torture for me, too."

"Then fuck me." When that didn't work, she brought out the big guns. Wide green eyes looked up at me and a small, sexy smile curved her lips as she whispered, "Please, Daddy. I need you."

Jesus fucking Christ, she's not out to kill me.

I'm already dead.

There was a mistake, and I got sent to heaven with this angel.

And I'll kill any motherfucker who tries to take her away from me.

"Push your shirt up and free your tits. Then use your fingers to hold your pussy lips open. Do not touch more than that, or I'll blindfold you so you can't watch."

She instantly followed my directions. My gaze alternated between her spread pussy, her tits, and her face. Hers stayed locked on my fist as I rubbed up and down my length—going quicker, squeezing harder.

The pressure built before the first shot of come hit her spread pussy. I aimed my fist just in time for the rest to land on her tits and stomach.

Fists to the bed on either side of her, I hung my head to catch my breath as I stared at my come splashed across her soft skin.

Mine.

Standing upright before my resolve weakened, I tucked my still hard cock away and redid my pants and belt.

"Are you really not going to make me come?" Juliet asked.

"No." Grabbing her wrists, I pulled her to sit before adjusting her bra and shirt back into place.

Pinching the fabric of her top, she pulled it away from where it clung to the stickiness. "I need to go shower."

"No," I repeated. With one last tease of my fingertip through her slit, I tugged her panties and pants up her legs, pausing to help her stand before sliding them over her raw ass.

"I can't stay like this all day."

"You will. No showering. No wiping it off." I gripped her chin and tilted it up. "And no playing. I'll know if you do. If you follow the rules, I'll eat your pussy when I get home. If you don't, I won't let you come for a week."

Panic filled her expression and voice. "A week?"

"Or longer." Lowering my mouth to hers, I kissed her hard, my tongue spearing in to taste her. I forced myself to end the kiss and move away. "I've got to go."

She looked disgruntled and dazed. "You're actually leaving?"

"I have to, I'm already late." I walked out to the hallway before turning back. "Remember the rules."

"I know, I know."

"Juliet."

"Maximo," she mocked.

So distracted by that smart mouth, I nearly left without my phone again.

CHAPTER TWENTY-ONE

This Could Be Fun

JULIET

I LIVE IN *here now.*

Not in this house, just in this shower.

I'd known the shower in Maximo's—*our*—room would be nice, but I hadn't known it would be so glorious, I wouldn't want to get out.

It had a waterfall that fell over my head and multiple shower heads that gave a water massage as they hit my body at different spots.

And since I was sore, it was much needed.

Maximo hadn't gotten home the night before until long after I'd gone to bed. Since I'd followed his rules, he'd woken me with his mouth between my legs. After I'd come from his tongue and fingers, he'd bent my knees up to my chest and fucked me at a mind-blowing angle while staring at our connection.

It'd been intense and hot and had left me tender in places I never knew existed.

When my stomach growled too loudly to be ignored, I turned the water off. I dried off and went to raid Maximo's joggers.

But when I opened the armoire, it wasn't only filled with his stuff.

The right half held my pajamas, too.

Huh?

Crouching, I tried the drawers at the bottom, and all his boxers and socks had been moved to the left. The ones on the right were empty.

On a hunch, I stood and went to the walk-in closet, flipping on the light as I entered.

Maximo's clothes were neatly hung to the left. His shoes, belts, and watches were in their spots at the side of the island.

Like the armoire, my clothes were on the right. My shoes and limited accessories were placed on that side of the island.

There was something about seeing my clothes with Maximo's that freaked me out a little but made me happy a whole lot more.

I'm not just sleeping in here with him.

I live with him.

Grabbing the ripped black crop I'd made, I put it on without a bra since I hadn't located those. I went commando for the same reason and pulled on a pair of my own joggers. Not bothering with socks or shoes, I left the room and headed for Maximo's office.

Despite the fact he was working from home, he wore black slacks and a dark gray shirt with the sleeves rolled. His shoulder held his phone to his ear as he typed on his computer.

Catching sight of me checking him out, a smile curved his lips. He pushed away from his desk and I went right to him, letting him settle me on his lap while he spoke to someone about orders or venders or something. I wasn't following the business-y conversation to begin with, but once his hand slid under my tee, my attention waned further.

Skimming up, he touched my bare breast before freezing. His arm reflexively tightened, as did the rest of him.

"What did you say?" he asked, tweaking my nipple before palming my breast.

I must not be the only one having trouble concentrating.

He waited for all of three seconds before saying, "Never mind, we'll talk about this later." He ended the call and tossed his phone to the desk before wrapping his other arm around my waist and shifting me so my back was flush to his front. Pushing under my shirt to palm my other breast, he dipped his head to nip my neck.

"Do they not feed you enough?" I asked, my voice breathy.

"Hmm?" he rumbled.

"You seemed a little *hangry* on the phone, hanging up like that. Now you're biting me. Should I ask Freddy to make you an omelet?"

"I like seeing you marked as mine," he said, his possessive words making me hot and wet and *happy*. Releasing his tight grip on my breast, he cupped me between the thighs. "And the only thing I want to eat is right here, little dove." He worked me through the fabric for a moment. "If you're not wearing a bra, does that mean you're not wearing panties?"

"I couldn't find them," I muttered.

Goosebumps spread across my skin as his lips skimmed my neck lightly. "Marco moved everything yesterday while you worked. I didn't want him touching those."

That was good, I didn't particularly want Marco touching them, either.

"I thought you sent him to make sure I followed the rules, not to be a moving man."

"That, too." He loosened his hold and shifted me so he could see my face. "Are you upset?"

"Would you let me move the stuff back if I were?" I shot back.

"No. I want you in my bed. In my space."

"I like being in your bed and space. Plus, it makes more sense to have my stuff there so I don't have to take a naked sprint down the hall after I shower in the morning."

"You can always take a naked sprint here." He tilted his head and rubbed his jaw thoughtfully. "Actually, that might be a new rule. It'd make the video conference calls more interesting." Even though he was the one who'd made the joke, his jaw clenched. "Never fucking mind."

I couldn't hold in my laugh, not that I tried too hard.

"Oh, you think that's funny?"

"Hilarious."

Maximo shifted me up so my ass was on his dick, and my laughter cut off at the feel of him hard beneath me.

I didn't think I'd ever get used to the way he felt. Or the way he looked. Or the way he wanted me.

"You drive me insane, dove."

"That feeling is very mutual."

His smile was equal parts tenderness and sinfulness.

God, how is this my life right now?

187

Averting my gaze because some things were just too beautiful to look at for long, I saw his phone was lit up with a ton of notifications. "What's on the schedule today?"

"I have another phone meeting in," he glanced at his watch, "five minutes ago. And then I need to go to Nebula and Star."

"Do you ever take a day off?"

"Not usually."

"Do other casino owners work as hard as you?"

"No, most of them delegate and collect money from other people's hard work. I'm too controlling for that."

"You? Controlling? Neeeeever."

He gave me *the look* and *the voice*. "Juliet."

"Maximo," I shot back, mimicking his deep voice.

"Brat."

"Control freak."

His sinful, sinister smile was back, causing a tremor to run down my spine. It should've been from fear, but it was from an overwhelming amount of lust.

"I can reschedule my meetings and stay here to show you how much of a control freak I can be."

I jumped off his lap and backed out of his reach. "No, no. I wouldn't want to get in the way of your work."

But even as I said it, wetness pooled between my thighs. The coil of need he'd loosened last night with his tongue and cock tightened inside me.

"Kiss me, Juliet."

I bent and pressed my lips to his, darting my tongue in to soak up the taste of bitter black coffee and Maximo.

Sinful.

Smoky.

Dark.

And so damn hot.

I stood when his phone started loudly vibrating on the desk.

"Jesus, someone wants to die," he bit out, reaching for it.

I hurried for the door, not wanting to hear him rip someone a new one.

"Black," he answered. "Yes. Yes. Hold on. Juliet."

I froze in the hallway and turned back to look at him. "Yeah?"

"Like the shirt. One of yours?"

I nodded.

"Looks like something one of the stores at Crystals would sell for a shit-ton. I'm impressed, dove." His expression hardened, and even though it'd only been a few days, I knew what was coming.

Daddy mode.

"But I don't want anyone else seeing the way your pretty tits peek out of those holes. Put a bra on."

"Got it."

"Freddy's bringing you breakfast in the sewing room. I'll be home for dinner. And I'll take tomorrow off. Anything you want to do, we'll do it."

I grinned, and his eyes dropped to focus on my mouth.

He sat forward like he was going to stand.

"Your call," I reminded him.

"Fuck my call."

I really hope he muted it.

"I don't have time to make out. I have to move my bras and panties into *our* room."

It was his turn to smile and my turn to stare.

"Juliet."

"Right." I went down the hall to the room that'd been mine for a whole year.

Considering how I'd come to live there, it was crazy that it ended up being the first place I'd ever felt safe. I'd been able to sleep without worrying Shamus would drag me from the bed—pissed and drunk and violent. Or that one of his drinking buddies would sneak in. Or that the faulty wires would start a fire, someone would break in, or any of the other stressors that'd kept me awake at night.

But as much as I'd enjoyed having my own space, sharing Maximo's was much better. I slept soundly because I knew I was even safer in his arms.

After putting on a bra, I grabbed the rest of my intimates and swimsuits before carrying them down the hall.

I dumped the load on the floor in front of the armoire before sorting them and putting everything away. When I was done, I went to my sewing room, following the scent of coffee that wafted through the air. I sat and grabbed the big mug off the tray, spinning the chair forward so I could sip my coffee and plan my project.

And then I nearly dropped the scalding hot liquid.

That sneaky bastard.

That underhanded, heavy-handed bastard.

Putting the cup down before I hurt myself—or him—I moved to the doorway.

Or maybe it was just a *way* because there was no damn door.

It was an open space.

Storming across the hall, I was ready to demand he put it back when I noticed he was still on the phone.

Maximo was leaning back in his chair, his legs kicked up on his desk and his cell pressed to his ear. But his gaze was on me as he ran his thumb along his bottom lip.

A lip that curled up in a satisfied smirk.

And then the smug, cocky son of a bitch winked.

Winked!

It was insanely hot and could work as porn for women all over the world.

But it was mine.

Not letting on that I wasn't actually mad, I glared for a few moments before returning across the hall to my coffee and my doorless sewing room.

"GRRRRR." MY FRUSTRATION grew as I reached for my scissors.

Considering I'd only been sewing for a few months, I was doing well. Not because I was gifted or effortlessly skilled. But because I worked at it for hours and hours every day. And even when I wasn't actually sewing, I was usually watching videos *about* sewing.

But as I glared at the wonky hem on the dress I was attempting, I was forced to admit I'd bitten off more than I could chew.

After tearing out the thread, I tossed the fabric to the side and went to our room.

There's only one thing that can help me relax right now.

But he's gone, so I'll settle for a swim.

I stripped down and slathered on sunblock before getting dressed in my swimsuit, coverup, and flip-flops. I grabbed my iPad and headed outside.

After dumping my stuff on the table, I slipped off my shoes and coverup before diving into the warm water. I swam a few laps before coming up to see Ash sitting on the patio couch.

"Hey," I said.

"Did you put on sunblock?"

"Yeah."

"Enough?"

"I could've slid down here on my belly like a penguin, I'm so greased up."

He gave me a dimpled smile. "Got a Diet Coke and water for you."

"Thanks."

I swam for a while longer, my mind working at the hem issue while the water worked at my tight muscles.

When my arms began to ache, I pulled myself out of the pool to chug my Diet Coke before it got warm.

"You headed in?" Ash asked.

"It's so nice, I think I'm going to stay out and read." I scanned his black tee and black slacks. Even though it was only in the low seventies, he had to be roasting in the sun. "You don't have to stay out, though."

He gave me his version of *the look.*

I rolled my eyes. "I don't know if you know this, but I've been staying home alone since I was four."

That had clearly been the wrong thing to say because his expression went hard.

I'd long ago forgiven Ash for pointing a gun at me. First of all, it wasn't like it'd been the first time someone had aimed a gun my way. At least he hadn't pressed it to my head—that hurt far worse than people assumed.

Beyond that, he hadn't done anything to make me feel unsafe since. He hadn't so much as raised his voice, even when we'd worked on math—and I was sure that experience had made him want to die a slow death in the desert.

But the anger that hardened his eyes and clenched his jaw reminded me that he wasn't just Ash with the chill vibe and dimpled smile.

Unconsciously, I took a step back.

His eyes lowered to take in the movement, his jaw clenching tighter even as his eyes softened. "Not mad at you, Juliet."

"But you *are* mad?"

"But not at you. And even if I was, you don't have to be afraid of me."

"I know," I said honestly, and not just because I was pretty sure Maximo would break his kneecaps if he so much as raised his voice at me. "Just instinct."

Again, that didn't seem to be the correct thing to say, but Ash locked his expression down. "Go read."

I nodded, snatching up my iPad and Diet Coke. Going to one of the loungers, I glanced back to see Ash typing something on his phone, his face set in an angry glare.

Stretching out, I opened one of the highlander romances Ms. Vera recommended.

I got so sucked into the world of grumpy warriors, stone castles, and sexy kilts, I didn't notice anyone approaching until they said, "Juliet."

Jumping, I nearly dropped the iPad. I raised my hand to block out the sun and looked at Cole.

"Call for you," he said, handing me a cell.

I put it to my ear. "Hello?"

"Good, it works."

At Maximo's deep voice, my body heated in a way that had nothing to do with the sun. "What works?"

Not answering my question, he said, "I'm sorry, little dove, something came up and I won't make it for dinner."

I worked to keep the disappointment from my voice, though I was sure I failed. "That's okay."

"It's fucking not, but it will be as soon as I get home to you. Hold on." His words were muffled as he talked to someone else before he came back. "Gotta run."

When the phone beeped to signal the call had been ended, I handed it to Cole.

"It's yours."

"What?"

Giving me a phone was yet another show of trust. Maximo wanted my trust, and he was extending the same to me.

Unbuttoning his suit jacket, he crouched next to the lounger. He swiped the blackened screen. Rapid firing off words as he flicked across the screens, he gave me the tour. "Browser. App store. Books. Music. YouTube. Texts. It's synced with your MacBook and your iPad, so your settings, books, music, everything transferred. Swipe from the bottom to unlock and you're good to go."

Only soaking in ten percent of what he'd said, my gaze went from him back to the phone.

My old cell hadn't been able to run games, apps, or anything else. It'd worked with prepaid cards, so more often than not, I only carried it in case I needed to call 911—the only thing I could do for free.

The phone in my hands was the antithesis of that.

One thing caught my attention most. "I can text?"

He lifted his chin and touched the speech bubble icon. Loading a new message, he began typing Maximo before selecting his number. "Easy as that."

This could be fun.

"Any other questions?" he asked.

I flipped through the screens. "How do I get to the contacts?"

Explaining tech to me was probably as frustrating for Cole as explaining math had been for Ash. But like Ash, he was calm and patient as he touched the screen a few times and brought me to the contact list.

Maximo, Ash, Cole, Marco, and Freddy were all on the list, along with someone named Miles. "Who's that?"

"Head of security for Black Resorts. If you can't get ahold of one of us in an emergency, call him."

Okkkaayyyy.

Let's hope that never happens.

"No number for Ms. Vera?" I asked.

"She hates technology. Won't even upgrade to a Kindle. Let me know if you have any issues." He went to talk to Ash before going into the pool house.

Why does he always crash in the pool house?

I brought back up the texts and typed in Maximo's name.

Me: Thank you.

I hadn't been expecting a message back, but it came instantly.

Maximo: It was selfish on my part. Now I can text you when I'm stuck in these boring as shit meetings. What're you doing?

I grinned, the flutter of giddiness settling in my belly like butterflies throwing a rager.

Me: Reading by the pool.

Maximo: Send me a pic.

I glanced over my shoulder to see Ash's face was still buried in his phone.

Feeling awkward, I opened the camera and switched it to front facing. I moved my arm around until I found a good angle and took a million pictures before getting a sendable one.

My phone vibrated a minute later.

Maximo: Christ, you're gorgeous.

Emboldened by his words, I brought the camera back up and took a picture aimed down my body. And then I took twenty more until I got a good one.

Holding my breath, I sent it before I lost my nerve.

The reply came within seconds.

Maximo: Fuck, are you trying to make me come home?

Maximo: Or just trying to make me come?

Yup, I was right.

This could be fun.

CHAPTER TWENTY-TWO

Sweet Patience

JULIET

"THIS IS WHAT you want to do?" Maximo asked, his lips tipped at one side as he looked at me.

Clutching the candy I'd pilfered from Freddy's stash, I nodded.

When I'd researched ideas for our day together, most of the things listed were geared toward tourists, partying, or were super expensive—or all three.

Going to a movie was the best option, but it seemed stupid when Maximo had a media room with recliners, a big projector screen, and a popcorn maker.

Not to mention, I got the feeling he rarely hung out and did a whole lot of nothing. Before I'd come there, I hadn't either. I'd always had more chores and errands than one person could do in a day. A year of being a homebody—by force and then by choice—had taught me how needed the occasional chill-day was.

"Phase one," I said. "Well, I guess this turned into phase three."

Phase one had been Maximo waking me with his mouth. He must've been at it for a while because by the time I woke, I was already on the edge. After I came, he'd carried me into the shower where he'd taken his time washing my body and hair before making me come again—that time with his fingers.

Phase two had been breakfast in bed where Maximo had listened to my hem frustrations. I'd listened while he'd told me about the boxer who'd dropped out of a fight with less than two weeks' notice because he thought he deserved more money. Neither Maximo nor his fight co-ordinator agreed.

Once we were done with breakfast, Maximo had thrown on a tee and his gray joggers, and I'd...

Well, I'd drooled everywhere.

But once I'd found my brain again, I'd thrown on the non-janky sleep shorts I'd made and the store-bought ripped crop. Then, much to his confusion and amusement, I'd dragged Maximo to the media room.

Grabbing the remotes as he moved, he went to the front and center recliner. I didn't try to sit in a different one. I dumped my bundle of goodies on the little table next to us before landing on his lap. I knew it was the right move when his arms circled me, hauling me closer.

He turned on the TV, clicked a bunch of buttons to load a list of movies, and handed me the remote. "Pick whatever you want."

Ultimate power.

I flipped through before landing on *Thor.*

Action movies weren't usually my preferred genre, but a Hemsworth made a girl do crazy things.

"Have you seen any of the Marvel movies?" he asked.

"Bits and pieces on TV but never all of one."

"Then we can't start here."

"What? Why?"

"Cinematic universes are made to be watched in order." He grabbed the remote and returned to the Cs. "We have to start at *Captain America.*"

A Hemsworth may make a girl do crazy things, but Chris Evans made them do batshit crazy things while he cheered them on and encouraged their individuality.

"Have you seen these?" I asked while it loaded.

"A few."

"Probably hard to binge a whole series of movies when you never take a day off," I teased.

As if I'd sent a message to the universe, his phone rang.

Me and my big mouth.

"Shit, I've got to get this." His expression was soft and apologetic as he hit pause.

"Hey, I'm the one who jinxed it."

I moved to get up, but he held me in place as he took his phone out of his pocket. "Yeah?" Whoever it was talked for a moment before Maximo bit out a harsh laugh. "That was the point." He was silent a beat. "Miles on it? Good. Get his picture around. I don't want their asses on my property, or it'll be worse. Yeah. Call if shit goes sideways."

When he ended the call and set his phone near the snacks, my curiosity got the better of me. "Everything okay?"

"My lawyers served the boxer who bailed with a breach of contract lawsuit. He called to apologize, trying to get back in. It wasn't going to happen, but we would've considered dropping the suit. Unfortunately for him, his manager got on the line and threatened Serrano."

"He should fire his manager."

"His manager is his father."

"That's a recipe for disaster."

"Now, because his old man thinks he's a made man with connections he wants to throw around, no one is going to book him."

I knew all too well what it was like to be punished for my dad's big mouth.

Poor guy.

As though he'd read my thoughts, Maximo added, "The prick apple doesn't fall far from the prick tree. Costa is a prima donna who thinks he's the Italian Mayweather."

"Why'd you book him then?"

"Because he may not be Money Mayweather good, but he's still good." His smile was cruel and cold. "And now he'll be lucky to work as an instructor at a kickboxing gym."

Yikes.

Maximo pressed his lips to my forehead before settling me back against him. He lifted the remote. "Ready?"

"Yup."

And if it sucks, I'm comfy enough to take a nap.

CAPTAIN AMERICA DID not suck.

Nor did *Captain Marvel.*

And definitely not *Iron Man.*

I enjoyed Chris Evans' good-guy, super soldier-ness, but I loved RDJ's snark and cockiness.

Apparently, I had a type.

"Iron Man 2 is next," Maximo said.

I glanced out the window to see the sun had begun to set.

Pressing the button to sit the chair upright, I stood and shook off the crumbs. "It's time for phase four."

Maximo stood, pulling me to him. "And what's that?"

"Dessert."

His gaze dropped pointedly to the empty candy boxes stacked on the table before returning to me.

"Those were snacks," I dismissed. "This is the official dessert."

"Isn't dinner supposed to come first?"

"Yeah, but then we might ruin our appetite for dessert." At his unconvinced expression, I crossed my arms. "Hey, you said I could plan the day. If you want to be a healthy adult with an appropriate diet, do it on your own time."

He smirked and gestured to the door. "Then by all means."

I grabbed his hand and pulled him toward the stairs. "First we have to change."

"Dessert is a formal occasion?"

Glancing over my shoulder to take in his furrowed brows, I laughed. "You'll see."

When we got up to our room, I released his hand and went to the armoire. Opening the drawer that held my swimsuits, I pulled out my favorite. The dark gray top had thin straps and a wrap-style front. The bottoms were tiny and white, with a dark gray feather pattern. I was pretty sure they were supposed to be palm leaves, but they looked more like feathers to me.

"Your idea of dessert is swimming?" Maximo asked.

"Just get changed."

So neither of us were tempted to jump the other while naked, I closed myself in the bathroom before stripping. I changed and pulled my hair up into a ponytail before opening the door.

I had good intentions with changing in the bathroom but there'd been a vital miscalculation in my plan.

Maximo still looked hot in his black trunks that hung way low on his hips, and I still very much wanted to jump him.

"You keep looking at me like that, Juliet, I'm gonna be ready to eat something even sweeter than dessert."

Realizing my eyes were aimed at the deep indent of his pelvic muscles, I darted them up to his face.

Oops.

But also not really.

Before I changed my mind and stripped out of my suit, I headed for the door. I didn't have to check to see if Maximo followed. I could feel him. Feel his eyes on me.

When we got downstairs, I turned to Maximo. "Can you light the fire pit?"

He lifted his chin and headed outside.

I stopped in the kitchen to get the skewers and marshmallows Freddy had stashed for me. When I got outside, the backyard looked like a small island paradise. Unseen lights dimly illuminated the path to the glowing blue pool. A fire burned in the center of the rectangular pit, the reflection of it dancing off the water.

But the most paradise-y part of paradise was Maximo in the hot tub. With his muscular, tattooed arms stretched along the ledge, he almost looked relaxed.

Almost.

But his eyes were too alert. Too watchful.

Too hungry.

The fire flickered to the right of him, casting shadows that played with his angular features.

Devilishly handsome and sinfully wicked.

Phase four is definitely my favorite.

Uh, phase one and then phase four.

Wait, phase two and three were also…

Fine, all the phases are my favorite. I planned a good day.

Maximo's eyes softened and lit with amusement when he saw my supplies. "Roasting marshmallows is phase four?"

"Technically phase four is just relaxing with the fire." I put a marshmallow on a skewer and handed it to him. "These are a bonus."

Getting my own ready, I set the bag down within reach and held Maximo's offered hand as I stepped into the water. The quiet jets were set low, the foam and bubbles soothing. It was the perfect complement to the fire.

It wasn't the first time I'd used the hot tub, but it was the first time I was using it at night with the fire pit. It was also the first time I was using it with someone.

Maximo settled me in his lap before putting his marshmallow in the fire.

In it.

Like some kind of monster.

"You're gonna," I started before his dessert turned into a torch, "burn it."

He blew out the flame. "That's the way I like it."

And then he ate the charred mess.

Again, like some kind of marshmallow monster.

"You're crazy." Positioning mine perfectly to the side, I spun the stick like I was roasting a pig on a spit. I was careful not to get it too close, unlike the insane person who grabbed another marshmallow, jabbed it onto his stick, and then jammed it into the flame. Again, he blew out his mini torch and ate it.

I waited until mine was just right before removing it from the heat. Careful not to burn myself, I slid it off and popped it into my mouth. The outside was perfectly browned with a hint of chewiness and the inside was liquid amazingness.

His arm tightened around my waist as he rested his chin on my shoulder.

Not dislodging myself, I reached back blindly until I felt the bag. Pulling a marshmallow out, I got it onto the stick and started my process again.

Once it was done, I shifted on his lap and offered him my beautiful creation.

After a couple bites, he nodded. "You're right, your method is better."

"Of course it is. Who in their right mind would eat a torched marshmallow?"

"I've never been patient."

"What? I'm *shocked.*"

He pinched my ass under the water.

"Hey!" I shook my head. "I shared my precious marshmallow with you."

Grabbing four new ones, he put two on each of our sticks. That time, he followed my expert slow cooking technique.

"I can't remember the last time I ate these," he said.

"You don't come out every night to toast marshmallows? I'm shocked again, what with all your free time and love of junk food."

He pinched my ass again, and I glared but couldn't hold it long.

Settling back against him, I ate my marshmallows that'd melted into one mega-mallow before sharing, "I've spent a lot of time out here."

"I know."

Why am I not surprised?

Maximo seemed to know every move everyone in the universe made. Taking my empty stick, he set it on the ledge behind us with his own.

"Hey—" I started before one of his hands went between my legs.

Never mind, this is better than marshmallows.

His other hand pushed into my top to tease my already hard nipples. Low and rumbly, he spoke into my ear. "Even when I shouldn't have, I'd sit in my office," he lifted his hand out of the water to point to the massive window that belonged to his office, "and watch you." Dropping his hand, he pushed it inside my suit bottoms, his finger teasing me. "Watch you swim. Watch you read. Watch you float around like you didn't have a care in the world."

Thanks to you, I didn't.

His finger slid into me as he used his hold to grind my ass against his erection. "I watched and I waited."

Swallowing hard, my word came out as a moan. "For?"

"For you. For when I could have you." Using the heel of his palm to rub my clit, he bit my neck, sucking the tender flesh hard enough that I knew it'd leave a hickey. He trailed his tongue up my neck and his lips grazed my ear as he whispered, "And just like your marshmallows, your sweetness was worth being patient."

If his hand wasn't already sending me over the edge, his words would.

My body tensed, my thoughts going hazy as everything faded.

It all snapped back when Maximo's hand stilled. He began teasing again, getting me close and then stopping.

He's trying to kill me.

The bastard.

So turned on, I was likely to explode from a strong gust of wind, I blurted, "I want to touch you."

It was his turn to go tense. "What?"

"Can I touch you, Daddy?"

"That's something you never have to ask permission to do, Juliet. Touch me any-fucking-time you want."

Turning so I was straddling him, I pulled his mouth to mine. I ran my fingers through his damp hair. I rocked my hips against him.

It was good.

So good.

But I wanted more.

Breaking the connection, I peppered smaller kisses along his stubbled jaw. "I want to taste you like you taste me."

"Christ." At his harsh curse, I pulled away, worried I'd messed up. But Maximo just cupped the side of my head in his possessive hold and stared at my mouth with heat that rivaled the fire. After a long moment, his hands dropped to span my hips and he lifted me to stand. He leaned forward to bite my nipple through my suit before rising to sit on the ledge. He positioned me on my knees between his spread legs.

A jet hit my thighs, soothing my skyrocketing nerves. In all our times together, I'd never gone down on him. I hardly got the chance to touch him before he took over.

Maybe I'd be awful.

"Take my cock out," Maximo ordered, leaning back.

Since his impressive length was already stretched up and sticking out of his waistband, I tugged the fabric the rest of the way down to free him. It really was just as beautiful as the rest of him. A vein ran up his thickness, and I really wanted to lick.

I waited for him to tell me what to do like he always did, but he just leaned back on his hands, watching me intently.

The one time I want him to tell me what to do, he's quiet.

My eyes landed on the pool house and a thought occurred to me far too late. "Is Cole—"

"At his own place."

Phew.

Tentatively, I gave in to the urge to tease my tongue along the vein. Maximo's low groan spurred me on, and I swirled my tongue over the head.

I took as much of him into my mouth as I could before sliding back up. I repeated the process, going a little farther each time. My rhythm was choppy and my positioning awkward, but I was enjoying myself.

More importantly, Maximo was enjoying himself if his grunts, groans, and roughly whispered praise were anything to go by.

I knew his patience and control were running thin when he started rocking his hips. And I knew they were gone when he wrapped my ponytail around his hand and took over completely.

Using his hold, he moved me how he wanted. Faster than I would've gone. Deeper than I would've gone.

After a minute, he slowed me to a leisurely pace. "Drop your ass to your heels."

I sat back but kept my torso forward so I didn't lose his cock.

"My greedy girl," he groaned, making my pussy pulse, constricting around nothing and just as greedy as my mouth. "Spread your knees."

When I did, the rush of water that'd been hitting my legs shot between them. I inched over until the jet was aimed at my clit.

Reaching over to pop open the inconspicuous control panel, Maximo adjusted the dials until the pressure increased.

Oh God. Too much.

Maximo moved my head again, jamming his cock all the way back until I had to fight to relax my throat.

Oh God. Not enough.

I didn't think I could come from water hitting my clit, no matter how hard the pressure. But paired with the obscene hotness of Maximo filling my mouth, it wasn't long before I was teetering on the edge.

The naughtiness of what I was doing.

Of what he was doing.

Of being outside.

Of *everything.*

It worked together, dragging every bit of pleasure from me until I was wrung raw. The onslaught of water was too intense on my oversensitive body.

It *hurt.*

I put my knees together, but Maximo pulled my hair and bit out, "Don't fucking close your legs."

Tears filled my eyes, and I used every ounce of willpower to spread them.

"Fuck. Yes. That's *my* good girl." His eyes went hooded as he released my hair and cupped the sides of my head. Using both hands to keep me in place, he thrust into my mouth.

He fucked my face.

Relentless and brutal and unhinged.

The power that came from making him lose his carefully held control was addicting. I didn't think I'd ever get enough of that rush or of him.

So fast, I wasn't expecting it, the overstimulated ache between my legs switched to bliss. The lines between pain and pleasure blurred as another orgasm tore through me.

"Close your legs and give me your eyes," Maximo ordered once I was done.

Lids I hadn't realized had closed snapped open as I gratefully shifted to protect my tender clit. His wild gaze went unfocused even as he maintained eye contact.

The intense intimacy was as terrifying as it was enthralling, and I couldn't look away. I couldn't even blink.

And I was glad I didn't because I got to watch as Maximo pulled my mouth off him and fisted his cock. Within a few rapid strokes, his deep groan sounded around us as his come shot out, landing on my lips and chest before dripping between us.

Panting like he'd run a marathon in under an hour, Maximo's eyes traveled my face. "I want to take a picture of you right now and hang it on every surface in my house." He paused before adding, "The ones no one else can see."

I was relieved he didn't have his phone because I didn't doubt he'd follow through. The sentiment was sweet, though. Obscene, but sweet.

Opening the control panel, Maximo turned off the hot tub and fire before standing and offering me his hand.

I climbed out and bent to grab the marshmallows and sticks.

I'm never going to be able to look at the hot tub the same again.

After returning the supplies to the kitchen, I followed Maximo up to the bedroom.

Stripping off his trunks—and giving me a beautiful view that I wanted to photograph and display where only I could see—Maximo pulled on his joggers, sans shirt. "What did you plan for dinner, dove?"

It took me a moment to prod my brain into working. "Pizza."

"So you're set on eating nothing of nutritional value today," he surmised.

"Hey. Our sandwiches had lettuce on them."

He arched an eyebrow but didn't argue further. "What do you want on the pizza?"

I'm not the only one who's more agreeable after coming.

Filing that away for future use.

Schooling my expression and tone to be nonchalant, I said, "Extra pineapple and anchovies."

Okay, this is also a moment I wish I could capture and keep forever.

Horrified disgust twisted his features as he grimaced. "I'll order two different ones."

I burst out laughing. "I'm kidding. Pepperoni with extra cheese. Like, a butt-ton of extra cheese."

"I'll tell them those exact words." Palming the back of my head, he pulled me to him and pressed his lips to mine, clearly not caring what was dried there. He broke the kiss and issued orders. "Go change and clean up while I order the pizza, then meet me downstairs. We'll watch the next movie while we eat."

I watched him—and his muscular back—leave.

Maybe I can convince him to take more days off.

I'll just be sure to ask after *I make him come.*

WHY AM I even surprised?

Standing in the doorway of the sewing room, I looked in at the shiny new Serger sitting next to my sewing machine. It was big and intimidating and unbelievable.

Turning around, I saw Maximo's office door was closed, which meant he was gone. Of course.

I walked over and grabbed the note off the machine.

Vera said this will help with your hem issue.

-Daddy

God. He was unreal. He'd paid attention, figured out what I needed, and then did it.

I'd never, ever get used to that.

Bringing up my texts, I typed out a few different messages telling Maximo he didn't have to keep buying me things. That I didn't need anything. That him listening to me while I'd vented had been enough.

I deleted all of them before deciding on something simpler.

Me: Thank you, Daddy.

His return message came within seconds, affirming I'd made the right choice.

Maximo: That's my good girl.

I'm so screwed.

CHAPTER TWENTY-THREE

Silver Tongue

JULIET

"*L*ITTLE DOVE."

"No dove here." I burrowed into the pillows to hide my eyes from the evil bedside lamp. "Only a raccoon."

"Need you to wake up for a minute, then you can go back to sleep."

Cracking one eye—it was the best I could do—I peered up at Maximo.

It didn't matter if he was up crazy late or just working from home, Maximo was always awake, showered, and dressed at an ungodly hour, like some sort of weirdo.

But he was a weirdo I missed.

It'd been almost two weeks since his day off with me, and I'd barely seen him. Each day, he'd been gone by the time I woke and got home after I'd gone to sleep.

"You awake enough to listen?" he rumbled, amused tenderness threading his tone.

"Mmhmm."

"I'll make it quick before you start snoring again."

That was enough to make both lids pop open. "I do *not* snore."

"Like a foghorn."

"No, I don't."

"Like a forest of lumberjacks sawing wood."

"Didn't you have something important to talk to me about?" I gritted out.

"You're coming to the fight tonight."

I shot upright, nearly hitting his jaw with my head. "What?"

"And staying the weekend with me at Moonlight."

"I am? We are?"

I'd been dying to visit his hotels. Any of them. All of them. I didn't care, I just wanted to see. But I'd kept that desire to myself. Part of it was I understood how busy he was. He didn't have time to entertain me or be a tour guide, and he'd likely feel obligated to do both.

Mostly, though, I'd worried he'd say no. Taking me to the underground fight where everyone had been wrapped up in their own depravity was one thing. But taking me to his place of work was far different. While logically I'd have understood if he didn't want his personal life aired at work, I knew I would've felt like his dirty secret if he refused me. That would've hurt.

And that hurt would've festered. It'd been easier to not even put it out there.

I couldn't get rejected if I never asked.

His lips tipped. "I take it you like that idea."

"A lot."

"It'll be a lot of waiting around."

"That's fine. I'm just excited to *finally* see one of your resorts."

His eyes narrowed.

Oops.

And shit.

"Have you been wanting to?" At my non-answer, he lifted his chin. "You've been wanting to. Why didn't you tell me?"

Not sharing the main reason, I gave him a smaller truth. "I know you're really busy, and I didn't want to be in the way."

"You'd never be in the way. A distraction, fuck yeah, but one I want. I didn't know you wanted to come. You never said anything so I thought…" His eyes went soft as he stroked my hair and finished, "I thought casinos would be hard for you because of Shamus."

"Gambling is probably ruined for me," I agreed. "But there's more than just that, right?"

"Right." His lips tipped before going serious. "If you want something, you need to tell me. Sometimes the answer will be no, but telling me what you want is a rule. Understood?"

"Understood."

"I'm betting you don't want to wake up and come with me now."

"I do not."

He grinned.

And it was beautiful.

"Ash will bring you later. I'll have Vera pack you a bag, so make sure you let her know what you want. One of your dresses ready?"

I wish. Maybe then I wouldn't want to put my head through the pretty dove canvas.

I shook my head. "But I've got—"

"I'll send something over."

"Maximo, I have…" I started before his eyes narrowed.

"Who am I?" he bit out.

"Daddy."

"And what does Daddy fucking love to do?"

"Take care of me."

"Then stop trying to take that away from me, or I'm not going to be happy. And neither will your burning, red ass."

Because he'd been gone so much and therefore unable to spank my ass, his threat made a surprising amount of longing surge through me.

And I must not have done a good job hiding it because Maximo's expression shifted from hotly stern to just hotly hot. "You like that."

I did.

A lot.

"Not the you-being-unhappy part," I clarified.

"Noted." Stroking my hair, he lowered his voice. "I haven't been doing a good job taking care of you. I'll make it right."

You're the only person who's ever taken care of me.

I opened my mouth to tell him that, but he stood and flicked off the light.

"Go back to sleep." His gruff order was softened by his sweet, lingering kiss. "I'll see you later."

Excitement and anticipation bubbled in me, and I didn't think I'd be able to sleep.

But I was out immediately—likely before he even got downstairs.

"SAY THAT AGAIN."

In the dark, dank room far below Moonlight, the squirrelly motherfucker tied to a chair spit out a mouth full of blood before repeating, "Viktor Dobrow paid me to hang around your resorts."

Viktor Dobrow.

Club owner, drug and woman peddler, and pain in my fucking ass.

"Why?" I asked.

"He didn't say, and I'm not stupid enough to question an order."

"But you're stupid enough to come here?"

"He paid me."

That was all we'd be getting from Tommy Janson because that was all he knew. He was exactly the kind of idiot who'd blindly follow whatever orders he was given—especially if he profited without having to do any actual work.

Even if said orders landed him on my radar.

And in The Basement.

Unless it was going to get too messy—like with Murphy—The Basement was where we brought people. People who owed me. People who crossed me. People who fucked me over.

And, in my eyes, Tommy Janson was guilty of all three.

Ash stood with Marco, waiting for my order.

Jerking my head toward Tommy, I said, "Dump his body outside one of Dobrow's clubs."

"What?" Janson shrieked. "Nah, man, no way. I'm not going down for just watching your place. I didn't see shit to report back. I didn't make trouble."

"Christ, I hate liars. You got caught with your hand in a woman's purse."

"Yeah, but I didn't steal anything from *you*."

"You steal on my property, you make my guests feel unsafe. That's costing me money."

Fucking dumbass.

"I'll work for you, man. You wouldn't even have to pay me. I'll tell Dobrow whatever you want, and I'll report back to you. I'll ask questions. I'll be your eyes and ears."

I had eyes and ears all over the city, ranging from high-level officials to card slappers, showgirls, and a very adult Buzz Lightyear who worked the Strip, posing with a variety of other *toys*. There were things to learn from everyone, but usually those who were dismissed and disregarded garnered the most useful information.

It was easy to overhear things when people forgot they existed.

But deals only worked when I trusted the person. And I didn't trust Tommy with a spork.

"I want to know when it's done," I told Marco.

"Wait! C'mon, we can figure this out. I can do something. I got good connections. I can score anything your clients need, I swear."

That wasn't a surprise. The sallow, waxiness of his pasty skin made it clear he knew his way around drugs.

I didn't like that shit in my casinos, I sure as hell wasn't going to supply it. Even at the makeshift arenas, coke, weed, and limited uppers were allowed, but anything else was confiscated by security during pat-downs and tossed. It hadn't taken long before people stopped trying to sneak it in.

Ash took out his little black kit, unzipped it, and pulled out a syringe. He glanced at it before putting it back and getting a different one. "Ready?"

"I hate this part," Marco sighed, approaching Tommy.

"Whoa, point made. Okay? Point made. I won't go back to Dobrow at all. I won't ever contact you. You'll never see me again, I swear it." The sound of something dripping on the floor came seconds before the scent of ammonia filled the small space.

Marco grimaced. "Damn, just once can't someone keep their piss where it belongs."

"Look how orange it is." Ash shook his head. "Jesus, drink a glass of water every once in a while." He smirked, undoing Tommy's belt. "Oh wait."

Cruel bastard.

"What're you doing?" Tommy shifted away as his belt was pulled free, panic widening his eyes. "Get away from me, you freak."

"Trust me, if I swung that way, I'd have higher standards."

After Marco pushed the sleeves of Tommy's grubby shirt up, exposing the plethora of scabs, scars, and track marks, Ash tightened the belt around Tommy's upper arm.

He had to know we weren't just giving him a free high, but that didn't stop him from watching the needle like… well, like a junkie getting his next fix. His movements and protests were half-assed, and it didn't take much effort for Marco to subdue him long enough for Ash to inject him.

I opened the door behind me and slipped out into the hall before the urine smell permeated into my clothes and not just my nostrils.

"Done?" Cole asked.

I lifted my chin. "Marco and you can handle the dump while Ash gets Juliet."

Cole would jam Dobrow's cheap security cameras so they could dump the body outside whichever of his clubs was most deserted.

Minus a few punches to Janson's mouth, there were no signs of a struggle. Ash's skilled rope work wouldn't leave any bruising or abrasions, Tommy hadn't put up a fight, and his own belt was used.

As far as anyone would be concerned, it was an OD.

But Dobrow would know.

"Get anything useful out of him?" Cole asked.

"Not unless you consider him pissing himself useful," I said.

His lip curled. "I think that room has seen more piss than the toilets in this place. Why is everyone's first instinct to piss themselves when they're about to die?"

Not everyone.

Twice Juliet thought she was facing death, and twice she faced it with strength.

"When I die," he continued, "it'll be with a beautiful woman riding my dick and another riding my face. And, unlike that diplomat at Nebula with the golden shower fetish, there will be no piss involved."

Little turned my stomach, but the reminder of how the diplomat had left that room did it. "Fucking hell, don't ever mention that shit to me again. I had to toss the whole bed and hire one of the crews that handle crime scenes to scrub that place out."

Cole smiled. "Did Serrano tell you the diplomat is trying to get tickets to the Angelo-Novak match next month? He wants to drop a shit-ton on bets and a suite."

"I don't give a shit how much he wants to spend, unless he's willing to sleep in a room coated in plastic, he's not welcome."

"Better tell Serrano that."

I checked my watch.

I had a shit-ton of preparations and inevitable fires to put out for the event that night. Stopping to deal with Janson had set me behind, so I needed to get caught up quickly if I wanted to have time for dinner with Juliet.

I didn't have time to argue with Serrano.

But I also didn't have the stomach to face a destroyed, golden showered room again.

Rubbing my palm down my face, I sighed. "I'll talk to him."

"Good luck. You know how he is with money."

Yeah, he liked it and wasn't big on turning away people willing to part with theirs. He'd set up a fight between chipmunks if he could get people to bet on it.

Pressing my thumb to the elevator's panel, the doors slid open and I went inside. It quickly traveled up before opening on the ground floor.

I took off toward the arena to see what fresh hell awaited.

And to argue with Serrano about a piss-happy diplomat.

JULIET

HOLY SHIT.

I'd known Maximo's casinos were beautiful. I'd also known they'd be better than my expectations because that was how it went with anything to do with Maximo.

But I had no idea Moonlight would be so absolutely breathtaking— and I'd only seen the outside.

Located not far off the Strip, the curvature and points of the main building resembled the phases of the moon. There was another taller building behind it, which I assumed was the hotel.

I had my nose practically pressed against the window as we drove closer.

"He's gonna be pissed," Ash murmured.

"What?"

"Nothing."

Fighting the urge to nervously fidget, I placed my hands in my lap before immediately moving my right one off so my tennis bracelet didn't snag the lace overlay of my magenta minidress.

Is this what the other half worries about?

Ruining their beautiful clothes with their equally beautiful jewelry?

Ash bypassed the main entrance and pulled up to a small road I hadn't noticed through the greenery. Rolling down his window to punch a number into the keypad, the barrier gate opened and he drove up the path that edged a pond.

In the center, there was a fountain topped with a beautiful sculpture of a woman in a flowing dress. Even though it was solid, the way the dress was sculpted made it look as though it were moving in the breeze. She held a bow with the arrow drawn, a mix of femininity and badassery.

"Who is that statue of?" I asked.

"Artemis. She's the Greek goddess of the hunt and the moon."

Continuing up the road, we drove under the overpass where a line of cars, limos, and idling taxis were backed up. Ash pulled into a tucked-away spot near security vehicles before killing the engine and getting out.

I opened the door and climbed out. "Do I need my bag?"

"I'll bring your bag up to the room."

I didn't argue because I likely would've toppled trying to lug that sucker around—Vera's idea of a weekend bag differed greatly from mine.

As we walked, he pulled his phone out and typed something. "Boss is near the shops."

"Since I have zero clue where that is, lead the way."

The electric doors slid open, and I stepped forward and gawked worse than a tourist seeing a line of showgirls for the first time.

Holy shit.

The outside was stunning, but it was nothing compared to the inside. The rounded glass atrium roof was covered in hundreds of thousands of twinkle lights that resembled the night sky. There was an attached twisting wrought iron arch spanning across with an illuminated half-moon.

Ash pointed to it, moving his hand with the curve. "Every hour it moves a spot to the next phase."

"It's so pretty."

Crowds of people posed in front of the massive lattice wall in the center of the room. More twisted iron spelled out *Moonlight* in a whimsical font, the name surrounded by vibrant green vines and beautiful white flowers that entwined through the lattice.

"Moonflowers," Ash supplied.

They found a theme and stuck with it, that's for sure.

Everything fit, down to the tiniest detail. Even the tile under my feet were a soft blackish blue with the occasional silver old-timey moon design stamped on one.

I glanced around at all the security guards, employees, and prominent signs making it clear no one under twenty-one would be permitted on the gaming floor.

"Uh." I stopped Ash and whispered, "Am I going to be allowed in?"

"You're Maximo's."

My heart squeezed at the sound of that.

He started walking, and I worked to keep the guilty expression off my face as I moved with confidence.

Or tried to.

My worry was for nothing, though, because no one glanced my way. A few people raised their chins at Ash, but otherwise we were given a wide berth.

Well, in an official capacity, at least.

Ash wasn't ignored by the women we passed, most of whom shifted to walk closer to him.

Surprisingly, he only gave them the same cursory glance he gave everyone else.

Keeping to the perimeter, we rounded a room packed with slot machines of every theme and style. Lights flashed, music and sounds rang out, people cheered or groaned.

It was sensory overstimulation times twenty.

We turned into a different area and went straight down the middle, passing table games of different types and limits. I averted my eyes from the blackjack and poker tables, my stomach clenching at memories I wished I could burn from my brain.

It seemed like we'd walked the entirety of the sprawling casino when we finally exited into a separate corridor. We turned and continued on, passing store after store. I glanced up at the second level that overlooked us, but I couldn't see what any of those were.

When we reached the end of the hall, it opened into a smaller atrium that resembled the main one. In the center, another statue of Artemis—I was assuming that's who it was—stood proudly above a waterfall fountain. It was beautiful.

But not as beautiful as the man who stood next to it with his hands in his pockets and his brooding eyes on me.

Belatedly realizing he wasn't alone, I glanced at the small cluster of people. Positioned behind him, Marco looked bored, as usual. Cole tapped away at an iPad before passing it to another man.

My gaze skimmed over the man talking to Maximo, and though he looked familiar, I couldn't place him. He continued talking even though he didn't have Maximo's full attention.

I slowed my steps, not wanting to interrupt.

It was the wrong move because Maximo shook his head and crooked a finger at me.

Oops.

Picking up the pace, my heels clicked on the tile as I hurried.

As soon as I got within reach, he hauled me to him and kissed me.

Right there.

At his work.

With people around.

As one of those people talked.

And it was not a quick peck. Or even a more affectionate yet still closed mouth one.

It was a *kiss*, with dancing tongues and nipping teeth. The kind that curled my toes and stole my breath.

Pulling away just enough so he could meet my eyes, Maximo said, "You look gorgeous, dove."

"Thank you for the pretty dress, D—Maximo," I hurried to correct.

At the name, his demeanor changed. His jaw clenched and his sharp eyes grew cold. His tone held that same coldness, stern and in full-on Daddy mode. "Who am I, Juliet?"

My gaze darted to the side—not that I could see anything but him.

Gripping my chin, he forced my eyes back to him. "I asked you a question, you know I expect an answer."

In contrast with his even one, my voice was barely more than a whispered squeak. "I didn't think you'd want me to call you that when there are other people around."

"I don't give a fuck who's around. Who am I, Juliet?"

"Daddy," I forced out.

"We'll talk about this later."

Oh shit.

I'm pretty sure talk *is code for* spank.

Keeping a possessive arm around me, Maximo turned me to face the others. He gestured to the man who looked like Derek Morgan from *Criminal Minds*. "That's Miles, head of security."

"I have your number," I said before throwing my whole self directly into the garbage—in my mind, at least. In real life, I stammered an explanation. "In my phone. In case of an emergency."

I could feel Maximo's silent chuckle.

Good, he's amused, not horrified.

Miles' lips were tipped.

Good, he's also amused, not planning a restraining order.

He offered me his hand. "I have your number, too. Nice to put a face to it, Juliet."

Maximo continued the introductions, pointing to the man I vaguely recognized. "This is Serrano. You *don't* have his number."

I'm never living this down.

Serrano unexpectedly pulled me into a hug that lasted all of two-point-five seconds before Maximo tugged me back against him, wrapping his arm around my chest. Serrano wasn't put-off as he grinned. "I understand you're the one to thank for my pay raise and bonus."

The pieces clicked together, and I realized were I recognized him from. He'd been the emcee at the warehouse, and I'd made a throwaway comment about how he deserved more money for amping up the crowd.

I had no idea Maximo would actually do it.

"You did a good job drumming up last-minute bets," I said.

Waving away my praise, Serrano shook his head. "Those rich assholes are all too happy to throw their money away." He leaned closer and lowered his voice. "But if you want to tell Maximo I deserve an extra week of vacation and a company car, that'd work."

"You have a company car," Maximo pointed out.

"It's almost two years old. Practically a *Flintstones* car." He shot me a wink before going serious as he gave Maximo his attention. "Anything else you can think of?"

"No, we should be set. Call if there's any issues."

"There's always issues."

"Call for the big ones." Maximo turned toward Ash. "All good?"

Ash lifted his chin. "Quiet day. You get my message?"

"I'll make plans," he said ambiguously before checking his watch. "Go eat and we'll meet at Supermoon in two hours."

With their orders, Ash, Marco, and Cole took off to the right, Miles went to the left, and Serrano walked down the way I'd come.

Turning me in his hold so I was facing him, Maximo tucked my hair behind my ear. "I'm so tempted to bring you up to the room, spank your ass until you can't sit, and then fuck you until neither of us can move."

I was right, talk *was code for* spank.

"But we need to eat. The rest will wait until later." He studied me for a moment as he skimmed his fingers down my neck. "Glad you like that idea, too."

I didn't bother denying it. Because even if I swore the pain sounded horrendous, the coil of need that tightened low in my belly said otherwise.

"I set reservations at the French restaurant, but we can switch to Asian or— "

"French is good," I answered instantly, my mind on bread.

Putting his palm to my lower back, Maximo steered me to a glass elevator. We rode it to the second floor and got off.

Like the downstairs, the long path was lined with stores and drink stands. We kept going until we reached a set of etched doors. Maximo opened one, holding it so I could enter first.

The interior of the restaurant was much different than the exterior, with brick walls, exposed wood beams, matching tables, and red chairs. Only a few subtle moons and wrought iron details tied in the Moonlight theme.

It was reminiscent of a French bistro—or what TV and movies portrayed one to be.

Bypassing the long line of people waiting, we approached the podium.

"Mr. Black," a woman in a sleek suit greeted, already standing at the ready with two menus in hand. "Right this way."

We followed her to a table against the floor to ceiling window. It overlooked a courtyard filled with palm trees and twinkle lights. Once we sat, she handed us the menus emblazoned with the name *Parisian Crescent*. "Liz will be right with you."

She wasn't kidding because no sooner had she stepped away did the server take her place.

Wide-eyed and terrified, her voice shook. "Good evening, I'm Liz. May I start you off with something to drink?"

"Just water for me, please," I said with a smile I hoped was reassuring.

"Club soda with lime, please," Maximo said, not looking up from his menu.

She nodded and rushed away like someone had lit a fire under her ass.

I watched her go, surprised she didn't just continue out the door to get away from Maximo. "Do you always inspire terror?"

"If I have my way."

Which meant yes because he always had his way.

"Isn't there some saying about catching more flies with honey than vinegar?" I asked.

"I don't want to catch flies. I want competent employees who do shit my way. Call me a bastard, an asshole, or even," his lips tipped, "a control freak. Their terror means I've made the expectations *and* consequences clear."

Thinking about the consequence I had coming my way later, I shifted in my chair.

Maximo didn't miss it. "Do I inspire terror in you, little dove?"

Swallowing hard, I admitted, "Sometimes."

"Smart girl," he rumbled, his eyes going hooded as he rubbed his thumb across his bottom lip.

I was beginning to recognize that was his tell.

And it told me he was thinking very naughty thoughts.

Before I could ask what they were, Liz approached with our drinks. "Have you decided what you'd like?"

Yes.

Maximo.

Naked.

Bossing me around and taking care of me.

Taking my silence as indecision, she pointed to an item on the menu I'd yet to even look at. "Chef Frédéric wanted me to tell you that he thinks you'd enjoy the gnocchi gratinée."

"Uh, okay I'll have that then," I agreed, even though I had no clue what gnocchi matinee or whatever she'd said was.

"Mr. Black?"

"Steak, medium rare, side salad with house dressing instead of frites."

I'm pretty sure frites are fries.

Who chooses a salad when they could have fries?

At the very least, have both.

"I'll put this right in," Liz said, taking the menus before hustling off like the boogieman and all her exes were chasing her.

"Quick question," I said before amending, "two, actually."

"Yes?"

"What's gnocchi gra-whatever?"

"It's baked mac and cheese but made with gnocchi."

Oh. That sounded delicious and exactly like something I'd order. Which led to my next question... "Who is Chef Frédéric?"

"Freddy. If he isn't working at the house or developing new recipes, he picks up shifts at the restaurants."

Freddy and Ash had already told me as much, but I hadn't put together Freddy was a nickname for Frédéric.

A thought occurred to me. "Since I'm assuming he isn't Freddy Frédéric, what's his first name?"

Leaning in, Maximo lowered his voice. "Don't call him it, or he won't bake you funfetti cake again."

I made the motion of crossing my heart because that was a consequence I couldn't handle. "Is it Milford? Mervin? Wilbur?"

"Laurent."

How anticlimactic.

My lips turned down. "I thought it'd be something unusual. Why doesn't he like it?"

"It's a family name."

"Okay?"

"He hates his family."

"That would do it," I muttered.

Between Ms. Vera, Freddy, and now me, it seems like Maximo collects strays.

Maybe he's more of a softie than he lets on.

I thought again about my impending consequences.

Never mind.

"FASTER, LITTLE DOVE."

Swiveling my hips, I moved up and down his length.

I liked the way Maximo looked at me always.

But I loved the way he looked up at me while I rode his cock.

So close.

Just need to find the spot.

"Faster," he repeated.

"No."

"You don't get to say no to Daddy," Maximo growled right before he flipped us. Slamming in, he hit the spot I needed.

It was perfect.

The entire night had been.

Dinner had been delicious.

When we'd gotten to the Supermoon Arena, Maximo had kept me with him while he'd checked on everything. Once he'd been sure there were no last-minute hiccups, he'd taken us to ringside seats, again settling me on his lap.

According to him, he hadn't been a fan of me sitting so far away during dinner.

According to me, I'd agreed.

As we'd watched, his hard expression had been imposing and intimidating to everyone else. But I'd gotten his sweet side. His funny jokes whispered in my ear. His teasing bites on my neck.

The fights may not have been as excitingly vicious as the warehouse ones, but the rest more than made up for it.

Once the last bout ended by TKO, Maximo had hurried me to his private elevator, impatient to get me alone.

To lift me in his arms and take my mouth during the ride up.

To carry me through his penthouse.

To strip me down.

To bend me over the bed and spank my ass.

To let me ride his perfect cock until we both went mad.

Riding him had been good.

But him putting all his strength into each thrust, relentlessly filling me over and over was *far* better.

My pussy tightened, the pulses of pleasure zipping through every last nerve ending in my body.

And then he slowed, stealing it all away.

Releasing a whimper of need, I wrapped my legs around him and dug my heels in, urging him to go faster.

He didn't, of course.

"Who am I?" he growled, his muscles taut as he held back and continued the torment.

Long strokes out, gentle thrusts in.

I tried to rock my hips, but his pace slowed even more.

"My Daddy," I rushed out.

"Only when we're at home?"

"Everywhere."

"Only sometimes?"

"All the time."

"Remember that, Juliet. Remember who takes care of you. Who knows what you like. What you *need*." His hips ground against me, and I was so full. Stretched. Impaled by his cock until I felt as though it were splitting me in two.

And I was happy to break if it meant the coil of need broke, too.

Maximo sped up, his hand going between us so his thumb could stroke my clit. "I don't give a shit who is around. I want people to know what a lucky bastard I am to have you. I want them to know you're mine, and I'm your Daddy. Is that understood?"

Unable to speak, I nodded frantically so he wouldn't stop.

But he didn't accept my nonverbal answer. He eased the pressure on my clit. "Whose are you?"

"Yours."

The pressure returned as he rubbed tight circles. "Say it again."

My neck arched, my orgasm hovering around the edge, so close to crashing over me. Drowning me. Forcing the words out while I could, I rasped, "I'm yours."

"Fuck. Yes," Maximo grunted as he lost control, fucking me harder than he ever had—which was saying something.

My orgasm tore through me, eviscerating me from the inside out. I didn't break. I *shattered* into a million shards, and Maximo was all that held me together.

Head falling back, Maximo groaned, harsh and low, as he came, filling me. His thrusts slowed before he planted himself deep.

Slumping forward, he gave me most of his weight as he licked and nipped my neck, collarbone, and breasts. "I could spend the rest of my life buried in this pussy and it wouldn't be long enough."

His touch was addicting.

But it was those obscenely sweet words he offhandedly spoke with his silver tongue that were the most dangerous.

Before I could respond—not that I planned to—he rolled off me. "Go get ready for bed, Juliet."

My exhausted body and I had no interest in arguing, so I climbed off the bed and opened my suitcase.

Helllooooooo.

Right on top, there was a sinfully decadent lacy gray bodysuit I'd never seen before. There was no way Maximo knew about it, otherwise he'd have told me to put it on before immediately ripping it off.

He was not a patient man.

This explains Ms. Vera's mischievous smile.

She's a great wing-woman.

Since putting on lingerie after sex was like ordering dinner after you were already full, I pushed it to the side and grabbed my toiletries before going into the bathroom.

When I returned, Maximo was on his phone. His eyes were on me, alert and furious—though that part didn't seem aimed my way. "Let me know."

"Everything okay?" I asked when he ended the call.

"Just some post-fight bullshit. It happens." He went into the bathroom, returning a couple minutes later smelling like mint and him. Rather than climbing into bed with me, he stood next to it. "Tired?"

I sprawled like a starfish. "Exhausted."

"The good kind?"

"The *best* kind." Yawning, I muttered, "I take it there's a reason you're not in bed with me."

"I need to make a few calls in the living room."

"Can I stay here and sleep?"

"Yes."

"Will you come in and spoon me?"

"As soon as fucking possible."

"Then enjoy your calls."

He bent to take my mouth, and God, his kiss had the power to wake me up faster than a triple shot of espresso.

Before things could get *really* good, he pulled away. "I'll be back."

"I'll be here."

"And thank fucking Christ for that," he muttered before leaving the room.

Sinfully charming with a silver tongue.

I'm in so much danger.

CHAPTER TWENTY-FOUR

Tease

JULIET

WHY AM I SO SORE?

Oh.

Right.

I need to stop breaking the rules.

Or maybe break them more.

I'm not sure which.

Aching yet content, I dropped my head against the shower wall and let the jets hit my muscles.

It felt good, but the one at home was better.

When I was finished and dressed, I started to pull my hair up into a messy bun when I caught my reflection.

First, I saw the small smile that seemed to permanently tip my lips.

That observation was quickly forgotten as I took in the love bites that marred the skin. They were not subtle, but they were undeniably hot.

What is that man's obsession with marking me?

Leaving my hair down to hide them, I went into the penthouse's living room to find Marco waiting.

Sitting in a chair with a cup of coffee, he barely glanced up from his phone as he pointed to the kitchen bar. "Breakfast."

I walked over to see a bowl of yogurt topped with fruit and granola. *My fave.*

Sitting on a stool, I faced away from the kitchen as I held the bowl and ate. I checked everything out since I hadn't seen it the night before. It was swanky, carrying over the color theme and wrought iron and mirrored details.

"What are those two doors?" I asked Marco.

He didn't glance up. "Second bedroom and bathroom."

He has the emotional range of a potato.

Setting the empty bowl down, I got up and...

Just stood there.

I knew I wanted to get out. Explore. See something. Do something.

I just had no idea what that *something* was.

After a few moments, Marco finally looked at me. "Want to go swimming?"

It seemed anticlimactic to do something I could do at home, but I did love a good swim. "Maybe."

"The pool downstairs has a lazy river around it. Or you can use the one on the balcony."

I'd thought he was kidding, but I should've known Marco didn't joke. Or smile. Or laugh. Or feel human emotions.

"There's a pool out there?"

He jerked his head toward the floor to ceiling windows.

Going over to the sliding glass doors, I peered out to see a small balcony with two lounge chairs and an infinity pool.

A pool.

All the way up, a billion stories in the air.

On the balcony.

It was terrifying. It was also beautiful, but there was no way in hell I was stepping foot out there when the design made it look as though I'd plummet to my death at any moment.

"I'd rather not die today," I muttered, backing away as my heart raced and my palms grew clammy.

"Then what do you want to do?"

I thought about what I'd seen the night before in the atrium. "Uhhh... Arcade?"

"Whatever you want."

"Or we can just hang here and watch movies?"

"Whatever you want."

"Oh! We could get those big twisty cups with the blended drinks." At Marco's look, I added, "Mine being non-alcoholic, of course."

"Whatever you want."

"Is that all you can say?" I asked Marco.

"No."

I growled my frustration, and it was small, but Marco's lips tipped. Just a hint.

Maybe I've given him a tic.

"Can we walk the Strip?" I asked.

"No."

My eyes narrowed. "You said whatever I wanted."

"Boss wants you on the property, so anything you want that keeps you here."

"So that means hookers, blow, and roulette are still on the table?"

Marco chuckled, and I wasn't sure I'd ever heard it before. "No." He picked up his phone and typed as he spoke. "There's the arcade, bowling, shopping—"

"You'd go shopping?"

"You wanna shop, we'll shop," he said without a hint of a grimace or dread.

Babysitting duty must suck. What kind of badass wants to follow a woman around all day?

"I can always go on my own..." I started before catching his glare. "Never mind."

Much like his boss, Marco was too observant and the pieces clicked. "You worried I'm gonna be bored?"

"Maybe," I muttered. "I just feel bad someone's always forced to babysit me instead of creating badass mayhem."

"We're not forced. Maximo asked, we agreed. We could've said no."

That was surprising. I'd just assumed it was an order.

Maximo was good at giving those.

"And I don't know what you think our daily life is," he continued, "but Ash is currently driving Maximo all over the city. Cole is banging his head against a wall, trying to supervise a new booking system installation at Star. That ain't mayhem."

"Seems like you've got the better assignment," I admitted because anything beat Vegas traffic or technology frustration.

"I do. But, Juliet, I'm a bodyguard. My job is to guard, not be entertained. I take it seriously. I take it even more seriously because one, I like you, and two, you're important to Maximo. And him trusting me with you means I'd fucking eat a bullet before I betrayed that trust."

It was the most I'd ever heard him say at one time, and he'd made it count. His words swirled around me like a warm sense of security I'd rarely felt in my life.

"Now I'll ask again," he continued, "what do you want to do?"

"Walk around and see the place."

He jerked his head toward the room. "Put some shoes on and let's go."

Hurrying into the room, I dug around my bag for my gray shoes and slid them on. I came out to find Marco ending a call. He took another minute to type something on his phone before scanning his thumb to open the elevator.

Once we were closed in, I asked, "Can you add my thumbprint to the scanner or do I have to be James Bond?"

"Ask Maximo."

"How many other people have access to this elevator?

"Ask Maximo."

"Has anyone ever told you that you talk entirely too much?"

He smirked. "No."

"I'm shocked."

When the elevator slid open at the main floor, I followed Marco because my sense of direction was off. Like the lack of clocks, the confusing layout was undoubtedly by design to keep people in the casino and spending cash. We walked a different route than Ash and I had, but we still ended up in the atrium.

I glanced around, but none of the shops looked familiar. "Wait, this is a different place than yesterday."

"Figured we'd start at one end and work our way across." He turned into the first store.

I hurried to follow into the minimalist store. There were shelves displaying purses and other accessories, but not much else.

"I wasn't planning on going in," I whispered to him.

"How else are you going to see the place?"

Fair enough.

I didn't make eye contact with any of the silent associates. I hoped they knew Marco and weren't about to call security on us. Since the store wasn't large and the bags all looked the same after the first few, it didn't take long before I was done browsing. "Ready?"

"You haven't seen everything." Marco led me through an entryway that opened into another minimalist room. Only that one had something far more interesting on the white display shelves.

Shoes.

Purses weren't my thing, and a year ago, I'd have sworn shoes weren't, either. But that was before I'd known how it felt to wear a pair of killer heels or the comfort of shoes with support.

Some of the shoes displayed were so ugly, I couldn't imagine anyone would buy them. There were others that were so gorgeous, I couldn't imagine how expensive they were.

I looked longingly at a pair of sexy and edgy black heels with studded straps. I tore myself away from them, and Marco followed me out past the still silent associates.

No Pretty Woman *moment happening here.*

The next store was filled with display cases of watches. Watches were even less of my thing than purses, so we didn't spend long in there, either.

We spent even less in the perfume store that gave me an instant headache and convenient mart with overpriced bottled drinks and candy bars.

I made up for my short time at the other shops when I stepped into a dress boutique. Some of them were gaudy or formal. Others were clearly intended for a Vegas wedding. But mixed in were some gorgeous pieces that ranged from cute sundress to sexy cocktail dress—including my lacy magenta one from the night before.

This explains how he sends me clothes so fast.

I took my time, my brain going crazy with inspiration I hoped I'd remember.

Once I was finished, we left and bypassed a men's wear store, ritzy suitcases and travel items, and an entire store dedicated to blown glass.

That one was beautiful, but I worried I'd trip and knock everything over like dominos.

We rounded the atrium before Marco announced it was time for lunch. Going for food court Mexican—a good taco was a good taco—

we sat in the crowded dining area and ate.

I had a mouthful of queso when Marco handed me his cell as it began ringing. "For you."

Swallowing, I hit accept and put it to my ear. "Hello?"

"I texted you, Juliet."

At the firmness in Maximo's tone, butterflies raved in my belly and my clit throbbed.

Shit. I still wasn't used to carrying a phone again.

"I forgot my phone in the room," I admitted.

"It stays on you at all times from now on. Understood?"

"Yes, Daddy," I said with only a moment's hesitation. My gaze darted to Marco, but his expression gave away nothing.

Maximo's tone softened. "Are you having a good day?"

"Yeah, it's been fun."

"I'll be back for dinner. Plan what you want." I could hear the smile in his voice when he added, "Just no hookers, blow, or roulette."

My eyes on Marco narrowed to a glare.

Snitch.

Movement caught my attention, and I glanced over as a large table of people stood, others rushing to take their place. In the midst of the chaos, I could've sworn I saw my dad's friends—well, former friend—Mugsy Carmichael.

Caught between wanting to hide in case it was him and wanting to confirm that it wasn't, I froze. A pit grew in my belly and blood rushed in my ears at the thought of explaining why I was there.

It's not him.

Just another wannabe gangster. Vegas is filled with them.

He may have spent more time in casinos than a nun in church, but it was still unlikely Mugsy Carmichael would be at Moonlight. It was even more unlikely he'd be in the food court area and not parked at a poker table until he ran out of money.

I knew that.

But it didn't stop my panicked mind from racing.

Keeping my head tilted away but my eyes alert, I searched for the man. But whoever he was, I'd lost him in the crowd.

"Juliet, are you there?" Maximo asked.

"Sorry, I think you cut out."

"I said I have something planned for later tonight, so don't overdo it." There were muffled voices in the background. "I've got to go. Miss you, little dove."

He clicked off, but I kept the phone pressed to my ear for a few long moments.

Maximo misses me.

To be fair, he never hid how happy he was to come home to me. He showed how he felt with his sweet kisses and frantic touches.

But it was the first time he'd said the words.

And, God, they'd sounded so good.

Danger, danger, danger.

MAYBE I SHOULD'VE napped.

After lunch, we'd changed paths so Marco could show me more of the resort—minus an area he'd said was off-limit. The tour had ended with the absolute best ice cream of my life before Marco had dropped me back at the room to get ready.

Eyeing the bed with longing, I forced myself to touch up my make-up—and my deodorant. I pulled my hair into the high ponytail Maximo loved, even though it would display the marks on my neck.

Or maybe *because* it would display them.

I stripped before putting on the gray bodysuit. The minimal fabric was soft, as was the lace. It gave the illusion of a corset without the organ rearranging and lack of breathing. I tugged on some dark wash skinny jeans that clung like a second skin and a slouchy sweater that fell off one shoulder, showing a hint of the lingerie strap.

A tease.

I put on a pair of gray suede ankle booties and hoped whatever Maximo had planned, it wouldn't involve a ton of walking. Otherwise, there was a good chance my feet and I would die.

Grabbing my cell off the bedside table, I went into the living room to wait.

I had three waiting texts from Maximo.

Maximo: I keep thinking about how fucking hot you looked riding me last night, little dove. It's making it hard to focus on anything else.

Maximo: I hope you're having fun but being a good girl.

That one sent a tingle through me.

Maximo: Juliet, a phone is useless if you don't carry it with you. What if there was an emergency?

That one sent a different kind of tingle through me.

Maximo hadn't seemed happy. And when Maximo was unhappy, it made him spanky.

I squirmed from both the phantom sensation of a burning ass and the heavy dose of lust that went through me.

There were a few dings before the elevator slid open. Maximo stepped out, looking like a model on a runway. Even after a long day out, his suit was crisp and perfect, as though it didn't dare wrinkle.

Stalking toward me, he was a hunter and I was his prey.

His very willing prey.

Cupping my head, he took my mouth with a desperation that said it'd been centuries since we'd last been together and not hours. His tongue thrust in and he tilted his head to deepen the kiss.

When he pulled away, I was breathing heavy as I asked, "What was that for?"

"Told you I missed you. I liked knowing you were here."

I couldn't hold back my grin, not that I tried hard. "I missed you, too."

His eyes dropped to my mouth. "Christ, you make me insane."

The words themselves may not have sounded good, but the intense way he'd said them did.

Releasing his hold, he stepped away and ditched his suit jacket before rolling his sleeves. "Did you decide on dinner?"

"Does the Asian restaurant have sushi?"

"Yes. Do you like sushi?"

I shrugged. "I have no idea, I've never had it."

"Let's find out."

As it turned out, I did like sushi. Just not the raw stuff.

Never the raw stuff.

Chang'e—named after the Chinese goddess of the moon, of course—was a Pan-Asian restaurant with an extensive fusion and dim sum menu. Contrary to my assumption that it would be casual, it was incredibly trendy and upscale. I was *way* underdressed, not that anyone would comment since I was with Maximo.

Maximo had ordered us an assortment of *mostly* delicious food—the uncooked spring rolls were almost as gross as the raw sushi.

It was obvious I wouldn't be going on a raw food diet in the future.

"What's the plan?" I asked when we finished eating.

"You'll see." Maximo checked his watch before standing and dropping a fold of cash onto the table.

Leaving the restaurant, we made our way across the main floor. When we reached the table gaming area, my attention caught on someone walking to one of the tables, a stack of chips in his hand. He sat and arranged them in front of him.

My steps slowed, and Maximo tilted his head to look down at me.

"I know that guy," I whispered.

"Who?"

I jerked my head subtly in the direction. "Gray shirt, bald head."

"How?"

"He came to visit Shamus a few times."

"Friend?"

"Not unless kicking his ass is a new way to express friendship. If so, Shamus was the most popular man in the world."

I remembered coming out from the backroom at the gym to the sounds of pained cries and shouting. Although that was the usual soundtrack at the training gym, that time had been different. The man had been sent to deliver a message with his fists.

It hadn't been the last time someone had shown up with a similar messaging method.

No, the last time had been the man who was standing next to me, his hand on my lower back. The man whose hands had been on every other part of my body. Whose bed I slept in. Whose arms were wrapped around me every night, his hold possessive and intimate.

A sudden burst of guilt clawed at me. It tore at the happiness I'd built, threatening to unravel everything like a loose thread.

Tug.

Tug.

Tug.

Surprise tears burned behind my lids, and I inhaled deeply, keeping them at bay. Shoving it all down.

"Juliet," Maximo said, making me jolt.

"Huh?"

His eyes were filled with concern. "Where'd you go, dove?"

"Sorry, what did you say?"

Catching my non-answer, the muscle in his jaw jumped, but he didn't push. "I asked if you're sure that's him?"

I nodded.

He steered me through the room, his pace brisker than it'd been. He paused near a pit boss just long enough to say, "Gray shirt, bald head, Omaha low limit. If he gets up before Miles or Ash gets here, have him followed."

Wait, what?

Since I sincerely doubted Maximo was avenging Shamus' beatdown, I had no clue why he was making a big deal of a small thing. Unless he recognized the guy, too. Knowing the company Shamus had kept, I wouldn't be surprised if the man was on his shit list.

The pit boss gave a barely perceptible chin raise before resuming his rounds like nothing was amiss.

I waited until we were walking before asking, "Why are you siccing security on him?"

Maximo didn't answer as he took his phone out, tapped the screen a few times, and put it to his ear. Whoever must have picked up because he repeated the description before adding, "He worked for someone McMillon owed. Keep an eye on him."

Once he hung up, I repeated, "Why are you siccing security on him?"

"Making sure he's only here to lose his money." He wrapped an arm around me and squeezed, though he remained somber.

"It's just a coincidence."

That wasn't the right thing to say because his eyes went colder. "I don't like coincidences."

"Okay, but to be fair, I think Shamus owed money to half the US population."

That got him to soften a little as he glanced down at me. "That much?"

I tilted my head and pretended to think before amending, "Half the *continental* US."

His lips tipped and more of the tension left him as we stopped.

I pulled my attention from his far too sexy expression to see we were at the entryway to the area Marco had said was off-limits.

Earlier, the doors had been propped open, and so many people had milled about, I hadn't been able to see what was in there. Right then, the doors were closed with a velvet rope secured across, so I still couldn't see what was in there. Signage marked it as closed for the evening.

Of course, none of that applied to Maximo, and he unlatched the rope and punched in a code to unlock the heavy door.

Holding it open so I could enter, he re-secured the rope and let the heavy door slam closed, the sound echoing in the quiet hall.

Beautiful photography and art lined the walls. Sculptures and floral displays were in the middle of the path. The theme, of course, was the moon, but also light. Bursts of it filled dark canvases—simple yet stunning.

Although it was lovely to look at, I was surprised by how busy it'd been earlier. The typical Vegas crowd didn't strike me as art aficionados.

Maximo took my hand, weaving his fingers through mine as he kept my pace, not rushing my very slow stroll.

Once we reached the end of the hall and the doors there, Maximo punched in a code. All six doors swung open, and we stepped into a dimly lit room.

The domed roof was velvety black, but there were no twinkle lights. Matching black benches were positioned in rows, but that was it.

"Sit," Maximo said. "Third row, right side of the aisle."

I went where he directed and sat on the padded bench. If nothing else, my feet were happy for a break.

Low classical music filled the room as the lights dimmed. Maximo sat next to me just as they went out, leaving us in pitch blackness. "Hold on."

Even with his warning, I yelped when the back of the bench slowly reclined.

Maximo didn't even try to stifle his laughter. Wrapping his arm around my shoulders, he curled my body into his so I was resting my head on his chest.

"If this is a nap area, this resort really does have everything."

"Give it a minute."

"A minute might be all I need to fall asleep."

Before I could even rest my eyes, the music grew louder and lights flashed as a laser light show was projected onto the ceiling. The music transitioned to Sinatra's *Fly Me to the Moon*, and I was completely entranced. Lasers shaped like the moon and solar system moved and changed along to the lyrics.

The music melded from the classics to classic rock. I recognized CCR's *Bad Moon Rising* from the first few chords.

Back when we'd lived in New York, Shamus had been all about classic rock. He'd listened to Springsteen until I'd wished I was born to run. It wasn't until we'd moved to Vegas that he'd switched to the Rat Pack to fit in with his wannabe mobster pals.

Once the volume faded, the bench slowly returned to normal and the lights slowly turned on.

"What did you think?" Maximo asked, his lips against my head.

"Can we watch it again?"

"Give me a second." He stood and went back to the control panel on the wall. Not touching it, he pulled out his phone and typed something before saying to me. "Shamus' pal lost his stack and left."

I'd been certain it'd been a coincidence, but it was reassuring to have confirmation—especially after the uncertain Mugsy sighting earlier.

Maximo pocketed his phone and pressed a couple control panel buttons. Within a few seconds, the lights faded as the classical music started. He sat and got us situated just before the bench lowered again.

Sinatra's croon floated through the air and the lasers started to dance. I noticed more details I'd missed on first viewing.

So wrapped up in what I was watching, I didn't think twice when Maximo's hand went from my ass to rub my back under my sweater. He froze, his voice rough when he rumbled, "What're you wearing under this, dove?"

"Uhhh…"

His hand trailed up the lacy fabric before he shifted me off him and stood. I couldn't see what he was doing in the darkness, and my heart raced with a jumpy anticipation.

A few moments later, the show and music cut off abruptly as the lights flared to life. Maximo pressed the door open and stared at me expectantly. "Let's go."

I didn't move. I just stared as he ran a tattooed hand across his jaw before sweeping his bottom lip with his thumb.

"Now, Juliet."

At that tone, I jumped up. That didn't stop me from muttering, "I'm coming, I'm coming. Sheesh."

"Just because I won't fuck you in here doesn't mean I won't bend you over a bench and spank your sweet ass."

"You won't fuck me in here?" Not that I'd expected him to, but he seemed resolute in his decision not to.

"Not with the cameras."

"But you'd spank my ass when security could see?"

"I know where the cameras are. I'd block your body and leave your jeans on," he said, like that made it better.

Actually, it did.

I contemplated throwing more attitude his way to see how it went.

And Maximo must've known I was thinking about it because lust blazed in his eyes as he adjusted the bulge in his slacks, trying to hide his hard-on.

Good luck with that.

"Don't look at me like that, or I won't be responsible for my actions."

The way he was watching me.

The way he looked so handsome yet so wild.

The threat—the *promise*—in his words…

It all worked for me. My nipples were painfully hard, my body was flushed and needy, and I was wet.

Soaked.

"You've got five seconds to get over here," he continued, "or I'm fucking you on a bench—cameras be damned."

I hurried over, remaining silent as we made our way down the long art corridor and back into the main area. Once the noises of the casino surrounded us, I couldn't resist tormenting him the same way his obscenely sweet words tormented me. I kept my eyes aimed in front of me and said, "I think I want to try riding your face."

The normally unflappable Maximo stopped suddenly in the middle of the walkway and nearly caused a collision.

"Juliet," he warned.

"You said communication was important, Daddy. So I'm communicating my desire to ride your face."

"Christ." He gave me a different version of *the look*. One that warned he'd punish me in the very best way.

We started walking again, moving through the crowds out for a wild Saturday. Our steps were forced to slow when a crush of people swarmed in with their party sashes, sparkling plastic tiaras, and big blended drinks.

Perfect.

Taking advantage of the slowdown, I tilted my head to look up at him. "I think I want to try sucking you while I ride your face. Do you think that'd work or am I too short?"

"I don't give a damn what I need to do, I'll make it work."

Well, this is backfiring spectacularly.

I think I'm more turned on than he is.

I remained quiet as we weaved through the partiers. Once we were in a less dense area, I asked, "Do you think there's a limit to how wet a woman can get before she risks dehydration? 'Cause if there is, I'm probably nearing that point."

"Jesus, Juliet. You and your filthy mouth are asking for trouble."

"Yay."

It was funny that, with everything else I'd said, my little *yay* was what made him crack.

Taking hold of my hand, the speed of his strides increased until I was practically jogging to keep up. Like a running back with his eyes on the end zone, he expertly maneuvered through the crowd, not slowing until we were at his elevator.

He opened it with his thumbprint, yanked me in, and hit the button to the penthouse. Before the door even closed, I was up in his arms, my back against the wall and his mouth on mine.

I wrapped my arms around his shoulders and my legs around his waist, taking everything he gave.

The blessedly fast elevator dinged, and Maximo carried me into the bedroom before setting me down. My feet were barely under me when he tugged my sweater over my head. His gaze raked over the lace and ribbon covering my torso. "Christ, Juliet, if I knew you had this on, we wouldn't have left the damn room."

"Surprise," I breathed.

"You're full of them."

"Is that good?"

His sinful smile was enough to steal my breath and make me danger-ously close to combusting. "The fucking best."

Definite backfire.

"Pants and shoes off, Juliet."

I knew once I stripped, Maximo would touch me. And once he did, I wouldn't have the self-control to tease him any longer. It was my last opportunity, and I was taking it.

Kicking off my shoes, my movements were slow as I unbuttoned and unzipped my jeans.

Maximo crossed his arms, but he didn't say a word.

Wiggling my hips—both for the appeal and because the jeans really were skintight—I slid them down my ass to my thighs. I turned, giving him my back as I bent at the waist to shove the jeans farther down my legs.

That was as far as I got.

Maximo came up behind me, shuffling me forward until I was bent over the bed. Holding the thin fabric that covered my pussy to the side, he ran his finger through my slit. Even though it was me his skilled finger was teasing, he was the one who groaned in frustrated pleasure.

There was a rustle of fabric before the head of his cock pressed into me. Unable to spread my legs with my jeans around my knees, every-thing was tighter and he felt huger than his already huge.

It skirted that glorious edge between torture and bliss.

When he slid out, I reached to try to clutch him to me, not wanting him to stop. His hands spanned my hips, lifting me to kneel on the edge of the bed. He pulled my jeans off before pressing a palm between my shoulder blades. "Back a little. Ass up. That's my good girl."

With my torso to the mattress and my ass tipped, the height lined up just right for him to slam in. The force knocked my knees out from un-der me, but Maximo repositioned me and slammed in again.

Lifting just enough to look over my shoulder, a fresh surge of arousal shot through me, nearly throwing me over the edge.

Holy shit.

He actually did it.

Like the threat he'd made our first night together, he was fucking me fully clothed, his slacks lowered just enough to free himself.

The actual visual was a million times better than it'd been in my head.

239

"DID YOU HAVE fun, little dove?" Maximo asked when we were finished and in bed for the night.

Amazing sex and two orgasms?

Definitely fun.

"Uh, yeah. I always have fun when we do that."

Maximo chuckled, and since his body was curled around me, I heard and felt it.

"I meant this weekend."

"Oh. Yeah, that was okay, too, I guess."

His arm tightened around me, his voice lined with amusement. "I'm glad you found my resort *fine enough.*"

Said orgasms, along with the long day filled with a billion of steps, caught up to me. My eyes were closed, my body was relaxed, and I was sated and happy.

And that was why I stupidly rambled. "I used to be so envious of the tourists here. They always had so much fun. Carefree fun. I never went to the Strip to sightsee or watch the shows or eat. The only time I've been was to pick up Shamus because he was too fucked up or fucked over to drive. That was *not* fun. Today was."

"Juliet," he muttered, tightening his hold.

"It's okay." I wiggled back into him and sighed deeply.

He didn't push the conversation, and I was grateful. I let it all go as I fell asleep.

CHAPTER TWENTY-FIVE

Carefree Fun

JULIET

𝒇OR ALL ITS vices and sins, Vegas really was beautiful.

The larger-than-life quality of the Strip reminded me of Times Square in NYC. Like most resident New Yorkers, we rarely went to Times Square or any of the sights that were deemed touristy. But my grandparents had taken me to ride the Ferris wheel inside the former Toys R' Us once, and I'd been amazed at the grandeur of it all.

Bright lights, huge buildings, and more people than seemed possible were a fitting description of the Strip *and* Times Square.

As Maximo stopped at a red light on Las Vegas Boulevard, I watched the people on the overhead walkways. Some posed for pictures, others hurried from one casino to another.

As I watched out my window, the pang of envy hit me, but it was far less than usual. Instead, my sour mood was because our weekend was over. I'd hoped we'd spend Sunday at Moonlight, but we hadn't even stayed for breakfast. Instead, I'd come out after getting ready to find my bag packed and Maximo waiting with a bagel and to-go coffee.

I was sure he had a lot of work to do, but it still sucked it was over.

Lost in thought, I didn't think anything of us turning until the car stopped. A valet was there in an instant, opening my door.

My brows lowered as I looked at Maximo, but all I saw was his back as he got out.

"Ma'am," the valet prodded when I didn't move.

Confused, I climbed out and muttered, "Thanks."

Maximo opened the trunk and pulled out two small travel bags. A different uniformed worker took them and hurried inside, not even asking where they needed to go.

Once Maximo was next to me, I didn't take my eyes from the towering glass building. "Where are we?"

"Cosmopolitan."

"Why?"

"I took today and tomorrow off. I thought we'd stay here for the night."

My wide eyes shot to him. "What? Why?"

Reaching out to twist the end of my ponytail around his hand, he yanked me against him. "For fun."

My insides turned to melty mush and my heart squeezed.

He was so damn thoughtful.

Like my veins were filled with champagne, excitement bubbled, leaving me light and happy. "What are we going to do?"

"Anything you want."

That is not *helpful.*

Correctly reading my thoughts, Maximo tugged my ponytail so my neck was craned back. "As long as I'm spending the day with you and the night ends with you riding my face, I don't give a damn what we do."

There were people around.

People close enough to hear his obscenely sweet words.

But I didn't care.

I didn't care about anything but the heat in his tender gaze, our impending day together, and ending the night riding his face.

Beyond that, it was carefree fun.

He released my ponytail. "Let's go to the room first."

Going into the beautiful building, I was stunned by its stylish ornateness. Massive crystal chandeliers draped over a bar and lounge area. People posed for pictures in front of them and a giant high heel.

Maximo and I walked through the lobby to where a concierge waited.

"Mr. Black." The man smiled, warm and professional, outstretching his hand to shake Maximo's and then mine. "We're thrilled to have you and your guest stay with us this evening. Would you care for a tour or may I show you to your room?"

"We're set, thanks."

The man handed him a key card. "Please let me know if there's anything I can do to make your stay perfect."

After thanking him, Maximo guided me to an elevator. Once we were inside, I asked, "Do you think they're going to send spies to tail us to make sure you're not here to poach their procedures and employees?"

He looked down at me with amusement. "Doubtful."

"Damn. Hotel espionage was on my to-do list today."

He chuckled, pulling me so my back was to his front before wrapping his arms around my waist. "I'll see what I can arrange."

Once we reached our floor, we walked to a door at the end of the hall. He unlocked it, holding it open for me.

Holy.

Shit.

This is unreal.

"How'd you book this last minute?" I asked, doing a slow turn to take everything in. A hammock hung in front of the row of floor to ceiling windows. There was a terrace outside, and the view was as beautiful as it was terrifying.

"It's invite only." Maximo's lips tipped. "And I have a connection."

Of course, he does.

In my shorts and distressed tee, I felt like a fish out of water. And not even one of those pretty neon fish. I was a guppy. Or a blobfish.

However, I didn't let it bother me—well, not much—because Maximo was even more underdressed in his gray joggers and black tee. Underdressed, but hot.

Everyone knew gray sweats were the equivalent of male lingerie.

His phone rang and he glanced at the screen. "Shit, I've got to take this."

"I'm sure I can find something to do," I deadpanned.

He touched the screen and put his cell to his ear. "Black." He stepped onto the terrace and closed the door behind him.

Left to my own devices, I scoped the place out.

Even after staying at Maximo's house for a year, my brain couldn't comprehend the luxury and opulence of how the other half lived. With so much to do in Vegas, most people only used their room as a place to crash. Yet the suite had a mini spa, a theater room, and more space than could possibly be utilized. It was unfathomable to spend a not-so-small fortune on a room with pointless amenities that would likely go unused. And if they were used, what was the point of visiting Vegas just to stay inside?

Backtracking to the living room, I eyed the fresh fruit in the bowl on the kitchen island.

I bet that banana costs forty bucks.

Next to it was a bottle of champagne on ice and a smaller bowl of strawberries.

The champagne is six hundred, at least.

And five bucks per strawberry.

The door slid open and Maximo stepped inside. There was more tension in his body, his face tight as he scowled.

"Everything okay?" I asked.

"Fine."

Ooookay then.

I wasn't surprised by his dismissive answer since he never talked about work. And I didn't blame him for not wanting to discuss it during his rare time off. So I did something that didn't involve words.

I kissed him.

And after a long, frozen moment, he kissed me back. And then he took control, gripping my ponytail to tilt my head so he could spear his tongue in.

Pulling away a minute later, he rested his forehead against mine. "How'd you know I needed that?"

"Lucky guess."

Dropping his head to my neck, he teased it with his tongue. "Perfect guess." He bit hard enough to make me cry out, a surge of moisture pooling between my thighs. "Sure you want to go out?"

"Nope, this works. This is definitely better."

If Maximo was one of the features of the room, I could understand why people would choose to stay in.

But he wasn't for anyone else. Right then, he was only mine.

"Let's go before I change my mind," he rumbled, releasing me.

"Fine," I said on a long, dramatic sigh.

"Brat."

"Control freak."

Maximo swatted my ass, but it was more playful than punishing. Unfortunately.

He unzipped his bag and pulled out a ball cap, sliding it on backward. At my gawking, he winked. "Got to go incognito for hotel espionage."

If he thinks he blends in, he is sadly mistaken.

We went down the elevator, getting off at a different floor than we'd gotten on. The hallway was lined with art and statues. One in particular caught my eye, and the longer I looked at it, the more bizarre it became.

"I liked the art at Moonlight," I started, fighting a smile, "but you don't have a statue of a naked man-dog and a naked man-bunny riding a donkey."

"Jesus, that's insane."

"Insanely awesome. Unlike your lack of animal-human hybrid erotica." I stepped closer to inspect it, surprised at the level of anatomical detail. "It must've been cold that day."

Maximo's rich laughter rang out around me, and I lost my hold on my own.

"If you're done ogling the statues," he said, "there's more to see."

"I don't think anything can top this, but okay."

We only walked for a short bit before I stood corrected.

Pausing in front of a restaurant, I pointed at the name.

Eggslut.

"I'm beginning to think this casino is run by a pervert." I tilted my head. "And now I don't know if I'm hungry or aroused."

"We can go back to the room so I can take care of both," Maximo offered, his tone playful while the look in his eyes was anything but.

Oh, this is gonna be a fun day.

Leaning into him, I grinned. "Later, Daddy."

"Why do I get the feeling you're going to earn a red ass before you ride my face?"

"Because I'm very lucky," I blurted without thought.

Maximo didn't respond verbally, but he did get a tender look on his face that hurt beautifully.

"Ready?" I asked when I couldn't stand the intensity any longer.

He answered my question with one of his own. "Are you actually hungry?"

"No, I'm good."

Keeping a possessive arm around me, Maximo gave me a tour of the expansive building. There was too much to see to waste time with window shopping, but I did pop into an eyewear place for a kickass pair of silver aviators for me and a black pair for Maximo.

When we got outside, I was grateful for the impulsive buy because the sun was blinding. I lowered my shades from the top of my head to cover my eyes as Maximo put his on.

How does he keep getting hotter?

This has to be some kind of witchcraft.

"Cosmopolitan is near the center of the Strip, so pick which direction you want to go," Maximo said.

I looked one way then the other before seeing what I wanted. "This way."

"Shops at Crystals?"

Since I was fairly certain they ran a credit check just to step foot inside, I shook my head. "Even better."

We walked for a bit before finally reaching New York-New York.

"You want chocolate?" Maximo asked, looking up at signage for the Hershey's store located in the resort.

"No." I paused before amending, "Well, yes. But I also want to ride the coaster and then eat a New York hot dog."

"You don't like heights," he pointed out.

"Which is why I want to ride first *then* eat."

My stomach already churned with a mix of excitement, adrenaline, and horror that left me queasy.

Despite the line for the coaster stretching on forever, Maximo sent one text and we were on the next ride. I chose safe seats in the middle, but there was only so much safety to be found on a coaster attached to the outside of a building. Luckily, Maximo sacrificed his hand so I could death grip it.

"Want to do it again with the VR goggles?" he asked when we got off.

My stomach dropped and turned. "No, once was enough. I just wanted to say I rode it."

He tugged my ponytail, but there was concern in his eyes. "You still want that hot dog?"

"Definitely."

Maybe.

Walking the winding halls of New York-New York was like stepping into an old NYC neighborhood. There was even a deli that looked nearly identical to one that'd been down the street from my grandparents' house.

The smells wafting from the restaurants were enough to make my mouth water. I stuck with my original choice of a hot dog and Maximo grabbed a slice of pepperoni pizza that was good, but not New York good.

"Does it look like the real thing?" Maximo asked as we threw our trash away and strolled through the rest of the fake neighborhood.

"I remember it being bigger," I joked. "But kinda."

I'd been born in New York and had moved to the city as a toddler. A big chunk of my life had been spent there, yet I'd never felt like a New Yorker.

I'd never felt like anything but a nomad.

Temporary.

That hadn't changed, but at least I felt some semblance of stability for the first time.

"Take a picture with me," I blurted suddenly, wanting a keepsake beyond the bellyache that was already fading.

Surprisingly, Maximo didn't hesitate. He pulled his phone out, brought up the camera, and handed it to a middle-aged passerby to take our picture in front of a fake stoop.

"Beautiful," the woman said, a hint of swoon in her voice. "Now one with you kissing."

Before I could laugh or say anything, Maximo cupped my head in his possessive hold and kissed me.

It may have been quick, but it was *intense.*

And I wasn't the only one who thought so, based on the woman's breathy, "Wow."

I second that.

Maximo took his phone from the wide-eyed woman and pocketed it. "Thanks."

She shot me a sly smile. "Lucky girl. Have fun, kids."

As we walked through the busy casino, I spotted a display advertising their Cirque du Soleil show with naughty new acts. "Can we go see that?"

"No." He wrapped an arm around my shoulders, his hand resting above my breast, his fingertips teasing the sensitive skin. "But we can go home and create our own version."

That sounded better anyway.

After a stop at the Hershey's store for a chocolate covered strawberry, we headed outside.

"I used to think the Strip was only a couple blocks of cramped hotels," I shared as I devoured my treat.

"What'd you think when you saw it for the first time?"

"I hated it." I shrugged. "None of my experiences here have been good."

"We'll change that."

We already are.

Maximo wiped a smudge of chocolate from my bottom lip. "What do you want to see next?"

I took a moment before giving him the only answer I had. "*Everything.*"

So we did. Fine, it may not have been *literally* everything because there was only so much we could do in one day. But we did a lot, including seeing the shark reef at Mandalay Bay and getting an up-close and terrifying visit with the flamingos, angry swans, and turtles at the Flamingo.

Once dinnertime hit, we stopped to eat in the promenade outside The Linq. I doubled up on my hot dog consumption—that time with the addition of fries.

"Are you having fun?" Maximo asked just as I stuffed my California dog into my mouth.

Chewing the delicious and semi-healthy goodness, I nodded emphatically. I swallowed and wiped my face before saying, "Minus the swans." I gave an exaggerated shudder. "I thought they were supposed to be elegant and graceful, not aggressive assholes."

"They're violent to protect their mate." His lips curved up on one side. "I can relate."

His admittance he'd be violent for me shouldn't make me happy.

Yet it does.

I took a needed drink and asked, "What about you? Are you having fun?"

Lifting his chin, he admitted, "More than I expected to. I've lived here my whole life but never bothered to do the touristy shit."

"Even when you were a kid?"

I tried to picture him as a child, but it was impossible. All I saw was a somber mini-adult or a brooding bad-boy teen—and something told me that wasn't far off.

He shrugged. "You're not the only one who used to hate the Strip."

"Why?" I asked, wanting to know more about him.

"Long story," he evaded, and I didn't push.

Sometimes—probably *most* times—the past belonged in the past. Heaven knew I didn't want to delve into my history.

I took another bite, half the toppings spilling out the other side of the bun.

"I'll grab a fork," Maximo said, already standing.

"And napkins."

And maybe a bib.

Watching Maximo move through the crowds, it didn't matter he wasn't at one of his properties. People still responded to his air of authority, his size, and the dangerous vibe that emanated off him. I could do without the way some women stopped to stare, but since he didn't so much as glance at them, it was whatever.

He was hot. It would be impossible not to notice.

Reaching for a fry, I stopped short and froze. The hairs on the back of my neck stood, and a chill slithered down my spine. I couldn't shake the feeling I was being watched.

Inconspicuously, I glanced over my shoulder, but nothing stood out.

I'd had the sensation off and on all day. Maximo's whole BDE-king-of-the-world thing attracted a lot of attention. As did his frequent PDA that went beyond *affection* and bordered on obscene.

We probably made for good people watching.

The feeling faded and another scan of the area confirmed nothing amiss, so I went back to what mattered.

Food.

After dinner—and a quick stop for a cupcake covered in sprinkles—Maximo asked, "Now that you tackled the coaster, are we going on the High Roller?"

The deliciousness I'd devoured churned like cement in my stomach at the thought of stepping onto the giant Ferris wheel.

Reading my expression, he chuckled. "Didn't think so."

He curled an arm around me as we continued down the street to ride the gondolas before visiting Bauman Rare Books. I hardly breathed as I scanned shelves of old, insanely expensive books.

When I finally dragged myself away from the treasures, we back-tracked down the Strip.

With the sun setting, the nightlife came alive and transformed Vegas from family friendly-*ish* to Sin City. The warm air was wired with excitement and depravity. People were ready to party as they hopped from one resort to another.

When we reached The Bellagio, I was bummed the fountains weren't active. We rounded the curved path, dodging plants and drunks on our way to the lobby.

Stepping in, I whispered an awe filled, "Whoa."

Glass flowers hung upside down from the ceiling, a burst of blossoms and light and beauty.

The crystal horse and floral gardens were gorgeous, but the world's tallest chocolate fountain was the star. Unfortunately, it was behind glass or I'd have dove in, open mouth first.

Maximo glanced at his watch. "Time to go."

Damn.

Walking outside, my disappointment grew when I saw the fountains still weren't active.

I stopped at the crowded edge of the path. "Can we stay a little longer?"

"No," was all he said before taking my hand and walking again.

Double damn.

Maximo rarely told me no, so I felt bad being pissy about it. It'd been a long day, especially for him since he'd likely been up at his usual five. That didn't stop me from slowing my steps like a petulant child stalling at bedtime.

Of course, he noticed. "Juliet."

"Maximo," I mocked.

"You're lucky I don't drag you back to our room, brat."

A shiver went through me, but I focused on his words and not the threat. "I thought that's where we're going."

He didn't respond verbally, but with his face in profile, I could see the tiniest hint of a smirk. At the sidewalk, he turned us in the opposite direction of our hotel and continued walking until we reached a security guard leaning against a concrete barrier.

"Black," the man said, moving aside so Maximo and I could take his place.

Maximo shook his hand. "Tell your boss I owe him."

"He knew you'd say that and said you're even."

As the man walked away, Maximo moved to stand behind me, his arms going to either side of my body, caging me in. Lowering his head, his low voice rumbled in my ear. "What was your favorite thing we did?"

"We haven't done it yet."

"You think the fountains will be your favorite?"

"No, I think riding your face will be."

"Christ, I should've just dragged you to the room. Any fucking room." Pressing in closer, he wrapped one arm around my chest, his hand casually resting against my breast.

I leaned back into him, sighing happily.

All the melty goodness that flowed through me like the warm chocolate fountain seized up when the sensation of being watched returned.

"What's wrong?" Maximo asked, all traces of heat in his voice replaced by alertness.

I tilted my head so I didn't have to shout. "I feel like we're being watched."

"We are."

My stomach dropped out. "What?"

"Marco was on duty earlier. Ash is on now."

"What?" I repeated.

Lowering his head next to mine, Maximo took a moment before pointing to where Ash stood along the side rail near some trees.

"They've been following us the whole day?" I shook my head. "How did I not notice?"

"Because they're good at their job."

"*Why* have they been following us?" I thought about Maximo's work—both the legal and illegal stuff. As worry tightened around my heart and lungs, making it hard to breathe, I turned and clutched his shirt. "Do you have enemies?"

"Every good business owner does. But nothing that puts me or, more importantly, *you* in danger. They're just doing their job."

I guess being a bodyguard is easier if you're in the vicinity of the body you're guarding.

I glanced at where I knew Ash was, but I could barely see him. "Do they always follow you?"

"Unless I'm at home or one of my properties. But I told them to keep their distance today." He turned me to face forward, wrapping me in his hold again. "I wanted you to myself."

I'm in so much trouble.

The first spray of water shot up from the fountain. Coordinated to music, the show was incredible and beautiful.

But just as I'd predicted, riding Maximo's face was my favorite part of the best day of my life.

CHAPTER TWENTY-SIX

The Fire

JULIET

"*Y*OU'RE COMING TO Star with me now."

I jumped at Maximo's voice as I stepped out of the bathroom in nothing but a towel. I hadn't expected him to be home, let alone in our room.

I'd had one glorious weekend with him at Moonlight and the Strip before Maximo's schedule had gone insane again. For almost three weeks, he'd been slammed preparing for a huge poker tournament. Most days, I only saw him when he woke me with his tongue, fingers, or cock, but there were nights he hadn't even done that.

It sucked, and I missed him.

And apparently that was mutual.

Excitement shot through me. We'd already planned for me to go for the start of the tournament, but spending the whole day was even better. "Okay."

"Vera will pack your bag, we'll spend the weekend."

"Okay," I repeated.

He stalked over to me, all graceful predator to my eager prey. "That easy?" Not giving me the chance to answer, he cupped my head and tilted it. Lust and something else blazed in his gaze as he murmured, "Always that easy."

Being called easy could be an insult, but since he said it with the same praising tone he used when he called me his good girl, I took it as a compliment.

Maximo's eyes dropped to my mouth. "Want those lips around my cock."

"Okay," I said instantly because I really was always easy for him.

"Don't have time," he continued, though he made no move to step away.

Taking advantage of his closeness, I worked to undo his belt and slacks. "Just for a minute."

The fire in him grew to a raging inferno as he watched me drop to my knees. His voice was raw and rough when he relented. "A minute."

I freed his already hard cock and licked the length before taking him as deep as I could.

It lasted longer than a minute.

Maximo didn't complain.

STAR WAS SMALLER than Moonlight, but just as beautiful.

Actually, it may have been more beautiful, with its swirling black and blue tile and shimmery-silver details.

And much like Moonlight, it had a theme and it stuck to it. The lobby was filled with starflowers. Projected shooting stars zipped across the black ceiling. Dots and swipes of silver were on everything from the walls to the gaming room chairs.

There was a giant blue and purple mural of a beautiful woman made entirely of stars.

"Who's that?" I asked, mesmerized by it. It reminded me of an optical illusion, and the longer I looked, the more it came together.

"Asteria, goddess of the stars."

I should've guessed.

As we walked the already crowded main floor, my eyes darted to take everything in. They landed on Maximo to find him watching me.

"What?" I asked, my face flushing.

He stopped suddenly and pulled me to him, not caring we were in public. PDA was never a problem for him. "I like seeing your reaction. Ash said I missed out at Moonlight." He studied me as if he could read my every thought and secret. "Glad I didn't miss it this time."

My heart squeezed, all his intensity aimed at me both overwhelming and exhilarating.

A ringing cut through the thickness.

"Shit, I have to take this." Maximo dropped his hand to pull his cell out. "Black." He was silent for a minute before biting out, "No, I want the one I chose." Another few beats went by as he rubbed a tattooed hand across his clenched jaw.

It was inappropriate to check him out while he was pissed, but I did it anyway.

So hot.

"Email it over." He hung up and gave me his attention. "You can't look at me like that when I'm on the phone. Christ, only you could make me hard while I'm dealing with bullshit."

God, his obscenely sweet words really are so good for my ego but so dangerous for my heart.

Keeping that thought locked away tight, I asked, "Everything okay?"

"Same shit, different day," he dismissed. "I've got to go to my office and deal with it. Did you or Vera pack your iPad?"

I nodded. "It's in my bag."

"I'll have Marco bring it to my office." His thumbs flew across his cell screen before he pocketed it and wrapped an arm around me. He steered me to a hallway with a black and silver *Black Resorts* sign over it. There was a row of elevators and then one with the thumbprint thing.

"Can you add my thumbprint?" I asked as the door slid open and we entered. I'd never gotten around to asking him at Moonlight—mostly because any time we were in the elevator, my mouth was otherwise occupied.

His lips tipped as he pressed a button. "Later."

"Yay."

"Christ, you're cute."

I liked when he called me little *dove* best and *brat* second. Calling me *cute* in his tender, amused tone was a close third.

The doors slid open a moment later, and we stepped off into a ritzy waiting room with glass and wrought iron. Empty chairs lined the wall opposite the row of elevators. A chrome and iron bar held a coffeemaker and supplies I was looking forward to utilizing.

Maximo gripped my hand and walked, pointing out things as he went. "Bathroom. Cole's office. Ash's—not that either use them for more than playing Madden. Conference room." He unlocked and opened the last door.

Huge, intimidating, and looks effortlessly expensive and infinitely powerful?

Yup, definitely Maximo's office.

Along with the typical desk with chairs in front of it, there was a couch and coffee table, a boardroom table lined with chairs, a bar that matched the one in the lobby—though his was stocked with alcohol, not coffee—and a wall of monitors like at home. The wide window behind his desk flaunted the beautiful view.

I could picture him leaning back in his chair, clutching a tumbler of whiskey as he stared broodily into the distance.

A king overseeing his kingdom.

I glanced around again before something occurred to me. "You don't have a receptionist?"

"Multiple."

I leaned out and looked pointedly at the empty waiting area. Lowering my voice with dramatic concern, I asked, "Can you see them right now? Do they talk to you?"

"Brat." Backtracking from the office, he hooked me around the waist, bringing me with him. We got onto the elevator, and he pressed a button for four floors down.

When the doors slid open, it revealed another expansive lobby. A long reception desk took up the entirety of the opposite wall, and at least five people sat behind it—though there may have been more I couldn't see. A massive version of the black and silver *Black Resorts* sign hung on the wall.

Eyes turned to us and lingered when they saw Maximo. They became fixated when they saw he wasn't alone. But he didn't acknowledge anyone as he took my hand and stepped out. He gestured to the desk. "Receptionists." He turned us toward a long hallway. "Offices and conference rooms." Reopening the elevator, we stepped in and he pointed up.

"Three more floors of receptionists, offices, and conference rooms."

Whoa.

Logically, I knew even Maximo couldn't singlehandedly run an entire resort, but it was surprising how extensive the business side was.

"Why don't you have any on your floor?" I asked.

"I like my privacy."

Knowing even a tiny bit about some of his business dealings, that made sense.

He unlocked his office again, moving aside for me to enter. My iPad was on the coffee table, along with a paper bag and a large disposable cup I was praying was filled to the brim with coffee.

Before I could investigate, Maximo turned me to face him. "If you get bored, you can go walk with Marco or hang out in our room upstairs."

"I'll be fine."

Who could be bored when they have coffee and a good book?

Moving behind his desk, he shook off his suit jacket and slipped it on a hanger. He rolled his sleeves to display his tattooed forearms before sitting at his desk.

Let me revise that.

Who could be bored when they have coffee, a good book, and an incredibly sexy man to stare at?

I was bored.

Reading in the office had been fun.

Though it felt a little stalkery, people watching on the wall of monitors had also been fun.

Fooling around frequently had been super fun.

But watching people play poker was *not* fun.

I didn't get the appeal.

I definitely didn't understand why they'd go bankrupt, get in deep with loan sharks, or lose their homes for it.

Clearly the fun was in playing, but it still seemed tedious. At least roulette had the big wheel. Craps had dice. Slots had blinking lights, loud noises, and bonus games. Those seemed more entertaining than staring at cards.

Standing to one side of the long room, Maximo talked with Georgie, the woman who ran the tournaments. I tried to see if anything interesting was happening at the tables.

Surprisingly, they didn't hurt to look at anymore. Guilt wasn't drowning me. I didn't feel anything.

Except the aforementioned boredom, of course.

I thought I was doing a good job hiding it, but Maximo wrapped his arm around me and curled me into him, my front pressed to his side. "Just another few minutes then we'll go eat."

"Take your time, I'm good," I half-fibbed because I'd been ready to leave five minutes after we'd arrived.

His eyes narrowed and his hand dropped to my ass. As he turned his attention back to Georgie, he tightened his hold on my cheek so hard, I had to choke down a yelp.

After another ten minutes, Georgie went to do her walkthrough and Maximo turned to me. "Let's go."

"Hold on, it just got exciting," I said, watching the table where two people had pushed their hefty stacks of chips all-in.

They flipped over their cards, but I couldn't see what they had. After the dealer added the turn to the row of cards, it was obvious one of the men lost by his curses and glower. He'd had more chips than his opponent, so he wasn't out, though his stack was significantly diminished.

Anticlimactic.

"I think I preferred when you were locked away at home," Maximo said, pulling me tighter against him.

"Why?"

"I'm greedy. I like having you all to myself. For only me to see."

Sure, he was a caveman level of possessive. And, yes, he was over the top. Insane. Straight up dysfunctional.

But I loved it.

"If anyone is looking at me," I put my hand to his chest, "it probably has something to do with you palming my ass like a basketball."

"No, they're looking because seeing you in that damn skirt makes a man wish he could pick you up and slam into that sweet pussy." As if his own words pissed him off, his eyes grew cold as he scanned the room.

The antipathy in his dark gaze should've scared me.

And it did, but in a good way. I liked the thrill. The power. The danger.

The fire.

So I played with it.

Stretching my leg out, I inched my skirt up a little. "This isn't even as short as the one I packed for tomorrow."

"Juliet," he warned.

"I'm not even sure that one covers the bottom of my ass."

"That ass is gonna be burning hot and red if you keep this up."

I tilted my head like I was thinking, but it was just to give him a clear view of the love bite he'd left on my neck and to draw attention to my ponytail—two things that drove him wild. "And now that I'm thinking about it, it might be too tight to wear panties."

"I hope you're having fun, Juliet, because now I'm replacing all your clothes with my sweats and tees so no one sees what's mine."

I was having fun. An immense amount of it.

Leaning into him, I whispered, "You know you're the only one who's ever seen me, Daddy."

His hold on my ass tightened, and there was no holding back my whimper. "And I'm the only fucking one who's ever going to see you." His voice was low and harsh. "That's my ass. My sweet pussy. *My* little dove."

Danger, danger, danger.

I couldn't take it when he said stuff like that.

Ignoring the way my heart swelled at his words, I gave him an innocent smile. "Anyway, the skirt still covers more than the swimsuit I brought. That thing is basically strings with tiny scraps of fabric."

That was the last straw.

Gripping my hand, Maximo stormed from the room. I had to practically jog to keep up with his long strides. I couldn't see his expression, but based on his pace and the rigid set of his muscular body, he wasn't happy.

Which meant I was about to get punished.

Yay.

Not slowing until we reached the elevator, the doors barely closed behind us when he had me up against the wall.

I love the fire.

259

CHAPTER TWENTY-SEVEN

Nothing

JULIET

I'VE CREATED A monster.
No, that isn't true.
He's always been a monster.
But now he's my monster.

Sitting in his office the next day, Maximo arranged me on his lap. He tightened his hold, grinding me against his hard-on. Working me through my shorts, he got me right to the edge before announcing, "I've got to go."

"But Daddy," I breathed, already whipped into a frenzy and ready to explode.

He'd been teasing me all damn day. Calling me to his desk, getting me needy, and then sending me back to the couch.

And even knowing what was coming—or not coming, in my case—I went to him when he called. I let him touch me.

I would let him fuck me if he tried, but, damn him, he never did. He just liked to whip me into a frenzy and let me suffer.

"I'll only be a couple hours, dove," Maximo said, his lips and teeth grazing my neck. "You can have Ash take you to check out the shops."

Yeah, big *no* to that one. I'd learned after the weekend at Moonlight that checking out the shops was *not* window shopping. I'd arrived home to bags and boxes of the items I'd eyed with longing—including the studded heels.

"We'll see," I hedged, guessing Ash was just as observant as Marco.

Gripping my hips, Maximo ground my ass against his cock one more time before lifting me to stand.

I sat on the edge of his desk and glanced at the double frame he had next to his monitor, smiling at the pictures of us in New York-New York. I'd wanted them for my own memories, but Maximo had printed enough copies to have a set on each of his desks. The one of us kissing didn't seem work appropriate, but he was the boss. What was he going to do, fire himself?

He stood, and I watched as he unrolled his sleeves, buttoning the cuffs before shrugging on his jacket.

It was like a reverse striptease, yet still managed to be hot.

"Whatever you do, make sure to be dressed and ready by five," he ordered in the authoritative way that made me wet. "We'll stop by the tournament then grab dinner."

"Okay," I said, even though the tournament part sounded less than thrilling.

There was a knock at the door, and Maximo called, "Yeah?"

Cole opened it and gave me a small smile before asking, "Ready, boss?"

Maximo raised his chin, turned off his wall of stalker security monitors, and pocketed his phone. "Do whatever you want but stay with Ash."

I stood and mimicked his chin lift. "Got it, boss."

He shook his head, but I could see the amusement curving his lip before I got his back as he walked out the door.

Once he was gone, Ash moved into the doorway. "What's the plan? Shopping? Swimming?" His dimples appeared even as he held back a smile. "4D theater? Lunch?"

"What was that?"

"Lunch? It's a meal you eat between breakfast and—"

I rolled my eyes. "The 4D theater part."

"It's like a theater, but in 4D."

"Smartass."

"Maximo said he didn't get to show you yesterday but thought you'd enjoy it."

I wasn't sure what a 4D theater was, but it was one more than 3D so it had to be good.

A 4D THEATER was way better than 3D. The immersive short movie made viewers feel as though they were riding a roller coaster through the solar system. The chairs moved and vibrated. Bursts of cool and hot air whipped around. Bubbles and splashes of water rained down.

And, best of all, my feet stayed firmly on the ground.

It was my kind of coaster.

So much so, I dragged Ash on a few times in a row.

When we were done, we walked across the gaming floor toward the restaurants. "Moonlight has the laser show and there's the 4D thing here. What gimmicks are at his other casinos?"

"Sunrise has a two-hundred-foot drop tower."

Two-hundred-feet? In the air?

Barf.

No thanks.

He smirked. "Didn't figure that'd be high on your list to try."

"Nope, definitely not. What about Nebula?"

"Nebula's gimmick is that it's expensive as—"

"Hey, asshole, watch where you're going!" someone shouted in front of us.

"Who the fuck do you think you're talking to?" another guy shot back.

Ash didn't step in or even pause to call security. Putting a hand between my shoulders, he stayed close and increased his pace to get us away from the brewing fight.

But it happened fast, calm to chaos in less than a second. The two men launched themselves at each other. Grappling, they slammed around before crashing into us. They fell to a heap, their wrestling bodies landing on Ash.

I was knocked on my ass, my head smacking the wall. Closing my eyes against the burst of pain, they shot open when someone gripped my arm and tugged. I expected a security guard or Ash, but it was Mugsy Carmichael's flushed and sweaty face staring down at me.

"Come on, Juliet," he said, his frantic eyes darting around as he yanked me up.

With warning bells sounding in my head, I tried to free my arm, but his hold tightened. "Ash!"

Covering my mouth with a palm that was moist and smelled like stale cigars, Mugsy shuffled us forward and used me to push open a darkened emergency exit. I braced for the alarm, but nothing sounded.

Nothing except the warning bells in my head growing to disaster sirens.

I tried to clutch the doorframe, but he shoved me outside so hard, I tumbled to the ground. Ignoring the burn of fresh scrapes on my knees and palms, I scrambled up to run. Before I could take a single step, he was in my space.

Gripping my upper arms, he gave me a smarmy smile, but frustration tightened Mugsy's features. "I'm here to rescue you. After they saw Maximo dragging you around yesterday, marked up and handled like a piece of property, I knew I had to get you out of here before it was too late. I'll take care of you."

They?

The way he spoke and the manic look in his eyes made terror coat my insides.

"Let me go!" I shouted.

Surprisingly, he listened and released one of my arms. I spun away, but his hold on my other arm remained firm, squeezing until I was sure I'd bruise.

Acrid bile rose in my throat when his hand dropped to touch my ass, but he only pulled my phone from my back pocket and threw it against the building.

Shit, shit, shit.

Now Cole can't track me.

Even as I fought it, Mugsy began shuffling us along the walkway before turning onto a narrow path that ran between two sections of the building. I lost sight of the door. I couldn't see *any* doors. But what I could see was a car parked at the end.

Oh hell no.

Fear tightened my chest and my breaths came in rough pants.

Be smart. Calm. This isn't the first time someone has come after me.

Frantically scanning the area, there was no one else around.

I doubted anyone inside would be able to hear me scream—a bone-chilling thought.

Since it was unlikely a rescue was coming, that meant one thing.

It was up to me to save myself.

I wasn't strong enough to take Mugsy in a fight, but I could effortlessly outrun him if he'd loosen his grasp. Outrunning a bullet wouldn't be so easy, but that was a risk I was willing to take.

Since tugging my arm free hadn't worked, I went for sympathy. "You're hurting me."

I should've known he wasn't capable of feeling concern toward anyone but himself. He squeezed harder, his tone earnest. "Maximo Black killed your father, Juliet. You need to come with me before he does the same to you."

And that was when, despite my best intentions to play it smart, I fucked up.

Because I forgot.

I forgot to act surprised. Distraught. Angry. *Vengeful.* It hadn't even occurred to me to pretend I gave one iota of a single fuck at learning of my father's murder.

Shamus would've been proud, I was finally acting like him.

Mugsy noticed my lack of reaction and his beady eyes narrowed. Any hint of faux concern was gone in a blink. "We thought Black was forcing you. Lying to you. But you knew he killed Shamus, didn't you? And you still slutted yourself out to him. You betrayed your father so you could live in that big mansion and feel like a somebody on the Strip."

Those eyes I felt on me at the Strip.

They weren't just Marco's and Ash's.

Mugsy sneered in disgust. "What kind of daughter would do that to her father? Thank God Shamus died before finding out his Jule-bug is a whore *and* a rat."

His words hit like a cannonball to the gut, taking my breath as they demolished the wall I'd built around my guilt. It flooded me, threatening

264

to rip me apart and take me down.

I held it together because if he got me to the end of the walkway, shit would go from bad to worse. I knew that down to my bones.

"Come with me, we'll make this right." His voice was patient and firm, like a father who was dealing with his misbehaving child. "You're lost. Confused. You wouldn't betray your own father like this."

"You need to let me go or Maximo will kill you," I lied.

Because it didn't matter what he did, Maximo was going to kill him.

"I'm trying to save you," he lied right back. "He's training you so he can sell you to the highest bidder or put you to work as one of his whores at the fights. It's his MO. He gets off breaking in naïve girls before shipping them off to make him money."

Maximo wouldn't do that.

Right?

I didn't respond beyond trying to twist away.

Clutching my face, Mugsy squeezed my cheeks until they ground painfully against my teeth. "Did you think you were special, Juliet? You mean nothing to him beyond sex and money." He shook his head with pity. "He's a billionaire who's dated actresses. Models. Socialites. Why would he want a white-trash-nothing when he could have anyone in the world?"

Again, his words aimed for a spot of weakness, and they hit their target.

They hit *hard*.

Why *would* he choose me? Having sex with me, sure, I understood that. But beyond the physical, why would Maximo—with all his good looks, power, and money—want to be with gutter trash? That question had lurked at the edges of my mind, invading randomly again and again. My insecurities were a loose thread and that question tugged at them, leaving me frayed. Like I could unravel.

Like I was temporary.

Was I just the latest in a long line of barely-legal girls and popped cherries?

Was he going to toss me aside when the next one came along? Or would he want me to be one of the girls at the fights, with politicians snorting coke off my breasts and big shots groping me?

I wanted to swear he wouldn't, but a lifetime of betrayal and heartache had taught me to never trust anyone.

And that definitely included slimy, shady, wannabe gangsters like Mugsy.

I tried once more to free my arm from his hold, but his grip was iron-clad. So I screamed as loud as I could. "Help! Someone help!"

"Shut the fuck up, bitch." He shook me so hard, I thought my neck would snap.

I got away from Marco that first night. I dodged Cole and locked him in a room.

I will not *be taken down by Mugsy Carmichael.*

Thrashing, I screamed bloody murder.

Smack!

Burning pain radiated across my cheek where he'd hit me.

His face was red as a tomato when he did it again. Violently yanking me closer with one hand, he used the other to hit me a third time. His stupid, gaudy ring caught my lip, tearing it open.

I wasn't sure what came over me, but at the metallic taste and the hot drops of blood sliding down my chin, I smiled.

No, I *grinned.*

"He's going to hunt you down," I said matter-of-factly. "He'll never stop. And when he catches you, he'll make sure your death is slow and painful."

All color drained from Mugsy's face, but he puffed out his chest and blustered, "He won't be able to get to me. But while he's trying, they'll pass you around like the whore you are. He won't even want you when they're done." His immense sweating turned into a waterfall down his jowled face as he pulled a gun. "Out of respect for your father, I said I'd get you to come on your own, but you're as greedy and money hungry as the rest. I should've let them have you."

When Maximo is done with him, he'll wish he had.

Jabbing the gun into my side, Mugsy smirked triumphantly. He began down the path, clearly expecting me to follow.

I didn't.

For whatever reason, someone wanted me. Whoever they were, they likely wanted me alive.

Which meant Mugsy wasn't going to shoot me. And if he did? Well, death was better than being passed around.

Calling his bluff, I screamed. I kicked. I swung my arms windmill style, hoping to connect.

I made so much damn noise, someone had to hear me.

Mugsy caught my ponytail in his sweaty palm, yanking hard enough to make my eyes water, but I kept going.

Even when he smacked me.

Even when he hit me in the eye with the butt of his gun.

Even when he made revolting threats that caused bile to rise from my churning stomach to lodge in my throat.

I was not going to be a victim. I'd die before that happened.

And I'd take that asshole with me.

Summoning every bit of will and energy and fury I had, I stopped fighting. I froze. Through blurry, already swelling eyes, I watched Mugsy's body relax with exhaustion and victory. Thinking he'd won, he let his guard down.

And that was when I attacked.

I threw my weight at him, catching him by surprise and knocking us both to the sidewalk. His head slammed against the unforgiving concrete, and he lost hold of his gun, the metal skittering up the path.

He tried to roll, but between me and his own gut, he was a turtle stuck on his back. "Fuck! Get off me, cunt!"

My fists rained down. My nails dug in.

I'll never be a victim again.

I'm not a little girl getting slapped around. I'm not small and defenseless against trained punches.

I'm not taking a knife for that bastard.

I decide who touches me. I decide my life.

Not a victim.

Not a victim.

"I'm not your damn victim anymore, Dad!" I screeched, blood and spittle spraying.

"You're fucking crazy, bitch," Shamus shouted back.

But it wasn't Shamus, of course.

Shamus was dead.

Maximo killed him.

Just like he was going to kill Mugsy.

Mugsy shoved me off him, and I rolled to the side. I braced for an onslaught of kicks or for him to pull me by my hair, but he was wheezing as he struggled to stand.

I was faster to find my footing. With him prone, I could've been the one to deliver the onslaught of kicks. As badly as I wanted to, I had an opening, and I was taking it.

Vengeance and violence could wait.

Running as fast as I could, I raced back to the door. I pulled and pulled but it was locked.

Shit.

Shit.

Shit, shit, shit.

Maybe I could make it past Mugsy.

Maybe the car at the end of the path was a coincidence.

Or maybe I'd be caught, dragged away, used up and spit out like a worthless nothing.

I couldn't let that happen.

I slammed my bloody fists against the door, hoping like hell I could be heard over the chaos of dinging machines, clacking chips, and conversation.

After a moment that felt like an eternity, the door swung toward me, nearly knocking me over.

Someone grabbed my arms, and I opened my mouth. My scream died in my throat and relief washed over me when I saw Ash's horrified gaze scanning my battered face. "Fucking hell."

"I'm fine," I offered, knowing I likely looked worse than I felt.

Which wasn't hard, really, because I didn't feel anything.

I was physically and mentally numb.

Pulling a walkie-talkie from his pocket, he said, "I've got her. Hall B-9. Search the rear path and delivery alley." His gaze returned to me. "Who?"

"Mugsy Carmichael," I said with zero hesitation.

He'd made his bed. He could rot in it.

Ash shifted us inside, closing the door and blocking me with his body. I was about to ask him to get me the hell out of there when I felt it.

Like the calm before a downpour, the room went electric and wired.

My eyes shot to the end of the hall just as Maximo stormed in. There was no cool, calm, blankness to his expression. It was unconcealed rage. Thunderous.

He wasn't a downpour.

He was a hurricane, ready to rip apart everything in his path.

I stared, captivated by how one man could fill an entire room with his fury and malice. And he stared back, as though nothing else in the room—in the *universe*—existed but me.

As he neared, I realized it wasn't only anger that darkened his expression.

It was desperation.

Panic.

Anguish.

Fear.

Unrestrained and raw, his dark gaze moved down me, taking in each scrape. Each cut. Each smear of blood and patch of dirt.

"Little dove," Maximo whispered roughly, as though the words were forced out through gravel and glass.

He lifted me in his arms, and I clutched the lapels of his suit jacket and buried my face in his chest. I wanted to fall apart, but the tears wouldn't come.

"Carmichael," Ash bit out.

Maximo didn't speak. He just held me tight as he began walking. After a minute, I heard the ding of the elevator before he stepped in and the noises of the casino were cut off. Even when we were alone, I didn't loosen my death grip on him.

I didn't do anything but shake.

The elevator slowed to a stop and Maximo stepped off. Only then did I let him go, but he didn't do the same. Cupping the back of my head, he held me to him. His lips pressed to the top of my head, and we stood like that for long, silent moments.

Just the two of us.

But not in our space.

I wanted *our* space.

"I want to go home," I said, my words muffled against his chest.

"Soon."

The elevator chimed and opened again. I tilted my head just enough to see Marco step off. I didn't think he could see much of the damage, but the rage in his eyes told me I was wrong.

He went to the kitchen and made a bag of ice, wrapping it in a towel before handing it to Maximo.

Maximo rearranged me in his hold and pressed it gently to my face. "Get Pierce here."

"I don't need a doctor," I tried, but I should've saved my breath because they ignored me.

"Ash already called," Marco said.

"Have security sweep the entire resort. Every fucking corner. Get Miles and Cole to go through the cameras from today."

"Yesterday, too," I said.

Both sets of angry eyes shot to me.

"What happened yesterday?" Maximo asked. His voice was low and even, but there was a sharp edge—as if I'd kept something from him.

I'm not the one with secrets.

"He said *they* saw you drag me through the casino yesterday. They thought you were pissed at me."

"Did he say who they were?"

I shook my head.

He gently sat me on the kitchen island. Curling his hands around the edge of it, he leaned down so we were brooding eye to swollen eye. "I need you to tell me everything, Juliet. Can you do that?"

I nodded.

"That's my girl."

I loved to hear Maximo say that, but right then, the words were hollow.

Empty.

Or maybe that was just me.

How did I let myself get in so deep?

How did I let him break through all my walls?

How could I be so fucking stupid?

Letting people in only leads to pain and disappointment.

I needed space from the man I'd willingly—*happily*—let take over every aspect of my life. The sooner I talked, the sooner I could get the distance I needed.

Starting at the drunks brawling, I did my best to recount everything that'd happened.

Well, almost everything.

I didn't tell them what Mugsy had said about me betraying my father. I also didn't share his claim that Maximo was training me. Using me. Breaking me in like I was just another naïve girl who meant nothing.

Who *was* nothing.

I couldn't bring myself to tell him because I didn't want to know the truth. I wanted to bury my head in the sand a little longer.

Even if I didn't speak the words out loud, they were there, a constant taunt running on a loop through my head.

Nothing girl.

Whore Jule-bug.

Rat Jule-bug.

Temporary.

As I described my counterattack and tackling Mugsy, Maximo must've realized the blood on my hands wasn't only my own. He moved away to get a damp, soapy towel. When he rubbed it across my raw skin, I hissed at the coarse texture and burning sting.

His force eased, but he didn't stop. "Got to get that motherfucker's blood off you." Mixed with the anger, there was a glimmer of pride in Maximo's eyes. "Ballsy. My ballsy girl."

Am I his girl?

Tears burned my eyes, though they had nothing to do with the pain in my hands. My heart hurt worse than any of my injuries.

Maximo cleaned the rest of the dirt and blood with the same tender care. Once he was done, I wrapped my arms around myself, sliding back farther onto the island.

And he noticed.

Of fucking course.

Concern furrowed his brows as he studied me. When he spoke, his tone was firm and demanding. "Is that everything, Juliet?"

I had to choke the words back because I wanted to obey my Daddy. To be his good girl. To trust him.

Just as he'd *trained* me to do.

"That's it," I lied.

His eyes narrowed, but before he could speak, the elevator chimed and opened to reveal Ash and Dr. Pierce.

The doctor stepped off, but Ash stayed inside. I offered him a smile, but rather than getting his dimpled one in return, I caught his flinch before the doors slid closed.

I must look worse than I thought.

Dr. Pierce and Maximo fussed over me, cleaning the cuts more thoroughly and slathering me with ointment. Thankfully there was nothing broken, requiring stitches, or needing a hospital.

Just as I'd said.

When they were finished, Doctor Pierce surveyed me. "The good news is, it looks worse than it is."

"That's not saying much because it looks like hell," Maximo rumbled before catching my frown. He reached out to stroke my hair back, and I didn't lean into his touch like I usually did.

I stiffened.

His jaw clenched, a muscle jumping, but Doctor Pierce grabbed his attention as he gave a short list of things to watch for before leaving.

Maximo gathered me to him and lifted me, turning to Marco. "Give me a minute."

Carrying me into the bedroom, he set me on the bed and rummaged through my suitcase and then his. He returned to stand in front of me and gripped the hem of my top.

I tried to scoot away. "I can do it."

He didn't respond verbally, but he gave me *the look*.

I stopped fighting, knowing he wouldn't relent. It was easier to get it over with.

Or so I thought.

Because Bossy Maximo was hard enough to resist. When he was gentle and attentive, treating me like I was precious, it was nearly impossible.

Once I was wearing a pair of my cotton shorts and one of his tees, he carried me back into the living room. Arranging me on the couch with an unneeded blanket, he said, "I'm going to talk to Marco and then we'll go home."

But it wasn't home. It was *his* home.

Just like my suitcase wasn't mine. My clothes weren't mine.

Nothing was mine.

I was nothing.

The pit in my stomach grew as the truth settled in.

It was the beginning of the end.

CHAPTER TWENTY-EIGHT

Knives To The Gut

MAXIMO

"SHE LIED TO me."

"About?"

Pacing the balcony, I ran my hand through my hair. "Something else happened with that motherfucker."

"She almost got kidnapped," Marco said. "She's scared shitless, roughed up, and in pain. It makes sense she's freaked."

"This is my fault." Guilt clawed at me like knives to the gut. "I stopped to check on the tournament without her because she was bored yesterday. If I'd have gone right to her, that bastard wouldn't have been able to get his fucking hands on her."

"This isn't on—"

"I'm supposed to take care of her. I'm supposed to keep her safe. But someone came after *my* woman on *my* property. And he almost got her."

"Boss, get it under control," Marco cautioned. "You go in there looking ready to murder someone, and you're gonna scare her more. This isn't about you. It's not about your guilt or Ash's guilt or even Carmichael right now. It's about her."

Fuck, he was right. I was being a prick, making it about me while she sat alone.

Dragging my palm down my face, I pushed aside my anger to focus. "Find out what they've got on the security footage."

"Miles is combing through it. He said the drunks claimed they were paid to make a scene and mess with Ash as a prank, but neither can describe the guy beyond the wad of cash he gave them."

Idiots.

"Ask around to see who Carmichael has been leeching on to," I said.

"Ash is already hunting. Doubt he'll sleep until it's done."

"That bad?"

Marco gave a half shrug. "You know how he is."

I did.

Fuck.

I'd have to deal with that, but nothing I said would mean jack-shit until we found Carmichael. It could wait.

Juliet couldn't.

"Make sure he doesn't lose his head when he finds him," I said.

If left unchecked, it was likely Ash would take Carmichael out. I needed information first. Then I wanted his blood to stain my hands.

Marco lifted his chin. "Where do you want him when we find him?"

"Meat plant."

At that, he gave me a rare smile.

"If it's not about this, I'm unreachable for the next week," I said. "I don't give a shit if the buildings are burning down, someone else can deal with it."

"Got it, boss."

I opened the door to get back to Juliet.

Still huddled on the couch and staring straight ahead, she looked tiny. Scared. She didn't move until Marco came in after me and closed the door.

Jolting, her wide eyes snapped to me before tracking Marco as he walked to the elevator. When he was gone, she dropped her gaze to her hands.

Christ.

I'm going to kill that motherfucker.

Locking it down, I crouched in front of her. "Ready to go home?"

She hesitated, and fuck if that didn't gut me. After a few stretching moments, she finally nodded.

I lifted her, and her legs automatically wrapped around my waist. She tried to drop them, but I lowered one of my hands to her thigh, holding it in place.

When we got into the elevator, she said, "I can stand."

"I know that."

"I can also walk."

"Know that, too."

"So put me down," she ordered.

"No."

I was relieved to hear the attitude and fire return. "You can't just say no."

"I can and I did."

"Control freak," she muttered, though her lips tipped up.

"Brat."

Whatever hint of lightness she'd had was gone in an instant. She may as well have been one of the statues downstairs with as stiff as she became.

"Put me down, please," she tried.

"No."

Averting her dull eyes, her voice was just as emotionless. "It's hurting my knees."

I didn't believe her, but I wouldn't risk it. I lowered her to her feet, and she immediately took a couple small steps away.

If her hesitating had gutted me, her putting distance between us fucking *killed*.

I wanted to pull her to me so I could reassure both of us she was safe and that I had her. But I didn't do it because, right then, I didn't have her. She was a million miles away.

We didn't talk on the drive home. Juliet stayed pressed against her door, as far from me as she could get without being outside. Her feet were on the seat, her arms hugging her bent legs.

Christ, my little dove looks lost.

When we got home, she climbed out before I even put the SUV in park. I followed her up the path and unlocked the door. By the time I'd turned off the alarm, she was already at the top of the stairs.

I followed her again.

She had me so wrapped up, so obsessed, so addicted, I'd have followed her anywhere.

I turned down the hall, and as expected, she was in her sewing room. But rather than sitting at her desk, she was standing and staring at the large dove picture.

"You need to rest," I told her.

Surprisingly, she didn't argue. "Can I do it by the pool?"

I nodded.

She approached, her eyes to the side as she waited for me to move out of the doorway so she could pass. Reaching out, I touched her loose ponytail.

And she flinched.

Fucking *flinched*.

I blanked my expression even as everything inside me was being eviscerated.

Either directly or by order, I had a lot of blood on my hands. I'd beaten. I'd killed. I'd tortured.

But nothing I'd done would come close to what I'd do to Mugsy Carmichael once we found him.

As badly as I wanted to take her in my arms, I moved to the side. "Go get changed."

Without a word, she took off toward our room.

And I watched her go, my gut telling me I was fucking up by giving her space.

Rather than following, I went to find Vera. When I found her in the laundry room, I asked, "How'd you like a week off?"

Her face lit, but it wasn't for herself. "You're taking time off?"

"The week."

"Good. You need it." She pointed up. "So does she."

Even more after what happened today.

I didn't share that because if Vera found out, there was no way she'd leave Juliet.

"When?" she asked.

"Right now."

Vera's eyes widened before narrowing with suspicion. "Why so soon?"

"I need some time with Juliet," I said, which wasn't a lie. "I'll get you a room at Nebula, everything on me."

Her eyes went huge. "No, that's—"

276

"I sprung this on you. Go home and pack. It'll be set when you get there."

Catching my dismissal, Vera sighed. "Young love." Heading for the side door, she grabbed her purse off the hook before turning back. "Enjoy your week. Relax for once."

I would.

Just as soon as I found out what had Juliet pulling away.

JULIET

I KNEW THAT was too easy.

Shielding my eyes with my hand, I looked up to see Maximo standing next to me in his aviator shades, low slung trunks, and nothing else.

"Aren't you going back to work?" I asked. When I'd gotten outside and he'd been nowhere to be found, I'd assumed he'd gone to his office.

"No." He handed me a Diet Coke and some pain meds, waiting until I'd taken them before ordering, "Roll over."

My mind may have been a mess of conflicted confusion, but my body didn't have the same problem. It heated at his demand. "What?"

He held out a bottle of sunblock.

Oh. Right.

I rolled over and closed my eyes as he crouched to apply the lotion to my back and nape, massaging it in. His skilled fingers moved down, nearing my ass.

My breath caught, anticipation rioting in me. It whooshed out in a disappointed rush when he stood, taking his touch with him.

No, this is good. If he touches me, I'll lose my head, and things will get even messier.

This is good.

Then why does it hurt so bad?

Without a word, he turned around and moved to the deck. Sitting on the patio couch, he stretched an arm across the back of it and stared down at his phone.

Tearing my attention from him, I flipped onto my back, but without my iPad to read, I was bored and restless. It was doubtful the chlorinated water would feel good on my face, so swimming was out.

Floating wasn't, though.

Going to the pool house, I grabbed a lounge floaty and dragged it into the water. Once I was situated with my Diet Coke, floating under the shade of the canopy, I'd hoped my mind and body would relax.

They didn't.

Because even in the peaceful quiet, my thoughts were at a roar.

Whore!

Rat!

Nothing!

CHAPTER TWENTY-NINE

Lies

MAXIMO

THREE DAYS.

Three long-as-hell days.

And with each passing one, Juliet pulled away more, sinking into herself.

I had no idea what to do.

I wanted to force her to tell me what she was thinking. I wanted her to not tense and flinch every time I touched her.

I wanted her to smile at me.

Sitting in my office with the door propped open, I didn't check any of the emails waiting for me. I didn't go through my messages, other than the reports from the men—all of which were dead-ends.

Instead, my eyes and my mind were on Juliet as she worked across the hall.

She needed time. I got that. But rather than things improving, they were getting worse.

Something had to change.

As though I'd summoned her with my thoughts, Juliet got up and came to stand in my doorway. Dressed in a pair of short shorts and a tee that hung off her shoulder, she was so beautiful, it fucking hurt to look at her. Her hair was pulled into a messy bun—she hadn't worn it in a ponytail since that day. My marks were gone from her neck completely. That bastard's bruises were there but fading.

Her body was healing, but the lost look in her green eyes said her mind was far behind.

When she didn't enter, I ordered, "Come here, little dove."

She didn't.

Staying where she was, Juliet straightened her spine, giving me a stubborn lift of her chin.

And then she gutted me when, in a casual tone, she dropped a bomb.

"I want to move out."

JULIET

MY HEART WAS jammed in my throat, choking me as it hammered away. I didn't want to look at Maximo, yet I couldn't tear my eyes away from his blank face.

"Repeat that," he ordered, statue still.

Inhaling deep, I repeated the words I'd barely been able to force out the first time. "I want to move out."

Maximo stood so fast, his chair slammed into the window, hitting with such force, I was surprised it didn't shatter. Despite how quickly he'd gotten up, his approach was slow. Prowling. Stalking.

Hunting.

It took all my willpower not to flee like a gazelle fruitlessly racing from a lion.

"I must have misheard you," Maximo rumbled, forced composure in his low, scary tone.

"I'm moving out," I said, firmer and more definitive, even though I felt anything but.

"No."

I'd known it wouldn't be easy—normal breakups rarely were, and Maximo and I were far from normal. But I'd anticipated more than a simple no.

"You can't just say no," I said.

"We've been through this, Juliet. I can and I did."

"Well… I don't accept your no."

"And I don't accept your asinine idea to move out."

"It's not asinine."

"It is."

I crossed my arms, growing more irritated. "Think what you want, but it doesn't change—"

"It does."

"I'm moving—"

"You're not," he interrupted again.

Letting out a frustrated huff because he was really starting to piss me off, I snapped, "You don't get to tell me what to do anymore."

"I'm your Daddy, little dove. That's exactly what I get to do."

"No, you're not. You never were. This whole thing is stupid and a mistake and I fucking *hate* it!"

Maximo's head jerked back as if I'd slapped him.

Even as I tried to tell myself my outburst was warranted, guilt ate at me. I didn't want to hurt him. I didn't want to lie to him. But he was making it so much harder than it had to be.

I couldn't deal. I had to get out of there before I did something stupid.

Turning, I didn't make it two steps when he caught my arm and spun me back. In a blink, he had me in his office with the door kicked closed and me pressed against it. With his forearms to the wood, he caged me in.

"Don't lie to me, Juliet. And don't lie to yourself. You love this as much as I do. You get off on it—your pretty little pussy always so soaked." Even with the control he had over his anger, there was unfettered desperation saturating his voice. "You need it. Need *me*."

God, it hurt.

I wanted to lean into his body. Tip my head back so he could take my mouth. Or tilt to the side so he could mark my neck. And for the briefest of seconds, I forgot why that was a bad idea.

But then I remembered.

Whore.

Rat.

Nothing.

Training.

Using.

Lies!

"I don't love it," I coldly lied. "And I don't need it or you. Now back up."

"No," Maximo gritted out, his own tone glacial.

"Why?"

"Why do you want to go?"

"I have my reasons."

He gave a harsh, humorless laugh. "This I've gotta hear."

"No."

"You can't just say no," he said, throwing my words back at me.

"If you get to do it, so can I." We were talking in circles, each one wrapping tighter around my neck until I could barely breathe. I tried to move to the side, but he didn't budge. "What does it even matter? We're over."

"We're far from over."

"We *are.*"

"Why?"

"Because I said—"

"Why?"

"I said so—"

"Why?" he roared, his palms slamming the door next to my head.

"Because you don't want me!" I roared right back, losing my temper and, with it, my filter. "I know about your MO. I know about *everything.* Now let me go!"

Undeterred by my anger, his tone was unnervingly calm. "What *exactly* is my MO?"

"Breaking in naïve girls and training them to work at the fights," I blurted, too pissed off and hurt to think.

I'd seen Maximo cold. Hot. Scary. Scary hot. I'd seen him shutdown, and I'd seen him totally open and at ease.

But never, in the entire time I'd known him, had I seen him so enraged. His body practically vibrated with it, his narrowed eyes filled with so much hatred, it tore at me. "That motherfucker tell you that?"

"Yes, but—"

"And you believed him?"

No.

Yes.

Kind of.

"Yeah, you believed him." His jaw clenched as he rubbed his hand over it. "That's fine 'cause he's right... I have been training you."

282

CHAPTER THIRTY

Truth

JULIET

*I*T'S TRUE.

At his blunt confirmation, the air was pushed from my lungs like I'd been pummeled. My heart shattered into a million pieces as the tiny shred of hope I'd clung to was violently ripped apart.

Looking to the side, I fought to keep it together until I was alone. Only then would I let myself be violently ripped apart, too.

Maximo shifted, and I thought he was going to let me escape with my tail tucked between my legs. But he gripped my hair and forced my head back so my eyes met his blazing ones. "I've been training you to take *my* cock the way *I* like. To suck it down your throat and to keep going even when you're gagging. To follow my rules, to listen to me, to *finally* fucking trust me. I've been training you to be *mine*. No one else's." He shook his head, scowling. "I want to kill every bastard who looks at you. You think I'd let someone else touch you? Touch what's mine?" His tone was sharp, its edge lethal. "Do you want to know what happens to someone who touches you, Juliet?"

I shook my head, not knowing what he'd say but still certain my answer was no.

"Too bad. I've been holding back, careful not to scare you. That was clearly the wrong move because it allowed that motherfucker to get in your head. That's Daddy's mistake, and it won't happen again. From now on, you get all of me because you're damn sure going to give me all of you."

If this has been him holding back, what's unrestrained?

Maximo's focus dropped to my side as he tugged my shirt up. Slowly, he ran a finger along the scar above my hip. A cruel smile curved his lips before he lifted his head to aim that smile at me. "Told you he'd be dead."

My breath came in rough pants.

He had told me. I just hadn't believed him.

By the time I'd known better than to underestimate Maximo, his threat, the Sullivans, and their goon were long forgotten.

"I didn't let him off easy. I took my time. I made it hurt. And when I buried my blade for the last time," he skimmed his knuckle along the scar, just as he'd done the first time he'd seen it, "it was right here."

He studied me, waiting for my response.

If I was a good person, I'd have screamed.

Bolted from him.

Called the cops.

But I wasn't a good person. Because rather than mourning a lost life or being horrified in the face of viciousness, warmth spread through me. Maximo had defended me when no one in my life ever had. He'd been willing to go to war for me. He'd taken care of me.

Which was why, rather than any of the sane things I should've done, I whispered, "Thank you."

There was a flash of something in his dark gaze before he pushed. "Thank you *who*?"

But I didn't give him what he wanted.

Maximo didn't look pissed at my silence. No, he smiled again—menacing and wicked.

Taking hold of my hips, he shifted us across the room to his desk. He turned me in his hold, bending me over the desk and keeping me in place with a hand between my shoulders. Papers and his keyboard fell to the ground, but he either didn't notice or didn't care.

He tugged my shorts and panties down to my thighs, kicking my feet apart so the fabric stayed taut, digging in.

My brain finally caught up, and I tried to stand, but his hold stayed firm. "Maximo—"

"I knew you didn't trust me yet, Juliet. I knew you were holding back. But I didn't think you trusted me so little that you'd believe Mugsy *fucking* Carmichael over me." His palm landed with a stinging slap to my ass. "We'll fix that."

My yelp grew to a shout when two more landed on the same spot.

Stop.

One single word.

One single syllable.

I knew it was all I needed to say, and he would stop instantly.

Yet I didn't say it. I didn't even think about it.

"What did Carmichael say to you?" he asked, as though it were a normal conversation and he wasn't spanking my ass crimson.

I opened my mouth to lie, but it was the truth that spilled out between my pained cries. "That you were training me to sell me to the highest bidder."

"Don't sell pussy like a damn auctioneer. What else?"

"Or make me one of your whores at your fights."

"I don't have whores."

"Fine, your girls who are there because those men have winning personalities."

"Attitude, Juliet," he warned, a hard slap landing on my upper thigh. "The girls come from escort services. I let them work the fights. That's the extent of my role."

"Well, how am I supposed to know what you do?" I bit out through the pain. "You never talk to me about your work."

"That's because when I'm with you, I don't want to think about that bullshit. I want to selfishly savor the peace and distraction you offer. But if it makes you feel excluded, then it's another of Daddy's mistakes." A blow hit the other thigh. "What else?"

"That I betrayed my father by being with you. That I'm a whore and a rat." The familiar guilt settled in my chest, making it hard to breathe. "He asked what kind of daughter would do that to her father."

"The kind with a piece-of-shit father who didn't deserve loyalty."

"I never even cried," I admitted as his palm caught the upper cheek, the sharp slap sounding around us. "I cried for the snake I killed in the desert but not my own father."

"He didn't deserve your tears, either."

"I never felt guilty for being with you. I felt guilty for *not* feeling guilty."

"You shouldn't feel guilty, period." Another two. "What else?"

"That I'm greedy and money hungry."

"You're far from either. In fact, you're a pain in my ass when it comes to accepting gifts without argument. What else?"

"That it's just sex."

"If all I wanted was this perfect pussy, I wouldn't hate our time apart. I wouldn't rearrange my schedule to work from home or bring you to the office with me. You're smart and clever and creative and stubborn and determined and loyal and countless other things I'm obsessed with." His hand connected twice, warming my ass as his words warmed my insides. "What else?"

At what was left, the warmth he'd created was replaced by jagged shards of ice that left my insides frozen and sliced apart.

I swallowed, unable to force the words out. I didn't want to tell him. I didn't want to bring it to his attention if he still hadn't figured it out himself.

I didn't want to shine a blinding spotlight on the truth.

At my hesitation, his hand came down on the same spot three times. "What else?"

"Nothing," I lied.

Wrong move.

The next one landed on my pussy, making tears burn in my eyes, though they still wouldn't fall. Spanking there again, he ordered, "Don't ever lie to me, Juliet."

Three more piercing smacks connected, and it was all I could stand. Like a dam in my mind was demolished, the words flowed out in an unbridled rush. "He asked why someone like you would want me. I'm not special. Just gutter trash. Temporary." Finally, the tears spilled free, and once they started, they wouldn't stop. My voice filled with so much sorrow, it couldn't hold it all and broke as I admitted, "I'm *nothing*."

His hand rained down a series of rapid-fire slaps, heat and tingles spreading across my skin.

And I sobbed.

Everything I'd kept buried deep inside came pouring out with my tears. All the fears and insecurities. The guilt. The self-loathing.

Mugsy had planted seeds of doubt. Thanks to my insecurities, those seeds had grown and spread like snaking vines to take over everything.

With his punishment, Maximo cleared away the mess that'd taken root in my head. My thoughts untangled and disintegrated as my mind went blissfully blank. Tension eased from my body, and I sank into the desk.

"That's my girl," he said, his hand connecting in a hard blow that soothed me like a gentle caress. "Let it all go."

His words offered absolution and his pain offered peace.

I wanted both.

Needed them.

"I believed him," I whispered on a shuddering exhale. "I thought you didn't want me. That you were moving on to someone else. Someone better." I couldn't keep the accusation from my tone when I pointed out, "You haven't touched me. Not even to hold me at night."

Three days.

Three days of him close, yet so far away. Not touching me. Barely kissing me. Hardly even talking.

Jealousy had twisted in my gut each time I'd seen him on the phone. Mugsy's words had echoed through my head, and I'd wondered if Maximo was talking to my replacement.

A new little dove.

"Jesus, Daddy fucked up." Maximo's palm skimmed over my sore ass. "I thought you needed space, but giving it to you fed right into his bullshit lies." He squeezed a cheek, the sting increasing until more tears spilled free. "Won't happen again. No space. No time. No leniency. No holding back."

That should've been terrifying, but instead, it sent a surge of relief and joy through me. I didn't give a damn if it made me needy or codependent, I wanted it. All of it.

All of him.

Releasing me, Maximo pressed his hand under me to cup my pussy. He curved his body over mine and curled his other hand around my throat. His hard cock pressed against my inflamed skin, making it burn. Making me burn. "And if you think I didn't wrap myself around you like this every night after you fell asleep, you're out of your mind. Can't sleep without you in my arms."

God, I'd been so stupid.

Keeping his possessive hold on me, Maximo straightened us to stand with my back pressed to his front. He pushed my shorts and panties the rest of the way off before turning us toward the wall of blank monitors. "I watched you. All the damn time."

My pulse went wild as my brain short-circuited.

Is he saying...

Even though he must've felt my thumping pulse, he continued, not holding anything back—just like he'd promised. "Camera in your sitting room. Had one in your bedroom until I didn't have the willpower to keep it turned off." Grazing his lips and teeth against my neck in a too light tease, he raised his head to my ear to whisper, "Want to know when that was?"

No.

I *needed* to know.

"I had it disconnected the morning after I watched you slide your hand between your legs. Seeing you touch yourself while you were wearing my sweats? It made me come harder than I ever had before. What were you thinking about?"

If I was wearing his sweats at the time, then it was the first time I'd thought of him while I'd touched myself. The night he'd carried me from the couch to my bed.

Licking my suddenly dry lips, I lied, "I don't remember."

His tattooed fingers around my throat gave a small squeeze. "You've already lied enough, Juliet. Do you want more punishment?"

A moan forced its way out. Seeing our reflection in the blank monitors was almost as exhilarating as feeling his hand around my throat.

"What were you thinking about?" he repeated.

"You," I admitted on a soft breath.

He groaned his approval, sliding a finger through my wetness. "Good. Because every time I stroked my dick, I thought of you."

Arousal shot through me and I tilted my hips, wanting him to touch me more, but his fingers only teased.

"Don't ever think," he continued, "even for one damn second, that I don't want you. I've always wanted you, even when I shouldn't have. All of you. *Everything.* Every piece of you."

Like only Maximo could, he overwhelmed me with his size, his touch, his obscenely sweet words.

I couldn't take any more. "Maximo—"

"Hush. You had your time to talk, now it's time to listen." Turning me to face him, he cupped my head with both hands, tilting it back. "Been obsessed with you since I saw you in that dump. The more time I spent with you," he jerked his head toward the monitors, "or watching you, the more that obsession grew. The more I needed you. I could never have better than you because there is no better."

It was too much. More than my brain and my body and my heart could take. "Maximo—"

"I said hush. Do you know why I started calling you *little dove*?"

I shook my head.

His cock jerked against my stomach. "Because I knew I was going to keep you in my cage. Even back then, I knew I'd never let you go."

And then he took my mouth, his kiss just as hungry as mine. His tongue speared in, demanding and greedy and hot.

Lifting me, he broke the kiss and began walking. Unable to keep my mouth off him, I kissed and nipped his jaw. When I bit down on his neck, wanting to mark him like he did me, he froze. I wondered if he'd just fuck me on the hallway floor, but after a brief pause, his long strides sped up.

My ass had barely hit the bed with a stinging ache when he had my shirt and bra off. I lifted onto my knees but didn't have time to undress him. He beat me to it, throwing his clothes off to land with mine before taking me down onto my back. His body covered mine, his hips between my spread thighs and his hard cock pressed against me.

But he didn't enter me. His hard length glided along my slit. It rubbed my clit, tormenting me until I had no choice but to beg.

"Please," I pleaded.

"Who am I?"

That time, I didn't hesitate. "My Daddy."

His eyes closed, his pleasure more than purely sexual. It was important to him. *I* was important to him. "Again."

Leaning up, I touched his cheek, his stubbled jaw, and down to the pointed crown that was inked on his neck. "You're my Daddy."

In one thrust, he filled me, slamming to the hilt and stealing my breath. "Who owns this pussy?"

"You do."

"Who owns you?"

Again, my answer was immediate because, dysfunctional or not, it was the truth. "You do, Daddy."

His movements were frantic and unhinged, his eyes wild at my words. With each powerful, savage thrust, the tension in my lower belly tightened. He pushed me closer to the edge until every nerve ending in my body was oversensitive and overwhelmed.

And then he stopped.

His thick cock buried deep was almost enough to launch me into bliss anyway.

Almost, but not quite.

Restless and needy, I rocked my hips with wanton abandon, happy to fuck myself on his length.

His weight pressed into me, pinning me to the mattress so I couldn't move those meager centimeters.

Maximo's voice was rough and harsh when he ordered, "Tell me you love it."

God.

Looking at him, his face far from blank or cold, I saw the blatant earnestness. The hurt. My words earlier were meant to be destructive, and they'd achieved their goal.

"I love it. I never hated it."

His hand moved from the bed to the base of my throat, his fingers curling around my neck. Although his touch was featherlight, the hold was intoxicatingly controlling and I wanted more. "Tell me you need it."

"You see what three days without this did to me. I'm a mess. I need it."

He started moving again, though I wasn't sure if he was even aware he was doing it. "Tell me you need *me*."

For all intents and purposes, I'd been on my own for as long as I could remember. Shamus had taught me early and often not to rely on others. Not to trust them.

Not to need anyone.

And I'd lived by that for a long time. Until Maximo had shown me what it was like to be taken care of.

"I need you," I told him, hoping he knew how difficult it was for me to willingly make myself vulnerable. "More than I've ever needed anyone or anything."

I should've known he'd get it.

Dropping his body tight to mine, he kissed me, long and hot and fierce. His pelvis rubbed against my clit as he ground into me. When we were both breathless, he tore his mouth away and tilted my head to nip my neck.

"Harder," I demanded, wanting the love bites back.

I missed them.

Maximo groaned against me before biting harder and sucking the sensitive skin until I gasped. Raising himself, he moved his hand back to my throat, his thumb stroking over the spot.

So close.

"No one takes you from me, little dove," Maximo growled. "No one opens your cage."

God, so close.

"Even you." His thrusts grew vicious, making my eyes unfocused and my thoughts hazy. "*I* decide when this is over."

My lids drifted closed, my neck arching.

"And it'll *never* be over. I'll never let you go because I love you, Juliet. 'Til the day I die."

What?

Did he really…

Try as I might to fight the crashing waves, I lost my thoughts, my breath, my mind. My orgasm tore through me, shredding me until I didn't think I could ever be put back together.

But one wasn't enough.

Maximo moved his hand from my throat to shove between us, his thumb stroking my clit how I liked. One orgasm barreled straight into the next, his thumb and dick working together to wring everything from me.

When I'd given him all I had physically, he brought his hand back up to grip my chin before he demanded more of me.

All of me.

"Tell me you love me."

I wasn't sure I'd ever felt familial or platonic love. I'd certainly never been in love.

Not until Maximo.

It was why I was so petrified. Because if Maximo lied, cheated, or let me down like everyone else, it wouldn't be an annoying disappointment. It would destroy me. Shatter me.

Admitting I loved him would hand him all my trust. There'd be no walls, no distance, no holding back.

Just like he wanted.

Like we both needed.

"I love you."

Lids closing, his head dropped back, exposing his strong neck. His shoulders were bunched, tense and taut with exertion as he slammed into me over and over. Rough and raw, he gritted out, "Again."

"I love you, Daddy."

His low groan made goosebumps spread across my skin. He continued driving into me as he came.

Once he was done, he gave me his weight, burying his head in the side of my neck as we caught our breath.

When he tried to lift away, I wrapped my limbs around him, whispering, "Just another minute, please."

"As long as you want," he whispered back, his lips teasing my neck. "Forever."

Surrounded by him, my meandering thoughts bounced all over.

Maybe I should've been disturbed by the fact he'd watched me.

Maybe I should've been horrified he'd killed the Sullivans' goon.

Maybe I should've been scared by his possessive declarations.

And maybe it was a sign of how fucked up and dysfunctional I was that none of it bothered me.

Not at all.

In fact, I *liked* it.

I didn't need a charming prince at my side. I needed a villain at my back. I needed someone who would love me with obsessive reassurance. Someone who wasn't afraid to get his hands dirty because I knew firsthand that the world was far from a fairy tale.

I needed Maximo.

My silence must've stretched too long for my villain because he lifted to look down at me. His brow was furrowed and his muscles tight, as though he were bracing for me to take it all back. "We good?"

Smiling, I ran my fingertips across his stubbled cheeks. "Perfect."

Relief flowed unfettered before he took my mouth in a bruising kiss. When he pulled away, he stroked my hair back, studying me—including the bags under my eyes. "You need rest."

He rolled to the side and tried to gather me to him, but I kept the momentum going, shoving him onto his back before straddling him with my ass on his abs.

His eyebrow quirked and an amused smile pulled at his lips.

I inhaled deeply. My shoulders were light, my chest was loose, and I could breathe easily.

Maximo gave me that.

So I wanted to give him something in return.

More of me.

CHAPTER THIRTY-ONE

A Deal's A Deal

JULIET

"MY MOTHER WAS a dancer at a strip club in Buffalo."

Maximo's eyes flared at my sudden admission, but he didn't speak.

"My dad met her when he went to celebrate a win. After a weekend together, he convinced her to move in with him. Used his charm and big talk, and she bought into it. She probably thought the next Ali or Holyfield was rescuing her from the trailer park. Instead, she ended up pregnant by a man who had problems with rage, gambling, alcohol, and fidelity."

She thought she was getting a prince but ended up with the villain. At least I've always known who I'm with.

"Nine months later, I was born on Valentine's Day. And in the most obvious omen to how their love affair would end, my mother named me Juliet because she thought *Romeo and Juliet* was romantic." I shrugged. "I don't think she ever read the book."

"Still a beautiful name," he said. "What happened to her?"

"She took off three months after I was born. Having a baby didn't soften Shamus. It didn't slow him down. He was still out drinking and fighting and fucking while my mother was stuck in a tiny apartment with no money, friends, or family other than a crying newborn. Claiming she had to get groceries, she left me with a neighbor and never came back."

"You sure she left on her own?"

I knew what he was asking. Before I was old enough to know better, I'd built up a fantasy that Shamus had forced her away and she was searching for me. Or that he or someone he owed had killed her. It was a gruesome thought for a kid to have, but it was better than my mother abandoning me.

"I'm sure," I said. "I found her online when I was twelve and made the mistake of reaching out."

"That bad?"

"Worse. She didn't ask how I was. She didn't ask if I was safe even though she knew damn well how Shamus was. She just fed me excuses about how she was too young to be stuck at home with a screaming kid. Then she told me not to contact her again because she had a new boyfriend and she'd lied about her age and didn't want him to know. And then she blocked me."

His palms glided up my sides. "Christ, I'm sorry."

"Don't be. I looked her up a couple years later because I hoped time would make a difference. It had, but not in a good way. She'd racked up arrests for DUIs, theft, that kinda stuff. I'd lucked out. Going with her would've been jumping out of the pan and into the fire."

Maximo sat and wrapped his arms around me. I greedily soaked in the comfort and attention before leaning back.

Taking another of those easy breaths, I unloaded the last bit of weight from my soul and shared something I'd never spoken out loud. Something I'd barely allowed myself to think. "I was *happy* you killed him."

A flurry of emotions ran wild across his handsome face. He opened his mouth, but I put my fingertips to them.

I needed to get it all out. Let it all go.

"Shamus being dead meant I wouldn't have to be on guard against his fists or his enemies' knives or his buddies sneaking into my room or bill collectors or any of the other shit I dealt with because of him. When you brought me here, it was the first time in my entire life I could sleep through the night. That I could relax. That I didn't look over my shoulder." Tears blurred my vision, slowly sliding free. "It was the first time I felt safe and like I had a *home*."

Even with loathing burning in his gaze, his touch was gentle when he cupped my cheek and wiped away my tears.

"Thank you for giving me that," I whispered through the lump in my throat.

When I dropped my cheek to his chest, he wrapped me tight in his arms and pressed his lips to my forehead. "I'll always give you everything, Juliet."

"I just want you."

"Always give you that, too."

Feeling emotionally drained, I'd shared all there was to share. It was his turn. "Tell me about your family."

I didn't think he actually would, but with only a brief hesitation, Maximo said, "My old man was a lot like yours. Greedy. Always out for more. Blinded by it. He never appreciated what he had," he gave me a pointed squeeze, "and he lost it all."

"How?"

"Remember I told you I inherited three of my casinos?" At my nod, he continued. "My great-grandfather built Moonlight and Star. My Grandpa Sal took over and added Sunrise. When he died, he didn't leave them to my father. He left them to me."

"Why?"

"Because my father would sell out at the first decent offer. He was an entitled bastard who had no interest in putting in the work, whereas I'd been learning the business since I was a kid. Grandpa Sal knew I'd die before I let our family's legacy go. Unfortunately, he was the one who died when I was sixteen, so my father got temporary control anyway."

Maximo got a faraway look in his eyes, the shadows of ghosts haunting him.

"We can talk about something else." I shifted to climb off him but didn't get far.

His palms slid to cup my breasts, the shadows in his eyes growing into a different kind of darkness. "Having these perfect tits right here is very distracting." He pinched my nipples, squeezing to the point of pleasure-pain.

When he released them, I moved fast, rolling before he could grab me again. A moment of panic widened his eyes, making my heart pang with guilt and regret. But I wasn't running. I just grabbed his tee off the floor and pulled it on before straddling him again.

He ran his thumb across his bottom lip. "You wearing my shirt is not helping me focus."

At his tell, I had to know… "What're you thinking?"

His lips curled into a hot, wolfish smirk. "That I can feel my come mixed with your sweetness dripping out of you."

A tremor went through me. He'd made me come so hard, there was no way my body could handle more. But I found myself willing to take the pain.

There's a reason I put on the shirt, and yet I don't remember why…
Oh. Right.

"Now who's being distracting?" I asked.

"Still you."

I understood if he didn't want to talk about his family drama, but I still wanted to know about him. "Tell me more."

He stroked the flyaway hairs from my face, his gaze landing on my messy bun and his jaw clenching. "Put your hair in a ponytail first," he shot back, like we were in some bizarre negotiation.

"That's all? And here I thought you were some big shot businessman. I'd have negotiated for more."

"In that case—"

"Nope, too late." I undid my bun and shook out my hair before refastening it in a high ponytail.

"You're a fucking wet dream," he murmured as if I'd performed a striptease rather than a hairstyle change.

"You keep this up, it'll be me with the unreal, massive ego."

"Good." His fingers absentmindedly played with my hair.

"A deal's a deal," I prodded when he remained silent. "Tell me more."

"Control freak," he teased, tugging my hair gently. Inhaling, he launched back into his story. "My father couldn't get over the insult of not inheriting Black Resorts. Sal left my parents an insane amount of money, but he wanted the power. Rather than letting Sal's experienced team run things, he took over."

"Which didn't end well," I surmised.

"He had no clue what he was doing. And since learning would've been too hard, he threatened, blackmailed, and double-crossed. He got in over his head and nearly lost everything. And then he died—alone and despised."

My eyes widened. "You didn't…"

"Kill my old man? No." He stared me down, unapologetically honest. "But I was going to, Juliet. I was going to pay him back for every punch, knife, and bullet I took thanks to his bullshit. And then I was going to put a bullet between his eyes. But there was a long line of people in front of me and one of them got to him first."

"You took punches, knives, *and* bullets?" My anger and outrage grew as I leaned back and scanned his beautifully-marred torso.

My eyes snapped back to his when I felt his silent laughter. It became outright laughter when I glared.

"Christ, you're perfect," he said, amused at my rage. "I just admitted I planned to kill my old man, and you're concerned with my old injuries."

"What else would I be concerned about?" I asked as my stomach loudly growled.

It was his turn to glare, looking displeased. "You haven't been eating enough."

I'd barely eaten for three days thanks to my churning stomach, so he was right. I climbed off him but didn't stop talking. "You said your dad died when you were nineteen. Have you been running the resorts since?"

"Unofficially. Sal's will had stipulations about college and age because he knew I'd try to get right to work and he didn't want me missing out. After my father died, Ma became the legal trustee, though it was in name only. I started running things and cleaning up his mess while I got my degree."

I didn't bother to ask how he'd cleaned up the mess because I was certain I didn't want those details.

Instead, I jerked my head toward the door. "Feed me, Daddy."

Standing, his body cut and muscular and *hard*, he rubbed his thumb across his bottom lip. "And when I'm done, you're gonna ride my face and feed me."

My nipples tightened and a fresh wave of arousal rolled through me. "Deal."

Maximo tugged on a pair of shorts, and we went to raid the kitchen. And after he fed me, we made it as far as the living room before his back was on the floor and I was riding his face.

Because a deal's a deal.

CHAPTER THIRTY-TWO

A Good Life

MAXIMO

"*H*OW DID THAT motherfucker just disappear?" I gritted out into the phone.

"He's always sweating," Juliet whispered from her spot on my lap. "It probably makes him slippery."

Christ.

Only she can make me smile when I'm pissed.

"None of his old crew has seen him," Ash said. "Half the people we talked to thought he ran away with Shamus to get out of paying his debts. The other half thinks Shamus is dead and that whoever took Carmichael out, too."

"Not yet," I muttered, my gaze locked on Juliet to watch for a reaction in case she could hear him.

There was none.

My girl was good.

No, she was *happy*.

She'd finally given me her trust, and with it, her submission.

And, fuck, it was even better than I'd thought it would be.

Each time she gave me more of that weight she'd always shouldered, the happier she got. Smiling more. Laughing more. Touching me more.

Her walls weren't down. They were gone.

I'd spent the first three days at home in hell, knowing she was pulling away. But the following three had been nothing but heaven.

Thinking about what Ash had said, my brows lowered. "Shamus has been... gone over a year. They haven't seen Carmichael since?"

"No."

Vegas wasn't a big town. It'd take work to disappear. Connections.

"Keep asking. Someone has to know who the bastard is leeching onto."

"Follow the trail of sweat," Juliet whispered, again making me smile when I wanted to punch a hole in the damn wall.

"She sounds good," Ash said.

"She is."

His voice lowered so she couldn't hear. "Take it that means the guest hasn't arrived."

My eyes stayed on Juliet, again watching for a reaction that didn't come. "No."

There was a hint of lightness in his tone. "Good luck."

I'm going to need it.

"Nothing?" Juliet asked when I clicked off.

"No."

"Damn." She tilted her head to the side. "You, uh, handled the Sullivan's goon. Do you think they—"

"No. He was making a mess for them, they were fine with me cleaning it."

"Then I'm back to nothing. Maybe whoever it is will give up."

It was doubtful, but the fact she wasn't scared as shit showed she trusted me to take care of her.

Which was exactly what I was doing.

Even if it made her lose her shit.

I gripped her hips to stop any escape attempts. "I need you to get ready. Someone is coming over."

"Who?"

"You remember meeting Ella Adams and her husband at the warehouse fight?"

She took a second. "The ones who sat next to us?"

"Yes. Ella's a psychiatrist."

Juliet's entire body went so rigid, I worried she'd shatter in my arms. Hurt filled her eyes, shuttering the easy brightness I'd had shining on me for three days.

Her voice was soft and wounded and flat. "You *do* think there's something wrong with me."

"Never." Cupping her face, I made her meet my eyes. "There's not a single thing wrong with you. You're perfect."

"Then why do you want me to talk to a shrink?"

"You've been put through a lot of shit. More than you should've ever had to deal with."

"I'm fine."

"I don't doubt it. But I wouldn't be a good Daddy if I didn't make sure of that."

She was quiet for a moment as she mulled it over. Reaching a decision, she slowly nodded. "I don't know if I'll be comfortable enough to actually talk, but I'll meet with her."

"Thank you."

She moved off my lap. "But you owe me sushi for dinner."

I grinned. "Anything you want."

"Should've held out for more," she muttered.

"What if I threw in going to a fight tonight?"

Excitement lit her face. "The warehouse?"

"Moonlight."

Her excitement dimmed a little. "Better than nothing."

She prefers the warehouse fights.

My girl is bloodthirsty.

Creating Juliet was the only good thing Shamus McMillon had done in his sorry excuse for a life, and that'd worked in my favor. Who I was and what I did wasn't an adjustment for her. She was used to violence and lawlessness. And since it wasn't directed at her, she thought it was a good life.

Starting for the hallway, she paused for a moment by the door before looking back. "I won't tell her about how we met or any of your work stuff," she said, again proving she was the perfect fit for me. "But should I act like we have a typical relationship?"

"Never." She still looked unsure, so I told her, "Ella and Tony have a similar relationship, just more casual."

Juliet worked to hide her smile. "So he's not a control freak, got it."

"Juliet…"

"Maximo," she mocked as she hurried from the room.

Limited time or not, I was about to go after her when my phone rang. *Damn.*

AWKWARD.

Soooo awkward.

Sitting in the center of the couch, I looked across the coffee table to where Ella Adams sat in an armchair. Unlike when I'd seen her at the fight, she wasn't glammed up in a Jessica Rabbit-esque dress. Instead, she wore simple jeans and a sleeveless blouse, looking stylishly professional.

I enviously watched as she took a drink of her giant iced coffee.

I should've held out for sushi and *a late afternoon coffee.*

She set it down on the table before smiling at me. "Awkward, right?"

I couldn't help but smile. "Right."

"I get it. And since Maximo is like Tony but cranked up to a million, I'm betting he sprung this on you last minute and didn't give you a choice."

"Right again."

"Figured." Crossing her legs, she seemed totally at ease whereas I was tense, my legs bent up to my chest. "Maybe it'll help if I tell you a little about me first."

"Okay." I was unsure anything would help but it couldn't get worse.

"I've been a psychiatrist for seven years. When I'm not working, I like to cook, garden, and chase after my two kids. Tony and I have been married for eleven years, but I've been his sub for thirteen. I found him and BDSM when I was this," she held her hand up with her index finger and thumb nearly touching, "close to dropping out of med school."

Her casual mention of being a sub was surprising. She spoke of it like it was just another fact about her, not something to hide or be ashamed of.

"Why'd you almost drop out?" I asked.

"Tony jokes that I'm not type-A, but a type-A-*plus* because an A isn't good enough. And since perfection is impossible in med school, I felt like a failure and was overwhelmed. I needed an outlet, and I found it in Tony and BDSM." She grabbed her coffee but gave me a pointed brow raise. "I'm sure I don't have to tell you how freeing it is to hand your worries and stress to someone you trust to take care of them."

Even after Maximo had become my Daddy, I'd held back so much of myself. It wasn't until after our blowup that I allowed myself to truly trust him.

And just as Ella said, it was freeing.

"I'm starting to learn that," I admitted.

"Good. Having someone in your corner who you can trust is important for your wellbeing."

"Are you and Tony, uhh, that way all the time?" I asked, both because I wanted to steer the conversation away from me and because it was nice to talk to someone who understood.

Blogs and websites could only go so far.

"We are and we aren't." At my confused look, she explained. "Back when we started seeing each other, if I wasn't in class or studying, I was doing whatever he said." She gave a small smile. "Now, between work and the kids, we don't always have time to fully sink into our roles the way we used to. But he's still my Dom and I'm still his sub."

Like all relationships, BDSM had a lot of variations. From what I'd read online, it seemed like most long-term ones were similar to Ella and Tony's.

"What about you and Maximo? Are you that way all the time?" she asked.

Damn.

Since she'd been so forthcoming, I felt rude not answering. "Yes."

"How do you feel about that?" At my hesitation, she held up her hands. "I know, typical shrink question."

Smiling, I thought about it for a moment. Would I rather we only occasionally played roles? Would it be better if there was more flexibility? Would I be happier if our dynamic was casual?

No.

Hell no, actually.

We were all-in, and I couldn't imagine us any other way.

So I shared a little. "Surprisingly, I love it."

She studied me intently. "Why surprisingly?"

I shrugged, wishing I'd chosen my words more carefully. "I figured it wouldn't do anything for me. That it was only his thing that I could accommodate for him."

"It's not?"

Shaking my head, I admitted, "I think I need it more than he does."

"How so?"

"I need the care and reassurance." I left it at that because I didn't want to get into why I needed that so badly. How years of neglect, abuse, and being alone had left me with insecurities and doubts that were only soothed by Maximo's brand of obsessive love.

Thankfully, she seemed to realize I was done and didn't push.

We spent a while talking about my sewing and her gardening. By the time we were done, the awkwardness was mostly gone and it was like a visit with a new acquaintance.

When we stood, she stepped closer. "I'd like to visit again, if that's okay with you and Maximo."

"Yeah, okay," I said, not as horribly against the idea as I thought I'd be.

"I'll be in touch with Maximo to schedule it," she said, taking the responsibility off me.

And then she left.

That wasn't torture.

Heading upstairs, I paused in Maximo's office doorway.

He looked up, concern etched on his handsome face. "All done?"

"For today."

Some of the concern eased, but not all of it. "You're going to talk to her again?"

I shrugged. "Depends on if you follow through with your end of this bargain."

He grinned, and God, I still couldn't believe he was mine. "Already made reservations."

"Yay."

"Get over here," he ordered, pushing away from his desk. When I was within reach, he pulled me onto his lap and cupped my chin, tilting my head back. "You okay?"

"Yeah. Ella is nice, so it wasn't too bad."

"Good."

It was good. I wasn't sure if I'd ever feel comfortable enough to really share, but there was something reassuring about knowing I had the option.

Kissing me quickly, he held my face. "Do you feel comfortable staying the weekend at Moonlight?"

That's why he still looks worried.

After what'd happened at Star, Maximo thought I wouldn't feel safe. But I knew I was.

"I'm good."

"You sure?" At my emphatic nod, he gave me a smile that sent a tremor through my body even before he said, "That's my girl. Vera already packed your bag. Go get changed for dinner."

He didn't have to tell me twice.

CHAPTER THIRTY-THREE

Earn It

JULIET

"YOU SURE YOU'LL be okay?"

Standing in the penthouse living room the next day, I looked over my shoulder to where Marco *and* Dan—one of Moonlight's security guards—stood. "Yeah, I think I'm covered."

Even with my reassurance, Maximo looked hesitant to leave. "Why don't you come with me?"

After a phone call from his realtor, Maximo had shared he was expanding Black Resorts with a new casino. Unfortunately, he'd yet to find the right land, which was one of the *usual bullshit* frustrations he'd been dealing with.

The realtor had found a handful of possible locations, and as much as I loved spending time with Maximo, sitting in the hot car and touring empty lots left a lot to be desired. More than that, though, it was important for us both to see I'd be safe alone.

Well, alone minus a bodyguard, security guard, and undoubtedly someone else watching on the cameras.

"I'm fine here, I promise. I'm going to sit by the pool and read. Maybe take a spin or fifty around the lazy river."

Maximo tugged his suit jacket on before pulling me closer. "I'll only be a couple hours."

"I know."

"I can come right back if there's an issue."

"I know."

"Keep your phone on you at all times."

"I know." At his narrowed eyes, I smiled and put my palms to his chest. "I'll be okay."

"I know," he said, stealing my line. Lowering his head, he kissed me like other people weren't in the room. "Be good."

"Never."

He grinned and let me go. "Love you."

"Love you, too."

I watched him get into the elevator before turning around. "He's gone. Let's throw a rager. Hookers, blow, the whole nine."

Dan's eyes went comically huge, but Marco didn't even blink as he said, "Go get changed."

I sighed. "Party pooper."

But I did as he said, stripping out of my sundress before pulling on my favorite feather print suit, a coverup, my aviators, and flip-flops. I got my iPad and headed for the door before backtracking to grab my new phone—Mugsy had shattered the old one.

All geared up, we went down the elevator to the main floor and out to the pool.

Marco led the way to a roped-off area that had one lounge chair, a giant umbrella, and a small table. I rolled my eyes, but truth be told, I was grateful for the seclusion.

I was okay.

I was safe.

But I was still on edge.

As soon as I sat down and got situated, my phone buzzed.

Daddy: Making sure you have your phone.

Me: You changed your contact name.

Daddy: Yes.

I shook my head but did it smiling.

Daddy: And now I'm disappointed you have it because I wanted an excuse to spank your ass raw tonight.

Me: Give me time, the afternoon is young.

Inhaling deep, I held my breath as I quickly typed out a message.

Something I'd been wanting to ask.

Something I'd been dying to try.

Something that terrified me just as much as it thrilled me—a common theme when it came to all things Maximo.

When my lungs began to burn, I exhaled as my finger hovered over the send button.

And then I pressed it.

Me: Then maybe after my ass is raw, you might want to fuck it?

Daddy: Christ.

Daddy: Jesus fucking Christ, Juliet, don't say shit like that when I'm not there with you.

Daddy: I nearly shot my load in my pants just reading that.

I grinned, loving that I had that kind of power.

Me: It was just a thought.

Daddy: Now it's a promise.

Daddy: Are you at the pool?

Me: Yes.

Daddy: Send me a pic.

Me: Don't you have work to do?

Daddy: And it's going to be frustrating, so seeing my hot as fuck little dove and thinking about fucking her tight little ass will make it better.

Well, how can I argue with that?

Going for inconspicuous, I took a quick picture. Then another quick dozen because I kept making a stupid face. I finally got a decent one and sent it just as a shadow descended over me.

I jolted, both from embarrassed guilt and being startled. When I looked up, Marco was there, holding out one of those tall, twisty cups. If he was judging my subpar selfie skills, he gave no indication.

Of that or any other human emotion.

"Is it rum?" I asked as I took the cup.

"No."

"Ah. Vodka then."

He shook his head and turned around to take a seat in front of me next to Dan.

My phone vibrated.

Daddy: Christ, how did I get so damn lucky?

Me: I ask myself that same question every day. Especially after I've come all over your tongue.

Daddy: Fuck, you're trying to kill me today.

I settled in to read another of Ms. Vera's Highlander recommendations in between drinking my virgin piña colada, dirty texting Maximo, and taking dips in the pool to cool off—from the heat *and* the messages.

A couple hours later, I was on my fifth rotation around the lazy river when Marco called, "Time to go, Juliet."

Damn.

When I reached the exit point, I gracelessly hauled my butt off my inner tube and exited the pool.

Marco was waiting with a towel. "He texted you."

We went back to my lounger, and I grabbed my phone.

Daddy: I'm going to be a little longer than planned. Did Vera pack you a dress?

Me: Just the one I was wearing.

The floral sundress was one of my own creations and the piece I was most proud of. The thin straps and high slit were perfect for the Vegas heat. There was a peekaboo cutout right under my chest that'd taken forever to get right, but it'd been worth it.

It was pretty, but casual.

Daddy: Go to Hilda's for a new one. We're celebrating tonight.

Me: You found a location?

Daddy: I found a location.

Me: Yay!

It wasn't my company, yet I felt a surge of pride and excitement.

"Apparently, we're going shopping," I told Marco.

He was his usual robotic self at the news.

Dan, however, had a face full of dread, as though he were in the midst of traumatic flashbacks involving endless hours at the mall with a girlfriend.

I'd have laughed had it not been for the glare Marco shot him.

Uh-oh.

Going up to the room, I showered and got ready before putting my sundress from earlier back on. We rode the elevator to the main floor, and I made a beeline for the boutique.

The woman behind the register smiled as we entered. "Hi. Welcome to Hilda's. Let me know if I can help you find anything."

A lot different than last time when I was ignored.

"Thanks," I said.

Within minutes, I found exactly what I wanted. Dark gray and completely off the shoulders, it was simple yet sexy.

As soon as I took it off the rack, the attentive sales associate gestured to an archway. "The changing rooms are right through there. Shout out if you need a different size."

"Thanks." Going into a stall, I tried it on to find it was perfect. I'd probably take the hem up an inch when I got home, but it wasn't the dress' fault I had short legs.

There was a soft knock before the saleswoman asked, "What size shoe are you?"

"Seven."

"Okay, hold on. I have a pair of pumps that would be perfect."

She returned a minute later and slid the box under the door. As she'd said, the gray suede pumps were perfect.

Switching back into my clothes, I opened the door to find Marco waiting. "All set."

He lifted his chin and took my purchases to the front.

As the woman rang me up, her gaze went to my outfit. "I love your dress. Where'd you get it?"

"Uhh, I made it."

"Really? What pattern did you use?"

"Just my own design," I muttered, wondering if she was mocking me.

I remembered how some of the mean girls in school used to ply their victims with compliments that were actually thinly veiled insults.

And, even though I was the one being judgy, the picturesque brunette looked like she could be queen mean girl.

"That's so impressive." She gestured around the store. "Most of what we sell is on consignment from designers. If you're interested, I'd love to carry that dress. I can't guarantee it will sell, so you might not make any money, but I bet it will. It's perfect for this time of year."

Stunned excitement roared through me even though I couldn't believe what I was hearing.

My dress.

My favorite dress that I labored and obsessed over for weeks will be for sale.

In a store.

A store in Maximo's resort.

The same store he told me to go to.

My heart went from racing to freezing, and my stomach dropped.

Oh.

Duh.

"No thanks," I forced out, disappointment choking me.

She gave me a kind smile. "No worries."

Marco signed for my purchases as I silently seethed. Once he had my bag, he asked, "Do you want to go anywhere else?"

I shook my head, growing angrier by the second.

I remained lost in my thoughts as we returned to the penthouse. Even though I changed into my new outfit, I no longer felt like going out. I stayed in the bedroom, pacing as my thoughts darted and my anger stewed.

Muffled voices came from the living room before the door swung open and Maximo filled the space. His eyes seared as he scanned my body. "Christ."

I opened my mouth to say hi, but that wasn't what forced its way out. "Why would you do that?"

"Do what?"

"You know what."

His eyes narrowed. "Attitude, Juliet."

"No," I snapped back. "I'm used to you being underhanded and manipulative. Most of the time, I even *like* it because I'm fucked up. But you've never been mean. This was just *mean*."

"Watch the way you talk about yourself." He crossed his arms over his broad chest. "Then start from the beginning because I've got no fucking clue what you're talking about."

I studied him, looking for signs he was lying, but all I saw was confusion mixed with anger.

Uh-oh.

"Hilda's wants to carry one of my dresses on consignment," I shared, still watching closely.

There was a hint of surprise and more than a bit of pride. "That's amazing."

I still didn't believe him. "Last time we were there, no one said a word to me. But today, she just happened to be chatty and offer to carry my dress?"

"Last time, people were told to leave you alone so you could shop in peace."

This wasn't his doing?

"I was there with Marco. Maybe she put two and two together and figured out who I am," I said as I fought to suppress my ever-growing hope.

Maximo shook his head. "Marco pulls guard and tour guide duty to VIPs on occasion. No one would think anything of it."

There was no holding it back. The excitement I'd had earlier bubbled through my veins, but it was accompanied by a sense of panic. For all I knew, I'd blown a once in a lifetime opportunity by turning her down.

Not to mention, Maximo looked ready to take me over his knee—dinner plans or not.

Shit.

I messed up.

"You really didn't have anything to do with this?" I checked.

"No, I didn't have to. If you want to keep sewing for fun, that's fine. You deserve fun. But if you decide to take it further, I knew you could do it without my help." He gave me a cocky smirk. "And I was right."

"Unless I blew it," I whispered.

Maximo stepped closer, menace and tenderness in his gaze. "Gotta work on your confidence, Juliet."

I had no doubt part of that would involve him spanking me until I begged and then fucking me until I came undone.

And I wanted that.

Just not right then.

"Later," I said, closing the distance between us. I grabbed his hand as I moved and continued toward the elevator. "I need to go talk to that woman before dinner."

"This isn't over," he rumbled as we descended.

Filthy anticipation mixed with my excitement. "I hope not."

We got off on the main floor and I continued like a woman on a mission, dodging and weaving people. When we got to Hilda's, I scanned the storefront, but the woman was gone.

"Damn," I whispered.

"I'll have Cole locate her number." At my unsure look, he squeezed my shoulder. "Sometimes connections are good."

"Yeah, okay."

I was about to turn around when she came out from the back and stopped. A smile spread across her face as she scanned me. And then it froze and her jaw dropped when she saw who I was with.

Okay, no way did she fake that.

"Hi. Hello. Uh, sir. Ma'am," she sputtered, flustered.

"Is the offer about consigning my dress still open?" I asked.

"Yes, of course. Definitely."

Probably more so now.

"Then I'd love to do it."

"I was hoping you'd change your mind." Going to the counter, she grabbed a business card and handed it to me. "The pieces we carry in different sizes sell best. The sooner you can get them to me, the better. If you have any questions, call me anytime."

Clutching the card, I grinned. "Thank you."

"You're welcome. I look forward to seeing them."

Maximo took the card and slid it into his pocket before taking my hand. "Enjoy your evening, Hilda."

"You, too, Mr. Black."

Hilda.

This is her store.

And she wants to sell my *dress in it.*

Once again, how is this my life now?

Maximo and I remained silent as we backtracked to the elevator. Once we were closed inside, he pressed the button to take us to the garage before yanking me to him.

Brushing my hair over my shoulder, he looked down at me. "You were right."

"About?"

A wicked smile curved his lips, and I braced even before he said, "I gave you time, and you earned that heated ass after all."

Oh no.

But also…

Yay!

CHAPTER THIRTY-FOUR

Belonging

JULIET

"WHERE ARE WE?" I asked, looking out the window.

When we'd left Moonlight, Maximo had taken me to the huge lot he'd put an offer on. Since he'd offered well over asking—and would pay cash with no contingencies other than an expedited closing—he'd heard back within an hour.

The land was his.

After we were done touring the site, we'd gone to dinner. As delicious as it'd been, I hadn't eaten much. My stomach had been a mess of anticipation and excitement and nerves.

I'd thought we were heading back to Moonlight, but I didn't recognize the area.

"Nebula," he said.

I whipped around to look at him. "Really?"

He lifted his chin, taking a turn and then following the path up to park near the main entrance.

Coming around, he opened my door and helped me out, not releasing my hand as we walked through the lobby.

Moonlight and Star were stunning, but Nebula was superior by far. It lived up to all its expensive and ritzy hype. Dark with splashes of bright colors, shimmery stars, and swirls of smokiness, it was like the VIP section of outer space. There were statues, murals, and dangling pieces of reflective mirrors.

I'd have loved to see more, but a cursory glance was all I could catch as Maximo practically dragged me through. We wound our way around the oval-shaped gaming floor and took a turn down a *Black Resorts* hallway before reaching the elevator.

Once inside, I was up and in his arms, my back to the wall.

"Will I ever not be so damn addicted to you?" Maximo growled against my neck before biting and sucking on my sensitive skin.

"I hope not," I breathed, making him groan.

The elevator slid open and he carried me into a breathtaking suite, that again, I barely got a glimpse of on our way to a bedroom.

"Why did you bring me here if you aren't going to let me see anything?" I teased as he lowered me to stand.

But there was no humor in his gaze. It was just fire and lust and desire. *Need.* "Because there is no one below us for three floors." His hand gripped my ass, his hardness pressed tight against my belly.

He didn't elaborate, but I got his meaning loud and clear—emphasis on the *loud.*

How bad is this going to be?

Or maybe how good?

Maximo took his time undressing me, his fingers and lips and tongue touching and caressing my skin. When I stood in front of him completely bare, he ordered, "Undress me, little dove."

I happily obeyed, though I didn't take my time. I greedily stripped him as though he were the present I'd wished for my whole life.

"Love the way you look at me." Taking my mouth, he shuffled us back until my legs hit the bed. He tore his mouth away and lifted me onto it, shifting us to the center before positioning me on my hands and knees.

Exposed and vulnerable and on edge, my nerves got the better of me. I started to close my legs, but his hand came down in a stinging slap and I froze.

Another nine peppered my cheeks and thighs. Warmth and pain spread through my body, wrapping around me to loosen my muscles and clear my head. My chest dropped to the mattress, and my ass tipped up.

Into his hand.

Into the pain.

"So perfect," he praised, one last sharp spank connecting. And then his mouth was on me. His tongue speared into my pussy, devouring me. Groaning as though he were the one in heaven, he licked and sucked and flicked, driving me to the edge of orgasm before easing away.

Over. And over. And over.

Spanking my ass had been punishment.

But getting me so close and not letting me fall was torture.

His tongue lifted to swirl around my tight hole, and my body tensed.

"Relax," he murmured against me.

"Easy for you to say."

"Juliet."

"But—"

"Hush."

Hearing that made my pussy squeeze around nothing, empty and deprived.

He resumed licking, his skillful tongue quickly driving me past the point of embarrassment. His thick finger pressed against my ass, but he only teased me before replacing it with his tongue.

"Please," I begged, my muscles so tense, my body ached.

Rather than giving me the release I needed, Maximo took his touch away. "Don't move."

"What?" As the bed shifted, I reflexively lurched upright to yank him back to finish what he started.

His wild eyes shot to me. "I said don't move. Don't make me repeat myself again, Juliet."

Dropping my face to the mattress, I couldn't see what he was doing. There was some rustling before he returned.

His teeth sank into my sore ass cheek, making me cry out. "When I tell you something, I expect you to listen."

The comeback I had on the tip of my tongue disappeared when the tip of *his* tongue speared into me. He worked my clit, pussy, and ass until tears of desperation burned my eyes.

I was vaguely aware of something clicking behind me before cold, slick lube coated my hole. That time when he pressed his finger against me, he continued, sliding it in.

My breath caught in my lungs from the pain. The fullness. The stretching.

"Breathe," he whispered, his other hand rubbing my clit as he pumped his finger in and out.

Easy for you to say, I wanted to repeat, but I couldn't form words. Especially not when he added a second finger.

If only two fingers made me feel like I was splitting apart, I didn't know how I'd possibly take his cock.

But the longer he worked me, the more I wanted to find out.

"I need you," I whimpered.

"We're just playing tonight," Maximo said, his voice strained and husky with arousal.

I may have been terrified of the pain and uncertain of the logistics, but that didn't mean I didn't want to do it. Or at least try. "Why?"

"I need to get you ready."

"I am ready." I rocked my hips back. "I need you."

"I'm still going to fuck this greedy pussy."

"I want to try."

Maximo hesitated for a long moment. "You sure?"

No.

"Yes."

Biting out a harsh curse, he removed his fingers and put more lube on me. I looked over my shoulder to watch as he coated the long length of his hard-on with it.

Length I was going to take.

What was I thinking asking for this?

But then I stared as he stroked himself and remembered.

I wanted him in every way I could get him. I wanted to continue trying new experiences because I trusted him.

Because I loved him.

He shifted to kneel behind me, the thick head of him pressed against my tight hole. "Tell me when to stop, Juliet. Don't try to take it if it hurts too much. Understood?"

"Understood, Daddy."

He eased in, and I felt like I was being shredded from the inside out. My muscles burned and stung with the intrusion, but there was an undercurrent of pleasure.

A very *under*-undercurrent.

"Relax, little dove," he gritted out, not sounding all that relaxed himself.

I did my best to inhale deeply, filling my lungs with much needed air as I forced my body to loosen.

Maximo inched in farther. "Christ. So fucking tight."

He fucked me with the tip, shallow and slow. Every few thrusts, he pushed deeper. It skirted along that thin line between pleasure and pain until I couldn't tell which was which.

Shoving my face in a pillow, I muffled my throaty moan. The pillow was snatched from under me.

"No one is on the floors below us," he reminded me. "I want to hear you scream."

When he thrust in harder, I gave him what he wanted because there was no way in hell I could hold back. My moan mixed with a harsh cry, forming a sound I didn't even know I could make.

And Maximo loved it. Groaning, his arm circled me to play with my clit, adding to the confusing rush of overwhelming sensations.

It hurt.

It was amazing.

I was so full.

I wanted more.

I was ready to explode.

I was sure it would kill me.

As his movements grew erratic and uncontrolled, I decided death by orgasm was worth it. I needed to come more than I needed my next breath.

Maximo must've felt the same urgency because his speed and the pressure he used on my clit increased. His voice was low and strained. "I'm not gonna last much longer."

"You're not even all the way in," I panted, my words clipped.

"Doesn't matter." That didn't stop him from pushing in deeper. "Every inch of you is mine now. Your sweet pussy, your fuckable mouth, and this tight ass."

His claiming words did it. A guttural scream ripped from me as the most intense, blinding pleasure-pain tore through my whole body. Destroying me. *Eviscerating* me.

One orgasm immediately rolled into another as his low groans mixed with my moans. His come filled me as he rumbled, "All of you. Mine."

We stayed locked like that for a long moment, slowly coming back to earth as we caught our breath. I hissed out a moan and winced as he slipped out. He didn't give me his weight like he usually did, which was good because I wasn't sure I could take it. As he climbed from the bed, I collapsed into a graceless heap.

I felt high—or what I guessed being high was like. My head was floaty and empty. My body was hyperaware of everything and yet nothing. I couldn't think or move or function. I was just... there. Happy and peaceful and detached and high.

I didn't even jolt when I was suddenly up in Maximo's arms, not having the energy or desire to ask where he was carrying me. A moment later, we sank into a hot bath before he settled me on his lap with his arms locked around me. Resting my cheek on his chest, I savored the bubble of serenity I was floating in.

The heat and water soaked into my tense muscles, soothing the raw skin and deep ache I'd gotten from his palm and his dick. I wasn't sure how much time had passed before I sat up and became aware of multiple things at once.

First, I was starving. My stomach was growling loudly for carbs and comfort food.

Next, I was completely at ease—mind, body, and soul. It was an all-encompassing tranquility I'd never experienced.

Last—and possibly most surprising—Maximo was hard. Long and thick, his cock stretched between us.

"How are you hard again?" I asked.

"Still," he corrected.

"*Still?*"

"Never fully went down."

"*How?*"

I'd have jokingly asked if he was popping little blue pills like Tic Tacs, but knowing Maximo, he'd have taken that as a challenge.

"Had my cock jammed in your tight ass," he said. "Made you come so beautifully. And now I've got you naked in my arms, happy and calm. Trusting." His dick jerked against me. "You've given me all of you."

I hadn't understood why my trust was so important to him. If I was already obeying, what difference did it make if I trusted him?

A lot, as it turned out.

I felt it every day, down to my bones. The happiness. The lack of

319

stress and anxiety. The stability. I no longer felt temporary.

I belonged. With him. In *our* life together.

Other than his love, that feeling of belonging was the best gift he'd given me. It was beyond anything I'd ever imagined was possible.

"Thank you for wanting all of me," I whispered.

His arms constricted around me. "'Til the day I die."

Not temporary.

Permanent.

'Til the day I die.

CHAPTER THIRTY-FIVE

Protect What's Yours

MAXIMO

"*G*OT A PROBLEM, boss."

Jesus.

For nearly a month, I'd worked every damn day, from early morning until late at night. I'd taken Juliet to work with me a handful of times, but I needed a day off with her. Since preparations for the new resort meant that wasn't possible, I'd settled for working from home.

Of course something would jack it up.

"What is it?" I asked Ash.

"Someone is here."

That got my attention.

No one came to the house without an invitation. Few people even knew where I lived. The route was winding and secluded, nothing for miles.

It wasn't a house someone would coincidentally stumble across.

"Who is it?" Setting down my mail and letter opener, I clicked a few keys to switch security cameras.

A man stood outside the gate next to a sleek red sports car. He leaned against it, patiently waiting.

"No idea and he wouldn't say," Ash said. "Just said he has something you might like."

There was nothing I wanted that I didn't already have. Except... "Carmichael?"

He tilted his head to the side for a moment. "It'd make sense."

That jowly bastard had been in the wind since going after Juliet. He had to know he was being hunted—and not just by me.

Ash and Marco had been quietly searching, watching the casinos and clubs off the Strip. When there'd been no sign of him, I'd made it known in the right circles I was looking.

That made Carmichael a powerful bargaining chip. Even his closest friends would turn on him if it meant I owed them a favor.

A lot of eyes were searching for him.

I just didn't know if the man in my driveway was one of them.

I grabbed my cell and texted Cole the plate number before asking Ash, "He wouldn't tell you anything?"

"Said he'll only talk to you."

I rubbed my jaw. "Set a meeting at Moonlight tomorrow."

"He said here and only here."

I didn't like anyone making demands of me, much less some unknown asshole who'd shown up uninvited. But my curiosity was piqued. I wanted to know what he had to offer.

More than that, I wanted to know where the hell he'd gotten my address.

"Juliet still watching a movie with Vera?"

"Yeah," Ash said.

"Confiscate our guest's cell, keys, watch, and anything that can be used as a weapon, including his damn shoes."

"On it."

He was almost to the door when I asked, "You got your kit?"

Tapping his suit jacket, he smiled with an edge of anticipation. "Always."

I lifted my chin. "Have it ready to go. Worse case, he takes a nap and we take a field trip to The Basement."

Ash's smile grew into a grin—the sick bastard. "There's always hope."

He left, and I leaned back in my chair to watch the cameras, switching them to follow their progress until they were inside. I shut off the monitors and checked my texts.

Cole: Rental. Give me a few, I should be able to find out who rented it.

That's not good.

I set my phone down just as Ash opened the door. Stepping aside, he let our mystery guest in before leaving and closing it behind him.

I didn't recognize the man, not even a flicker of familiarity. He was around my age, but the years hadn't been kind. He had gray in his brown hair and his face was scarred from a life hard lived. His gaze was set in a glare as he scanned the room.

In Juliet's words, he looked like a 'goon'.

"Thanks for seeing me." His tone held a sharp edge as he offered me his hand.

I didn't take it, and he didn't look surprised. "You didn't leave me much choice."

Despite my lack of invitation, he took a seat. "Sorry about that, but we felt it was best to talk in private."

"*We*? Do you have a mouse in your pocket?"

He smirked. "My partner and me."

Bullshit. It's his boss calling the shots and he's an errand boy dressed up to look like a somebody.

"And who is your partner?" I asked.

"I'd rather not say."

His boss told him not to say.

Talking in circles and coded bullshit lost its luster fast. "Tell me why you're here."

Unlike me, he wasn't annoyed. He enjoyed feeling like a big man. "We have something you want."

"And that is?"

"Mugsy Carmichael's location."

It could've been a bluff. I hadn't been subtle about making it known I wanted Carmichael.

His eyes traveled the room before landing on me again. "And we'll give him to you, delivered with a bow."

"In exchange for what?"

"Giving our boxers a shot in your circuit." He raised a brow, the implication heavy. "Either one."

Coming to my home uninvited and making demands was stupid and shortsighted.

Following that up with implied knowledge of my business was stupid and suicidal.

He was silent for a moment, waiting for a reaction. When he didn't get one, his glare hardened.

As if I'd wronged him.

"What did you say your name was?" I asked, though we both knew he hadn't given one.

He didn't answer, but it wasn't a strategic avoidance. His attention was aimed out the window.

Shit.

I should've had made sure Juliet stayed in the media room until we gave the okay. I'd assumed their movie would last longer, but based on his stare going from nosy to rapt, I knew she was outside.

Turning my chair to the side, I watched Juliet bend at the waist to set her iPad and Diet Coke down. She shoved off her shorts and slowly lifted her tee to reveal her gorgeous body in a white bikini that barely covered anything.

Shaking out her hair, she gathered it before securing it in a high ponytail.

My wet dream was putting on a show that was only supposed to be for me.

I spun back to the man and cleared my throat.

It took him far too fucking long to drag his eyes away from her. When they met mine, they were calculating and sharper than I'd given him credit for. "Our offer is generous. You get Carmichael and your pick of fresh boxers. They're good. Fast, young, and ambitious." He smiled, but it wasn't a friendly one. "We're doing you two favors."

His words were affable, but his tone spit fire and disgust. The longer he sat there, the heavier the chip on his shoulder became. And the harder it was for him to hide it.

I'd pissed off a lot of people personally. Even more by domino effect. It was impossible to keep track of everyone who hated me.

But this man was undeniably one of them.

It was evident in his eyes, his voice, and his body language.

I just had no clue why, and he clearly wasn't going to tell me. Not why he hated me. Not who he was.

And not why he was actually there.

Because I was willing to bet Nebula the only boxing he was involved with was the cardboard variety.

I was about to call bullshit on the whole thing when my phone rang. "I have to take this," I said before hitting accept. "Black."

"Car was rented by William Janson," Cole said, his voice quiet.

Why's that name sound familiar?

Shit.

Tommy Janson.

He'd been the squirrelly little shit caught stealing at Moonlight. The one who'd worked for Viktor Dobrow.

"Is it the same as last time, Sophia?" I asked, keeping an eye on my guest.

His own eyes were busy darting around my office and out the window, searching for something.

"Brother," Cole said.

"Okay, put it on my schedule." I hung up and smiled at the man across the way from me. Just like the smile he'd thrown my way, it was far from friendly.

I stood fast, and Janson jolted and tensed. Pocketing my cell, I rounded my desk and sat on the edge of it in front of him. "Tell me more about the boxers."

He relaxed, leaning back in his chair. His expression morphed from loathing to victorious. "You'll have to see for yourself."

Even with me closer, he wasn't smart enough to stay on guard. His focus drifted out the window to Juliet, gawking even as his features tightened.

"Trying to figure out how a bastard like me got someone like that?" I asked as I casually leaned back, rearranging my hands until I felt what I needed under my palm.

He gestured around, his jaw clenched. "I can guess."

"No, it's not the pool or the house or the clothes or any of the other shit my money buys her. She's mine because I keep her safe. And I don't let other bastards eye-fuck her, Janson."

His brows shot up.

Couldn't have planned that better if I tried.

Gripping my letter opener, I swung fast but with restraint because I didn't want to kill him—yet. The sharp steel sank into its target, his eyeball making a sickening *squelch* as blood and fluid spurted.

His blood-curdling scream was music to my ears.

Ash threw the door open but stayed in the doorway.

Janson jerked back, the pointed steel dragging and more blood spurting.

"I could kill you right now," I said calmly, gripping the handle. "Another couple inches and this is buried in your brain."

His cries of pain didn't stop, but his thrashing did.

"Do you work for Dobrow like your brother did?" When he didn't answer, I twisted the opener until he retched. "Do you work for Dobrow?

"Yes!" I slid the steel free, and his hands covered the massacred eye. "You're fucking crazy."

He wasn't wrong.

Especially when it came to Juliet.

My possessiveness got the better of me and didn't think twice before stabbing him in the other eye.

The dumbass should've expected it.

Always protect what's yours.

"Fuck!" he screeched before throwing up on himself.

"At least it's not piss," Ash pointed out.

Janson covered his face, bloody tears streaming.

"Why'd Dobrow send you?"

The only answer I got was another retch and more screams.

"Use the rental and take him to the plant," I told Ash.

Ash lifted his chin, his anger palpable.

Despite Juliet and I insisting it wasn't his fault, he had a lot of pent up rage and guilt about Carmichael getting to her on his watch.

Rage and guilt that was about to be transferred to that motherfucker.

Disappearing for a minute, Ash returned with two towels. He tossed one to me and shoved the other against the man's face as he hauled him up.

Wiping some of the blood from my hands, I followed them out of the room and found Vera waiting.

Unfazed, she scanned me for injury, coming to the correct conclusion that none of the blood was mine. "Mr. Ash said you'd need me."

I jerked my head toward the open doorway. "My office—"

"Maximo?"

326

My gaze shot to Juliet's pale face as she took in the gore.

I fucked up.

Again.

"Close your eyes," I barked, harsher than intended.

She did as I said, but asked, "Are you okay? That's not your... right?"

"I'm good." I wanted to touch her, but not with my hands coated in blood. "Keep them closed."

Vera reached behind me to slam the door shut as Ash covered Janson's mouth and dragged him down the stairs.

I took off for our bedroom and locked myself in the bathroom. After rinsing my hands, I pulled my cell from my pocket and called Marco.

"Boss," he answered.

"I need you at the house."

"Be there in twenty."

I dialed Cole.

"What's going on?" he asked by way of greeting, already on alert since I wouldn't be calling if it weren't important.

"Where are you?"

"Home."

"Need tech and possibly a GPS wipe."

"Where?"

"The plant."

"I'll gather what I need and leave in ten."

Tossing my phone down, I turned the shower on as hot as I could stand before climbing in. The scorching water mixed with the deep red blood, turning it pink as I scrubbed.

My thoughts switched between Janson, Dobrow, and unfamiliar regret. Stabbing Janson hadn't been a mistake. Doing it while Juliet was home had been. I'd let my temper get the better of me.

I'd fucked up.

My job was to protect her, and instead I'd traumatized her.

Turning off the water, I dried myself and wrapped the towel around my waist before opening the door.

Pacing the room, Juliet froze when I stepped out. Her gaze dropped to inspect my naked torso for injury.

"I told you it wasn't my blood."

"Just making sure."

Pulling her into my arms, I was glad she didn't resist. I inhaled her sunshine scent as I ran my hands across the soft skin of her back. "You okay?"

"A little freaked," she admitted.

Guilt hit my gut harder.

Seeing it, she rushed to explain. "It's not that. I'm just freaked because I thought you were hurt. I didn't really see anything." A sad smile I hadn't seen in a while curved her lips. "Even if I had, you know I've seen a lot worse in my life."

I should dig Shamus out of his unmarked grave and shoot him again.

"I have to go," I said.

"I figured."

"No more outside today. Marco will be here soon. Vera is always armed. You'll—"

"*Vera* is armed?"

"She lived a rough life before coming here."

"I know," Juliet said. "I didn't realize she was packing heat. Makes me glad I've always been polite."

As usual, Juliet managed to make me smile despite the shitstorm brewing. "'Packing heat'?"

"It sounds badass... just like Vera, apparently."

"Which is why you'll be safe."

But my girl didn't need reassurances.

"I know. I'm worried about you." Her voice shook and her arms wrapped tightly around my waist, making me painfully aware that we were only separated by a towel and her thin swimsuit. My dick hardened and her eyes snapped to mine. "Really? Right now?"

Cupping her head, I tilted it back. "With you? *Always.*"

"You're insane." But that didn't stop her from pressing tighter against me.

As tempted as I was to sink into her and fuck away my anger, I didn't have time. "I need to get dressed."

She opened her mouth but closed it and released her hold. "I'm going to grab a quick shower before more hell breaks loose."

After she closed herself in the bathroom, I pulled on a suit and holstered my Glocks before going to my office.

The blood was already gone from my desk, and the scent of disinfectant hung thick in the air. The carpet was sudsy with cleaner.

"How is she?" Vera asked, looking up from her supply tray. She grabbed a scrub brush before switching it out for a larger one.

"She's good."

"Of course. We're women. Women are always strong."

I couldn't argue with that. "You got your Ruger?"

She smiled and lifted her pant leg to show her ankle holster. "Women are also always prepared."

"Good. Marco is on his way. I want everyone locked in until I get back."

Approaching, she patted my cheek the way my mom used to—as though I were a mischievous little boy and not a grown man with murder on his mind. "Be safe." Her features tightened, ruthlessness taking over. "But do what you have to do to make sure you and Juliet continue to be safe."

"That's the plan."

She turned and pulled on gloves before crouching to clean the blood from the carpet, as though it were nothing more than spilled wine. "Then once it's settled, you can get started making beautiful babies."

Jesus.

Leave it to Vera to be blunt.

It wasn't the first time I'd thought about putting my baby in Juliet, but I was a selfish fucker. I wanted her to myself for a while longer.

Shaking my head, I backtracked to the bedroom just as Juliet finished getting dressed.

I closed the distance between us and cupped her head before kissing her hard. "Be good."

"Never." At my look, she rolled her eyes. "Fine."

I started to step away but she gripped my lapels, worry evident on her pretty face. "Be careful."

"I'd never let anyone take me from you."

With one last kiss, I headed downstairs just as Marco arrived.

"What happened?" he asked.

I recapped Janson-number-two's visit and the Dobrow connection.

Scowl growing, Marco remained silent while I spoke. Once I was done, he shook his head. "Fuck."

That summed it up.

CHAPTER THIRTY-SIX

Target

Maximo

WALKING INTO THE plant, I went straight to the limp body hanging from a meat hook by his bound wrists. I slowly circled him. He'd been stripped to his underwear to check for wires, trackers, or anything else he may have hidden.

I wasn't surprised there was nothing. Dobrow wouldn't shell out for pricey tracking equipment since he didn't give a shit about anyone but himself. Janson wasn't smart enough to take any precautions—the dumb fucker had rented a car with his own license just to feel like a big shot.

Ash had bandaged Janson's eyes, but it wasn't out of care. It was so he didn't die or pass out before we learned what we needed.

"You work fast," I said.

Ash's smirk was at odds with the rage on his face. "It's not work when you love what you do."

I looked at where Cole sat with his computer. "The rental?"

"Wiped and dumped." He typed before speaking again. "William Janson. Thirty-five. Born in Carson City. Did time for possession of drugs *and* illegal weapons, and then again for petty theft *and* grand larceny."

He looked up from the screen at Janson. "You overachiever, you."

"How do you know all that?" Janson asked, his words slurred from the pain and the adrenaline crash.

"I'm that good." Cole paused before adding, "Also, public records are public, dumbass."

I circled Janson again, purposefully making my steps louder. With each footfall that sounded around him, his body grew tenser as he braced.

Finally, he lifted his head. "Even if I had something to say, you're going to kill me. So just get it over with."

"Where's the fun in that?" I shook off my suit jacket, hanging it on the back of a chair before rolling my sleeves.

Starting slow, I worked his torso.

Hook to the kidney.

Pause.

Two quick jabs to the chest, knocking the wind out of him.

A longer pause.

Another two hooks to the same kidney.

I made noise as I moved back, just for Ash to step in quietly with a surprise uppercut and a jab followed quickly by a right cross to the mouth.

Janson drooled blood down his chin. "I don't even know anything."

"Christ, I hate liars."

I came back in with more body shots until he was groaning and swaying. Taking a break so he didn't pass out, I grabbed a water bottle and leaned against the table. I glanced at Cole's computer screen. "What've you got?"

"He's been working as a bouncer at Ace in the Hole for the past three years."

Ace in the Hole was one of Dobrow's unsubtly named strip clubs.

"He was dating a dancer for a while, but… oof, tough break. Bunni is currently shacked up with the bartender."

"She's *what*?" Janson bellowed. His moment of outrage must've taken all his energy because he drooped. His weight pulled at his arms and shoulders, doing our work for us.

"Do you not follow her online?" Cole asked

"She blocked me."

He gave a low whistle. "I can see why. Lotta X-rated pics of her and her new man."

"That cunt."

Cole laughed. "Funny 'cause according to her Facebook post, she caught you in bed with one of the other dancers."

"It's different for men," he scoffed.

"It's not," I said, not that it mattered for him anymore.

Since Janson was no longer on the verge of passing out, Ash and I resumed working him. We took turns, waiting and striking. Manipulating his mind as much as his body.

I took another break. Drank my water. Circled him.

Played with my target.

"I can keep going," I told him. "Not for hours or days. I can keep you here and alive for *weeks*. Broken bones healing painfully wrong. Wounds becoming infected until your flesh festers and rots. I'll keep patching you up just to tear you apart again."

His body shook, his pulse visibly racing as his breaths came in sharp pants. Terror wafted from him.

Opening his mouth, saliva mixed with blood and vomit dripped down his chin. "Go for it," he forced out. "While you do, Viktor will be using your whore for *weeks*. And then he'll tear her apart. Mutilate her until a disfigured shell is all that's left. You deserve it for what you did to my brother."

My hand hovered over my gun, everything in me screaming to make him eat a bullet. But getting answers was more important, so I didn't kill him.

I hurt him.

Putting my thumbs to his bandaged eyes, I pressed. His shrieks echoed around us until he was choking on them.

Easing the pressure, I asked, "What does Juliet have to do with this?"

He sobbed, bloody tears leaking through the bandages.

I glanced at Ash. "Serrated knife and needle-nose pliers."

A lot of men could take a punch, especially if they were used to it. True pain was a different matter.

Janson gulped hard, his lips pressing together until the skin around them turned white.

A moment later, Ash handed me what I'd asked for, purposefully making them clink together. I ran the rough edge of the knife across Janson's side, just hard enough to sting and make blood pebble. I eased it away, watching Janson slump before I dragged the blade harder, slicing open his skin. His screeches grew louder as I cut again, drawing an *X*.

Pushing the cold pliers against the gashes, I said, "I wonder how much skin I can peel from his body before he passes out."

I pinched the bloody skin between the tip of the pliers and began to pull.

"Wait!" Janson screamed, nearly hyperventilating. He angled his body away from me. "If I tell you what I know, will you let me go? I'll move across the country. You'll never see me again." His earlier bravado was long gone as he sobbed, his voice thick as it cracked. "My brother was an asshole. Viktor is a greedy prick. I don't want to die for either of them."

"You'll tell me everything?"

"All of it. Just don't kill me." His body shook, rattling the hook above his head, which only made him shake worse. "I don't want to die," he wailed over and over.

"Tell me."

"You won't kill me?"

"Not if you tell me everything."

His head fell forward, his chest heaving. "Shamus owed Dobrow. A lot. More than he could pay."

A sinking pit filled my gut as ice water flowed through my veins. "And?"

"And he gave his daughter as payment."

Why am I surprised? Even from the grave, he makes Juliet's life hell.

I should've brought that motherfucker here instead of going easy on him with a quick bullet between his eyes.

Not for the first time, I thought about how lucky it was that my little dove had shown herself that day.

God knew what she would've faced had I not taken her.

"We thought Shamus took her away to protect her," Janson continued. "When Viktor pressed Mugsy Carmichael to find them, Mugsy told him he suspected you killed Shamus."

I thought about Carmichael's visit to my office. He'd acted concerned about Juliet but had only wanted to trade her to save his own ass.

"What else?" I asked.

"We watched and waited for a while before Viktor got bored and moved on. But then word got around you did have the girl, and he got interested again." He paused, wheezing. "I need water."

Rolling his eyes, Ash grabbed a bottle and poured it down his throat like he was waterboarding him.

Janson turned his head and coughed, bloody spittle shooting everywhere.

"Why'd you come today?" I asked once he quieted.

"To offer Carmichael and set a meeting." He took a shuddering breath. "And to scope out your place to see how to break in."

Juliet was smart. Sweet. Funny. She was ballsy and adventurous and stubborn and creative and ambitious and beautifully submissive in her gilded cage.

But Viktor didn't know any of that.

"Why all that effort for one woman?"

"To get back at you. You have power. Clout. He wanted to use that to expand his reach, but instead, you banned him and others followed. He lost connections and money. Two of his clubs went under. He blames you. You took from him. He wants to take from you."

Guilt sat heavy on my shoulders. Her old man may have been the one to put a target on her back, but dragging Juliet into my life had grown it.

"Anything else?" I asked, fighting to reign in my rage and guilt.

"That's it. That's all I know." He inhaled deep before shaking his bound hands. "Now let me go."

"Where's Dobrow now?" I asked Cole.

Janson thought I was talking to him. "I dunno, probably one of his clubs. I can give you a list."

Cole clicked a few buttons then turned the computer so I could see. A map took up the screen, a blinking light flashing. "He was bouncing around to some of his clubs earlier, but he's been here for a while—All or Nothing."

"Another strip club?" I guessed.

"His most popular because the girls do more than dance," Janson shared. "He does a lot of his business out of a backroom. The only door on the right."

Cole closed his computer and packed his gear. Ash had already locked up the tools and was heading for the door, ready to go.

Janson must've figured out we were leaving because his head jerked around despite the fact he couldn't see. "Wait! What about me?" He rattled the hook, thrashing his body. It was pointless, he'd never get free.

Even if he did, once the door locked behind us, there was no opening it. He'd be trapped.

I was just stepping out when he screamed, "You said you'd let me go!"

Looking over my shoulder, my lips curved into a cruel smile he couldn't see. "I lied."

CHAPTER THIRTY-SEVEN

Highway To Hell

Maximo

*W*HAT A PISSHOLE.

Parked around the corner from All or Nothing, I felt like I needed a shower, and I hadn't even stepped foot inside. The entire area was run-down—blocks of abandoned buildings and discarded trash.

"We sure he's in there?" Ash asked.

"Don't let Cole hear you doubt him or he'll thoroughly explain the cell tracking process until your eyes glaze over."

He grimaced. "Forget I asked."

We had eyes on the front door and Cole was parked around back, watching that exit and the tracker for movement. Unless there was a hidden tunnel we didn't know about, Dobrow was inside.

Ash drummed on the steering wheel, already wired. "What's the plan?"

What I wanted to do was walk in, empty my magazine into Dobrow, then go home to Juliet. Unfortunately, the packed club ensured that wasn't an option.

"Wait until everyone leaves, snatch Dobrow, get out before I catch something from the air." Taking out my cell, I texted Marco.

Me: Everything good?

Marco: Quiet. Vera roped Juliet into watching another chick flick.

Me: Call if anything changes.

It took a handful of hours for the cars to clear out. It was another hour before the staff left. The place was dark and quiet.

It was time.

I messaged Cole.

Me: Heading in the front.

Cole: I'll go in the back.

"Ready?" I asked Ash as I pulled on gloves. But he was already gloved up and heading out.

Ash and I stuck to the shadows as we made our way to the door. He aimed his gun at the lock. "Pick it or shoot it?"

I pulled the handle, and the door swung open.

He shrugged. "Or do it the boring way, that's fine."

We walked into the main room of the darkened club, the stench of sex, body odor, cheap perfume, and alcohol saturating everything. Heading past the large mirrored stage, I pushed through the swinging door to the long hall. Cole was already positioned in the open doorway at the other end, a grimace locked on his face. I only had to wait a moment to figure out why.

The sounds of skin slapping and fake moans came from behind a door on the left. It wasn't the one Janson had told us about, but it also didn't sound like Dobrow was conducting business.

Ash mimed gagging.

Reaching out, I turned the handle and opened the door, bracing for whatever horror awaited.

I didn't brace enough.

Rather than Dobrow, it was a naked and sweaty Carmichael banging a bored stripper from behind. His body jiggled with each thrust.

That time when Ash gagged, it wasn't mimed.

"Maximo!" Carmichael stopped and scurried back, flashing everything in the process.

"Never say my name while you're naked." I wanted to turn away, but I wasn't stupid—just scarred for life. "Jesus Christ, I'll never get this image out of my head."

The stripper flopped down and yawned, her dazed gaze aimed toward the desk. It took two-point-five seconds to realize she was high as a kite.

Anyone fucking Carmichael would have to be.

Ash went back into the hall as I stalked across the small, makeshift bedroom. I checked Carmichael's pants for a weapon before throwing them and his shirt at him. "Get dressed."

Unstable and shaking, he struggled to put them on, already starting his excuses. "I can explain. It's Viktor. I owe—"

"Where is he?" I asked. "His Escalade's here."

"It needs new brakes and repairs. He's driving a Benz."

"Rooms are empty," Ash said. "His cell is charging in his office."

Shit.

There was a possibility Janson not returning had tipped Dobrow off. There was also the possibility while I was staking out his place, Dobrow was doing the same to mine.

Panic shot through me. My place may have been Fort Knox with two people armed and on guard, but shit happened. Even with every precaution, something could go wrong.

I pulled my cell out, but Cole's blockers meant no signal.

"Cole, check in with Marco," I called, knowing his setup could bypass them.

"On it."

Returning my focus to Carmichael, I asked, "Where would he go?"

He rapidly shook his head, looking two seconds from a heart attack. "He collects bank from his other clubs at the end of the night, but I don't know where he'd go after. We're not actually friends. I was only getting close to keep Juliet safe. He wants to *sell* her."

"The same Juliet you tried to kidnap?" Ash bit out.

"That was to protect her, too." His eyes shot back to me. "I didn't know you were serious about her, I thought she was—"

"I heard exactly what you thought. Now shut the fuck up."

If he was smart, he'd have listened.

But no one could ever accuse Mugsy Carmichael of being smart.

"I was wrong, I see that now." He held his hands up in surrender. "But my intentions were good."

Ash strolled closer, but Carmichael's eyes were on me and the gun in my hand.

Another mistake in a worthless lifetime of them.

"Don't you know what they say about good intentions?" Ash pulled a syringe from his pocket. "They pave the highway to hell."

Carmichael finally looked to the side, but it was too late. Ash jabbed a needle into his neck and within seconds, he was down. His unconscious body dropped like a sweaty bag of bricks onto the still naked stripper.

"I don't think that's how the saying goes," I told Ash.

"I was ad-libbing."

I glanced around to figure out how we were going to get him out of there. "You couldn't have waited until he carried himself to the car?"

"He was annoying me."

Even wearing gloves, I touched as little of the DNA splattered blanket as possible, spreading it on the floor. I'd barely gotten it positioned when the stripper got some life back into her and gleefully shoved Carmichael onto it.

As soon as his weight was off her, she jumped out of bed, and I trained my gun at her. She didn't notice as she skipped to the table, popped a handful of pills, and downed them with a few chugs from a vodka bottle. Stumbling back to the bed, she flopped down with one leg hanging over and passed out.

She didn't care—and likely wouldn't remember—we'd been there.

I looked at Ash and lifted the blanket. "Grab a corner."

We got Carmichael out to the hallway just as a door slammed from the main area.

"It's the two in our two-for-one sale," Ash whispered.

A moment later, Dobrow yelled, "Janson is gone! Pull your tiny dick out of that whore and get out here!" The swinging door shoved open and his eyes went wide when he saw two guns aimed at his head.

That was all we got before he turned and ran.

Ash and I followed as he slammed out the door and raced toward a car. I shot once, the bullet whizzing by him to shatter the driver's window.

"Fuck!" Dobrow screamed, dodging to the left and racing past the club. He turned the corner before darting to the side into the alley between two dilapidated and abandoned buildings.

I had to hand it to him, for such a bulky fucker, he was fast. Every time I thought I had a clear shot, he changed paths or used the dumpsters and stacks of garbage as a shield. Unlike the guns in action movies, my bullets weren't infinite and I wasn't wasting them. Dobrow didn't have the same theory, squeezing off wild rounds over his shoulder that didn't hit anywhere close to us.

He took a sharp right and we followed just in time to see him scaling and hopping a tall wooden gate down the alley.

"Has he been training for the Olympics? Varsity track? Shit," Ash panted.

Hoisting myself onto the gate, there was no sign of Dobrow. I was almost over when he stuck his upper body around the corner and quickly fired three shots.

Burning pain exploded in my shoulder, making me lose my hold on the gate and fall forward to hit the ground.

"Fuck!" Ash landed on his feet next to me, his gun trained down the path.

"Go," I ordered.

He didn't argue.

Standing, I took a few seconds to fill my lungs with the breath that'd been knocked out of me. I ran a different route, reaching the end just as Dobrow turned in my direction.

His focus was aimed behind him as he tried to shoot over his shoulder, but the only thing the empty gun did was click. When he faced forward and saw me, his eyes went wide and his steps stumbled. Recovering quickly, he spun, only to find Ash blocking his way. He took a shuffling step backward toward a narrow alley, but before he could turn, Cole's gun dug into his back.

Trapped, Dobrow glared at me with hatred burning in his eyes. He opened his mouth—likely to hurl insults and spew bullshit—but he didn't have the chance. A syringe stabbed into his neck, and he was flat on his back within seconds.

"Between him and Carmichael, one of us is throwing our back out," Ash said, already hefting Dobrow's dead weight.

Or soon-to-be dead weight.

We hauled him down the thin path and dumped him on Cole's backseat. Cole and Ash dealt with Carmichael's body while I grabbed a bottle of cleaner and rag from the trunk. I wiped everything down, including my blood from the fence and ground.

It was overkill—no one would look into Viktor Dobrow's disappearance. Even if they did, the area was likely covered with so much DNA, there would be no separating it.

Returning to the car, I tossed the supplies in the trunk and slammed it shut.

Ash took a look at my shoulder—it was just a graze but it burned like a bitch. "We need to clean that."

"Once we get there."

Cole rounded the car. "The plant?"

I shook my head. "I have a better idea."

CHAPTER THIRTY-EIGHT

Perfect

MAXIMO

STANDING IN THE fenced-off construction site, I looked down at the men secured inside the deep but narrow pit. I didn't smile.

With them out of the way, Juliet would be safe. No looking over her shoulder. No reminders of her piece of shit father or her life before me.

She'd given me her trust.

I was giving her peace.

Which was why I didn't smile.

I grinned.

Circling the hole, I waited out of view.

An unseen monster in the dark.

My anticipation cranked up when one of them finally croaked, "Where am I?" He coughed, his hoarse voice louder when he yelled, "Hello? Is anyone there?"

"Shut the fuck up," a different voice bit out.

"Who the hell are you?"

"Someone with a fucking headache who doesn't want to listen to you crying like a little bitch."

I stepped closer, though they didn't notice me as they struggled against their bonds, trying to get free.

Viktor Dobrow looked pissed.

Mugsy Carmichael looked ready to piss.

And William Janson looked... at nothing. He couldn't see.

Smirking, I kicked some dirt in—a hint of what was to come. Two of the three men finally looked at me, and I kicked another pile their way.

"No, no, no," Carmichael blubbered.

"What was that? What's happening?" Janson shouted, terror shaking his words.

Dobrow was silent, but his expression quickly morphed from anger to panic-stricken as he realized what was about to happen. When he finally spoke, his tone was thick and earnest—the voice of a desperate man. "I can pay you. I have family who can get you anything and everything. Whatever you want. Ransom me. I'm worth more to you alive than I am dead."

It was bullshit. While we'd waited, Cole had done the electronic research and Ash had spoken to a few contacts so we could prepare for potential retaliation.

There'd be none.

Dobrow's men were already fighting over his throne of garbage. His limited family had cut him off long ago.

No one would pay a cent for him. Even if they would, there was no amount that would make me consider keeping him alive.

He'd tried to fuck with my business.

For that alone, he'd die.

He'd tried to take Juliet.

For that, he'd die a painful, terrifying death.

"I'm going to build my office on this spot," I shared. "I'll add to my empire here. I'll make billions here. I'll live and breathe and fuck Juliet on top of your grave. And soon, I'll forget any of you ever existed."

With the knowledge I'd won in every way possible consuming their last thoughts, I picked up the hose and held up my hand.

The men screamed, their faces red as their mouths moved frantically. Their useless words were lost in the rumble of the mixer. And as wet concrete filled the hole and their lungs, their useless lives would be lost soon, too.

Slowly.

Agonizing.

Exactly what they deserved.

Once they were covered, I lifted my hand and the flow stopped.

There was nothing but satisfying silence.

Steve—the head of the construction company—started the excavator and filled the hole the rest of the way with dirt, tamping it down and packing it in until it looked like the rest of the area.

Climbing out, he came over. "We're pouring foundation this morning. By the afternoon, this will be covered."

"You good with me staying until then?"

"Figured you would."

I handed him an envelope filled with a shit-ton of cash. "Thanks for coming in early. I owe you."

"No, I still owe you."

Since I'd gotten him out from under the mafia's thumb before they'd killed his wife and kids, I was betting he'd never feel like his debt was repaid.

Tucking the envelope away, his solemn expression lightened to a grin. "But if you're feeling generous, I've been trying to sneak Maria away for a weekend at Nebula. If you wanted to pull some strings to free up a room, I wouldn't say no."

"Name the weekend."

"I'll be a damn hero."

Heading to where Ash and Cole stood guard at the gate, I said, "It's done."

Ash exhaled, over a month's worth of rage and tension releasing as satisfaction coated his expression.

Maybe now he can let the guilt go and move on.

Going to the SUV, I peeled off my filthy, bloodied shirt. The bandage Ash had stuck on was still clean, so I didn't change it before pulling on the fresh shirt I kept for emergencies.

"You going home?" Ash asked.

"Not until the slab is laid."

"I'll wait around, too."

"No, go home. Take the week off. Enjoy a break before the next shit-storm blows in."

"You just want to keep the excavator and bulldozer rides to yourself," Ash bitched, but he was already heading for Cole's car.

Going back into the worksite, I grabbed a cup of shit coffee from the office trailer.

Then I waited for concrete to be poured, which was almost as thrilling as watching paint dry.

SHIT, I'M BEAT.

Pulling into my driveway that afternoon, I killed the engine and got out just as the front door whipped open.

Juliet came flying out, running full speed. I braced as she launched herself at me. Her arms wrapped tight around my neck, and I winced at the pressure on my shoulder.

That didn't stop me from cupping her sweet ass and lifting her into my arms. "Where are your shoes?"

"You're home," she breathed instead of answering. She leaned back to meet my eyes. "Is everything okay?"

I'd once told Juliet she was worth starting a war for, and I'd meant it.

But I hadn't started the war. Viktor Dobrow, Mugsy Carmichael, and her own piece-of-shit father had.

I'd just finished it.

Which was why my words were nothing but the truth when I said, "Everything's perfect."

"It always is," she whispered.

My gaze dropped from her tired green eyes to the dark circles under them. "Did you not sleep, Juliet?"

Her body trembled at my tone. "Not really. You know I can't sleep without my Daddy wrapped around me."

So damn perfect.

When I carried her inside, Marco was waiting.

"Everything set?" he asked.

"Done. I'll fill you in later. You guys have the week off."

"Got it." He closed the door behind him.

"Sheesh, so chatty," Juliet muttered.

I was anxious to get her upstairs, into the shower with me, and then in bed on top of me. Unfortunately, I'd barely taken a step when Vera came from the living room.

She opened her mouth, but I spoke first. "You've got the week off."

"I'll grab my things." Smiling, she added, "And you can get started on what we talked about."

With that, she rushed from the room.

"What's she up to?" Juliet's narrowed eyes tracked Vera. "She had a mischievous smile. It's her tell."

"What's my tell?" I asked, avoiding her question.

Her eyes went hooded. "I'm not saying because then you might stop, and I like watching it."

"I like watching, too." Squeezing her ass until she whimpered, my voice was low and rough. "Right now, we're going to shower and then I'm going to fucking *love* watching you ride Daddy's cock."

A harder tremble went through her. "I can do that."

"That's my good girl."

Carrying her up the stairs and into the bathroom, I lowered her to stand. My fingertips skimmed and teased as I stripped her. Distracted by the sight of her naked body and desperate to feel it against me, I didn't think before unbuttoning my shirt and peeling it off.

At her gasp, I looked down at her furrowed brow. Her gaze was aimed at the blood-stained bandage on my shoulder. "What happened?"

"Just a graze," I said, pulling her close.

Her big green eyes darted to mine. "You were *shot*?"

"Grazed."

"By a bullet?" Juliet's body tightened and fury poured from her.

Everyone had their limit. At the way she glared at me, I wondered if I'd found Juliet's.

Before I could offer an explanation, her rage-filled eyes shot to mine. "Did you kill them?"

I should've known better than to doubt her.

Because from the very beginning, Juliet understood who I was. She knew the monster she was getting involved with. Who she was falling in love with.

Who her Daddy was.

And she'd never tried to change me. She wanted me exactly how I was, handing me her body, trust, and heart because she knew I'd kill to protect them.

Right then was no different. My girl wasn't pissed at me.

She wanted vengeance *for* me.

I lifted my chin. "Carmichael, too."

Her brows shot up as the pieces clicked together. "Wait, Mugsy Carmichael was involved? Did you find out who he was working for? And why he tried to take me?"

I wouldn't lie to Juliet, but I wouldn't tell her the whole truth, either. Shamus had already done enough damage. Knowing he'd sold her to clear his debts would destroy her.

I shouldered some of the blame, but to protect her, I'd shoulder it all.

Gripping her ponytail, I used my hold to tip her head back to meet my eyes. "It was part of some bullshit revenge against me and you got dragged into it. I fucked up."

Any hurt or anger she had would've been justified for the target I'd helped put on her back.

But when she looked at me, there was nothing but gratitude and relief and love. "No, they fucked up. And now I never have to worry about creepy Mugsy again." As if saying the words out loud made them sink in, she whispered, "It's really over, isn't it?"

"It's over."

After a long moment, a slow grin spread across her face and the last bit of tension she carried melted away. "You always take care of me."

"'Til the day I die."

Her eyes heated as her fingertips danced down my abs. "I want to take care of you."

"Then we better shower fast."

Throwing the rest of my clothes off, I turned on the water and hauled her under the jets. I scrubbed the dirt and grime from myself before teasingly soaping her.

"I need you," she murmured, clutching my upper arms as I worked between her legs.

Juliet was strong. Stubborn. Independent. After being on her own for so long, she didn't easily need.

But she needed me.

And that made me crazed.

Killing the water, I quickly dried us off before lifting her.

Carrying her to the bed, I dropped her back to the mattress and covered her body with mine. Her skin was warm and flushed. Soft. Fucking

347

beautiful.

Just what I needed after dealing with so much ugly.

Needing to feel her, I fisted my cock and lined it up with her wet pussy.

"Wait," she interrupted just as I slid the tip into heaven. Putting her hand on my good shoulder, she shoved. "You said you wanted to watch me ride your cock."

Christ.

Using the time to find my control before I came embarrassingly fast, I let her roll me to my back. I grabbed a pillow and propped my head up so I could see every-damn-thing.

Juliet straddled me, her pussy tormenting me as she wiggled around to find her position. Lifting onto her knees, she wrapped her fist around me before lowering to take my dick.

Agonizingly, torturously, painfully slow.

Once I filled her, her head fell back and she let out a sexy as hell sigh. Her movements were cautious and unsure until she found her rhythm, rocking and grinding.

Jesus Christ, she's going to kill me.

My gaze stayed locked on our connection as I watched my dick stretch her. Using my thumbs, I spread her lips wide so I could see more as I stroked her clit.

Her breath caught and she picked up speed as her caution changed to frenzy. Hard and fast, she rode me until her body tightened and her movements became halting.

Taking over, I gripped her hips and lifted her all the way up my length before sliding her back down.

"Harder," she demanded on a moan. I did as she said, but it still wasn't enough. "Harder, Daddy, please."

I repeated the motion, raising my hips as I slammed her down.

The force made her cry out. "Yes, like that."

I gave her more. Everything I had. No holding back. No gentleness. No control.

Rough and hard and savage, I fucked her.

Juliet took it. All of it. All of me. Exactly how I was, how I gave it, how I needed it.

And she loved it.

Squeezing my dick like a vise, she came hard. Coating me in her sweetness as her greedy pussy sucked me deeper, setting off my own abrupt release. Filling her. Marking her.

Mine.

Mine.

So fucking *mine*.

Slumping forward, her lips lazily skimmed across my chest and up to my neck.

She bit, making my spent cock jump as I growled, "Juliet."

"Maximo," she mocked.

"If you didn't look ready to pass out, I'd spank your ass raw."

"I'm not that tired," she tried, but the yawn that followed contradicted her.

Shifting us to our sides, I wrapped myself around her before cupping her throat and pussy. At the possessive hold, she took a deep breath and released it in a peaceful sigh.

"Love you so damn much," I murmured against her head, tightening my hold.

"Love you, too, Daddy." When I still didn't relax, she asked, "Are you sure everything's okay?"

Dobrow and Carmichael were dead, and with them, the last of the threats from her life before me.

She was in my arms, relaxed with no walls or mental guard up. Body, heart, and soul, I had all of her.

Not to mention, my dick was coated in her come and her pussy was full of mine.

Which was why I repeated my answer from earlier. "Everything's perfect."

With my little dove, it always was.

EPILOGUE

Juliet

A Few Days Later

"TIME TO GET out, Juliet."

Damn.

The weather was scorching, but thanks to the overcast sky, the pool temp was perfect. I wasn't ready to get out.

"Or you could come in," I tried, treading water with just my head exposed to the heat.

Maximo crossed his arms. "Now, Juliet."

Maybe I can stay in just a little longer...

Underwater, I tugged the two strings holding my top in place. I stood so he could see my breasts as I tossed the scrap of fabric his way and repeated, "Or you could come in."

"Jesus Christ," he muttered, his cock hardening to push against his joggers.

It didn't matter how often it happened, I'd never get used to the way Maximo wanted me. It was a heady power that made me bold.

Bold enough to slip off my bottoms and toss them with my top.

That did it.

In record time, Maximo stripped and jumped into the pool, landing near me. He palmed my ass and easily lifted me in the water. I wrapped my legs around him as he began walking.

Disappointment filled me as we neared the ladder.

Oh well. I probably earned a punishment later, at least.

But Maximo didn't go to the ladder. He took us through the waterfall to the hidden alcove. Turning me around, he set me on the bench and positioned me on my knees facing away from him.

"This is going to be hard and fast because we don't have much time, so play with your clit."

"Okay, Daddy."

"That's my good girl," he praised as he slammed into me.

My hand went between my legs to do as he said, the pad of my middle finger rubbing tight circles on my clit.

Each ruthless thrust took me higher, forcing moans that echoed in the small space. His hand suddenly covered my mouth, taking me by surprise.

But then I heard it.

Muffled voices.

There was no way they didn't notice my bathing suit or Maximo's discarded clothes.

Mortified, I tried to shift away, but Maximo wouldn't let me.

Lowering his front to cover my back, his mouth was at my ear. "I didn't tell you to stop."

Since his hand prevented me from speaking, I shook my head frantically.

"Play with your clit or I'm going to pull out of this sweet pussy and slam into your tight little ass instead. I'll fuck it so hard, neighbors miles down the road will hear your screams."

As tempting as that threat was, I resumed rubbing my clit. It was wicked and wrong and so damn hot.

His pace slowed, but the power in each plunge remained brutal.

He's getting off on this depraved torment.

Despite our company, my body began to tingle and a rush of electricity and lava flowed through my veins.

And so am I.

Thankfully, the voices faded quickly because I wasn't sure how much longer I could hold out.

"You close?" Maximo asked, harsh and raw as his thrusts took me off my knees.

I nodded as my finger worked my clit with frenzied strokes. My release hit hard, crashing over me like the water around us. Even with his hand over my mouth, my cries were loud.

"Thank Christ," he grunted before coming with a low groan.

At the sound and the feel of him, another aftershock of pleasure rippled through me.

Rather than giving me his weight or rearranging us so he could hold me like he usually did, Maximo backed away. "Jesus, you make me lose control."

Of all the compliments Maximo gave—sweet or obscene—that was the most profound because he didn't lose his carefully held control often. But I could make him do it.

I turned and smiled up at him.

"Don't think you can give me that sexy smile and you'll be off the hook," he said, but the only heat in his voice was from lust not anger. "I'm still going to spank your ass raw for not listening to me, but it'll have to wait because now we're late."

"For what?" I asked, but he didn't answer.

Ducking out of the waterfall, he paused for a moment before turning back. "Come on." When I swam out, he gave me *the look* and ordered, "Wait here."

I did as he said, enjoying the view as he climbed out in all his naked glory. He grabbed my towel from the lounger and dried himself as he returned. "Out."

My gaze lingered on his cut, tattooed body. "You know—"

"Now, Juliet."

"Fine," I said, but only because I was curious where we were going. I climbed the ladder and took the towel, wrapping it around myself as Maximo tugged on his joggers.

I ran through what I knew of his schedule but came up empty. There were no events at the resorts. No warehouse fights.

"Where are we going?" I asked as he started for the door.

"To get married."

That was it.

That was all he said.

He didn't ask.

Didn't explain.

Didn't even pause.

Simple as that.

"What?" I shouted, my heart freezing before pounding frantically in my chest as butterflies created a mosh pit in my belly.

He reached the door before turning around. "You better hurry or you're getting married in that towel. We leave in an hour."

"What?" I repeated, both because of the bombshell and the time crunch.

"I tried to give you more time." He opened the door and closed it behind him.

I stood and stared, completely stunned.

Married.

He wants to get married?

Married!

Remembering the limited timeframe, I rushed after him, but he was nowhere to be found. I clutched the towel and ran upstairs.

When I opened the bedroom door, there was still no sign of Maximo. There was, however, a gray dress and shoes on the bed. It may not have been the traditional white, but there was no mistaking what it was.

Holy shit, a wedding dress.

Hurrying to shower off the chlorine, my thoughts raced like crazy, but none of it was bad. No panic. No terror. And not even the tiniest hint of doubt.

Just excitement.

Okay, confusion at the abrupt sneak attack and a hefty bit of shock, but mostly excitement.

After my shower, I blew out my hair. Knowing how much he loved my hair in a high ponytail, I pulled the bulk of it up but made it stylish by wrapping the remaining pieces around the elastic and sliding some gemmed bobby pins into place. I added loose curls to the ends and the pieces framing my face.

Once I was done with my makeup, I hurried into the bedroom. Skipping a bra, I tugged on a pair of minuscule lace panties before carefully sliding on the thick strapped dress over my head. It was understated but stunning, with a deep V between my breasts and a high slit up my thigh. Sitting carefully, I secured the matching strappy heels into place and moved to stand in front of the mirror.

I'm wearing a wedding dress.
Because I'm getting married.
To Maximo.
But not if I don't hurry up.

After a few quick touch-ups, I rushed from the room. I expected to find Maximo in his office, but it was empty. As was the rest of the hall.

Nearing the stairs, voices traveled up from the foyer. I clutched the banister so I didn't tumble down the steps on my trembling legs. I was grateful for my tight hold when I caught sight of Maximo. He must've showered in one of the other bathrooms because his hair was still damp. He wore the black suit and shirt combo I loved so much, but with the surprising addition of a gray tie that matched my dress.

When I dragged my eyes up his body to meet his, I lost my breath. There was so much intensity, fire, and love burning unrestrained in them. He stared as if watching me walk was the most mesmerizing thing he'd ever seen.

He moved, reaching the bottom of the stairs as I did before taking me in his arms. I got the distinct impression—based on the desire in his brooding eyes and his hardness pressed against my belly—that he liked what he saw.

"You look so damn beautiful," he whispered roughly, "and I'm so damn lucky you're mine."

My heart squeezed at his sweetly possessive words. I didn't fight to block them out in a feeble effort to protect my heart.

He already owned my heart.

And I knew he'd die to protect it for me.

Before I could speak, he said, "We have to go."

But he didn't release me or move.

After a long moment, Ash cleared his throat. "Boss."

"Right." Maximo took my hand and walked to the waiting Lincoln. Once we were in the backseat, Ash began driving.

Unable to hold it in, I asked the question that kept ricocheting through my head and dancing on my tongue. "Are we actually getting married?"

"Yes," Maximo said simply.

"Like, legally-legit married?"

"Yes."

"You didn't even ask me," I pointed out.

"I told you things would be done my way and that I'd seldom ask,

354

even for major things. Is that a problem?"

That was true, he had told me. I just hadn't realized it would apply to lifelong, legal commitments.

Concern filled his gaze as his brow furrowed. "I asked you a question, Juliet, and I expect an answer."

Was it a problem that Maximo Black wanted to marry me?

Hell no.

It was the opposite of a problem.

Shaking my head emphatically, I smiled so wide, my cheeks felt as though they'd split. "I'm just in shock. It's very sudden."

"Not for me. I've wanted to marry you for months, but I knew you weren't ready. I've been patient. I've waited. And I'm done. I want you tied to me in every way you can be, wrapped up like I am."

"I already am."

"And now it'll be official. You'll be completely mine."

I knew what people would think if they heard the way he talked. They'd think he was deranged. Dysfunctional.

Obsessed.

And maybe he was.

But so was I.

Because his possessive, controlling words didn't scare me. They thrilled me. They wrapped around me like a security blanket, warm and comforting. They flowed through my veins, breathing life into me and filling my heart until I thought it would burst with happiness.

We rode the rest of the way in heavy silence, lost in our own thoughts. My impatience and excitement grew in equal measure with each passing mile.

After a while, I recognized one of the buildings in the distance.

"Are we getting married at Nebula?" I asked.

"Yes. We're staying there tonight and catching a flight tomorrow afternoon."

I'd never flown before. In all our times moving, we'd just loaded our limited belongings into our car and a small rented trailer we'd towed behind us.

As terrified of heights as I was, the thought of flying was actually exciting.

Another in a long line of new experiences thanks to Maximo.

"Where are we going?" I asked.

"You'll see."

My curiosity couldn't leave it at that. "Is it on the west coast or east coast?"

"It's not in this country."

"Is this why you had me get my passport?" I asked. He'd had Marco take me before a trip to the fabric store, claiming it was so I could travel for business with him.

"Yes."

"That was months ago."

"I told you I've waited months."

Before I could respond, Maximo unlatched my seatbelt and nudged me toward the door I belatedly noticed the valet was holding open. Another took Ash's spot in the driver's seat.

Once I was out, Maximo wrapped an arm around my shoulders and guided me through the packed building. We got into the elevator, and I got my first glimpse of us in the reflection of the gleaming steel. It was no wonder people had stared.

He looked powerful and commanding in his suit.

I looked lovely in my dress.

We looked beautiful.

Like we belonged together.

The elevator opened, and we stepped out into an open room with twisting light features hanging from the ceiling and a long bar to one side. Ash kept going toward a set of frosted double doors, but Maximo stopped and turned me to face him.

"I wanted to marry you at one of my properties." He glanced around. "Someplace I'll see often."

"It's perfect."

I'd have married him at any Elvis chapel, gimmicky destination, or street corner.

His eyes seared into mine as he finally asked, "Do you want to marry me, little dove?"

My answer was immediate and honest. "More than anything."

"I'll control you, every aspect of your life," Maximo warned, similar to when we'd first become *us*. "I'll always be your Daddy. I'll tell you what to do and punish you. I'll love you and work every damn day to make sure you never regret giving me you. This will be your life from now on. Is that what you want?"

"'Til the day I die," I said, giving him the words he often gave me.

Reaching into his pocket, he pulled out an engagement ring before sliding it onto my finger.

It's important to commemorate our two-hour engagement.

"Ready?" he asked, though he was already walking.

"Wait." I didn't move, and Maximo stopped, worry evident on his tense face. Undoing his tie, I slid it free and tossed it onto a potted plant. "You don't wear ties if you can help it." I popped his top button free. "Perfect."

It was a small gesture, but Maximo kissed me like it was huge. When he pulled away, he looked even more impatient as he guided me to the frosted double doors.

They opened on our approach, and I lost my tenuous hold on my tears.

The balcony was bursting with beautiful flowers and greenery. Like the night sky, twinkle lights arched in a canopy over us. With the sun setting in the backdrop, it was magical.

A fairy tale with a princess and her villain.

MAXIMO

Two Years Later

"WHERE ARE MY pills?"

I fought to hide my smile as my frazzled wife rushed into my office. She had a soft measuring tape draped over her neck, pins stuck in her shirt, and multiple colored pencils jammed through her hair.

I'll never get over how damn beautiful she is.

"Come here," I ordered, evading her question. Not because I didn't want to answer it, I just enjoyed playing with my little dove.

She didn't move. "My pills?"

"Now, Juliet."

At my tone, she rushed over and took her spot on my lap.

I started pulling the colored pencils from her hair. "How's the dress?"

"Good. I finally found the perfect color combination to complement the design so it doesn't look like a clown outfit or something out of an eighties club."

"I knew you'd figure it out. You always do."

Even if her outfits were ugly, I'd have secretly bought every last one if it meant she was happy. But that hadn't been necessary. She'd made Dove Couture a success all on her own.

Ever since consigning her dresses with Hilda's, she'd had more order requests than she could accept. We'd knocked down one of the walls to expand her workspace into a spare bedroom, and it wouldn't be long before we'd have to expand again. People liked her designs and the approachableness in the style. It fit with Vegas life.

I'd told her she could put her own store in Black Moon once it opened, but she'd turned me down. She didn't want to be so overloaded, she lost the availability to create for fun when inspiration hit.

I'd always support her, but I'd be lying if I said I wasn't happy she'd declined her own store. It would've been an intensive time commitment, and I was a greedy fuck. I liked having her time and attention to myself.

But I was ready to share her.

"I threw them out," I told her, pulling the sewing pins free and dropping them into the container I kept on my desk for that purpose.

"Threw what out?"

"Your pills."

Her brows lowered as she leaned back to look at me. "Why?"

"Because it'd be hard for me to put my baby in you if you're on them."

Her lips parted as she sat in stunned silence for a moment. "You want to have a baby?"

"Two babies. Maybe three." I removed the tape measure last but kept it close in case I wanted to tie her wrists with it. "We'll see how it goes."

"Babies? *Plural?*"

"Is that a problem, Juliet?"

Usually my tone would make her eyes go hooded, but instead they were filled with panic. "I… It's just…"

Softening my expression, I cupped her head. "It's what?"

A tear streaked down her cheek followed closely by another. And another. "What if I'm a bad mom? Neither of my parents were a shining example." Her words were choked when she forced out, "What if I fuck up our kid?"

Christ, she broke my heart.

With each passing day, Juliet had managed to shake off more of the damage from her parents. For the most part, she lived free from their toxic memories.

Or, as she said, she lived carefree.

But every once in a while, their ghosts came to haunt her.

"Your parents were a good example of who you didn't want to be, and you've already proven you're *not* them. You're selfless, loving, patient, and everything they never were." There wasn't a hint of doubt in my mind when I said, "You'll be the best mom."

She didn't speak, but her tears slowed.

Opening the top drawer on my desk, I grabbed her birth control pack and handed it to her. "We'll wait until you're ready, little dove. And if you never are, that's fine, too. But don't let your shitty parents control you."

She gave a sniffling laugh. "I know, that's your job."

"'Til the day I die," I shot back with no hint of humor.

She fell silent again, flipping the pack in her hand. "You really think I'd be a good mom?"

"The best."

"Would we still have time together?"

"I'd make sure of it."

"Would you still be my Daddy even after you're a dada?"

I pulled her closer so her ass was firmly on my hard-on. "Try to stop me."

She grinned and tossed the pack toward the wastebasket.

I didn't watch to see if it made it in.

I was too busy bending my little dove over my desk so I could tie her to me in a new way.

JULIET

One Year Later

"YOU SURE ABOUT this?"

No.

"Yes."

I didn't want to do it, but I needed to.

Maximo helped me off the four-wheeler like I was made of delicate glass and the world around me was made of lethal knives. Even once I was standing, he kept hold of me as we walked through a thin path

359

between the trees.

Dread coursed through me like thick sludge, but I forced myself forward.

He stopped at a small clearing. "This is it. Do you want me to stay?"

"No, I'm okay."

He looked hesitant to leave.

"I just need a minute alone with him."

"I'll be right over there," Maximo relented. "Call if you need me. And keep an eye out for scorpions, insects, any animals. Even birds can—"

"Daddy," I interrupted, pressing in as close as I could, "the only predator who wants to eat me is you."

"Christ, don't say shit like that, or we'll have a repeat of me fucking you on the four-wheeler until we break the axel."

"That was fun."

"It'd take a hell of a lot longer to walk home from here."

"It'd still be worth it."

"Juliet," he said in the voice that sent a tremor down my spine.

That didn't stop me from taunting, "Maximo."

"I'm gonna spank your ass when we get home." His words were harsh, but his expression was filled with heat and tenderness and concern.

And love.

So much love.

He kissed me, soft and sweet. "I'll be right over there."

"I know."

He was always close whenever I needed him.

And I always needed him.

With one last scan of me and the area, Maximo backtracked through the narrow path.

I waited until I couldn't hear his footsteps before looking down at the dirt in front of a large rock.

"Hey, Dad," I said, though the name felt weird on my tongue.

Even when he'd been alive, he'd never been a dad to me. Any good memories associated with him were covered in asterisks because there was something bad attached, too.

This is stupid.

After checking the ground for bugs and boogeymen, I sat down. "I bet if the afterlife is real and you're looking up at me, you're furious, huh? Your Jule-bug married to the man who killed you." I rubbed my round stomach. "And having his baby, too. It's a boy, due in two months. I like the name Rhett. Or Rocco. I can't decide. Maximo doesn't care, he's just over the moon I'm giving him a son."

I waited for hellfire to erupt in front of me because Shamus had sweet-talked the devil into letting him come back to make my life hell one last time.

It didn't happen, of course, so I continued carrying the conversation.

"Ella—the therapist I see sometimes—suggested I talk to you. She said I need closure. I think I'm supposed to air my grievances into the universe so I can forgive you and let it all go."

Again, I paused like Shamus was going to sprout through the ground and tell me to take my hippie bullshit to a commune.

"But because you were such a greedy coward, I met Maximo," I pointed out. "And he saved me from whatever shithole I'd have been buried in thanks to you. Now I have an amazing life. A perfect husband. Good friends. A business. A baby boy soon. And I have love. So much of it, sometimes it feels like my chest will explode because it's so full."

With perfect timing, my son rolled in my stomach.

"That's why I'm not here to bitch you out," I told my dad or the universe or whoever. "I'm here to thank you." Using the rock, I stood and looked down at his grave. "Your death was the only good thing you ever did for me because it brought me Maximo. So, thank you."

With that, I walked away from my father's grave and knew I wouldn't be back.

I cleared the thin path onto the trail where Maximo waited. As soon as he saw me, he hurried over to take my hand so I didn't trip on a rock.

It wouldn't be the first time I did that.

Concern furrowed his browse as he scanned my face, likely searching for tears or—more likely—rage. "You okay?"

"Perfect."

"Did you say everything you needed?"

"Yup."

Ella was right, I felt a sense of closure, even if I hadn't said what she'd suggested.

Straddling the four-wheeler, I didn't sit. Instead, I pulled my husband closer and kissed him. "I love you, Daddy."

"Love you, too, little dove."

I sat and scooted to make room for him. When he didn't climb on, I asked, "What's wrong?"

"Nothing. Give me a second."

I watched him go down the path I'd just come from.

As curious as I was to know what he was up to, I stayed where I was. I soaked in the beauty around me and the beauty that was my life.

I was happy.

Safe.

Carefree.

Permanent.

MAXIMO

STANDING ABOVE SHAMUS' grave, I looked down and hoped like fuck he was in hell looking back up at me.

"Only good thing you ever did in your life was make Juliet. And you fucked her up. Fucked her over. But I fixed it. Killed the prick who stabbed her. Killed Carmichael and Dobrow for trying to steal her from me because you used her as payment. I take care of her. And in return, I get the perfection that's Juliet *Black*."

I tugged my joggers down, freeing my dick.

And then I pissed on Shamus McMillon's grave, grinning as I watched it soak into the dirt.

"I won, motherfucker."

THE END!

OTHER BOOKS BY LAYLA FROST

THE HYDE SERIES
Hyde and Seek
Best Kase Scenario
Until Nox: Happily Ever Alpha World
Until Mayhem

THE AMATO SERIES
With Us
The Four
Styx
Stoned

STANDALONES
Give In
Little Dove

Made in the USA
Monee, IL
14 July 2021